DEAD OF NIGHT

A BERLIN WARTIME THRILLER

By Simon Scarrow

SIMON SCARROW

DEAD OF NIGHT

A BERLIN WARTIME THRILLER

HEADLINE

First published in Great Britain in 2023 by
HEADLINE PUBLISHING GROUP

1

Cataloguing in Publication Data is available from the British Library

ISBN 978 1 4722 5858 8 (Hardback)
ISBN 978 1 4722 5859 5 (Trade paperback)

Map and artwork by Tim Peters

Typeset in Garamond by Avon DataSet Ltd, Alcester, Warwickshire

Printed and bound in Great Britain by Clays Ltd, Elcograf S.p.A.

Headline's policy is to use papers that are natural, renewable and recyclable
products and made from wood grown in well-managed forests and other
controlled sources. The logging and manufacturing processes are expected
to conform to the environmental regulations of the country of origin.

HEADLINE PUBLISHING GROUP
An Hachette UK Company
Carmelite House
50 Victoria Embankment
London EC4Y 0DZ

www.headline.co.uk
www.hachette.co.uk

For my friend Bharat Goswami,
who taught me how to think about thinking

The Berlin Area, 1940

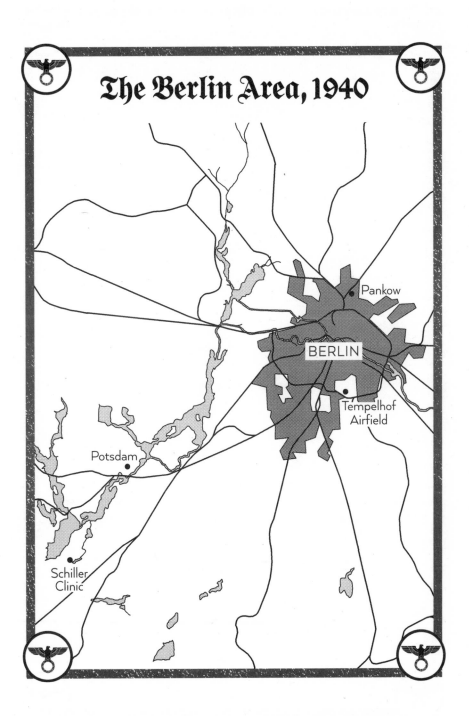

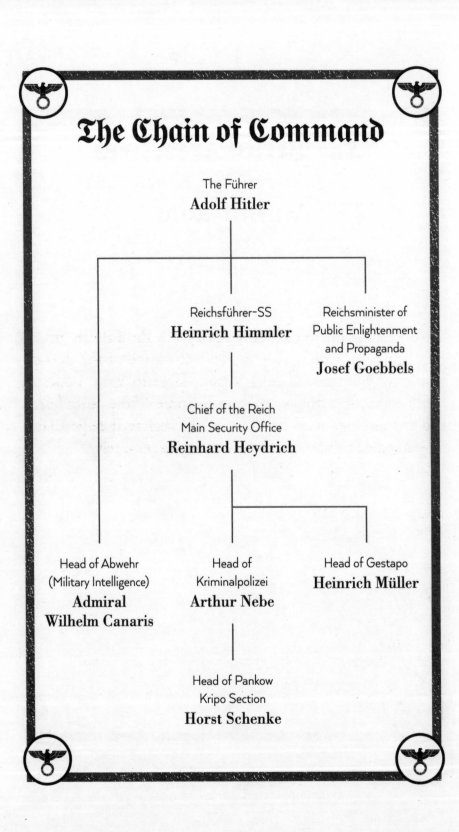

The Chain of Command

The Führer
Adolf Hitler

Reichsführer-SS
Heinrich Himmler

Reichsminister of
Public Enlightenment
and Propaganda
Josef Goebbels

Chief of the Reich
Main Security Office
Reinhard Heydrich

Head of Abwehr
(Military Intelligence)
**Admiral
Wilhelm Canaris**

Head of
Kriminalpolizei
Arthur Nebe

Head of Gestapo
Heinrich Müller

Head of Pankow
Kripo Section
Horst Schenke

Author note

Writing about life in Germany during the Third Reich inevitably brings an author face to face with some of the darkest aspects of human nature. It's impossible to write honestly about the time without referring to some of the attitudes of and terminology used by those in the regime. I hope that I have handled this aspect of the novel with sensitivity.

Prologue

Berlin, 28 January 1940

The choir and orchestra reached the end of the reprise of 'Fortuna Imperatrix Mundi', and with a final sweep of his baton the conductor brought the performance to an end, bowing his head as if in exhaustion. At once the audience at the Philharmonie let out a cheer and applause thundered through the hall. As the conductor turned, some of the audience rose to offer a standing ovation and the rest began to follow.

Dr Manfred Schmesler sighed as he stood stiffly. Like those around him, he was wearing his overcoat and gloves but no hat, so that he might hear the music more easily despite the cold. Because of the shortage of coal in the city, the heating had not been turned on, and even after an hour and a half of the audience crowding into the hall, the air was frigid. Schmesler wondered how the performers had been able to carry on in such conditions. Perhaps the need to concentrate had distracted them from the icy atmosphere.

He felt a light pressure on his arm and turned to his wife, Brigitte. She said something inaudible, then cleared her throat and spoke loudly as he dipped his ear towards her.

'I said, they did wonderfully.'

'Yes,' he replied. 'Under the circumstances.'

The applause continued as Wilhelm Furtwängler gestured to his orchestra to take a bow, and then the choir. The clapping subsided and there was the usual bustle as the crowd edged towards the aisles and made for the exits. Schmesler guided his wife out, along with the couple who had accompanied them to the performance, Hans Eberman, a lawyer, and his wife, Eva. The Schmeslers had met the Ebermans at a party a few months earlier, and had shared a number of social events since then.

Eberman caught his eye and commented just loudly enough to be heard, 'How fortunate that the tickets were free.'

Schmesler knew his companion well enough to sense the irony, and smiled back briefly. Since the Nazi Party had taken power, they had driven a host of musicians and composers into exile and limited the repertoire of those that remained to mainly German music, which meant the capital's concerts were becoming repetitive. At least they had been spared an evening of Wagner, thought Schmesler.

As the crowd edged forward, people fumbled for scarves and mufflers and put on their hats in preparation for the cold out in the street. Berlin was in the grip of the bitterest winter in living memory: the canals and the River Spree were frozen over, and snow covered the city. And the nation was at war again. Schmesler was old enough to have served in the previous conflict, and his memory was scarred by the terrible suffering he had witnessed on the Western Front. The war to end all wars, they had called it, and yet scarcely twenty years later, war had returned to Germany. And with it had come food rationing and the nightly blackout that smothered Berlin with darkness once the sun set.

The increasing scarcity of coal meant that heating was a luxury for the few, mostly senior members of the Nazi Party or their cronies. Although Schmesler was a member, he had joined as part of the wave of professionals who had seen the way things were going and realised that membership would become the *sine qua non* of any successful career, as well as serving a more private purpose. And so it had proved for doctors and for lawyers like his new friend Eberman. Those who had joined the party in the days of the Weimar Republic looked down on the newcomers with contempt for their new-found enthusiasm for the cause. More importantly, they were not inclined to share their supply of coal.

It was strange, Schmesler reflected, that a resource once so commonplace was now a rare and valuable commodity. Even the coal that did turn up in the capital tended to be the degassed variety, lacking the greasy sheen of the better-quality type that generated more heat. He and Brigitte were obliged to burn wood in the stoves of their house in Pankow to stay warm and heat enough water to wash with. The boiler that supplied the building was only fired up at weekends and on Tuesday and Thursday evenings, when coal supplies allowed. Even wood was becoming scarce, and Schmesler prayed for the prolonged spell of freezing weather to end.

As they approached the exit into the foyer, he heard a harsh voice cut through the hubbub of conversation.

'Winter Aid! Winter Aid collection!'

He saw four men in greatcoats with the brown caps of the party paramilitaries. One had raised a tin and rattled it loudly before he repeated his cry.

'Damn them,' Eberman muttered. 'Don't they fleece us enough already with their bloody collections?'

Schmesler reached into his coat pocket and took out a handful of badges. Poking through them, he found the special Winter Aid badges he had earned through previous donations. He handed one to Eberman before fixing his own to his lapel, where it would be seen. His companion smiled at the thought of getting one over on the party's henchmen clustered about the exits, where they intimidated those passing into handing over money for the cause. A visitor to Berlin might think this was charity, whereas the inhabitants recognised it for what it was – one step short of being mugged.

A man blocked the way of the group ahead of Schmesler and his lips curled in amusement. 'Spare some change to help those in need, friend.'

There was no trace of a polite request, merely an instruction, and the concert-leavers without donor badges paid up and hurried away. An SA man stepped in front of Schmesler and held up his tin.

'Winter Aid.'

Schmesler angled his shoulder slightly to display the badge, and the SA man waved the two couples past before confronting those behind them. Schmesler took his wife's arm and increased their pace as they passed through the foyer and out of the revolving door onto the pavement. At once the freezing night air bit at their exposed skin, and they hunched their heads into their collars and breathed swirls of steam.

Eberman made to return his badge, but Schmesler shook his head. 'Keep it. Who knows how many more SA parties are on the streets tonight.'

'Thanks.'

Despite the blackout, there was enough illumination from the narrow beams of masked car headlights and the loom of mounds of snow for them to see their way, and Schmesler led them along the street towards the U-Bahn station. Once he was clear of the crowd emerging from the theatre, he slowed so that the other couple could fall into step beside him and Brigitte. The trampled snow had compacted into ice, and she clung to his arm to avoid slipping. The conditions discouraged any further conversation until they reached the steps to the station, where they would part company; Schmesler and his wife catching a train to Pankow while the Ebermans walked the remaining distance to their apartment on the next street.

'Shall we go to the Richard Strauss event next Friday?' asked Eva.

Her husband sniffed. 'Not that there's much of a choice these days.'

She swatted his shoulder. 'Strauss may not be the kind of first-class composer you are so fond of, but at least he's a first-rate second-class composer.'

All four laughed knowingly before Eberman continued, 'It seems that no piece of German music should be so sophisticated that it could not be belted out at a Nazi Party rally, eh?'

'Come now,' said Schmesler. 'It's music all the same, and it's a pleasant distraction from the war. It'll be good for us.'

'I suppose . . .'

'Then it's settled. And it's your turn to get the tickets, my friend.'

Schmesler glanced towards the station entrance at the sound of an approaching train. 'We have to go.' He turned back to his companion. 'Are we still meeting for lunch next Monday? About that matter you wanted to discuss?'

Eberman shook his head. 'It's not important any more. Another time perhaps.'

There were handshakes and farewells as the couples parted, the Schmeslers hurrying down the stairs into the station. They reached the platform just as the northbound train pulled in. Doors clattered open and shut as passengers alighted or boarded; the guard blew his whistle. The train jolted into motion and Schmesler and his wife nearly lost their balance as they made for an empty space on one of the benches. It reminded them both of an evening when Schmesler had invited Brigitte out after they'd first met. The motion of the train had thrown them against each other and he had instinctively put his arm around her to stop her from falling. It had broken the ice and they had laughed nervously. Now they smiled at each other in delight at the unbidden memory of that night.

Conversation was difficult on the U-Bahn trains, and in recent years people tended to be careful of what they said in case an inadvertent comment attracted the attention of an informer. The two of them held hands and sat in silence, counting off the stops until the train pulled into their station in the Pankow district. Stepping out of the carriage, they walked quickly through the cold, dark streets of the smart residential neighbourhood until they reached their home.

It was a modest two-storey building dating from the middle of the last century. Schmesler had acquired it three years earlier from its Jewish owners, the Frankels. He had studied at Berlin University with Josef Frankel, and they had once been close friends. After the Nazis had come to power, the friendship was no longer advisable and they had kept their distance, socialising in secret. With Frankel no longer able to operate his business, he had left Germany with his family as restrictions tightened around the country's Jewish community. He had sold his house to his good friend Schmesler for a bargain price, and taken what little capital he had in order to make a new life in New York. However, the family had been forced to leave behind a younger daughter, Ruth, when they had failed to find her birth certificate, and now that war had broken out, she was trapped in Berlin.

The couple climbed the steps from the street and scraped the snow from their shoes on the iron bar next to the covered porch. Schmesler unlocked the front door, and they stepped inside and closed it before turning on the lights, so as not to provide an excuse for the local block warden to fine them for breaching blackout regulations.

It was cold enough indoors to require them to keep their coats and gloves on, and only their hats were hung on the stand beside the door. Schmesler kissed his wife on the forehead.

'You go on up to bed. I'll be along a bit later.'

'Work?' She sighed.

He nodded. 'We're short-handed at the centre, thanks to conscription.'

'Did they have to take all your assistants?'

'In time of war, the army needs all the doctors it can find, my love.'

Brigitte shook her head. 'War . . . So much for the Führer's claim of being a man of peace.'

Schmesler instinctively glanced round before he could catch himself, and smiled guiltily as he responded. 'Make sure such words stay at home. Be careful who you share your doubts with.'

'I would hope I'd be safe speaking my mind to my husband of twenty years.'

He winked at her. 'You never know . . .'

'Oh, you!' She pinched his cheek.

'Give the Führer a chance, Brigitte. Now that Poland is obliterated, there is no reason for France or Britain to continue the war. We may have peace by the time spring comes. Hold on to that hope, eh? Now, to bed with you, before I tell the Gestapo you are sharing un-German propaganda.'

He watched as she climbed the stairs to the galleried landing, turned on the light and disappeared from view. Then, making his way to the parlour, he sat in the chair in front of the stove and opened the hatch. The heavy iron was still warm, even through the thickness of his gloves, and he saw a dim glow within. When he opened the vent, the heat intensified and smoke curled up. Taking some kindling, he arranged it over the first small flames to flicker into life. He waited until there was a healthy blaze before he added some split logs and shut the hatch. Already he could feel the warmth radiating from the ironwork, and he let it seep into his body, smiling with contentment.

He glanced at the desk beneath the blackout curtains. There was a briefcase sitting there that contained a folder of reports awaiting his attention. He had been putting off the moment all day at the office, and now again at home. It could be delayed no longer. He eased himself to his feet and crossed to the small side table where he kept a decanter of brandy and some glasses, and poured himself a generous measure. Then, settling in the leather desk chair with the warmth of the fire at his back, he opened the case and took out the file. Reaching for a pen, he flicked open the cover and glanced over the first report, considering the hand-written recommendation at the bottom. His right hand moved, and the nib hovered over the report.

He hesitated, then knocked the brandy back, feeling the fiery liquid surge down his throat. Setting the glass down with a rap, he marked the final box on the page with a '+', moved the sheet to the side and considered the next document.

The clock on the mantelpiece marked the passage of time with a steady *tick tock*. Every so often, Schmesler stirred to place another log in the stove as he worked late into the night processing the documents into two piles: one for those marked in the same way that the first report had been, and a smaller pile where he had left the box empty and merely signed the report instead.

Upstairs, his wife slept alone in her thick nightdress beneath several layers of covers. She lay on her side, breathing deeply, sleeping in a dreamless and untroubled state until the early hours of the morning, when a sharp crack sounded from downstairs and jolted her awake. For a few heartbeats she was not sure if she had imagined the sound. She reached under the covers to where her husband usually lay, but he was not there, and the bedding was cold and clammy. She waited for several minutes, listening for further sounds before she stirred. Turning on the bedside lamp, she squinted at the sudden brightness as she looked at the alarm clock. Just past three o'clock. An absurd hour for her husband to still be working.

She swung her legs from under the covers and slid her feet into her slippers before making for the top of the stairs.

'Manfred,' she called out. 'Manfred . . .'

She waited for a response, but there was silence, and she tutted irritably as she descended the stairs and made for his study. As she opened the door, warm air washed over her, and with it came the acrid odour of gun smoke.

'Manfred . . . ?'

She did not see her husband immediately. There were papers scattered across the desk and on the floor nearby. The chair lay on its side, and an outstretched arm projected from behind it. A short distance from the curled fingers of the hand lay the dark shape of a pistol.

Chapter One

31 January

It was shortly after midday when the door to the Kripo section office opened. Sergeant Hauser looked up as a man in a dark coat hung his hat on the stand inside the entrance. He crossed to the stove in the centre of the room and turned to warm his back before nodding a greeting. The sergeant was doing his best to write up some notes while recovering from a gunshot wound to his shoulder. Although it had been a flesh wound, he still wore a sling from time to time when he needed to ease what remained of the pain. Now he set his pen down.

'How did it go, sir?'

His superior, Criminal Inspector Horst Schenke, had attended a funeral that morning. Count Anton Harstein and his wife, an elderly couple who had been family friends, had been murdered shortly before Christmas. Thanks to the paperwork associated with the investigation and the delay caused by frozen soil, it had taken five weeks before the bodies could be buried. Count Harstein had once managed the Silver Arrows motor racing team that Schenke had driven for before a crash had ended his racing career and left him with a limp.

After the accident, Schenke had needed a new direction in life and had joined the police.

He took a deep breath. 'As well as such things can.'

Despite the Harsteins being aristocratic and well connected, few mourners had turned up to the funeral. Apart from Schenke and his girlfriend, Karin, there had been no more than ten others, including the Harsteins' son, an army officer who had been given compassionate leave to attend. The bitter winter had kept away most of those who might otherwise have been there, and the priest had stumbled through the service with chattering teeth, somewhat faster than was decent. The murders had cast a pall over what little Christmas cheer there had been, and Schenke was still grieving for them in his private moments. He did not want to give his feelings away.

'How's the wound healing?' he asked Hauser.

'Slowly enough to save me from household chores.' Hauser grinned. 'Helga's starting to get suspicious, though, so I'm having to show some signs of recovery.'

'You live dangerously, my friend.' Schenke had only met Hauser's wife on a handful of occasions, but that was more than enough to realise that she was formidable. 'Even without being shot at.'

Both men were quiet for a moment as they recalled the incident at the Abwehr headquarters where Hauser had taken a bullet, then the sergeant turned to a thin man in his mid-twenties sitting at another desk. He had fine white hair over a gaunt, bespectacled face, and unlike the others he wore no coat but sat in a simple dark suit and tie, apparently oblivious to the cold. He was reading the front page of the *Völkischer Beobachter* newspaper. The headline story concerned the gallant resistance of the Finnish army as it held back the Russian invasion and defied the ill-equipped and incompetent legions of Stalin. Even though a pact had been signed with Russia the previous August, the article was clearly sympathetic to the Finns. *Russia put in its place*, the headline ran. Schenke wondered how long such a treaty could endure between two nations with such diametrically opposed ideologies? It was odd, Schenke thought, that a very real war was taking place with high numbers of casualties – at least on the Russian side – while the land war Germany was involved in seemed to be little more than an occasional exchange of shots and the dropping of propaganda leaflets since the fall of Poland. Although, like many people, he still hoped for a peaceful resolution, he was beginning to fear that worse was to come.

'Liebwitz, go and see if the man from the lab has finished examining those ration coupons that came in this morning.'

'Yes, Sergeant.' Liebwitz rose quickly and gave a nod before he strode out of the office.

Schenke felt a stab of guilt. Liebwitz had been sent to the Kripo section to assist with the investigation into the killings before Christmas. Recruited into the Gestapo, his stiffly formal attitude had not endeared him to his colleagues, and Schenke suspected that he had been assigned to the Kripo to get him out of the way. Now he was waiting for official confirmation that his transfer was permanent. The wheels of bureaucracy were turning at their usual glacial pace, so for the moment, Liebwitz was still officially Gestapo, and that made him a target for Hauser, who treated him as the office dogsbody.

'You could go easy on him,' Schenke said.

'He has to pay his dues, like any member of the team.'

'He has nothing to prove. He's done a good job.'

'So far . . .'

Schenke could see that he was not going to shift the sergeant's feelings towards the new man and looked round the office at the empty desks. 'Where are the rest of the team this morning?'

'Frieda and Rosa are interviewing a woman about a domestic assault. Persinger and Hofer are out rounding up a few of the known forgers and fences for interrogation about the fake ration coupons. One of them must know something about it.'

Schenke nodded. Persinger and Hofer were veterans of the police force. Both were big men who had a talent for getting information out of suspects, even without having to resort to violence. There was a no-nonsense demeanour about them that was usefully intimidating. Frieda Echs was in her forties, solid and efficient, with enough lived experience to handle situations sensitively. The section's other woman, Rosa Mayer, was slim, blonde and striking, and was good at her job and at fending off attempts to flirt with her.

'Schmidt and Baumer are down at the Alex attending a political education seminar.'

'I'm sure that will broaden their minds,' Schenke responded quietly as he considered the political training sessions held at the Alexanderplatz police headquarters. Schmidt and Baumer had joined the force since the Nazis had seized power, and were therefore deemed more likely to be responsive to the regime's propaganda. Hence their summons to the seminar. Even so, Schenke had sufficient faith in their intelligence and detective training that he was confident they would privately question what they were told. Even though Hauser was a party member, the sergeant similarly had little time for some of the activities of the Nazi Party. The notion that there was an 'Aryan way' of conducting criminal investigations struck both men as a ridiculous waste of time.

'I dare say we'll be sent for political training at some point.'

Hauser shrugged. 'No doubt. In the meantime, let's just do the job, eh, sir?'

There was a subtle warning in the retort to remind Schenke that the occasional critical comment about the party was acceptable, but not to push the issue.

The door opened, and both men turned to see Liebwitz holding it ajar to admit an overweight man with a sour expression. He wore an unbuttoned coat over his suit and swept the folds aside to stuff his hands in his pockets. While Liebwitz hurried past him to his desk, the visitor glanced at the two Kripo men by the stove and fixed his eyes on Hauser.

'Inspector?'

The sergeant pointed at his superior. 'Try him.'

The man shifted his gaze. 'Doctor Albert Widmann, from Chemistry Analysis at the Werdescher Labs.' He didn't offer a handshake.

'Criminal Inspector Horst Schenke. You've had a good look at the latest batch of coupons we seized. What do you make of them?'

Widmann collected his thoughts. 'They're good. Easy to take for the real thing, to the unpractised eye. For an expert like myself, of course, the forgeries are obvious to detect.'

'Oh?' Hauser arched an eyebrow. 'How so? From an expert's point of view, of course.'

Widmann puffed his chest out slightly. 'Certain irregularities on the perforations, for example. You wouldn't notice if you were presented with a single coupon, but it's clear to see when you have a sheet of them in front of you.'

'How do they compare with the others we already have?' asked Schenke. 'Do they come from the same source?'

'From first inspection, I'd say so, but I'll have to take them back to the lab to test the composition of the dyes and the paper before I can confirm that. Do you suspect they are the work of one man, or one crime ring?'

'We don't know. It's a possibility.'

'If so, it should make them easier to track down.'

Schenke shared an amused glance with Hauser, and Widmann frowned.

'What?'

'If it's the work of one crime ring, then we're dealing with a sizeable organisation. One that's managed not only to avoid the previous round-ups but is sufficiently well hidden from police eyes that we haven't encountered them yet. If it's more than one ring, there's a chance we'll already know about some of them and we can use our informers to uncover the links between them.'

Widmann nodded. 'I see. Very good. Makes sense.'

Hauser cleared his throat. 'Perhaps you should spend some time with us. Be good for you to see how Kripo does its work out on the streets.'

'In this weather?' Widmann said. 'Fuck that. I'll stick to my nice warm lab, thank you.'

All three shared a brief laugh before Widmann buttoned his coat. 'I'll fetch those samples and be on my way.'

'Let us know the results as soon as you can,' said Schenke.

'You're not the only investigators calling on my time. I've a few other jobs to do first.'

Schenke stepped between Widmann and the door. 'If we don't put a stop to these forgers, many people will have to go without food this winter. I'm not sure how sympathetic starving people are going to be about your priorities. And if the people are unhappy and that gets back to Heydrich's office, I doubt he'll be sympathetic either. What do you say, Liebwitz? You're a Gestapo man. You're better placed to know how the Gruppenführer will react.'

Liebwitz looked up from his paperwork with his usual deadpan expression. 'I think he would be displeased to hear of any dissatisfaction amongst the people, sir.'

At the mention of the name of the director of the Reich Security Main Office, Widmann's eyes widened. He swallowed nervously.

'I'll see what I can do.'

Schenke smiled. 'I'm sure you will. Thanks.'

Once the scientist had closed the door behind him, Schenke turned to Liebwitz with a grin. 'Couldn't have done a better job myself of putting the shits up him.'

'I merely expressed the truth, sir. Heydrich pays close attention to the social intelligence reports. I have seen his response to those he does not like at first hand.'

Schenke was not yet certain how much the new team member's attitude was down to dedicated professionalism and how much was due to defective social skills.

'Of course you have,' he responded, and then glanced at his watch. 'I'm going out for some lunch. If Persinger and Hofer get back before I do, tell them to start the interrogations without me.'

Hauser nodded, and the inspector turned to leave, pulling up his collar in readiness for the bitter cold of the street.

* * *

Even though the snowfall had been fitful since New Year, the streets had not yet been cleared. Stained mounds lined the pavements, shoulder-high in places, with gaps left at crossing points. Grit had been laid on the paths and gave the icy surface a dirty speckled appearance. Despite the cold, there were plenty of people out, moving quickly, chins down as they left trails of breath in their wake. Those buildings lucky enough to have regular heating were betrayed by the absence of snow on their roof tiles, and Schenke noted the bare roof of the local party office. An SA man was outside, pasting a replacement over a blackout poster that had been defaced by a brush moustache and a lick of dark hair over the forehead of the skeletal head of death as it rode a bomb dropped by a British plane.

The SA man glanced round, and for a moment Schenke feared he would raise his arm in the 'German greeting', which would oblige Schenke to remove his hand from his pocket to do the same. But the man glanced at the pasting brush in his right hand and rolled his eyes instead, and Schenke smiled as he strode by.

At the end of the street, he turned left into a working-class neighbourhood where there were a number of traditional beer cellars and cafés. He crossed the street and made for the entrance of Wehler's, where it was still possible to buy coffee. The bell above the door clanged as he entered and closed it quickly behind him. A warm fug of smoky air filled a large space packed with tables and chairs. A counter ran the length of the rear of the café, and the mirrors mounted on the wall behind it made the place feel twice as large.

Wehler's was popular with those taking a midday meal, but Schenke was able to find himself a seat in a cosy booth beside a window overlooking the street. He unbuttoned his coat and loosened his scarf as he waited for one of the waiters to come over. The condensation on the inside of the window made it impossible to see out clearly, and those passing by were only visible as dark blurs. So it was that he missed the figure who had followed him from the precinct and now stood hesitantly on the far side of the street.

His mind played over Widmann's comments about the forged ration coupons. If it was the case that they were dealing with a previously unknown crime ring, then their prey was going to be difficult to track down. One thing the Nazi regime had achieved was the rounding-up of most of Berlin's criminal organisations and the execution or imprisonment of their members. In the frequent absence of legal niceties such as evidence and due process, such measures had succeeded in reducing organised crime, though the crimes of individuals continued: theft, fraud, assault, mugging, rape and murder. Whatever regime was in power, such crimes would always live alongside humanity. He forced his mind away from work and thought about Karin instead. They had arranged to watch the latest film starring Heinrich George at the local *Ufa* cinema that night. He was looking forward to seeing her.

A woman lowered herself onto the bench on the other side of the booth. Schenke glanced up with a polite smile, ready to welcome any companion for lunch. Then his smile froze as he saw her face, and he felt an icy prickle of anxiety grip the back of his neck.

Chapter Two

Ruth Frankel was slight and wore a threadbare brown coat. The seam on one of her gloves was pulling apart and her face looked pale, even for a Berliner in the middle of winter. Her dark eyes regarded him nervously beneath fine eyebrows and a widow's peak of dark curly hair that fell beneath the brim of her felt hat.

'Hello, Horst.' She forced a smile. 'How are you?'

Schenke glanced round the café, but no one seemed to be looking in their direction or paying them attention. He spoke quietly. 'What are you doing here?'

'I need to speak to you. There's no one else who can help me.'

He leaned forward. 'What do you want? Money?'

She frowned slightly and shook her head. 'That's not why I'm here. Why would you think that, I wonder? Wouldn't have anything to do with all those posters and newspaper smears about money-grabbing Jews the party is so fond of printing? You think I'd risk trying to blackmail you? Is that it?'

Schenke inhaled deeply to calm himself. 'I'm sorry, Ruth.

But you know the danger we both face if anyone realises what you are and informs on us.'

Her expression became frigid. 'You make me sound like a thing rather than a person. Is that what I am to you?'

Schenke was stung by her comment, then felt guilty. Ruth had been instrumental in catching the killer who had been using the blackout to murder women in the last months of the previous year. She had nearly been a victim herself, and had she not fought off her attacker and provided crucial information to Schenke and his team, the killer would still be at large. In the brief time he had known her, he had felt pity, and guilt, for her predicament. If they had lived in another Germany, she would be someone he would be keen to know better.

'I didn't think I'd see you again.'

She smiled sadly. 'I had no intention of seeing you either. I wanted to disappear into the shadows and stay out of sight as much as possible, long enough for people to forget my face in the newspapers. That was your doing, remember.'

'I had no choice. The orders came from the head of the Gestapo.'

'So you say.'

A waiter was heading towards them, and Schenke beckoned to him while Ruth sat back and pretended to rummage in her handbag as if looking for something.

He nodded a greeting to the man. 'I'll have the soup of the day and coffee.'

'No coffee, sir. We have a substitute, if that will do?'

Schenke recoiled at the thought of the bitter ersatz coffee. 'Tea, then.'

'Very good, sir. And what will the lady have?'

Schenke was taken aback by the question. He had not

intended to share a meal with Ruth and had hoped that she might be persuaded to speak her piece and leave him alone as swiftly as possible. Every moment he spent in her company endangered them, her most of all. Any Jew caught consorting with an Aryan in a public place was likely to be sent to a work camp, from where she would not return. Schenke would be kicked out of the police and imprisoned for several months before being released to scratch a living on the margins of society. They must bluff it out now and act as if this was a normal, and lawful, lunch date.

'I'll have the same,' said Ruth.

'Very good.' The waiter turned to make his way back through the café. They would be left alone for a while, and Schenke folded his arms to make it clear to anyone watching that they were not a couple. Even so, he saw from her pinched, pale face that Ruth could use a decent meal, and he felt an urge to help her.

'What is this about?' he asked in a gentle tone. 'You said you needed my help. Why me particularly?'

'Because you're a policeman.'

'I'd have thought that was the very last kind of person you'd turn to.'

'In any other circumstances, yes. But I know you, Horst. I know you are a good man who wants to do what is right.'

'I want to uphold the law and bring to justice those who break it. That's all.'

She gave him a knowing look. 'That's what you might tell others. You don't have to spin me that line. I know you have more integrity than most. And compassion.'

It was pointless to refute her observation and pretend that a hard heart dwelled beneath the professional veneer he tried to cultivate. He had treated her with some kindness and consideration during the murder investigation; at the very least he had shown her sympathy. He was tempted to feel more for her, and quickly stifled the impulse.

'All right. I will hear you out, but I can't promise to do more than that. Even if I want to.'

'I understand.' Ruth paused and looked down at her gloved hands as she collected her thoughts. 'I'm here on behalf of a family friend. A good friend. She lost her husband a few days back. You may have heard about it. His name was Manfred Schmesler.'

'Schmesler?' Schenke searched his memory and recalled a brief obituary in the *Völkischer Beobachter*. 'Yes, I saw the report. A doctor, as I recall. He lived in Pankow.'

'An SS Reich doctor,' said Ruth, and he saw the flicker of distaste on her face. 'But he was a family friend long before he joined the SS, and the party. He was close friends with my father when they were at university, and they remained close until that was no longer possible. But they stayed in contact, being careful that it was done in secret. Schmesler and his wife supplied us with extra rations and money from time to time.' She paused. 'Needless to say, I trust you not to repeat any of this. I would not want his widow to get into trouble. She already has enough to cope with without falling foul of the police or the Gestapo.'

'I understand. Go on.'

'Although the newspapers do not give the details of his death, the official version is that Manfred Schmesler committed suicide. That's what the police concluded after they were called to the scene. His widow is adamant that he would never have killed himself. He was under pressure at work, but he enjoyed life and loved his wife.' There was something in the tone of her voice when she said 'wife' that struck Schenke as odd.

'That's how it appears sometimes,' he said, 'but people can hide their true feelings well enough for their family to be unaware. Did he leave a note?'

'Yes,' Ruth conceded.

'So?'

'His wife says she can't believe that it can be true.'

'What *does* it say?'

Ruth shook her head. 'I don't know. She was too upset to tell me. Only that he had never given any indication that he was ashamed of his work and did not deserve to live. She is certain that he did not die by his own hand.'

'Murder?' Schenke frowned. 'How did it happen?'

'He was shot through the head. She discovered him in his study with a gun close to his hand.'

'His own gun?'

Ruth nodded.

'And the note was where?'

'On the desk.'

'Written in his hand?'

Ruth thought a moment and nodded. 'That's what Brigitte, his wife . . . widow says.'

'I have to say that on the face of it, the death could well be a suicide.'

They were interrupted by the return of the waiter carrying a tray bearing two steaming bowls, two teacups on saucers and a teapot. He set them on the table, along with spoons, and withdrew. Schenke made sure the man was out of earshot before he spoke.

'Where do I feature in this situation?'

'Brigitte Schmesler wants you to look into her husband's death and say whether you think it was really suicide. She knows that I helped you find the man responsible for killing those women last year. I told her you were a good man. She thought her request would be better coming from someone you know personally. So I agreed to approach you.'

Schenke nodded slowly as he stared across the table. 'You're taking a big risk on behalf of someone you say is a family friend,' he prompted, but her expression remained fixed, so he continued. 'If the police have concluded it was suicide, they must have their reasons.'

'Brigitte is convinced they are wrong.'

Schenke realised that it would look strange if they neglected their meal, so he picked up his spoon and sipped his soup cautiously. Ruth did the same. Both were silent for a while as he thought over what she had told him. If there had been any doubt about Schmesler's death, the matter would have been referred to Schenke's section at the Pankow precinct. Clearly the regular police, the Orpo, were content that it was a suicide. That was a rush to judgement that struck him as unusual, given Brigitte Schmesler's conviction that her husband had not taken his own life. Even with all the disruption caused by the war and the shortage of men due to conscription, someone should have referred the case to the Kripo. The fact that the Orpo had decided that no further inquiry into the death was required made it difficult for him to raise the matter without giving an explanation for his interest. All the same, he hoped it would not ruffle too many feathers if he merely asked a few questions. Enough to persuade Brigitte that it was suicide after all.

But what if she was right? Or at least, what if the answers

were not sufficiently convincing? What then? With the investigation into the forged ration coupons taking up nearly all Schenke's time, any new investigation would be an extra burden. However, if it hadn't been for Ruth, it was likely that the police would still be hunting for the killer stalking the capital's railway system before Christmas. He owed her a favour.

'What are you thinking?' She was staring at him. 'Will you look into it?'

'And what if I think it *is* suicide? Will you let the matter go?'

She nodded. 'I've risked enough just to approach you. If you tell me you think the official decision is correct, I'll inform Brigitte and leave you alone. But I can't answer for what she may do.'

'Fair enough. I'll see what I can find out. Give me two days.'

'Shall I meet you here?'

'I'd rather not. It's not safe for you. There's a newspaper kiosk outside the U-Bahn station. We'll meet there at noon. It won't take long, either way.'

She glanced down at her soup hungrily, and Schenke realised she had been counting on another meal. 'All right, we'll meet here. Just make sure you aren't being watched. If I see anyone following you, we'll meet at the kiosk the next day. Agreed?'

Ruth nodded. 'Thank you.'

They ate in silence and mopped up the dregs of their soup with the dark bread before Schenke sat back and regarded her sympathetically. 'How are you coping? Still living with the old woman who took you in?'

'She kicked me out as soon as she heard I'd been involved with the police.'

'Where did you go?'

'A friend let me stay with her for a few days,' she replied with a guarded expression.

'You have nothing to fear from me,' said Schenke. 'I have no interest in the comings and goings of you or your people. I have bigger fish to fry.'

She picked up her cup and drank some tea. 'And what happens when the Jews become the bigger fish?'

'Hopefully that won't be my problem.'

'But it will be mine. And if your superiors make it yours? Would you hunt me down if you were ordered to?'

Schenke considered the question briefly. 'Only if you had committed the kind of crime that falls within the usual remit of the Kripo. Otherwise, no. I'd find a way to leave you be.'

'I hope I never have to hold you to that, Horst. But with the way things are going, the outlook for the Jews is bleak. From the rumours I hear, the Polish are being treated like animals by your masters. If that is the case, what hope have my people got?'

'What will you do?'

'If the time comes when the party decides to remove the Jews, I have a plan.'

'You won't be able to hide for ever.'

'I may not have to.' She dropped her voice to a whisper. 'Just long enough to survive until Germany is defeated and the Führer and his scum are swept away.'

Schenke shook his head. 'That's insane. The war may already be over. Poland has been conquered and Britain and France have no reason to fight. Even Britain's colonies are starting to see the light. General Hertzog and his Boer party are pushing the South African parliament to declare a separate peace with Germany. If they succeed and other parts of the empire follow suit, Britain will not be able to fight. I believe there's still a chance we'll be at peace in a few months' time.'

'You think so? You think the Führer is the kind of man who believes in peace? He doesn't. He thrives on war. One day he will pick a fight with a more powerful nation and Germany will be crushed.'

Whatever he might think of the present regime, Schenke was a patriot, and he was offended by her words. 'You saw how easily our armed forces swept through Poland. Other nations will have seen that and been warned of the consequences of waging war with us. Germany will not be defeated, and it is treason to wish it.'

Ruth regarded him thoughtfully. 'I always thought that the lesson of history was that treason is measured in the damage done to a nation by certain people. It is often the case that those who most vociferously claim to be patriots turn out to cause the most harm. I think that's true of the Führer, his party and those who blindly follow him . . . don't you?'

Schenke did not reply, feeling his anger rise, and at the same time, a spark of fear that her words might turn out to be true. Just as had been the case in the war that had taken place earlier that century.

Ruth finished her tea. 'I'd better go. I have an evening shift at Siemens.'

'I'll see you in two days' time.' He reached across the table impulsively and took her hand. 'Be careful, Ruth.'

They exchanged a look for a beat before Schenke withdrew his hand and cleared his throat awkwardly.

'I'll be fine.' She forced a smile, then stood and left, making sure not to hurry and draw attention to herself.

Once she had stepped out into the street, Schenke gave a deep sigh, finished his tea and indicated to the waiter that he was ready to pay. As he emerged from the café, he saw that the grey sky had become darker and an icy breeze had picked up, swirling the first small flakes of snow that had begun to fall. He pulled up his collar, shoved his hands into his pockets and strode back towards the precinct.

Chapter Three

The Kripo section office occupied one end of the precinct building, a former barracks built during the Bismarck era, when the Prussian army had seemed invincible after crushing their Austrian and French foes. The stables at the rear had been converted into garages and storerooms, while some of the original accommodation was preserved for the use of police units whenever officers were called in from other forces to provide additional security for parades. The days when they might be required to put down communist demonstrations or to limit the transgressions of far-right paramilitaries during the troublesome years of the Republic had long since passed. The uniformed police took up most of the main building, and Schenke went to find the officer in charge of the district where the Schmesler residence was located. Hauptmann Sperlemann had been recently transferred to Pankow, Schenke knew through the precinct's 'mouth wireless', but their paths had not yet crossed.

Sperlemann's office was at the end of a corridor on the third floor of the building. A polished brass plate outside had his name and rank engraved on it in the old-fashioned block type that the party liked to use to promote the distinctiveness of German culture. Schenke rapped on the varnished wood. There was no reply, and he knocked again and waited before trying the knob. The office was unlocked, and he eased the door open before stepping over the threshold.

The interior was panelled, and two windows on the far side overlooked the courtyard behind the precinct. A lit stove to one side provided a comfortable warmth throughout the room. A large desk stood opposite, with two wooden trays placed neatly side by side to the right and a penholder and inkpot to the left. A telephone sat in the middle. Behind the desk was a leather chair above which hung a portrait of the Führer in a three-quarter pose as he stared, as if deep in thought, in the direction of the ice-rimmed windows.

Schenke was considering whether to leave a note for Sperlemann when he heard footsteps and turned to look down the corridor. An officer in a double-breasted greatcoat was approaching, a frown on his face. 'You're letting the heat out of the bloody room. Get inside.'

Schenke did as he was told, and a moment later the other man closed the door and pulled off his leather gloves as he regarded his visitor.

'You're from the Kripo section, aren't you?' His voice was clipped, and he removed his hat and scarf to expose fleshy jowls and a scar on his left cheek. It was small enough to indicate a carefully supervised duel, or it could have been the result of an accident. Sperlemann's eyes were brown, like his hair, which had been cut short at the sides, combed back from the forehead and held in place with sugar water. His head was potato-shaped and his complexion was poor. He appeared to be in his mid forties, so it was unlikely that he would be promoted much further.

Schenke cleared his throat. 'Criminal Inspector Horst Schenke. Section head.'

Sperlemann looked him over. 'I'd have expected an older, more experienced man. More to the point, I'd have thought someone your age would have been called up by now.'

'I was excused conscription on account of an old leg injury, sir,' Schenke explained.

'Leg injury, eh?' There was a hint of scepticism in the man's voice that caused Schenke's pulse to quicken with anger. Sperlemann was old enough to have fought in the previous war, and might well be the kind to harbour resentment at those unable to serve in the armed forces. Schenke himself felt a degree of shame that he couldn't fight for his country, but there was nothing he could do about it.

'What kind of leg injury?' Sperlemann pressed.

'A motor-racing accident.'

'Motor racing?' He cocked an eyebrow, and then his eyes widened as he made the link. 'Schenke! Silver Arrow Schenke.'

'That's what some of the papers called me,' Schenke reluctantly acknowledged.

'You're too modest. I saw you race once. You came second to some damned Italian. That was the race before . . .' Sperlemann paused, an awkward expression on his face.

'The crash, yes.' Schenke did not like to dwell on the past. On a career that had been painfully torn from his grasp. Gone were the heady days of being a sporting star. All that remained from that part of his life was an occasionally painful restriction of movement in his leg that caused him to limp. Now he was a criminal investigator, putting his brain to the test instead of his body.

Sperlemann sensed his disquiet and did not pursue the subject. Instead he hung his hat and scarf on the pegs to one side of the door and began to unbutton his coat, revealing an Iron Cross ribbon on his uniform jacket. 'What's the purpose of your visit to my office, Schenke?'

'I have a few questions about a recent death that might merit further investigation.'

'A death? What death is that?' Sperlemann slung his coat across the back of a chair and moved to the stove to warm his back, hands on hips.

'SS Reich Doctor Schmesler. He was found dead in his study by his wife.'

'Yes, I know. The man committed suicide. Blew his brains out. What of it?'

'I understand there was a suicide note.'

'Yes. Short and to the point. Schmesler said he was feeling depressed following a terminal diagnosis for a brain tumour. He wanted to avoid a prolonged and painful death.'

Brain tumour? Why had Ruth kept that from him? Schenke wondered. 'Was there anything else in the note?'

Sperlemann thought a moment and shrugged. 'A few loving words to his wife, asking her for forgiveness.'

'That's all?'

'What more do you want? A bloody existential treatise on the meaningless of life? By all accounts the man was a gifted doctor at the top of his game, with everything to live for. The tumour changed that. So it goes. The matter is closed. I'm sure the Kripo have better things to do. Why do you want to look into it? You think the Orpo have botched it?'

Schenke was prepared for the question. 'Schmesler was a member of the SS. I would imagine that Himmler would not take kindly to the death of one of his officers being brushed under the carpet. I could call the Reich Security Main Office to notify them that I believe the case should be re-examined, or we could keep the matter in house while I deal with it.'

Sperlemann looked at him in silence, and Schenke could guess the thoughts running through his head. To obstruct Schenke might entail provoking the ire of a senior member of the SS. Fear of their superiors had taught many subordinates to adopt an unofficial policy of obeying orders before they were given.

'Very well, what do you want to know?'

'It would be simplest if you let me read the file. I am sure you are a busy man; I wouldn't want to intrude on your time any more than necessary.'

Sperlemann was not the kind of person to give in with good grace. 'I can let you have it until tomorrow. I want it back on my desk in the morning. Is that clear?'

'As you wish.'

He crossed to his desk and took a brown file out of one of the trays. Schenke stepped forward to take the proffered file and was relieved to see that it was slim enough to contain few documents.

'Thank you.' He turned to the door and made his way back into the corridor.

'Tomorrow morning, remember,' Sperlemann called after him as Schenke closed the door.

Back at the Kripo section, he entered his own office and left the door open to admit some of the heat from the stove outside the thin partition of wood and glass that separated him from his team. He ordered Liebwitz to bring him a mug of ersatz coffee, then sat down to read through the details of Schmesler's death. He fanned through the documents: the brief statement of the first officer on the scene, the more detailed report of the officer in charge, together with his conclusions. There was a crudely drawn diagram of Schmesler's study, notes from the interview with Brigitte Schmesler, and several photographic prints of the body from various angles. He scrutinised the photos carefully. It was possible that the doctor had shot himself while seated and had fallen to the floor between the chair and the desk. It was more likely that he had been standing when he shot himself.

Assuming that was how he had met his end.

The position of the gun was equally ambiguous. Sometimes a suicide victim's hand clenched around the weapon, sometimes spasms caused it to be released. Turning his attention to the rest of the room, Schenke saw that the blackout blinds were in place, there was no sign of forced entry, and the doctor's paperwork was arranged neatly, though there were dark stains where blood had sprayed across the top of the desk. The splatters looked relatively spread out, as if the point of origin for the blood and brain matter was from a lower height. It seemed that Schmesler had been seated then, he decided.

There was a photograph of the suicide note. Schenke read through the doctor's last words.

My dearest Brigitte,

I cannot tell you how hard it is to leave this world, and you, behind. We have had a long and happy marriage and it pains me to end it this way. You will have noticed my change of mood recently. I have been suffering increasingly severe headaches the last few months, and consulted a specialist, who confirmed what I feared. There is a malignant tumour in my brain and it is growing so swiftly that I have months if not weeks to live. My end would be an agony I would not inflict on you or myself. So I must go. May God forgive me for what I am about to do.

Your adoring husband,

Manfred

'Like Sperlemann said, short and sweet,' Schenke muttered to himself. When he read it through again, though, the terseness seemed to strike a false note. He tried to imagine himself in the doctor's place and how he would phrase the note he might pen for Karin to find. It would certainly be more emotional, more sensitive to her feelings. Perhaps Schmesler was a bit of a cold fish. Or he was trying to spare his wife too many details . . .

He looked for the coroner's report and found it towards the end of the file, just before the form completed by Sperlemann closing the case and authorising all relevant documents to be sent to the records office in the basement of the precinct. The coroner reported that death had resulted from a gunshot injury to the forehead. There were scorch marks on the flesh around the entry wound that indicated the muzzle of the pistol was close to or touching the skin at the time it was discharged. The coroner's summation was almost as concise as the note, and confirmed that suicide was the cause of the doctor's death. The absence of any comment about the brain tumour struck Schenke as odd.

There seemed to be an air of indecent haste hovering over the documents in the folder. It did not feel right. Schenke sifted back through the papers until he found the notes from the interview with Brigitte Schmesler. As he read them, he tried to picture her being questioned as the body was removed from the study and taken to the morgue for the coroner to inspect. The notes described the interview in the plain style used by the police, but reading between the lines, the raw emotion and shock was easy to imagine. Brigitte was adamant that her husband would not have killed himself, the tumour notwithstanding. Nor would he have kept the knowledge of his fatal condition from her. Their marriage had been happy, and they had trusted each other and kept no secrets. And yet she could not name any person with a grievance against her husband that might motivate them to harm him. Schmesler had had many friends and was respected and regarded with affection by all who knew and worked with him.

Schenke was aware from his Kripo training days that people were prone to denial when the police confronted them with evidence of their spouses' darkest secrets. In some cases, they even denied what was obviously true. Shock and grief would do that to most people, so he was not surprised by the interview notes, and knew it was not wise to put too much store by Brigitte's comments at this stage.

Moving on, he found the report on the weapon. A broom-handled Mauser, something of an unusual firearm given the preference for smaller and more portable pistols these days. One round had been fired, and the spent bullet had been found embedded in a book on the shelf at the side of the room. He examined the photo of the Mauser closely and then set it down and tried to visualise the dimensions as he made his right hand into the shape of a pistol and aimed it at the centre of his own forehead.

'It's not that bad, surely?'

Glancing up, he saw Hauser standing in the doorway of his office. He grinned with embarrassment as he lowered his hand.

'What's that you're looking at?' Hauser asked, tilting his head as he glanced at the contents of the open file.

Schenke hesitated before answering. He was on potentially dangerous ground, having withheld the real reason for his interest in the case from Sperlemann. It would be unfair to draw the sergeant into the matter. Even so, the rush to judgement by the Orpo and the promise he had made to Ruth made it hard to let the matter rest. There was enough doubt in his mind to warrant a closer look into the circumstances of Schmesler's death.

'I'd like you and Liebwitz in on this. Bring him in and close the door.'

Chapter Four

Once Schenke had explained the circumstances of Schmesler's death, he paused and looked at his subordinates directly.

'Before I go into any further details,' he began, 'you have to know that I was not made aware of this case through the usual channels. I was contacted by a civilian who was concerned that the Pankow police had made the wrong call when they put Schmesler's death down as a suicide.'

'Who contacted you, sir?' asked Liebwitz.

'It's best that I don't give you a name at this stage. Let's say it was a friend of the Schmesler family.'

Liebwitz blinked. 'Sir, as far as I understand the process, any request to question the findings of a closed case has to be referred to the local commander. In this case, Oberst Kleist.'

'I haven't made an official request at this stage,' Schenke responded. 'And I won't if we come to the conclusion that suicide is the most likely explanation. I'll return the file to Sperlemann and that will be an end to it.'

Hauser smiled slightly. 'I'm getting the feeling that you're already not convinced about the official verdict.'

'There are some aspects that cause me to doubt it,' Schenke

replied. 'But I won't say any more until you've had a chance to look at the file. Before we do that, I want to make it clear that I am not ordering you to help me. It may be the case that someone higher up has decided it would be best for Schmesler's death to be recorded as a suicide. In which case I'll understand if either of you doesn't want to get involved . . . Well?'

Hauser and Liebwitz exchanged a glance before the latter responded. 'Even if this is not according to protocol, we are police officers. We are duty-bound to investigate, sir.'

'I take it that means you are willing to help.'

Liebwitz frowned. 'I believe that is the gist of what I said, sir.'

Schenke nodded. 'Thank you, Scharführer. How about you, Sergeant?'

Hauser jerked his thumb towards the former Gestapo man. 'Same as what he said, I think.'

'Good. Then let's get started.'

The three men pored over the contents of the file for more than an hour. They worked in silence, broken occasionally by a request for a specific document to compare details. Hauser was a thirty-year veteran, and his experience of crime and human nature was unmatched in the Kripo section. By contrast, Liebwitz was young, though his naivety and lack of social skills were in some measure compensated for by the quickest mind that Schenke had ever encountered amongst the police officers of Berlin. His piercing eyes swept from side to side behind the round lenses of his glasses as he scanned the documents, and he paid no attention to the other two men. At the opposite end of the desk, Hauser nodded to himself and muttered under his breath. A study in contrasts, Schenke thought with amusement as he glanced at them.

Dusk was gathering outside when Schenke went to brew more coffee. He returned with three mugs, which he set down on his desk. Once he was seated back in his chair, he cleared his throat.

'I think we've read enough to have come to some views about Schmesler's death. So, is it suicide or not? What do you say, Hauser?'

'We've got the suicide note, the gun by the body and no obvious enemies. Even his wife agrees with that. Of course, she says he had no reason to feel suicidal, but I've heard that before in suicide cases. Shock and denial often go hand in hand. I dare say if we interviewed her a month from now, she'd feel a little differently about it.' The sergeant paused and scratched his chin. 'I'd say it was likely to be suicide, based on what's in the file. Which isn't as detailed as I'd like, admittedly.'

Schenke nodded and turned to Liebwitz. 'What's your view?'

The younger man scanned his notes briefly before he responded. 'I agree with most of what Sergeant Hauser has said.'

'That is gratifying to hear,' said Hauser.

Liebwitz looked at him and spoke in his habitual flat tone. 'There are many reasons why a suicide verdict could be educed. However, Brigitte Schmesler is convinced that her husband had no reason to contemplate ending his life.'

Hauser sighed wearily. 'Like I said, I've heard the same thing before from husbands and wives of suicides . . .'

'Granted, you have more experience,' Liebwitz conceded. 'But that does not mean that this instance has to be the same as the others.'

'There's always a first time, I suppose.'

Liebwitz seemed unaware of the sergeant's sarcasm as he continued. 'If it was suicide, it can't have been easy. The pistol is a Mauser, a handgun with an unusually long barrel. Schmesler was shot directly from the front. The alignment of the entry and exit wounds prove that. It's a difficult shot to attempt. If I was to shoot myself, I'd choose a different weapon.'

'Come the day,' Hauser muttered, and Schenke frowned at him.

'It would have been easier for a third party to shoot him from the front.'

'That's what I was thinking,' Schenke agreed. 'Go on.'

Liebwitz indicated the file. 'There is no medical confirmation of the tumour mentioned in the suicide note. If Schmesler had consulted his regular doctor, it would be reasonable to expect him to tell his wife about the tumour diagnosis. It is possible that he chose to use another doctor in order to keep the condition a secret from his wife until it was confirmed to spare her from worry. Brigitte Schmesler says the note is in his handwriting.'

'Quite,' Hauser intervened.

'Schmesler could have been coerced into writing it,' Liebwitz suggested. 'A further possibility suggests itself . . . An autopsy might be expected to search for proof of the tumour to confirm the validity of the note. But given the extensive damage to the brain, the individual conducting the autopsy might assume that the presence of the tumour had been obliterated by the trauma caused by the bullet. The paucity of the coroner's notes leads me to suspect he made no attempt to search for evidence of a tumour.'

Schenke nodded thoughtfully. 'If the coroner was aware of

the evidence pointing towards suicide, he might be tempted not to look for another explanation.'

'Yes, sir. And if Schmesler was forced to include the reference to a tumour in the note, the person responsible might have reasoned that the police and the coroner might not search for the presence of the tumour if they thought the note was genuine.'

'True, it would be tricky and rather unpleasant to go to the effort of confirming what the note said. It would be a lot easier to take it at face value.'

'I agree, sir. The investigative standards of the Orpo are somewhat deficient in my limited experience.'

Hauser tried to hide his amusement at the Gestapo man's hubris.

'So your conclusion is that we're not looking at a suicide?' Schenke pressed him.

'I cannot be certain either way, based on the limited evidence available, sir. However, I am surprised by the speed with which the decision was reached that the death was a suicide.'

'I see.' Schenke folded his hands together as he went over his subordinates' evaluation of the evidence.

'What do you think?' said Hauser.

Schenke gave a mirthless laugh. 'I think I'm about to make myself very unpopular with Hauptmann Sperlemann, and Oberst Kleist into the bargain.'

'Not suicide, then. Murder, you reckon?'

'I'm not prepared to suggest we're looking at a murder when I speak to Kleist. I'll tell him that Sperlemann's decision is not based on sufficient evidence and that further investigation is required.'

Hauser shook his head. 'You know damn well that Kleist will put you on the spot and demand to know why you think Schmesler might have been murdered. How will you answer that? There's nothing in the evidence that comes close to suggesting a motive.'

'I know. But that doesn't excuse us from looking into his death. That's our job. It's what we're trained to do and what we're good at. If I'm honest, I hope we can confirm that it *was* suicide and save ourselves the trouble of an investigation. We've already got plenty on our hands dealing with the ration coupon forgeries. Kleist won't be happy about any more delay in tracking down the forgers.'

'Then why in God's name are we making more work for ourselves?'

Schenke stared at the sergeant. 'Hauser, you're a career criminal investigator with a fine record. You didn't get those commendations and promotions by turning a blind eye to the possibility that a crime had been committed. A man may have been murdered. If that's true, then his wife and family deserve justice. It's our job to see that they get it.'

Hauser closed his eyes and frowned briefly. 'All right. How do you want to play this, sir?'

'I've got until tomorrow to return the file to Sperlemann. I'd like to be sure I'm on firm ground before I notify him and take the matter up with Kleist. We need to see the crime scene in person, and speak to Brigitte Schmesler.'

'Now?'

'Can you think of a better time?' Schenke swept the sheets and photographs back into the file's plain cover. 'We're going to need a pool car. Liebwitz, see to it. I want it outside the main entrance in ten minutes. '

'Yes, sir.' The Scharführer hesitated.

'What is it, Liebwitz?'

'Shall I arrange for a driver as well, sir?'

'No. You can drive.' As soon as Schenke spoke, he grasped what the Gestapo man was getting at. 'You *can't* drive, can you?'

'No, sir.'

'Really?' Hauser looked amused. 'You've got a doctorate, you shoot like an Olympic champion, and you are highly trained in unarmed combat, yet you can't drive?'

A pained expression formed on Liebwitz's face. 'Is that a problem?'

'It is now.'

'Then I will attend to it as soon as I can, Sergeant. I will arrange for driving lessons at the first available opportunity. So . . . who will drive the car?'

Hauser raised his arm in its sling slightly and tilted his head towards Schenke. 'Ask the motor-racing star.'

'Fine,' Schenke growled softly. 'I'll drive.'

Chapter Five

As Schenke turned the Opel into the street where the Schmesler residence was situated, Hauser cuffed the condensation away from the side window and peered out. There was just enough light left to make out the details of the houses on either side.

'I used to play around here when I was a kid. My mother cleaned for a Jewish family in that house on the corner. In fact most of the people living in this street were Yids.'

'I doubt that's the case now,' said Schenke, as he squinted to make out a number on a weathered pillar. 'Nice neighbourhood like this is sure to have attracted the attention of well-heeled party officials and their friends. They'll have picked up a few bargains once they put the squeeze on their former owners.'

'Pardon me,' said Liebwitz. 'Squeeze?'

Hauser glanced at him and laughed. 'What?'

'I am not certain I fully understand. You seem to be implying that the Jews were victims of unfair business deals. But there are no reports of such practices in *Das Schwarze Korps*.'

Hauser shook his head. 'My God, you believe everything you read in the SS rag?'

Schenke cleared his throat loudly to interrupt the conversation. Though Liebwitz was a useful new member of the team, he had served in the Gestapo and had a proven inclination to take the party's propaganda at face value. It was not wise for Hauser to speak so freely about his doubts in front of another party member, even one who was part of the Kripo section. As far as Schenke knew, Liebwitz's loyalty was to the party, the police service and his professional comrades, in that order.

'That's the place, just up ahead.' He raised a hand from the steering wheel and pointed, and his companions ceased their exchange.

Schenke pulled up in front of the house. He switched the engine off before he addressed the others. 'We have to go easy. This is not an official investigation. Not yet. I don't want to give Brigitte Schmesler any reason to call the precinct and complain about anything we might ask her. Equally, I don't want to get her hopes up about a possible murder investigation.'

'So what do we say?' asked Hauser.

'We say that we have been sent to clear up a few outstanding details so that the precinct can complete its report into her husband's death.'

'We tell a lie, then,' said Liebwitz.

Hauser twisted towards him. 'You have a problem with that?'

'Not at all. Since working with Kripo, I have seen how the deployment of lies can enhance the effectiveness of an investigation.'

'Good.' Hauser nodded towards the house. 'Shall we?'

As they climbed out of the Opel, Schenke glanced both ways along the street. There were two other cars passing each other cautiously a short distance away, as well as several pedestrians on the pavements. The houses lined the road on either side, with only a handful being opulent enough to have small driveways. All were set close together.

'One of the neighbours might have heard the shot. They might have seen something.'

'There were no interviews with neighbours in the file, sir,' Liebwitz pointed out.

'Then it's time someone spoke to them. See what you can find out, Scharführer. Speak to the occupants of the houses on either side, and those opposite.' Schenke pointed. 'Then join us inside.'

'Yes, sir.'

As Liebwitz strode across the street to the house on the left, Hauser let out a sigh. 'I know I've said it before, but he's a strange one. I'm not sure I'll ever get used to having him in the section. I know the others feel the same way.'

'It's your job to make sure they get used to the idea. The Scharführer has been assigned to us. Besides, we can well use his abilities.'

'Just as long as he's not using us . . .'

'Maybe we're better off thinking he is still working for the Gestapo. Might make some of us think before we speak,' Schenke added, before climbing the steps and rapping the knocker. The blackout siren had not yet sounded, but the dark curtains had already been drawn at the windows.

The door opened fractionally, and a woman's face peered out.

'Frau Schmesler?'

'Who are you?'

Schenke pulled the straps of his lanyard from under his coat so that she could see his identity disc. 'Criminal Inspector

Schenke, Kripo section of the Pankow precinct. This is Sergeant Hauser.'

The woman opened the door slightly wider, and he could see she was in her mid sixties. Rather too old to be Schmesler's wife, he thought. 'I have some questions for Frau Schmesler.'

'The police have asked her enough questions already, not that you've done anything about it.'

'May I ask who you are?'

'I'm Brigitte's mother, Ilse Neuman. I'm staying here for a few days to comfort her.'

'Might we come in? It's too cold to talk on the porch.'

She stared back with a sour expression, and then opened the door. 'Come in. Quickly. And get that snow off your shoes.'

The door closed behind them, and as Schenke removed his hat, he caught the odour of the house: floor polish and a faint smell of leather. The hall was panelled with a lighter timber than was usual for a house of its age. There were other touches of modernity. A long iron table topped with glass stood to one side, a geometric design running along the edges. Two tall floor lamps of polished steel illuminated the hall, with a framed portrait of the Führer between them. Schenke wondered what he might think about being on display in a hall that reflected a bohemian aesthetic.

'Mother!' a voice called. 'Who is that?'

'The police. They want to speak to you, girl.'

Schenke heard the soft clack of shoes crossing a wooden floor, and a slim woman emerged from a doorway. Her dark hair hung loosely about her face, and she had applied no make-up. She wore a dark blue dress with a thick black knitted

49

sweater over it, and regarded her visitors with the same frosty suspicion as her mother.

Schenke introduced himself and Hauser again, and Brigitte glanced at the sergeant's sling. 'What happened to you?'

'Injured, ma'am.'

'Sergeant Hauser is too modest,' Schenke interrupted, sensing an opportunity to ease the tension. 'He was wounded in the line of duty.'

Ilse's expression softened. 'You poor thing. What happened?'

'I was shot.'

'Shot?' She touched a hand to her cheek.

Hauser nodded. 'You remember that business about a killer stalking women on the trains before Christmas? It happened when we were hunting him down.'

'Oh! I remember. Shocking business. You are a brave man, Sergeant.'

Hauser pursed his lips modestly.

'You must be cold. Let me get you boys something warm to drink. Chocolate?'

'That will do nicely.' Hauser smiled. 'You are too kind.'

'Nonsense. Anything for one of our police heroes.' The older woman turned to her daughter. 'Take them into the parlour. I'll bring you some as well.'

Brigitte frowned and shook her head. 'I don't want—'

Ilse patted her hand. 'It'll do you good.' She turned and bustled off to the door at the end of the hall and disappeared.

Brigitte stared after her and spoke softly.

'My mother is driving me mad . . . She has been here since the morning after Manfred was killed. Come.'

She led them to the door she had come out of and waved them inside. The interior was warmed by a stove and followed the same modern style as the hallway. Two single chairs and a two-seater settee were arranged before the stove, and small tables sat between the furniture. Smoke issued from a cigarette lying at an angle in an ashtray, and a book was face down beside it. *The Magic Mountain* by Thomas Mann. Brigitte crossed the room quickly, closed the book and placed it in a bookcase on the far wall before turning and smiling politely.

'Sit, please.'

Schenke took the chair opposite the door and Hauser the settee. As Brigitte sat opposite the inspector, she pulled the hem of her dress down and brushed a strand of hair behind her ear.

'What's this about? Has there been a development in the investigation into my husband's death?'

'Not exactly,' Schenke said. 'We're seeking clarification at this stage. I need to ask some questions, and then it would be useful if we could look at the room where your husband was found.'

'I don't see why that is necessary. I told your colleagues everything, and they went over the room carefully enough. Why are the Kripo involved now? Has someone come to their senses and realised a murder has been committed?'

Schenke leaned forward. 'Murder?'

'My husband did not commit suicide.'

'That's not what the official report concluded.'

'Then the report is wrong,' Brigitte said tersely.

'You say that, but the police found the gun and the suicide note. There was no sign of forced entry, nor of any intruder in your house.'

'That's because the killer came in through the back door. We lost the key a week ago, and the locksmith wasn't able to come and see to the lock until the day after Manfred's death.'

'And the note? You agreed it was in your husband's handwriting.'

'I did,' Brigitte conceded. 'But the words did not sound like his. Manfred would have been less cold and more sentimental if he ever had to write something like that.'

'He might have had his reasons for using the tone he chose. He might have been under stress. He might have felt the need to hurry and get the deed done.'

Her eyes widened. 'Don't you think I have considered all that? Manfred was happy in his work. Happy in his life. We'd just come back from an evening out with friends. We'd had a wonderful evening. There was no reason for him to take his life.'

'Except that he had been diagnosed with a brain tumour,' said Hauser.

Brigitte's gaze fell to her hands, and she folded them in her lap. 'Yes. So the note said.'

'You don't believe it, ma'am?'

'I knew my husband. If he'd had a medical condition like that, the first thing he'd have done would be to tell me.'

Schenke shrugged. 'Perhaps he was trying to protect you. Perhaps he didn't know how to tell you.'

'You weren't married to him, Inspector. I knew him. There were no secrets between us.'

Schenke softened his tone. 'With respect, there are always secrets between people, no matter how close they think they are.'

She was silent before she nodded reluctantly. 'You're right. But on a matter like that, I know he would have confided in

Lucan Library

Issue Summary

Patron: Nolan, Eddie
Id: B241***
Date: 07/12/2023 11:08

Loaned today

Item: SD400000015009
Title: The black dress
Due back: 20240318   000000

Item: SD000000230034
Title: The Nuremberg rallies
Due back: 20240318   000000

Item: SD200000050735
Title: Dead of night
Due back: 20240318   000000

Item: SD900000108709
Title: Operation Barbarossa : Nazi
      Germany's war in the East,
      1941-1945
Due back: 20240318   000000

Item: 05214590959667
Title: The Second Reich : Germany,
      1871-1918
Due back: 20240318   000000

Thank you for using self service

me. He would have thought it cowardly to end his life before telling me the truth.'

Ilse entered the room with a tray on which were four steaming cups, delicately manufactured and simply decorated with a rich purple stripe around the rim.

'Here we are,' she smiled. 'This will do us all some good.'

Brigitte glanced at the tray and frowned. 'Mother, I need to speak to these men alone.'

'Surely they wouldn't mind if I remained? To support you.'

'I don't need your support. I need you to listen to me.' Brigitte spoke tersely. 'Thank you for the chocolate, but now you need to leave us alone.'

Ilse shrugged, picked up her cup with a faint huff and was about to leave the room when there was a knock at the front door.

'Who is that now?' she muttered.

'Another of my men,' Schenke explained.

She put her drink down and hurried out. Schenke rose and helped himself to one of the cups, and passed a second to Hauser. Brigitte made no effort to take one for herself. A moment later, Liebwitz entered the room, his face pallid and pinched from the cold. He nodded a curt greeting to Brigitte and stood stiffly as he reported.

'I have finished questioning the neighbours, sir.'

'You can tell me about that later. Take a seat.'

Liebwitz sat down next to Hauser and helped himself to a cup without asking.

Ilse stopped on the threshold, her eyes narrowing as she saw the cup in his hands. 'I . . . Well I never.'

She turned and bustled away. Schenke waited until her footsteps had faded before he spoke. 'This is Scharführer

Liebwitz of the Gestapo. He is attached to my section and is assisting us in this matter.'

'Gestapo?' Brigitte looked him over. 'Good to see someone is taking me seriously.'

Liebwitz stirred, and Schenke cut him off before he could speak. 'The Scharführer is a valuable member of our team. I am sure he will pay close attention to what you are able to tell us.' He took a sip of the scalding chocolate and winced before continuing. 'You seem convinced that your husband was murdered. Why do you think that? Did he have any enemies? Someone who hated him enough to kill him?'

'He had professional rivals. Men who had not been promoted as swiftly as him. There were also people in the party who were envious of him because he had come to the attention of some senior party figures. But there's no one I can think of who might have wanted to kill him.'

'Then who do you think it might have been?'

'I don't know!'

Her sudden flash of temper stilled the room, and she breathed hard for a moment before slumping back in her chair.

'I apologise . . . It's been terrible, a terrible shock. I don't know who might have murdered him. For all I know it could have been a burglar he caught in the act. But I doubt a burglar would have gone to the effort of making it look like suicide.'

'Well, yes. Quite.'

'What I do know is that it was definitely not suicide. It's the job of the police to find out who murdered him and why. It's *your* job, Inspector.'

'We take our job seriously, Frau Schmesler. If we decide that it wasn't suicide, you can be sure we'll spare no effort to track down his killer.' Schenke let his words sink in. 'Perhaps you could tell us a bit more about his position. What kind of medicine did he practise?'

'Manfred trained as a paediatrician and worked in a Berlin clinic for most of his career. After the party came to power, he specialised in racial hygiene. He helped train other doctors and nurses in the field. That was until just over a year ago, when he accepted a post in a new organisation set up by the government. Still working in the same specialism, he told me.'

'What organisation?' asked Hauser.

'He couldn't tell me. It was strictly confidential.'

One of those secrets between people, Schenke reflected wryly. 'Was there any change in his attitude after he began this new job?'

'If you're asking me if the work got him down, then no. He was excited by it. Very eager to see it through, he told me. In time he would be recognised as having rendered a great service to the German people, he said.'

'But no specific details about what the work entailed?'

Brigitte shook her head.

'Did he mention the names of any of the people he worked with?'

'No.'

'Do you know the name of the organisation?'

'No.'

'Or where it is situated?'

'Sorry, no.'

'I find it unusual that you have so little information about your husband's occupation since he took on the new appointment,' said Liebwitz.

She shot him a dark look. 'I find it unusual that a Gestapo

man would be unaware of the degree of secrecy that has become a part of everyday life in recent years.'

Liebwitz nodded. 'I am aware that there are many matters deemed worthy of secrecy for the good of the Reich, Frau Schmesler.'

Her brow creased in puzzlement.

'I will have to make some enquiries about your husband's work through official channels,' said Schenke. 'We may be able to question his colleagues about anyone they might know with a grudge against him.'

'Good luck with that.'

He took another sip of chocolate and then set the cup down. 'If we could see the room where your husband was found . . .'

'What would you hope to find that your colleagues might have missed?'

'They were Orpo police officers. The Kripo are trained to see things others might miss.'

'Really?' She smiled hopefully and eased herself up from her chair. 'Follow me, gentlemen.'

Chapter Six

As they stepped into the study, Brigitte reached for the switch. Light blazed from some fittings on the wall and a small chandelier hanging in the centre of the room. She immediately realised her mistake and dashed to the window to pull the blackout blinds across, then turned towards the three policemen with a guilty expression. 'Sorry about that. I have been avoiding this room. I forgot about the blinds.'

'We're not block wardens.' Schenke smiled reassuringly. 'You're safe on that front.'

She looked relieved, then gestured towards the side of the desk nearest the door. A small rug lay at an angle across the floor.

'That's where I found him. I haven't had a chance to clean the floor, so I covered the stain with the rug and . . .' Her shoulders trembled and she clasped her hands over her face, sobs shaking her small frame. Schenke placed a hand on her arm.

'We can take it from here, Frau Schmesler. Why don't you go back to the parlour? It's warmer there.'

She nodded, then shuffled to the door and closed it behind her.

The three men stood in silence as they looked round the study, taking in its modern design. One wall was lined with glass-fronted bookcases upon which were neat rows of medical manuals and journals, novels and history books, along with skiing trophies and framed photographs. The largest, in a gilt frame, was a wedding portrait, and Schenke felt pity tug at his heart as he looked at the smiling couple. The desk was large but minimalist, and there were still a few dark smears that had not been wiped from its surface. There was a telephone, a penholder and an inkwell on the desk. An unlit stove stood in a fireplace, the door open to reveal a heap of grey ashes. After the warmth of the parlour the study felt chilly.

'Did you get anything useful out of the neighbours?' Schenke asked.

Liebwitz shook his head. 'No one heard the shot or remembers seeing anything unusual that evening.'

Schenke took the file from the inside pocket of his coat, opened it on the desk and fanned out the police photographer's pictures of the scene.

'The paperwork's been removed.' He tapped a photo, and Hauser and Liebwitz craned their necks to see. Part of Schmesler's body was visible at the bottom of the frame, together with several sheets of paper that had fallen from the desk. On top lay two piles of documents, and more were spread across the polished surface.

'We'll need to ask about that,' Schenke decided. 'Make a note, Liebwitz.'

The Scharführer took out his notebook and wrote swiftly. Hauser crossed to the window and eased the blackout curtain aside to check the frame and the metal catches that locked it in place.

'No sign of any tampering there,' he concluded. 'Looks like Frau Schmesler was right: anyone who entered the house probably came in through the back door. Assuming someone else was involved, of course.'

Schenke crouched, wincing as pain shot through his left knee and up his thigh. The old injury seemed to be troubling him more the longer the bitter winter weather endured. Reaching for a corner of the rug, he raised it and looked down at the dark stain on the carpet where Schmesler had died. There was a large patch, and several smaller spots and smears presumably caused by his death throes.

'That's a lot of blood,' Hauser murmured.

'A feature of head wounds,' said Liebwitz. 'Then there's the brain matter with all the attendant blood vessels. A typical person has—'

'I get the picture,' Hauser responded. 'Just saying.'

Schenke stood and eased the desk chair back over the bloodstain. 'Let's accept that he committed suicide for the moment and was at his desk when the shot killed him. Most likely he'd have been sitting here when he wrote the note. Then he puts the pen back in its holder, takes out his gun . . .' He lowered himself onto the seat, took out his Walther pistol and removed the clip. Pulling back the slide, he checked that there was no round in the chamber, then snapped the slide in place. He raised the weapon and positioned it so that the muzzle was close to his forehead.

'That's an awkward angle,' Hauser observed.

Schenke adjusted his elbow. 'Not easy to hold it that way. Much better like this.' He moved the muzzle to the side of his head. 'Or this.' He pointed the barrel under his chin, then opened his mouth and inserted it briefly before lowering the weapon. 'That's the best way to be sure of doing the job. But it's still possible that he could have shot himself from the front.'

'Unlikely, given that he used a Mauser, sir,' said Liebwitz.

Schenke nodded and raised the pistol again, holding it further away from his forehead. 'That about long enough for a Mauser's barrel?'

Liebwitz nodded.

'Well, it's damned uncomfortable for me. Unless Schmesler had freakishly long arms and flexible joints, I'd say he would have found it no easier to accomplish.'

All three were silent for a moment, before Hauser spoke. 'It's not looking good for the suicide verdict, is it?'

'It isn't,' Schenke agreed. 'Which begs the question, how did the Orpo miss such an obvious factor?'

'Maybe they didn't,' Hauser replied. 'Maybe they were told to leave it out of their report. I don't like the sound of that.'

Liebwitz frowned. 'That would be a serious failing of investigative practice.'

'It would, wouldn't it?' Hauser looked at him and sighed. 'Do I have to draw you a picture?'

'Sergeant?'

'Someone is keen to have Schmesler's death put down to suicide.'

'Why?'

'That might be a question it is better we do not try to answer.'

'Then the question is who is behind it?'

'I refer you to my previous answer.' Hauser turned to Schenke. 'What do you think, sir?'

'We'll deal with that later. Let's get on with the job. We know that Schmesler was shot through the front of the head, and the exit wound aligns with that. There was something in the file about the bullet striking the bookcase.'

He turned the chair and saw a small shattered pane in one of the doors of the bookcase. Behind it was a series of volumes of a paediatric journal. There was a ragged hole in the volume at the end, which had been replaced upside down, presumably after a policeman had extracted the slug.

'So he was facing at a right angle to the desk when the shot was fired.' Schenke traced an imaginary line through the air with his finger between the bookcase and the chair. He paused. 'Hauser, sit in the chair.'

The sergeant did as he had been instructed. Schenke squatted by the bookcase. 'Hello . . . that's an odd angle. He'd have to be tilting the weapon down when it was fired to hit the glass here.'

He looked through the broken glass at the damaged book and saw that the angle between the hole in the glass and the entry place on the volume's spine was impossible. He opened the door and took the book out, replacing it the right way up, and now the height of the passage of the spent bullet was consistent. But the direction was not.

'From the difference in the angle, it looks like Schmesler must have been over there, by the stove.'

Liebwitz leaned closer. 'Excuse me, sir.'

He plucked the book out and eased it into the correct numerical sequence amongst the other journals. 'I think you'll find that provides a more accurate angle.'

Schenke glared at him, and then focused on lining up the damage to the book and the broken glass and estimating the angle back to the chair some two metres away. 'That still doesn't look right to me . . .'

He glanced round the room and spotted a slender walking cane beside the door. Picking it up, he slid it through the broken glass and pressed the tip against the damaged book. The cane was almost parallel to the floor and a metre above it.

Hauser pursed his lips. 'Interesting . . . Well, that rules out Schmesler standing up when it happened, or even sitting in his chair. It looks as if . . .'

'As if he was kneeling on the floor when the shot was fired.' Schenke completed the suggestion. 'Not quite the position you'd expect a man to assume if he was to take his own life. Hauser, move the chair out of the way. Liebwitz, get on your knees behind the bloodstain, about a metre back from the centre of the blood pool. Face the other way.'

The younger man positioned himself and Schenke visualised two scenarios.

'If he shoots himself, the angle would strike the bookcase higher up. If someone else shoots him, you'd expect the angle to dip towards the books. But this looks like the shot was fired in a flat trajectory through his head towards the bookcase.' He turned to Hauser. 'I'd say Schmesler was on his knees facing someone sitting in the chair when he was killed.'

Hauser studied the angles and nodded. 'I think you're right, unfortunately.'

Liebwitz looked over his shoulder. 'Unfortunately?'

Schenke gestured to him to get up. 'Seems that Frau Schmesler is correct. It's murder. That complicates matters for a lot of people. I'm going to have to inform Kleist. He's not going to be happy to have the Orpo verdict challenged. He'll be even unhappier if he was under pressure from higher up to have Schmesler's death put down as a suicide.'

'Are we going to inform Frau Schmesler?' asked Liebwitz.

'No,' Schenke replied. 'It'll be hard for her if she thinks there's any chance of getting justice for her husband only for a Kripo investigation to be closed down when it has barely started. We'll tell her when the time is right, if at all. Is that understood?' He looked at his subordinates intently. 'I don't want to give a grieving widow false hope.'

'Yes, sir.' Hauser nodded.

'Liebwitz?'

The Scharführer looked troubled. 'Sir, I don't think there's much doubt that her husband was murdered. In which case, she should be told the truth. And her husband's death should be investigated by our section at Pankow.'

Schenke felt an impulse to smile at the Gestapo man's use of 'our', and also a surge of frustration about the possibility of the investigation being quashed by higher powers for reasons that Schenke and his section might never discover.

'I agree with you, Liebwitz. But other people control what we can and cannot investigate. That is the reality. I will push for an investigation, but if I am not given permission to proceed, that will be the end of it. Clear?'

'Yes, sir.'

Schenke replaced the cane and swept the documents back into the file before replacing it in his pocket. 'Let's go. Wait for me in the car. I'll speak to the wife.'

Brigitte looked up expectantly from her seat in the parlour when he knocked and entered. Her mother was sitting close by, knitting, and it was she who spoke first.

'Well, Inspector, did you discover anything new?'

'We've made some observations. We'll be looking into them in the morning. If there's anything I need to tell you, I'll be in touch with your daughter.' He turned to Brigitte. 'There's one question I'd like to ask you.'

'Yes?'

'The police photos show that there were some papers on your husband's desk at the time of his . . . death. The top of the desk is clear now. Do you have the documents he was working on?'

'No. They came to take them away the morning after Manfred was killed.'

Her mother tutted, but focused on her knitting.

'They?'

'Two men who said they were from his office. They wore SS uniforms. They said the papers were confidential.'

'Did they give you their names? Or tell you who had ordered the recovery of the documents?'

Brigitte smiled. 'Like many people, I've learned that you don't ask too many questions of those who work for Heydrich.'

'Your husband was in the SS.'

'Quite so, and I never pried into his business. He only signed up for the good of his career. If you don't want to languish in some junior post, it is wise to join them. I'm sure the same is true of the police.'

'Not quite yet, I hope.' Schenke put his hat on and nodded. 'I'll be in touch, Frau Schmesler.' He glanced towards her mother. 'Thanks for the chocolate.'

Outside, he climbed into the Opel, then eased the car into the street and headed back towards the precinct.

'Well?' asked Hauser.

'I'll ask for permission to launch a murder investigation first thing in the morning.'

'Thought you might.'

Schenke looked at him. 'Do you have a problem with that?'

'Not me, sir. But someone might. And they could make it our problem . . .'

He was right, Schenke conceded, but there was the question of duty. It was the proper thing to do to request permission at least. What happened then was out of his hands. They drove on in silence until they reached the precinct.

'It's getting late,' said Schenke. 'I'll keep the car for the night.'

They exchanged farewells, and Liebwitz made to salute before lowering his hand awkwardly as he recalled that these men he worked with were not minded to reply in kind.

'Goodnight, sir.'

Schenke drove away thinking over the details of the evening, before pushing thoughts of Manfred Schmesler aside and concentrating on the prospect of returning to his flat and Karin's warm embrace.

Chapter Seven

The hall of his flat was cold when he let himself in. Music was playing in the living room, and he hung up his hat, coat and scarf on the pegs by the door before taking off his gloves and rubbing his hands to restore some feeling. As he entered the room, a wave of warm air embraced him. A small pile of firewood stood by the stove, and the only light came from a standing lamp, which lent the room a cosy and romantic air. Karin was sitting on the sofa with her legs curled under her as she read a magazine. Her hair had been cut in a short bob and dyed black, as it had been when he'd first met her.

Schenke smiled. 'Going for the Louise Brooks look again?'

'You like it?'

'Very glamorous.'

'Weasel words, my darling. I asked if *you* like it.'

Her new hairstyle reminded him uncomfortably of Ruth, and the dangerous spark of affection that she stirred inside him. A thought he suppressed as soon as it flickered into his mind.

'Well?' Karin prompted.

He planted a kiss on her lips. She tossed the magazine onto

the floor and curled a hand behind his neck, pulling him closer as she returned the kiss with passion. At length they drew back from each other and she spoke softly. 'Criminal Inspector Horst Schenke, it is almost criminal how much I am in love with you. I just hope the party does not make it an offence for people to love others more than they love the Führer.'

He kissed her again and smiled fondly. 'You are teasing me again. I don't think even the Nazis would dare to make that an offence.' He was largely sympathetic to her political views, but had come to accept that the party was not going to relinquish power, nor was it going to permit any rival ideology or political movement to contest its supremacy. It was fruitless to even try. That way led to the harsh regime of one of the camps, or disappearance with the prospect of your battered body being discovered in a wood or river with a bullet wound to the head. In such a world, Schenke focused on what he could do to bring criminals to justice. Making the streets of Berlin safer was a higher priority than fighting a regime where crushing defeat was the only outcome.

'How was your day, darling?' he asked, shifting the focus away from the issue.

She pushed him away. 'A very subtle change of subject there. I barely noticed . . .'

She eased herself back on the settee and slid her feet over Schenke's thigh so that he could massage them gently as they talked.

'You'll be pleased to know that I have volunteered to do some shifts at the army hospital. I was offered light nursing duties, since I have no training in anything more useful. I've been given a uniform and shoes. Would you like me to show you?' she teased with a purr.

'Perhaps later. When do you start?'

'First thing next week. Eight in the morning.'

'That's going to be a rude shock for you.'

Karin frowned, and her tone hardened as she continued. 'I know you think I am the pampered daughter of some wealthy household, but I am not.'

He instantly regretted his slight. Karin was the daughter of a man who had killed himself rather than endure the shame of poverty, and a woman who had thought nothing of abandoning her child in order to join her lover in Paris. If it had not been for Karin's uncle taking her in, she would have struggled to make a living. She was always aware of that, and grateful to her uncle.

'I'm sorry,' he said. 'It's a good thing what you are doing. I'm proud of you for volunteering and I am sure that Admiral Canaris will be equally proud when he hears of it.'

'You think so?'

'Your uncle may come across as a little haughty occasionally, but he is not so proud that he would object to you doing your duty for the fatherland. Besides, there will be many who will need your help, especially if there is no peace in the spring and the war continues. If that happens, your hospital is going to be very busy, I fear.'

They both stared towards the glass window of the stove. The burning wood cast a wavering red glow that evoked as much fascination as warmth. Fire, thought Schenke: the means of civilisation as well as the possibility of its destruction.

'Another war, then,' Karin said quietly. 'Given that the party has a thirst for violence.'

Schenke shrugged. 'There are some who claim the Führer is a man of peace.'

'Those who say that are fools.'

'Then be glad that I am not one of them,' Schenke replied.

'I know. I just wish you would be more open on that front. You can trust me. We can talk freely about anything.'

'Yes. But what if we allow ourselves to become accustomed to speaking freely, and inadvertently we say something in another place and are overheard by an informer?' He took her hand. 'You know very well how unforgiving they will be. It's safer not to talk about such matters in the first place.'

'I know. What has become of Germany that we should feel this way?'

'It will change. Things always do. No government lasts for ever.'

'I wish I shared your optimism . . .'

They fell silent again. Outside in the street, a motorcycle backfired, and the sound drew Schenke's thoughts to the Schmesler investigation. As if she sensed his preoccupation, Karin shook her head.

'I am sorry, Horst, I haven't asked you about your day yet. Any progress on the forgery case?'

'Not really. We've handed some more examples to the lab for testing. If they were printed using the same dyes and there's only one crime ring involved, we can put an end to it once we track them down.'

'Until another ring takes its place.'

'True . . .' He yawned. 'There was another thing.'

'Oh?'

'I was asked to look into the death of a doctor. The local police recorded it as suicide, but the wife insists he was not the kind of man to kill himself.'

'She thinks he was murdered?'

Schenke nodded. 'I went over the file with Hauser and the new boy, Liebwitz.'

'Gestapo Liebwitz?'

He laughed. 'I wonder if that's going to be his nickname from now on.'

'Maybe he'd like that.'

'He wouldn't give a damn either way. He's a strange one. Acts more like a machine than a human sometimes. But he's smart, and I'm glad he's working with us. Anyway, there were some details in the file that raised questions, so we went to the house to speak to the wife and look over the scene.'

'And . . .' Karin prompted.

'It looks like murder.' He shook his head. 'I wish it was suicide. We've got enough to do as it is. However, it's our duty to investigate. Then again, there's something about the haste with which the decision was made that worries me. I don't want to get drawn into any of the games being played by political factions within the party. I had enough of that during the case before Christmas.'

'Poor thing.' Karin squeezed his hand. 'I could ask my uncle to look into it for you. If anyone can discover what's going on, it would be the head of military intelligence.'

'I don't want to get him into any trouble. And I don't want him stirring up trouble for me and the others in my section. But thank you.'

'All right then.' Karin nodded. 'You must be hungry. I made some soup. It'll be cold now, but I can heat it up in ten minutes or so.'

She made to rise, but Schenke drew her back and eased her

down onto the rug in front of the stove. Lying beside her, he reached for the buttons of her trousers.

'We can have the soup later . . .'

Schenke flopped onto his back and held Karin's hand to his bare chest, spent with lovemaking. Blinking away perspiration, he stared up at the ceiling.

'That was . . . rather intense.' She laughed. 'Something you needed to get out of your system?'

'Not really. It's just the effect you have on me sometimes. I see you from a certain angle, or there's a look in your eyes, or the way you move . . . and I want you.'

'That's good to know, darling. I shall have to practise that move.' She turned onto her front and raised herself on her elbows so that she could look down at him. 'Would you like that soup now?'

'It can wait. Let's just enjoy the moment.' He closed his eyes and breathed in the scent of her perfume and the faint odour of sex. His heartbeat was slowing, and contentment enfolded his body and swept away all his concerns. Karin's soft skin seemed to merge into his own flesh where their sides touched. For a moment, all other troubles seemed far away. He drew her close, and she put an arm across his chest and rested her head in the curve between his chest and shoulder. He felt a sudden desire not to let such moments escape him. He had been fortunate to find this woman . . .

He felt his heart quicken as the familiar urge to put the question consumed his thoughts. What if she said no? What if she was happy to be his lover and venture no further commitment? Then there would always be doubt between them. There was only one way of finding out. He sighed and breathed deeply before he spoke.

'Karin, will you marry me?'

She stiffened. 'What did you say?'

He opened his eyes and stared into hers. 'Will you marry me?'

Her lips parted in a smile. 'You seduce me, have your way with me and then spring a question like that?'

'Is there a better time to ask? Besides, we have an understanding. That night at the Adlon when we agreed we were in this relationship for the long term. So . . . what's to stop us?'

'Nothing.' She planted a kiss on his chest. 'Nothing at all. To answer your question – yes. I wish it with all my heart.'

'Thank you, my love.' He felt elated now that he had her reply, and he felt very tired. 'I will be . . . I will do my best . . .'

'Shh.' She touched a finger to his lips. 'You don't need to say anything. If you are half as good a husband as you are a criminal investigator, I am a lucky woman indeed.'

'I think I'm the lucky one.'

She frowned ironically. 'I hope we shan't start on a disagreement.'

'I agree.'

He ducked as she made to swipe him across the crown of his head.

'Oh, you!'

They laughed together, and then she asked, 'What about the soup?'

'I don't want to eat. Let's go to bed.'

* * *

Later, after they had made love again, and were entwined beneath the bed coverings, they made small talk about the future. Where they might live, where they might travel and if they might have children. It was close to midnight when they finally fell asleep. Schenke did not dream, unusually for him, and when he woke, he could hear Karin breathing gently beside him. He was aware of the need to relieve himself, and slipped out from under the covers; she murmured a protest and shifted towards the spot in the bed where he had been. It was cold enough for him to be as quick as he could. When he returned, she was awake, and cuddled up to him, laying her head against his shoulder and reaching an arm across his chest.

'Still willing to marry me?' he asked.

'I believe so,' she teased.

'I wondered. The cold light of dawn – well, pre-dawn – has a way of making some people reconsider their decisions from the night before.'

'Really? How flippant of them.' She twisted a finger into the hairs on his chest. 'Horst . . .'

'Yes.'

'I need to ask you something.'

'I'm not already married. I am free of syphilis and there is no insanity in my family.'

She smiled. 'That's all good to know. But the question relates to something else.'

'Ask away then.'

'It's something serious.'

He felt a tingle of anxiety. 'What do you mean?'

'I hate to put this on you when you have so much to deal with already. But there's a person I know who needs to ask you a favour.'

73

'What kind of favour?'

'It's a legal matter, as far as I understand it. My friend knows that you are a policeman.'

Schenke stirred and turned onto his side to face her. 'Who is this friend exactly?'

'He's a writer. A newspaper correspondent.'

'I don't like the sound of him already.'

'Don't be like that. He's a good man. If he wasn't, I wouldn't be asking you to help him.'

'Can you at least tell me his name and who he works for?'

'I can't. He asked me not to say. He swears that the help he needs is legal and will not put you in any danger. All he wants is a few minutes of your time. I said we had plans to meet for lunch tomorrow at Liedermann's. He could join us there. You have a quick chat, and he goes on his way.'

'Simple as that, eh?'

'That's what he told me. I believe him. And I believe he needs your help. I told him you were an honourable policeman, a rare enough thing these days.'

'Don't try to flatter me, Karin.'

'It's the truth. I wouldn't ask this of you if I thought my friend could get help somewhere else.'

Schenke did not like the prospect of meeting a journalist whose name and purpose he did not know. He was equally unhappy about being steered into it by Karin. But he had asked her to marry him and she had accepted, and that meant that her life and interests were now bound into his. She needed a favour from him, and he could see that it was a test of his commitment. It would sour things between them if he refused.

'All right, I'll speak to your mysterious friend. But that is all. And I expect to be told his name and who he works for when we meet.'

'He said he would be open with you.'

Schenke laughed. 'That would be a novel experience, judging by nearly every journalist I have ever met. Why not just tell me his name now?'

She hesitated, then turned his face towards hers and stared intently at him. 'Because he thinks it would be enough to scare you off.'

Chapter Eight

1 February

Oberst Kleist's frown deepened as he read through the summary of the evidence presented by Schenke to support his application to open a murder inquiry into the death of SS Reich Doctor Schmesler. Every so often the commander of the Pankow precinct let out a soft hiss of disapproval and made a mark on the report with his pencil.

On the other side of the desk, Schenke stood with his hands clasped behind his back, waiting for his superior to finish reading. He noted the framed print of Hitler behind the desk, the bookcase with a handful of reference works, and the small framed pictures of what he took to be members of Kleist's family. Pride of place went to a gilded frame of Kleist himself with his wife and four children, the youngest of whom – a girl – was looking up at an odd angle as if oblivious to the photographer, or perhaps defying him, Schenke mused with a faint smile.

At length Kleist tossed the document to one side and eased his spectacles up on top of his bald head so that he looked like a teacher about to admonish an errant schoolboy.

'You seem pretty sure of yourself, Inspector.'

'My conclusion is based on a survey of the evidence at the crime scene. I am by no means confident that Schmesler did commit suicide, sir.'

'Despite the suicide note, the lack of evidence of a third party in the room and the absence of any suspect with a grievance.'

'The absence of any known suspect,' Schenke countered. 'Once the Kripo launches a murder investigation, I am confident we will identify one.'

Kleist leaned back. 'You Kripo types think you leave us uniformed policemen in your dust, don't you?'

Schenke had encountered such comments before. There were many good policemen in the ranks of the Orpo, but there were more who were little better than petty despots, strutting their beats ready to give a hard time to anyone they encountered who failed to show them the respect they thought was their due, or who fitted one of the categories the party had created to define those deemed 'un-German': beggars, lippy youths, prostitutes, gypsies, homosexuals, and above all, Jews. It was hardly surprising, since many of the Orpo came from the ranks of the Free Corps, the Steel Helmets and other paramilitary groups imbued with the intolerant nationalist zealotry peddled by the party.

'Not at all, sir. We are trained for different duties. The Orpo does a fine job of keeping order on the streets, while Kripo officers are trained to detect serious crimes. Both are necessary for the preservation of the law.'

Kleist stared at him with steel-grey eyes. 'Are you patronising me, young man?'

'No, sir.'

'Well I wouldn't even think of doing so if I were you.' He

leaned his slender frame forward and tapped Schenke's outline report. 'Your request is turned down.'

The words caused Schenke's heart to sink a little. He had made a good case for the investigation, and he deserved more than this curt dismissal.

'May I ask why, sir?'

'For any number of reasons, Inspector. Firstly, in my judgement, the evidence you have produced is circumstantial and insufficient to warrant changing the decision about the cause of Schmesler's death. Secondly, your section is already up to its neck in another investigation. To date, you've made little progress in tracking down the source of the forged ration coupons, and I am not happy about that. Indeed, I am inclined to lodge an official complaint about your failure to carry out your duty.'

'Investigations take time, sir. Particularly when we are reliant on scientific work at the forensic labs to corroborate the evidence we have secured.'

'That sounds like an excuse to me, Schenke. No, don't interrupt. I haven't finished. Thirdly, I have it on good authority that Schmesler's colleagues had noticed a marked change in his mood over recent months. He had become withdrawn and depressed and was overheard talking about this matter to his wife on the telephone.'

'She made no mention of it when we spoke to her.'

'Then she must have forgotten, or chosen not to tell you.'

'Who claims to have overheard this telephone discussion, sir? Who is the person who told you about Schmesler's colleagues?'

Kleist slammed his hand on the desk. 'Damn you, Schenke! How dare you question me in this manner. I am not a fucking suspect. When I tell you what I have heard, that is an end to the matter. People better placed than me and higher in rank have made the decision, and you will not contradict them, or me. Manfred Schmesler shot himself because he was too weak to carry out the duties to the Fatherland that were asked of him. The case is closed. Make sure you return the file and all its contents to Sperlemann at once. You are dismissed. Get out.'

He stabbed a finger towards the door, daring Schenke to defy the order. There was no prospect of taking the matter any further. The decision to report the death as suicide would stand, and there was nothing the Kripo could do about it. Brigitte Schmesler would be on her own, and Schenke doubted she had the resources to pursue a personal investigation.

He bowed his head smartly and turned to walk from the precinct commander's office, closing the door behind him. He stood for a moment in the chilly corridor and gritted his teeth.

'Shit . . .'

'That's too bad,' Hauser said. 'I thought we did some good police work last night.'

'I don't understand,' said Liebwitz. 'Although the evidence was not conclusive, there was enough to warrant an invest-igation, surely?'

Hauser patted him on the back. 'Welcome to the real world, Scharführer Liebwitz. This is where truth and justice come up against political expediency, and expediency wins every time.'

'Expediency?'

'Of course. Someone jumped the gun and said it was suicide, or they were told to say it was suicide. So Kleist has a choice. He either looks like a fool for being responsible for a bad decision, or he risks having a strip torn off him by someone higher up, or he ensures that neither of those things happens by slamming the lid on the case. That's how it works.'

Liebwitz spoke through gritted teeth. 'It's wrong. This goes against every reason why I chose to join the security services. Someone in authority must be made aware of the deliberate attempt to prevent an investigation.'

Hauser frowned, and then laughed. 'You can't be serious . . . What were you back in the day? A choirboy in a monastery?'

'I sang in a choir,' Liebwitz admitted.

'Really? You do surprise me. Did you ever leave that choir of yours?'

'Of course. My voice broke late in puberty. I was no use to them.'

'And I bet they really missed your sunny personality.'

'Enough of that,' Schenke interrupted. 'There will be no investigation and, like the Oberst said, we have other work to do. Has there been any news from Widmann about the dyes used on the forgeries?'

Hauser nodded. 'I called the lab while you were with Kleist.'

'And?'

'Widmann's not there. He was called away first thing this morning. Temporarily reassigned to other duties.'

'What other duties?'

'The secretary at the lab would not say.'

'Any idea when he will be back?'

Hauser shook his head.

'Who is taking over in his absence? Did you get a name?'

'There's no one taking on his casework. His assistant was conscripted, and he hasn't been replaced yet.'

Schenke clenched his fists in frustration. 'What the hell are we supposed to do then? We need confirmation that the dye is the same so we can track the forgeries to their source.' He breathed deeply. 'All right. Keep pushing the other lines of investigation. See what further forged coupons and documents we can come up with. Have our lads put pressure on their contacts on the street. We need some leads while we wait for Widmann to get back to his job. Liebwitz, you have contacts at the Reich Security Main Office. I know the SD compile reports on what the people are thinking. Find out if there is any mention of forged rations coupons or disputes relating to them. Get the details and report back here.'

Schenke returned to his office and sat behind his desk. The Schmesler file lay open in front of him, and he sighed as he flipped the cover over the contents. He must return it to Sperlemann, but that could wait until he had carried out a more pressing duty. Closing the door, he picked up the phone and asked the switchboard to connect him with the telephone number of the Schmesler residence.

It rang several times before there was a click and a female voice spoke. 'Hello?'

'Brigitte Schmesler?'

'I am her mother. Who is this?'

Schenke cursed under his breath. 'Inspector Schenke. I spoke with your daughter last night.'

'The policeman?' Her tone flattened. 'Well, Inspector, I have to tell you she is resting at the moment and I don't think she should be disturbed.'

'With respect, I need to speak to her. Please tell her.'

'Oh . . . as you wish!'

There was a pause as the receiver was set down, then Ilse called her daughter's name in a piercing voice that grated on

Schenke's nerves. How much worse it must be to be in the same house, he reflected. He had sympathy for Brigitte's predicament. Grieving, initially appreciative of the support, and now wishing her mother would vanish and leave her alone, as she had intimated the previous night.

'Inspector Schenke?' Brigitte sounded breathless. 'Has there been a development?'

'No. The precinct commander has confirmed the findings of the initial report that your husband killed himself. There will be no further investigation by the police.' It was a short statement, delivered tonelessly, but he resisted the impulse to add a more human touch. He did not want her to cling to any false hope.

'It's not true,' she responded. 'I know it's not true.'

'Oberst Kleist reviewed the evidence this morning. He has determined that the cause of death was suicide.'

'What's your opinion, Inspector? Do you agree with him?'

'It doesn't matter what I think, Frau Schmesler. I presented my observations to the Oberst, and he considered them before confirming the original report.'

'What did you observe then, Inspector?'

'I cannot say. It's a police matter. Such details are confidential.'

'My husband was murdered. I have a right to know.'

'I'm afraid you don't. I wish I could be more helpful, but my hands are tied with regard to such matters.'

'I won't tell anyone what you tell me,' she continued in a softer tone. 'I give you my word.'

'I can't help you. I'm sorry.'

Her voice took on a bitter edge. 'This is a mistake, and because someone has made a mistake, the police won't admit it. I'm right, aren't I? And you, you're closing ranks to protect them. You should be ashamed of yourself, Inspector. Does no one have any backbone any more? Does no one stand up for what's right?'

'I do my duty and obey orders,' Schenke replied. 'That's all.'

'I'm sure that's a great comfort to you . . . Damn you and your kind!'

There was a click, and the line went dead. Schenke replaced his receiver in the cradle. She did not understand how things worked in the police force, but that did not mean she was wrong to say the things she had said, and it made him uncomfortable and embarrassed.

He picked up the file, collected his hat and coat and stepped out into the section office.

'Hauser, I'm returning the file to Sperlemann. Then I'm out for lunch. I'll be back by two.'

Hauser looked at the clock and raised an eyebrow to indicate that he felt it was too early for such a break. Schenke ignored him. Now that the Schmesler investigation had died a stillbirth, there were other concerns to needle him. The man Karin had arranged for him to meet at lunch. Who was he, and what did he want?

Chapter Nine

Ten minutes later, he was walking down the street in the direction of Liedermann's, a restaurant that had once been the favoured haunt of artists, writers and intellectuals. Now, its clients spoke in guarded tones and there was little to differentiate it from other eating places. He did not hurry; there was plenty of time before the appointment to meet Karin and her unnamed friend. He went over the previous night, and once again could not come to any other conclusion about Schmesler's death. If not suicide, the most likely conclusion was murder. As things stood, the murderer would escape justice, and Schmesler's wife was condemned to spend her remaining days convinced that the police had failed her. The thought ate into his conscience.

He arrived fifteen minutes early and was shown to the table Karin had reserved, a booth tucked away in the corner of the restaurant and screened from other diners by a row of tropical potted plants. He ordered a brandy to warm himself and drummed his fingers on the glass as he waited.

He caught Karin's voice in conversation with a man who spoke accented German, and a moment later they came into sight.

'Horst, darling!'

He stood up, and they kissed before she stood aside to indicate her companion. He was a tall, thin man in his mid thirties, wearing glasses. He took off his hat to reveal a high forehead with thinning hair. Well groomed and with expensive-looking clothes, he did not much resemble the dowdy reporters of the Berlin newspapers that Schenke was used to.

'Horst, this is my friend William Shirer.'

The man held out his hand and smiled. 'Karin has told me a great deal about you, Inspector.'

'Has she?' Schenke shot her a cold look. These days it was wise to share as little about yourself as possible.

He focused his attention on the man as the three of them took their places in the booth, Schenke and Karin together, seated opposite the journalist. Schenke recognised the man's accent and connected it to the name. 'I have heard of you. You're that American correspondent. The one Goebbels is not too keen on.'

Shirer grinned. 'Guilty as charged!'

Schenke turned to his girlfriend. 'It is not safe to be in this man's company,' he muttered. 'Why have you done this?'

She placed her hand on his wrist. 'We weren't followed. William made quite certain of that. He knows how things work in Berlin and he's used to evading his Gestapo tails. He met with me only after he was sure that he was not being watched, and we took further precautions before we came here. We're safe.'

'Safe?' Schenke said. 'It's never safe to meet people the party does not regard as friends.'

Shirer coughed lightly. 'I understand what you are saying,

Inspector Schenke. Or may I call you Horst?'

Schenke felt a ripple of unease. The question might be motivated by the informality of the American character, but it might equally imply a level of familiarity with Karin that made him wary. There was an element of jealousy too. How did she know this American she called a friend well enough to take such a risk? Schenke knew that she opposed the Nazi Party, and that was dangerous in itself, but this man Shirer was a sign that she was in greater jeopardy than he had realised. They would need to talk about this. For now, he fixed a cold stare on the American.

'I'd prefer it if you did not use my first name.'

'As you wish, Inspector Schenke.' Shirer's gaze switched to Karin. 'Are you still certain we should involve, uh, Inspector Schenke? He does not seem to be very receptive.'

'You can trust him,' Karin replied. 'And once he knows the details, he'll help us. Horst is a man who knows right from wrong and puts justice first.'

'I am a policeman,' Schenke intervened. 'I enforce the law. I am not a moral philosopher.'

Karin smiled fondly at him. 'I know your heart, darling. There is rather more to you than the stern-faced policeman you present to the world. William wants to talk to you about a matter that concerns justice as much as the law.'

'Then he should go to the precinct and make an official statement.'

'I have already tried that,' said Shirer, 'but no action has been taken. The police don't seem to be interested and refused to look into the matter.'

'Then why should telling me make any difference?'

'Because I hope you will at least hear me out. Then perhaps you might do what your colleagues should already have done. To be frank with you, I have exhausted all other possibilities. None of my German press contacts are interested or willing to look into what is happening, nor are the police or any lawyers I have approached. When I spoke to a party official, I was threatened with deportation. You are my last hope.'

'Karin must have told you that I am a Kripo investigator. I only deal with the most serious of criminal matters.'

Shirer adjusted his spectacles and glanced round the restaurant before he continued. 'I believe this *is* a serious criminal matter. Will you hear what I have to say?'

Schenke hesitated. If Shirer had been rebuffed by all those he had mentioned, it was likely that there was either no virtue in investigating whatever allegations he was making or, worse, a danger in taking it any further. But there should be no harm in merely listening to what the man had to say. He could at least do that, and satisfy Karin. If, as he suspected, there was no role for him, the matter would be closed and life could continue as before.

'Very well. But I cannot guarantee that you will have any more success with me than you have had with the others you have approached.'

Shirer rubbed his hands together to warm them. 'I should tell you that I have learned more than when I first took the matter to the police.'

Schenke glanced at his watch. 'I have to get back to the precinct by two. It's best you address the matter directly.'

'As you wish.' Shirer paused to arrange his thoughts. 'Just over six weeks ago, I was approached by a family who told me that they had recently lost their youngest child. Paul had been born with a spinal deformity that meant he was confined to a bed for much of his life. He could only be taken outside the house in a wheelchair. But he was an intelligent and lively boy and he had friends who liked his company and a family who loved him. Then, last October, he had a mild chest infection and was taken to hospital. He was there for a month before the family were advised he needed to be moved to a specialist clinic away from the city, outside Potsdam, where the clear air would help his recovery. They agreed, and he was transferred there.

'For the next month, they were given regular reports saying he was recovering, albeit slowly, and then, just after Christmas, they were told he had died as a result of pneumonia, and that his body had already been cremated and his effects donated to other patients. An urn containing his ashes was delivered to the family a day later. When they asked for a full report, it revealed little more than what they had already been told. So they grieved, and arranged for the ashes to be interred in the family plot at the local Catholic church, and tried to get on with their lives.'

'It's a sad tale,' said Schenke, 'but a familiar one. Many children with birth defects die early.'

'That's true. However, almost exactly the same thing happened to a friend of Paul. He had some form of mental impairment, but was healthy in other respects. He was sent to the same clinic outside Potsdam after he had been assessed at the hospital where he had got to know Paul. He was reported to be doing well, but his family were told it would disturb him if they were to visit before he had got accustomed to his new surroundings. And then they were told he had died from heart failure, even though he had been physically healthy when they last saw him. It made no sense as far as they were concerned. The parents of both families thought there was something suspicious about the deaths.'

'A coincidence, surely?' Schenke responded. 'Parents sometimes refuse to accept the truth about the death of a child when they are in the care of others. Suspicion is natural.'

'I understand that, Inspector. But the same physician authorised the paperwork committing both children.'

'Another coincidence.'

'I thought so too. But then I tracked down a young orderly who works at the hospital, and he told me that dozens of children had been moved to the same clinic since summer last year.'

'And are they all dead too?'

'He wouldn't say, but he suggested I look into the public records of registered deaths.'

'And?'

'There was a marked increase in mortality of young people with mental and physical disabilities in the closing months of last year at that clinic.'

Shirer paused, and Schenke considered what he had heard before he spoke. 'I admit that it sounds suspicious, but this is surely a matter for the local police. They're the ones who should be looking into it.'

'And yet they refuse.'

'You could try talking to the Kripo section in Potsdam. Whoever you speak to, though, you're going to need more evidence before any investigation can be justified. Have you approached any of the other families?'

Shirer smiled sadly. 'Most refused to meet with me once they knew I was a foreigner and a journalist, but some were willing to speak off the record. They had butted their heads up against authority and got nowhere.'

Schenke took a deep breath. 'What are you suggesting, Mr Shirer?'

'Don't be obtuse, Horst,' Karin chided.

'I want to hear him say it,' Schenke insisted. 'Well?'

Shirer leaned closer. 'Someone is killing these children. I don't believe their deaths are natural and nor do the parents I've spoken to.'

'If what you say is true, surely the number of deaths must look suspicious. I doubt anyone killing on that scale is going to go unnoticed at the clinic concerned. I would have thought someone is already looking into the matter.'

'I don't know. All I can confirm is that the records I investigated show that the number of deaths has increased significantly compared to previous years, and that the circumstances of the deaths and the manner in which the families were informed are eerily similar. Enough to suggest that someone in authority should look into them. But when the matter has been raised, by these parents and myself, all we get is a cold rebuff that there is nothing to investigate and it would be a waste of public resources to pursue the matter.'

'Why are you so interested in this affair, Mr Shirer?' Schenke asked. 'What's your stake in this? After a good story to sell to your American newspapers about the seamy side of German society? Is that it?'

'No.' Shirer shook his head sadly at the accusation. 'It's more of a personal matter. Paul's aunt has been my cleaner since I arrived in Berlin. I get on well with her and believe she is a good person. So when she told me what I have told you, I offered to help in what small way I could. For no other purpose than to help someone in need. Once in a while, even the most hard-boiled journalist does something for altruistic reasons. God knows, many in my trade deserve the reputations they have earned. But most are good men and women.'

'I see. And why did you drag Karin into this affair?'

'We've been friends for a number of years now. I mentioned what I had discovered to her before I knew that you were a Kripo officer.'

'It was my idea for William to speak to you, Horst.' Karin took his hand. 'I told him you were a good man. Was I wrong to say so? I'll admit I did not want to involve you at first, but I could not think of anyone better to turn to when I heard his story.'

'But what do you think I can do about it? Any investigation needs to come through the correct channels. Unless the Orpo refer the matter to me, I cannot get involved.'

'You were involved in the death of that doctor,' Karin pointed out. 'You looked at the evidence on the say-so of a relative.'

Schenke gritted his teeth. 'That was different. The matter had already been investigated by the Orpo, so I had the authority to review their findings. It would not be regular for me to initiate an investigation before the Orpo had got involved.'

'What if,' Shirer interrupted, 'you were to speak to the families of the victims? I know one couple live in Pankow. I could arrange it for you. Then you can make your own mind up. If you feel there is nothing that can be done, I will not impose on you any further. Your word will be good enough for me. If, on the other hand, you decide the matter needs to be investigated, you could accompany them to the precinct and persuade the uniformed police to report the complaint and pass it up to Kripo to look into.'

'That is not the usual procedure,' Schenke replied sharply. 'It is not how things are done in Berlin. I appreciate you Americans like to play fast and loose with the law, but this is not some frontier town in the Wild West. We do things by the book here in Germany.'

'I fear you have been watching too many American movies, Inspector.' Shirer paused, and then continued with a slight smile. 'In any case, I hardly think your current government pays more than lip service to the rule of law and doing things by the book.'

He was right, but it offended Schenke's sense of patriotism to hear the truth about his country spoken by a foreigner, even as he agreed with the American. The party treated the law with contempt. They accused judges of being enemies of the people when they passed judgements they did not approve of, and used protective custody as a cover for mass arrests of political opponents. The Nazi Party and its leaders were no better than the gangsters and evil cattle barons depicted in the films Shirer had referred to. Only they were not make-believe.

He noticed that Karin was watching him closely, and he felt an aching weariness over all the compromises he had made since the party had seized power. One could either go with the flow and feel one's soul wither and die by quotidian increments. Or one could feel clean again by standing up for what was right and face the consequences that entailed.

'I'll do it,' he said quietly. 'I'll speak to the family. Make the arrangement and let Karin tell me the details. I'd rather not be seen in your company or contacted directly unless it is necessary.'

'I understand.' Shirer nodded. 'I know this won't be easy for you. Thank you.'

'I'm not doing it for you.'

'Fair enough, but I thank you anyway. I wish there were more like you in Germany. I wish more of your people had spoken up while they had the chance.'

Schenke smiled sadly. 'So do I.'

Shirer glanced at his watch. 'I have to go. I have an appointment with one of Goebbels' aides to discuss the speech your Führer gave at the Sportpalast the other night to mark the seventh anniversary of the Nazis taking power. Did you happen to hear it on the radio?'

'I heard some of it,' Schenke replied.

'His comments about Chamberlain, Daladier and Churchill were rather damning. But it was what he said about the war that struck me: "They started the war. They will get all the war they want . . ."'

'So?'

'It struck me as a peculiar phrase for one who claims to be a man of peace. I would have thought that such a man would not have ordered his army to invade Poland and provoke the conflict. What do you think, Inspector?'

Schenke stared at him. 'I think some Germans might agree that is a fair comment, Mr Shirer.'

The American returned his gaze shrewdly. 'Thank you, Inspector . . . I'll leave you and Karin to have your lunch.' He eased himself out of the booth. 'Goodbye for now. I hope we meet again under happier circumstances.'

Once Shirer had left, Karin turned and kissed Schenke on

the cheek. 'You are doing the right thing,' she said.

'Oh, I have no doubt about that.' Schenke raised his hand and beckoned to the waiter to indicate they were ready to order. 'The question is, am I doing the wise thing?'

Chapter Ten

Lunch had been a joyless affair. Schenke was tempted to blame Karin, but the truth was he had made his choice, for better or worse, and that was his responsibility. Nonetheless, she had applied some moral pressure on him, trading on his affection for her, and that did not sit easily with him. So they had made the smallest of talk as they ate, mindful of the need not to attract any attention. Both knew there would be a more earnest exchange that evening in the privacy of his flat. They finished the main course, but skipped dessert and coffee. Schenke settled the bill, and they parted outside the door with a perfunctory kiss and went their separate ways.

As he walked, Schenke shoved his gloved hands into his pockets and lowered his chin into his muffler as most Berliners had grown accustomed to doing since the freezing winter had gripped the capital. Heads lowered, shoulders hunched, looking up only to see their way along the pavement or to cross a street. The city seemed to be populated by strangers.

As he turned the corner towards the precinct, a woman in the entrance of a shop glanced at him and then stepped into the street and increased her pace to catch up with him.

'Horst?' She spoke loudly enough for him to hear but not so loudly that a stranger might turn round out of curiosity.

He recognised the voice at once and continued a few steps before stopping to look into the window of a toy shop. There was still some Christmas bunting around the frame, and a couple of dolls, with blonde roundels of hair on either side of their heads, stared back unblinking. Below them were arranged a few toy cars, and he felt a twinge as he saw that one of them was a Mercedes model he had once raced for the Silver Arrows team, before the accident that had ended his career. Around them were toy tanks, artillery pieces and planes, all bearing the red, white and black design of the party, which had long since replaced the former national emblems.

She stepped up beside him and he glanced round to make sure no one else was nearby.

'What are you doing here, Ruth? We weren't supposed to meet until tomorrow.'

'You spoke to Brigitte Schmesler. You told her you could not investigate Manfred's death.' Her tone was accusing.

'I did.'

She glanced at him. 'Why not?'

'My superior is confident that the original verdict is correct and that the death was caused by suicide.'

'Is that what *you* think?'

'Not from what I have seen. It's possible he was murdered.'

'Then why aren't you looking for his killer?'

'I can't. I was ordered to leave the case alone. The decision came from higher up the command chain. They want the case closed.'

Ruth turned towards him, spoiling any pretence that they were two passers-by who had happened to look in the shop window at the same time. At once Schenke felt vulnerable. He looked round quickly, but the other people on the street seemed oblivious. She glared at him with her intense dark eyes.

'Why?'

'I don't know.'

'You're not concerned by that?'

'Of course I am. But there's nothing I can do. I put my neck on the line for you on this. I agree with your friend. It wasn't suicide. But unless the case is reopened and assigned to the Kripo, I am powerless to do anything more for you.'

'I see . . . Then tell me, how is Brigitte to secure justice for her husband?'

Schenke shrugged.

'You could investigate it yourself,' she said.

'No.' He was angry at her now. 'I am not a private investigator. Besides, I would not know where to start without the resources of the Kripo and the authority to question people. And if my superiors got wind of it, I would be in trouble. You must understand that.'

'I suppose so. Then I'll have to do it by myself.'

'For God's sake, that's madness. It would be risky for me, far more so for you.' He did not need to spell it out. They both knew how dangerous it was for a Jew to draw the attention of the authorities. But he could see the determination in her expression.

'Why are you getting involved in this?' he demanded. 'You are a Jew. Schmesler was a member of the SS, the organisation responsible for the injustices done to you and your people.' He shook his head. 'You're crazy.'

'I can't help that.' She smiled faintly. 'I have my reasons.'

'Oh? And what might they be?'

'Manfred joined the SS for a reason.'

'What do you mean?'

'He wanted to protect his wife.'

Schenke frowned. 'Protect her?'

Ruth hesitated for a moment before she responded. 'Brigitte was illegitimate. Her mother claimed that her father was a Dane she met briefly in her youth. Later, after Brigitte met Manfred, Ilse told her the truth. Her father was a Berlin Jew.'

'And yet Manfred still married her.'

'Why wouldn't he?' Ruth shot back. 'They were in love. Their secret only became a problem after the Nazis came to power. So Manfred joined the SS to protect her. Most doctors join to help their careers. It was natural enough for him to follow suit and claim that was his reason.'

Schenke digested this briefly. 'That was a big risk to take, for both of them.'

'Maybe, but now you understand why I want to help.'

'You may come to regret that pig-headedness of yours.'

'Very likely. But it's a chance I am prepared to take to do the right thing.' She looked at him directly. 'I think I know you well enough to know that you feel the same way.'

She was right, and it annoyed him that his moral code was so obvious to her. 'Look here, it isn't wise for either of us to get involved with this, but I owe it to you, Ruth. It was thanks to you that we caught the killer of those women before Christmas. That said, if I sense that it's getting too dangerous, then the matter's over, for both of us. Those are my terms. Agreed?'

Ruth was silent for a moment. Then she nodded.

'I want your word on it,' he pressed.

'Yes. I agree.'

'All right . . . If you are so determined to see justice done, and if you want what help I can give you, then we need information. You need to ask Frau Schmesler for any names she can provide of people who knew her husband professionally. Any places he may have mentioned in connection with his work. I'd be surprised if she was unable to provide at least a few leads.'

'I'll speak to her about it.'

'That's the easy part. If she comes up with anything, you will need to do the initial legwork. Find the people she mentions, where they work and where they live, then pass the information on to me.'

'And what will you do?'

'I'll have to be careful. I can't question them about Schmesler's death directly in case word gets back to my superiors. I'll have to find some other way to approach them. If I uncover any leads strong enough to justify reopening the case, maybe my superiors will do what they should have done in the first place. But don't build your hopes up, Ruth. And the same goes for Brigitte. Chances are you won't discover anything that helps us take the matter further. In which case, it will have to end there, as we agreed. Understood?'

Ruth nodded. 'How shall I contact you if there is any information to pass on?'

The next shop along was boarded up. A faded sign above revealed that it had once been a Jewish haberdashery. Party posters had been pasted over the boards. There was a door set back from the street and Schenke indicated it. 'If you need to speak to me, chalk a swastika at the bottom of the door. When I see it, I'll erase it and meet you here at twelve thirty during my lunch break. I'll do the same if I need to contact you. Is that clear?'

'Yes. Though I'm not happy about scrawling a swastika on the door of a Jewish shop.'

'What Jew would be? That's why I suggested it. To help protect you if anyone sees you doing it.'

'And what if they see me wiping yours off?' she asked with a wry smile.

He had not thought of that. 'Do it as discreetly as you can. We should not be seen together at any other time, for both our sakes. We'll be taking enough of a risk as it is. I have to go now.'

A pained expression flitted across Ruth's face. 'Very well. Stay safe, Inspector.'

Schenke turned and walked off towards the precinct and did not look back. In his estimation, there was little chance of her discovering any information that would help track down the person responsible for Schmesler's death. Moreover, there was a danger that her investigations might get her into trouble with the authorities and she would be sent to one of the camps. He stopped and looked back, ready to go after her and persuade her to change her mind. But she had gone.

There was a note from Oberst Kleist on his desk when he returned to the section office. He scanned the demand for an update on the forgery investigation. For a moment he was tempted to let his superior know that the case was being held up by the delay in receiving Widmann's report on the dyes now that the latter was temporarily occupied by other duties. But as soon as he thought of it, he discounted the idea. It would only make him look like one of those officers who was always making excuses. At the same time, it would be dropping Widmann into the soup, even if he was not to blame for being set another task. Schenke knew from experience that when a subordinate was handed jobs by two different superiors, neither would accept that anyone else's demands should interfere with the orders they had handed down. Credit for solving cases had a tendency to rise up the chain of command, while responsibility for delay or failure flowed in the other direction. It would be best to resolve the matter personally.

He told Hauser that he was going to the labs where Widmann worked to chase up his report, and left the precinct for the drive into the centre of Berlin. The forensic labs were in a plain modern building a short distance from the Reich Security Main Office's headquarters on Prinz-Albrecht-Strasse. Schenke parked at the rear of the building. The light was already beginning to fade as he walked round to the entrance at the front and showed his badge to the uniformed policeman on the reception desk, a lean man in his fifties with grey hair.

'I need to speak to someone in the chemical section.'

'Do you have an appointment, sir?'

'No.'

'I see. A moment, please.' The policeman lifted the receiver of the phone on the desk and asked to be connected to the chemistry laboratory. A moment later, Schenke heard a tinny female voice but could not make out any words. The policeman relayed his request, then looked up. 'Who do you wish to speak to, sir?'

'The person who has been left in charge by the chief of the Chemistry Analysis unit, Doctor Widmann.'

There was another brief exchange. 'Doctor Widmann has been temporarily transferred, sir.'

'I know that, dammit. I need to speak to the person responsible for his work during his absence.' He leaned forward and glared. 'Now.'

The demand was repeated, and after a short delay the policeman replaced the receiver on its cradle. 'Someone is coming down to see you, sir.'

He indicated a waiting area lined with benches at the rear of the entrance hall, but Schenke refused to sit, and instead paced up and down irritably as he tried to ease the ache in his left knee. It always troubled him more during the winter months, and the unusually bitter cold of this season had made the discomfort worse.

He paused at the sound of footsteps, and a young man appeared. Mid twenties, prematurely bald, but sporting a thin brush moustache, he gave a nervous smile as he approached. 'Inspector Schenke?'

'Yes, and you are?' Schenke responded brusquely.

'Laboratory Technician Hilfrich, sir.'

'*You're* the one Widmann left in charge,' Schenke said doubtfully.

'Yes, sir.'

He shook his head. 'You'll have to do, then.'

'I will endeavour to do my best to assist you.' Hilfrich did not hide his resentment.

'Good. I need to know what progress Widmann has made on the comparative tests he was running on the forged ration coupons my section provided. Do you know anything about that?'

'Indeed, sir. We were running the tests when Doctor Widmann was called away. I will be writing up the analysis as soon as I get the chance.'

'So you have the results?'

'Yes, sir.'

'And you did not think to call Pankow to inform me?'

'I had not been told it was urgent.'

'Well I am telling you now that it is urgent. So?'

'The tests show that the dyes are a match, sir. All of them.'

It was the first piece of good news Schenke had had in days. 'I want the analysis report completed at once and sent to Pankow. Is that clear?'

'Yes, sir.'

'I may need to speak with Widmann when he returns. Do you have any idea when that will be?'

'I was told it would be no more than two weeks.'

'Two weeks?' Schenke frowned. 'If it's not a confidential matter, what was the purpose of his assignment?'

Hilfrich shrugged. 'It's no secret. He's been assigned to a committee drawing up guidelines on the use of pesticides in hospitals, barracks, prisons and camps. That sort of thing.'

'Not the best use for the talents of a senior forensic scientist.'

'Orders are orders, sir.'

'Yes, they are. And now you have yours. I want that report on my desk first thing in the morning. I suggest you get started on it at once, Hilfrich.'

Schenke turned away and strode out of the building. Outside, the gloom was thickening, and he increased his pace as he returned to the car he had signed out of the motor pool. A covered lorry stood a short distance further along the street. As he approached, a man in a dark hat and a short leather jacket climbed out of the cab.

Schenke reached the side of his car and stopped, his hand fishing for the key in his pocket.

'Inspector Horst Schenke?'

He turned towards the man, a sixth sense causing a faint prickle of anxiety to seize the back of his neck. 'Who are—'

Too late he heard the soft crunch of a footstep behind him on the snow-covered pavement. Before he could turn, there was a blinding flash of white. He did not feel the blow to the back of his head, or the impact of the ground, as he fell senseless into the dark pit of oblivion.

Chapter Eleven

A sudden violent jolt brought Schenke back to consciousness. He opened his eyes, but all was pitch black. He became aware of something covering his face, the material coarse against his skin. An engine snarled, and beneath him he felt the rattle of a lorry. He rolled over and caught the side of his head against something cold and unyielding, and groaned in pain.

'Lie still, you fool,' a voice ordered as he was hauled onto his back and pressed down under what felt like a boot. He tried to resist, but his ankles and wrists were securely bound, and he slumped back. He had a shattering headache and felt nausea well up from his stomach, so that it took a huge effort to keep from vomiting. His tongue was dry and swollen for some reason, and he had to draw up some saliva and moisten his mouth and lips before he could speak.

'What the fuck is going on?'

'Keep your mouth shut!' The booted foot pressed down savagely.

'Who the hell are you?' Schenke raised his voice to a shout. 'Help! Help me!'

A sharp blow to his jaw cut off the cry, and a voice snarled close to his ear, 'Any more noise out of you and I'll beat you so hard it'll be hours before you come round again.'

Schenke groaned in fresh agony as he tasted blood from a split lip. 'I'm going to be sick.'

'I wouldn't. Now keep your mouth shut, Inspector.'

The lorry bounced over another bump and the road gave way to uneven ground. Schenke was jerked violently from side to side. Bracing himself as best he could, he tried to recall what had happened. He remembered the man who had called his name, then nothing. He tried to work out who might have cause to abduct him from outside the crime laboratory. That had taken confidence, and the smoothness with which he had been distracted at the critical moment suggested careful planning and training.

The lorry changed down a gear and began to slow, and the noise of the engine took on a more resonant note. Schenke realised they must have entered a building. The vehicle pulled up sharply and the engine turned over for a few seconds before it was switched off and the vibrations beneath him stilled. He heard the metallic clink of a chain and a grating scrape as the tail was lowered.

'Get him out!' a new voice ordered, and he felt someone grasp the collar of his coat and drag him a short distance before he was passed down to other hands. There were at least three of them, he decided. He was hauled upright, pinned by the arms as someone untied the rope around his ankles. As the bonds fell away, he tensed his body and braced his feet, knees slightly bent.

'Don't even think of making a break for it. You won't get far and you'll only piss us off,' the second voice warned him.

'Who the hell are you?' Schenke demanded.

'It is best for you not to find out, Inspector Schenke. It'll do you no good. Get him onto the chair.'

He was dragged across a concrete floor and forced down onto a plain chair with a back. Raising his head, he could see light through the material covering his eyes and realised he was sitting in front of the lorry, lit up by the headlights shining through the blackout slits. A shadow passed in front of him, and he heard the grinding of boots on the grit covering the floor.

'We'll make this quick if you cooperate and answer my questions truthfully. If I think you are lying, this is what you'll get.'

Something heavy struck him hard on his left arm. The effect of the blow was instant and agonising.

'Truth or beating. Your choice. Is that clear?'

He gritted his teeth as he waited for the pain to subside, then nodded.

'Good. Let's begin . . . What's your interest in Dr Schmesler?'

'Schmesler?'

'Just answer the question. Why were you looking into his death?'

'His wife was certain he hadn't taken his own life. She claimed he was murdered. So the Kripo was called in.'

'Who gave you the order to investigate the death?'

'There was no order. I acted on my own initiative.'

Another blow landed on the same spot as the first, and a burning pain seared his arm, making him feel nauseous again. He let out a sharp cry.

'You are wasting your time. No one can hear you. I told

you what would happen if you lied. Again, who gave the order?'

Schenke grimaced before he could manage a response. 'It's true, I swear to God. I decided to look into Schmesler's death.'

'The bastard's lying,' another voice growled, to Schenke's left. 'Hit him again.'

'No!' Schenke shook his head. 'It's the truth.'

'Not the whole truth,' the first man continued. 'You don't just decide to look into such a matter for the hell of it. Why did you take two of your cronies to poke around the Schmesler place?'

So these men had been watching the house, thought Schenke. *Who the hell were they?*

'I was approached by someone close to the family. They said the Orpo had rushed to record the death as suicide, but Schmesler's wife was convinced it wasn't and she wanted the police to launch a murder investigation. I said I'd read the file and look over the evidence to see if there were adequate grounds to justify reopening the case.'

'Who approached you?'

Schenke's pulse quickened with anxiety. He did not want to provoke another blow, but he was not prepared to give Ruth up to these men, whoever they were.

'A cousin of the family. He called my office to raise Frau Schmesler's concerns and—'

'A cousin?'

'He said he was a cousin, but I didn't believe him.'

'Why not?'

Schenke shook his head. 'Just the way he spoke. Something was off about him.'

'Then why did you listen to him?'

'There were details in the file that did point towards murder. Enough to convince me it was worth a fresh look. If it was murder, it was my duty to turn it into a criminal investigation.'

'Who do you think the man who contacted you was?'

'I honestly don't know.'

His interrogator was silent for a moment. 'What did you conclude when you'd looked at the evidence?'

'I ruled out suicide.'

'How can you be certain?'

Schenke described his examination of Schmesler's study and his doubt that the doctor had been able to shoot himself as the Orpo had reported.

'What happened when you challenged the initial report?'

'The precinct commander ordered me not to pursue the matter. He told me the case was closed and to leave it there.'

There was a tense silence before the man spoke again. 'Why do you think your superior refused to accept your findings?'

'He was ordered to make sure that the death was recorded as a suicide. But you'd know that. There's not much happens in Berlin that you Gestapo thugs don't know about.' It was deliberate provocation, and Schenke strained his ears for any indication that would confirm his suspicion about who had snatched him off the street.

'Someone told your superior to ignore the evidence?' The interrogator's surprise was clear. 'Who?'

'He didn't give any names. Just told me that word had come down the chain of command that the official line was that Schmesler had committed suicide and the matter was closed.'

'Shit . . .' another voice muttered. 'What the fuck are they playing at?'

'Silence!' the interrogator snapped. 'I'm the only one speaking to the cop. The rest of you keep your mouths shut. You hear?'

The rest of you? How many? Schenke wondered. He tried to place any sounds of movement around him and estimated there were more than the three he had identified so far.

'Who are you people?' he asked. 'Who do you work for? Müller? Heydrich?'

'Like I said, you don't want to know,' the man replied. 'Let's just say that the people we work for like to keep things neat and tidy. So they were not best pleased when you poked your nose in where it wasn't wanted. What about the men who were with you? Do they know what you know?'

'Yes.'

There was a sharp intake of breath. 'That's not helpful to us, Inspector.'

Schenke saw a glimmer of hope. 'If anything happens to me, you'll have to silence them too. I can imagine that the deaths of three officers from Pankow's Kripo section is not going to be taken lightly. That'll destroy any hope your superiors may have of the truth about Schmesler's death being covered up.'

A shadow took up position in front of him. 'Do you really think so, Inspector? I find it hard to believe you could be that naive. The Kripo's standards must have slipped if they are appointing fools like you to run their business. You know the score, Schenke. Those in power – those we work for – have no regard for legal niceties. Thousands of bodies have already been buried under the foundations of the new order; why would my superiors be concerned about three more?'

He let the threat hang in the air for a moment before

continuing. 'That said, it would be a shame to rob the Kripo of three good men when they are needed for other duties. This is what is going to happen. You are going to forget Schmesler's death. You and those in your section who know anything about it. You will not speak of it to anyone. If you do, we are sure to find out, and next time we will not be so understanding. Is that clear, Inspector?'

'Yes.'

The figure stepped closer, and something hard pressed into the side of Schenke's head. He felt a sharp stab of terror as he realised that it was the muzzle of a gun. The weapon jolted as the slide was pulled back with a click.

'Listen to me. If you mention our little conversation here tonight to the police, you will die. If you attempt to reopen the Schmesler case, you die. If you speak to Brigitte Schmesler again, you die. If you attempt to find out who we are, you die. If you make any comment to the press about the Schmesler case, you die. If you attempt to get any superior officers to have a second look at Schmesler's death, you die . . . Is all of that understood?'

'Yes.'

'Good. Then our business here is concluded. I understand that you are a good policeman, Schenke, so direct your efforts to other cases and forget you ever heard Schmesler's name.'

Schenke felt hands grab him and pull him off the chair. He was bundled back into the lorry and dumped onto his side. Men climbed in around him as the engine restarted, and then the vehicle rumbled out of the building and into the night. He was jolted about as the lorry negotiated a rough track for perhaps twenty minutes before meeting a more even road surface. After another ten minutes, they turned onto another track and drove a short distance before the vehicle drew up. He had heard no one speak for the entire journey. As soon as the lorry was still, he was hauled out and dragged a few paces in the snow, then lowered to his knees. Once again he felt the muzzle of a pistol pressed against his temple.

'In a moment, I am going to free your hands,' the man who had questioned him explained. 'You will remain still and you won't remove the hood. If you do . . .'

'I die.' Schenke nodded. 'I get it.'

There was an amused sniff before the man spoke again. 'I believe we are making progress, Inspector. We'll back the lorry away. You'll be visible in the headlights, so don't feel tempted to move too early, or we'll come back for you and tie you up again, and this time we'll leave you here. It's going to be a long, cold night. Cold enough to freeze to death. Once you can no longer hear the lorry's engine, count to a hundred and then you can remove the hood and untie your feet and go home. Forget this happened.'

'Not much chance of that. I'd be a liar if I said I'd forget. This is not the kind of thing that happens to people often.'

'You'd be surprised, and many of those we have a quiet word with don't get to go home. You've had your warning. Don't push your luck any further. Germany needs good men. What she doesn't need is troublesome men.'

'Thanks for the tip.'

The muzzle of the gun was still pressed against his head, and yet Schenke felt a curious sense of elation along with the fear that gripped his body. The slightest pressure on the trigger was all that would be required to blow his brains out. His tough-guy attitude was an act. It was all that kept him from giving in to naked terror.

The gun was removed, and there was a soft click as the safety catch was engaged. A moment later, he felt hands working at the ropes around his wrists.

'Remember, keep still until we are gone.'

Footsteps crunched across the snow, and he heard the doors of the lorry slam shut, the engine roaring into life as the driver gunned the accelerator. With a rattle, the vehicle backed away, the thin beams of the headlights playing across the coarse material of the hood over his head. Schenke sat still, not tempted to remove it. Then the light was gone as the lorry turned and drove off. He waited for the engine to fade, and then all he could hear was the distant hiss of a train and the clatter of heavy wheels passing over a set of points.

He lifted the hood off his head and felt a wash of icy air on his face. It was dark; the only illumination came from the dull gleam of the surrounding snow. He was sitting in a small clearing, with trees either side of the track the lorry had driven along. He pulled off his gloves, untied his ankles and set off along the track in the direction the lorry had taken.

After fifty metres, the trees gave way to a large open patch of ground. On the far side he could make out the dull mass of a vast building stretching out on either side. He made his way into the open and across the flat expanse of snow-covered ground, breaking into a trot despite the ache in his bad leg. As he drew closer to the building, he saw several large objects standing in front of it, and a moment later realised that they were aircraft. This was the Tempelhof airfield, whose sprawling structure resembled a vast eagle when seen from the air.

A door opened, the dim light within briefly silhouetting the shape of a man in overalls, and then closed again. A match flared briefly, and Schenke saw the tiny red glow of a cigarette.

'You there!' he called out as he stumbled across the snow past the dark bulk of a Junkers transport plane.

'Who's that?' a voice responded, and Schenke saw the lighted tip of the cigarette swing down. 'Who is it?'

He slowed to a limp as he drew closer. 'I need help.'

'Who are you?' the man demanded.

'Police. Let me inside the building,' Schenke panted. 'I can show you my badge.'

The dark shape moved ahead of him and opened the door. A blade of light stabbed across the snow, and Schenke brushed past the man into the warmth of a workshop lit by a single bulb. To the right, shelves lined the wall, extending all the way across the room. On them were cardboard boxes and spare parts for aircraft engines. Opposite was a long series of windows overlooking a cavernous space containing a plane with trestles around the engine on the port wing. The surrounding area was illuminated by a pair of kerosene lamps. The workshop was heated by a gas device that hissed as the ceramic plates glowed red.

The door closed behind him, and Schenke turned to face the man. He was shorter by a head and looked to be in his mid forties. There were streaks of dark grease on his stubbly jowls, and his overalls were similarly soiled. He reminded Schenke of the mechanics he had known in the days when he had driven for the Mercedes Silver Arrows.

He regarded Schenke suspiciously. 'Police, you said . . .'

'That's right.' Schenke fumbled for the chain lanyard around his neck and held out the metal disc bearing the details of his unit and his identity number. 'Inspector Schenke. Kripo.'

The engineer inspected the badge and then glanced up.

'You're a mess. Looks like you ran into a wall face first while you were blundering around in the dark, Inspector.'

'Some men dumped me on the far side of the airfield.'

'The Lufthansa depot?' He arched an eyebrow. 'Thought that had been locked up for the duration. Though I saw some men over there a few days back.'

'No, in the trees,' Schenke said.

The engineer scrutinised Schenke's face. 'I'll get you some water and a towel. You can warm up by the heater meantime.'

'Is there a phone in here?'

'On the bench there, next to the heater.' The engineer made his way to the end of the room, where there was a door behind one of the projecting shelf units, and disappeared from view.

Schenke crossed to the heater and sank down on a small rocking chair with a threadbare stained cushion. He pulled off his gloves and winced at the burning pain in his bruised arm before reaching for the telephone receiver. He dialled the number of the office at the Pankow precinct, and after a few rings there was a click.

'Kripo section, Pankow precinct,' a voice intoned. 'Scharführer Liebwitz speaking.'

Schenke was grateful to hear the Gestapo man's voice.

'It's Schenke. I need you to get a car and a driver and pick me up at the Tempelhof airfield.'

'Tempelhof. Yes, sir. How soon do you require me, sir?'

'At once will do nicely, Scharführer.'

'Yes, sir.'

'Wait a moment!' Schenke turned to the door as the engineer reappeared with a jug and a towel bundled under his arm. 'Which part of the airfield is this?'

'Hangar 4. Just beyond the east terminal wing.'

Schenke repeated the location and Liebwitz acknowledged it before hanging up.

'Here you are, sir.' The engineer set the jug and towel down beside the telephone. 'Afraid I haven't any drink to offer you at this hour.'

'What about a mirror?'

'That I can do.' He reached into his overalls and pulled out a leather wallet. It contained a small mirror on one side and a comb and toothpick on the other. It smelt of oil.

Schenke examined his face. There was blood all over his chin and a graze on his temple where the muzzle of the pistol had been jammed. He shuddered as he recalled the moment when he thought he was going to die. Pouring some water onto the corner of the towel, he began to wipe the blood away. The cut on his lip was painful as he dabbed at it.

'Looks like you were given a working-over. Who did that to you?'

'I really don't know.'

'Kripo inspectors don't get beaten up every day.'

'I said something similar to them . . .'

Schenke thought through what had happened to him. Someone was going to great lengths to make sure that Schmesler's death was not investigated. He took a last look at himself, anxious not to alarm Karin when he returned to the flat, then handed the mirror back to the engineer.

'Thanks. What's your name?'

'Klaus Zebrinski. Am I in any kind of trouble?'

'I just wanted to know who to thank. If I need to speak to you again about tonight, I'll be in touch. Are you on night shifts?'

The engineer shook his head and gestured towards the

aircraft in the hangar. 'Rush job on the engine. I'm here during the day normally. I'd better get back to work, if there's nothing more you need from me.'

'I'm fine.'

Schenke turned his back towards the heater as the engineer made his way into the hangar, warming his body as he waited for Liebwitz to arrive. All the time his mind pondered the identity of the men who had abducted and beaten him. At the time he was certain they were Gestapo men, but on reflection some of their comments made him doubt that. But if not the Gestapo, then who else? Who else would threaten to kill him?

Chapter Twelve

'I'll see you in the morning, Liebwitz,' Schenke said as the car pulled up outside his apartment block. 'I'd be grateful if you kept quiet about picking me up. There's no need for anyone to know.'

'Yes, sir. As you wish.'

There had been no conversation between them on the drive back from the airfield; Liebwitz had appeared to be looking straight ahead as Schenke sat beside the uniformed driver. Now the Gestapo man just stared back with his usual deadpan expression. He asked no questions.

'Right then. Thank you for fetching me.'

'Yes, sir.'

Schenke opened the door and climbed out. As the car drove off, he shook his head. Much as he appreciated Liebwitz's intelligence, eye for detail and other accomplishments, there was as yet no sign of a personality he could warm to. Even so, Schenke was coming round to regarding him as a comrade, with the obligations that entailed. Then again, a month ago Liebwitz had been working for Müller, the head of the Gestapo. Müller had assigned him to Schenke's section to report on the

Kripo's progress in the murder investigation before Christmas. It was possible that Liebwitz still owed more loyalty to the Gestapo than to his new colleagues.

'He's an odd one . . .' Schenke muttered.

Bracing himself for Karin's reaction to his appearance, and the inevitable questions, he entered the building. As he climbed the stairs, he thought about Ruth. She must be told what had happened. In order to protect them both, he would have to persuade her not to ask any more questions about Schmesler's death.

When he entered his apartment, music was playing from the living room. He hung up his hat, coat and scarf before making his way along the corridor. Karin was sleeping on the sofa in the pool of light cast by the reading lamp. She lay curled up at one end, her head on a cushion, dark bob framing her finely drawn features. A fashion magazine lay on the floor beside the sofa, together with a pair of satin slippers. A red glow came from the smeared glass window of the stove, and the room radiated domestic cosiness. Schenke paused a moment to drink in the scene and relish the comfort it afforded him. Whatever might happen in the world outside his front door, here at least there was peace of a kind he could happily get used to.

It sometimes surprised him that she had chosen to be with him when she could have picked someone with a more glamorous occupation and outgoing personality. In the years since Schenke had been forced to give up motor racing, he had withdrawn from the society he had once known. He recalled the looks of pity after the accident when he limped into a room, imagining the whispered asides: *the poor fellow. He was once tipped for greatness on the motor-racing circuit, you know. But now? What's to become of him?*

Karin stirred, and her eyes opened as she mumbled drowsily, 'Horst . . .'

She eased herself up and rubbed her face as he sat down at the other end of the sofa and stretched out his legs. She smiled at him, and then her jaw sagged.

'My God, your face!' She grabbed his hand. 'What happened to you?'

'Someone took me for a little drive to a quiet spot and asked me a few questions.' He touched his swollen lip. 'Unfortunately they got carried away in their enthusiasm to find out what they needed to know.'

'Horst, save the hard-boiled detective hero stuff for the office.' She traced her fingers over the graze on his temple. 'Are you hurt anywhere else?'

'A few bruises and a tender pride, but nothing more serious.'

He settled into the sofa and let his head ease back so that he was staring at the shadows on the ceiling. 'I thought they were going to kill me.'

'Who did this to you?' Karin demanded.

'If I had to guess, I'd say they were Heydrich's henchmen. It certainly felt like their style.'

She stood up, crossed the room to the small table where Schenke kept his spirits and poured a glass of brandy. 'Here. Tell me what happened.'

He downed the contents in one, wincing as the fiery liquid stung his lip. It burned in his throat before settling in his belly, warming him through. He considered how much he could safely tell her. The leader of the men who had abducted him had given him an unambiguous warning and the more Karin knew then the more she too would be in danger. On the other hand, Schenke needed to talk it through with someone he could trust. She sat still, listening attentively until he had finished.

'What does your Gestapo man, Liebwitz, know about it?'

'Nothing more than that I asked him to pick me up from Tempelhof.'

'Could he be in on it? Could he have told the Gestapo where to find you?'

Schenke had considered the possibility already and shrugged. 'I don't know. He's not the deceitful type. I doubt they'd risk involving him in the kidnapping.' Schenke gave a wry smile. 'He'd protest it was not lawful.'

'He didn't remark on your appearance?'

Schenke smiled. 'He's not generally the curious type. Until he is told to be.'

'Something of an oddity, then.'

'You can't imagine.'

She took the glass from him. 'Another?'

'Thanks.'

She refilled his glass and poured one for herself before sitting down next to him and leaning into his shoulder.

'Careful.' He winced.

They sat in silence for a moment before she muttered, 'The bastards. We're ruled by gangsters, Horst. That's what they are. They use violence with impunity. What has happened to this country?'

'We waited too long for the party's star to fade. We didn't take them seriously until it was too late. And now?' He shrugged helplessly.

'There's still something that can be done – about this, I mean.' She gestured towards his face. 'My uncle has his sources.

If anyone can find out who those men were, it's the people at military intelligence.'

'No,' Schenke replied. 'Absolutely not. I don't want Canaris involved. If he puts the word out about my abduction, it will be sure to get back to the men who took me. Their warning was clear. Next time I won't be allowed to walk away.'

'What if he were to speak directly to Heydrich? Just to warn him off.'

'Warn Heydrich off? You overestimate the influence of your uncle. Canaris may be an admiral and occupy one of the most important military posts, but don't think for a moment that that will impress Heydrich. For him, the interests of the party come first. He won't hesitate to defy your uncle.'

'If he's the one behind this attack.'

'True,' Schenke conceded. 'But who else is it likely to be?'

'That begs a further question, my love. Why are they so keen to ensure that Dr Schmesler's death is not investigated? You seem sure it was not a suicide.'

'More than ever.'

'So what are they hiding?'

'I don't know. He might have crossed swords with a senior figure in the party. He might have been caught with his hand in the till – normally they like to make a public example to fool people into thinking they do not tolerate corruption. Faking a suicide is not their usual method. But right now I don't know what the real reason is for trying to pass his murder off as a suicide.'

'If you found the men who kidnapped you, they could be made to tell you.'

'I doubt it. They'd deny any connection to the Reich Security Main Office, even if Heydrich chose to throw them to

the wolves. That's how he operates. The man is the very devil.'
He shifted so that he could look at her directly. 'I mean it,
Karin. You can't tell Canaris anything about this. It would
only put me in danger. More importantly, it might put you at
risk. I couldn't bear that.'

She smiled and kissed him.

'Ouch!'

'Oh, sorry! I forgot.' She raised herself a fraction to kiss him
on the forehead. 'Poor darling.'

Schenke took another sip of brandy, then put the glass
down on the floor beside the sofa. 'There's nothing that can be
done. I'll just have to get on with the coupon forgery case.
That's something I can do without getting into trouble with
the party.'

'There's still the other matter,' Karin said warily.

'What other matter? You mean that business of Shirer's?'

She nodded, and he frowned.

'It's a separate matter, Horst. You can still speak to the
parents William told you about. You did agree to,' she added
with slight emphasis.

'I know, I know. Just give me a few days to get this evening
behind me.'

A brief look of guilt flitted across her face, and Schenke
knew immediately what she was about to say. 'You've already
arranged a meeting, haven't you?'

'Yes,' she admitted. 'I didn't see any reason to delay once
you had agreed to it. That was before this, of course.' She
gestured to his face again.

He gave her a knowing look. 'And perhaps you didn't want
to give me the chance to change my mind.'

She met his gaze for a moment, then nodded. 'That too.'

'Why is this so important to you, Karin?'

She looked surprised. 'Someone is responsible for the deaths of those children. Isn't that a good enough reason? I don't believe you could walk by on the other side of the street.'

She knew him well then, Schenke conceded. He wasn't yet sure if that was a good thing. In his line of work it was important not to give too much of yourself away. He knew that Karin kept her own secrets. Until the meeting with Shirer earlier that day, she had never mentioned his name, and yet they clearly knew each other well. What else was she keeping from him? Her opposition to the regime ran deeper than his own, he knew, but she had not mentioned any connection with others of a similar persuasion, and he had not asked. In fairness, she had as much right to her secrets as he did, but it troubled him all the same.

'All right, then. When do I meet them?'

'Tomorrow. Shirer has arranged for them to be at Liedermann's at twelve thirty.'

'Not there. That's where we met him last time, and the waiters may recall the three of us being there together. You'd better find somewhere else, and make sure Shirer keeps away. If he lost his tail last time, the security police will make damn sure it doesn't happen again. Not unless they're prepared to risk incurring the wrath of their superior.'

'Aren't you overplaying this? It's not a matter of state security. And if there is something serious going on, it's fair game for the criminal police.'

'That may be. But there's a foreigner involved. Shirer is not a friend of the regime. Goebbels tolerates him because he thinks he can be used to present Germany in a favourable light to his readers back in America. If he is responsible for stirring something up over the deaths of these children and word of it reaches the US press, that will be another black mark, however small, against the reputation of the Third Reich.'

'You think there aren't already enough black marks? You could fill volumes with the sins of Hitler and his followers.'

His heart felt heavy with weariness. 'Karin, I don't disagree with you. Truly. That is why we have to tread carefully over this matter. It's easy to make powerful enemies these days. For our own sakes, as well as these parents', we have to proceed with caution.'

'Caution?' Her lip curled. 'What is the saying? Caution makes cowards of us.'

'Not quite.' Schenke smiled. 'Besides, it's not a saying. It's a line from a play: "Conscience doth make cowards of us all." *Hamlet.*'

'Same difference,' she replied. 'It's cowardice that got Germany where it is.'

'You are right, but we can't change that now. That is why we must act with caution when we wish to exercise our conscience. Otherwise we'll go the same way as Hamlet, destroying ourselves and those around us and achieving nothing of any value. There is still room for acts of nobility, but anyone who tries anything too foolhardy just disappears as if they never existed. What good can they do then?'

She held him close and muttered in his ear. 'I'm afraid, Horst. I feel surrounded by danger. Sometimes I even dream of it. I find myself in familiar settings terrified of speaking the truth.'

He gritted his teeth as her embrace put pressure on his badly bruised arm. She sensed him flinch and drew back.

'What is it?'

'Nothing. I'm just tired. Let's get an early night. I want a fresh mind tomorrow.'

She kissed him on the cheek. 'An early night sounds good,' she purred.

There was no mistaking the meaning of her tone.

'Go easy on me . . .'

Chapter Thirteen

2 February

As he approached the precinct the next morning, Schenke paused by the window of the toy shop and waited for a gap in the stream of those walking to work before stepping into the entrance of the boarded-up shop next door. He reached into his coat pocket for the length of chalk he had brought with him and bent down to make the code mark he had agreed with Ruth. He prayed that she had not yet begun to ask any questions awkward enough to draw the attention of the men from the previous night.

The place he had chosen to draw the swastika was smeared with grime, and the chalk did not leave much of a trace. He swore under his breath and rubbed at the dirt, then hurriedly scrawled the symbol. As he straightened up and pocketed the chalk, he saw the brown cap of a middle-aged SA man who had slowed down out of curiosity, and who now winked with approval as he raised his arm.

'Heil Hitler, friend.'

Schenke swallowed and nodded. 'Heil Hitler.'

'That the best you can do?' The man tutted. 'Should be bigger so those Jewish rats can see it. Remember next time, eh?'

He continued along the street, and Schenke watched him for a moment before exhaling with relief. He glanced back at the mark and was satisfied that it was small enough not to draw the eye of anyone else. He looked both ways along the street on the off chance that he might see Ruth, or anyone who might be watching him, but the people hurrying by in both directions ignored him. He pulled his collar up and made his way towards the entrance of the precinct.

Hauser arched an eyebrow as he saw his superior's face when Schenke entered the office.

'You walk in front of a truck, or something?'

'Or something,' Schenke replied. Mindful of the warning he had been given the previous evening he quickly changed the subject. 'Anything from the labs?

'Don't know what you said to the lab boys, but it worked.' Hauser grinned as he slapped an envelope down on Schenke's desk. There was a note on the front from Hilfrich to the effect that the report had been hand-delivered at seven that morning, which caused Schenke to smile. He broke the seal and took out several sheets of paper. Besides the typed copy, there were two pages of tables detailing the results of the tests. He glanced over the conclusion before sliding the sheet of paper across to Hauser, and then noticed that the sergeant was not wearing his sling.

'You seem to be recovering well.'

'Who said anything about being recovered?' Hauser grinned. He raised his arm and made a pained expression before he let it drop. 'The longer I can convince Helga I need time for the arm to recover, the longer I can avoid domestic duties. Besides, the damned sling is a nuisance.'

Hauser picked up the paper and scanned the lines. 'Good. All from the same source, then. I think it's time we pulled in some of the usual suspects for questioning, sir.'

'Agreed. Is everyone in the office?'

'Baumer's down in the canteen and Rosa Mayer's not in yet. She had a date with a naval officer last night . . .'

'Enough said. Round them up for a briefing at . . .' Schenke glanced at the clock on the far wall of the section office, 'nine thirty. If Mayer's not here by then, we'll start without her and I'll have a quiet word later on about not letting naval officers get in the way of her duties.' He pulled the report together and tapped the papers on the desk to signify that the exchange was over.

'Right, sir.' Hauser nodded and closed the partition door behind him before shouting his superior's orders across the office.

Schenke settled down to read through the report in preparation for the briefing. Although the document bore Hilfrich's signature, the frequent flourishes of arrogance were pure Widmann, and it was clear that the technician had cobbled the document together from his superior's notes. The tests carried out at the labs proved that all the forged coupons Schenke had submitted for analysis had been printed using the same dyes. Better still, one of the dyes was particularly unusual, being formulated for exclusive use by the Ministry for Food and Agriculture to ensure that its documents could not be easily forged.

'Not so exclusive as Reich Minister Darré would like to think,' Schenke muttered to himself. He felt a wicked sense of gratification at the thought of some senior officer at the Reich Security Main Office reading over the final report on the forgery investigation once it had been completed and discovering that someone had had the hubris to use the government's own ink to forge ration coupons. An internal investigation would follow in order to root out those responsible for supplying the forgers, and they could expect no mercy from Himmler if they were identified. Schenke felt a moment's sympathy over the ultimate fate of the corrupt officials, but then drew some comfort from the possibility of Germany's burdens being lifted a little by the disappearance of a handful of the regime's inner guard.

As he pored over the columns of figures, his mind began to drift, and before he was aware of it, he was feeling anxious about Ruth Frankel. She had neither the resources nor the training to carry out an investigation on her own, and now that the thugs had beaten and threatened Schenke, it would be too dangerous to work with her to find those responsible for Manfred Schmesler's death. If Brigitte was being watched by the same shadowy figures who had abducted him, there was a good chance they would observe any meeting between her and Ruth. They would be sure to follow Ruth and try to find out what she was up to. If they discovered that she was a Jew, she would be subjected to an interrogation far more painful and terrifying than the one Schenke had undergone. He resolved to warn her off, in the firmest possible manner, at their appointed encounter.

He forced himself to focus on examining the lab report. By the time he had finished, the clock on the office wall showed there was ten minutes left before the briefing. He hastily made a series of numbered points, read over them to ensure that he had not missed anything important, and then glanced through the glass partition. The rest of his section had already gathered around the open space in front of the blackboard and notice-board at the side of the office and were chatting to each other. The noticeboard displayed a number of pictures of those suspected of involvement in forging the ration coupons, as well as a map indicating places where the coupons had been discovered and other related documents. Rosa and Frieda were sitting at a table to one side, deep in conversation. The younger woman seemed radiant, and Schenke found himself envying her moment of happiness.

He picked up his notepad and went out to join them, taking a position in front of the blackboard. The others fell silent, watching him expectantly. He was aware of the scab on his swollen lip and felt self-conscious for a moment. *Dammit, I don't owe them an explanation.* He cleared his throat and began.

'As Hauser may already have told you, we have the results from the lab. All the samples we sent in, and those acquired from other districts of Berlin, were printed using the same ink.'

There were a few murmurs before he continued. 'So, good news at last. If just one line of enquiry can be traced back to the crime ring responsible for printing the forgeries, then we can put an end to the whole business. When the villains are brought to book, the drinks are on me.'

'Careful, sir,' Baumer grinned. 'You know how much beer the sergeant can put away.'

Hauser nodded. 'Damn lucky my drinking hand wasn't wounded when I was shot.'

'Somehow I think you'd have managed,' said Schenke, and the other members of the section laughed. 'Anyway, to work. We'll continue to go after the suspects Persinger and Hofer have been hunting down – the known forgers and fences, as well as those with connections to the black market in Pankow. I don't want word getting out that we're on the hunt, so we'll take as many as we can in one swoop.' He held up his notepad. 'I've drawn up a list of those I want brought in and held in the cells.'

Liebwitz raised a hand and Schenke nodded.

'Will that be protective custody, sir?'

Schenke had already considered that. Protective custody was a widespread device for keeping criminals and suspects in the cells without having to charge them. Since seizing power, the party had also used it to arrest and detain political opponents, trade unionists, uncompliant journalists and any others who had defied them. It was a blunt instrument, but effective. Some individuals had already spent many years in police cells or the camps under the protective custody rule.

'Yes. We may need to keep them for a while before we get what we need. A few days of prison rations usually loosens their tongues.'

Hauser cleared his throat. 'And if that fails, a few days of being questioned by our new Gestapo colleague will loosen their teeth. Is that not so, Scharführer?' He nodded to Liebwitz, but the latter did not seem to understand the gentle dig.

'Extraction of teeth has proved an effective method of interrogation, Sergeant,' he replied. 'But there are many other techniques the Gestapo has perfected. I have been trained in most of them.'

The mood in the office became more sombre, and Schenke was keen to make up for Hauser's flip remark before the relationship between Liebwitz and his new colleagues was damaged any further.

'Trained? You mean you have learned about them? In theory.'

'Mostly theory, sir.' Liebwitz nodded. 'But I would be able to apply my learning if it was required.'

'Ah, thank you for the offer. I'll keep it in mind.' Schenke returned to his notes. 'You'll be given the names of those we want to speak to. Two uniformed policemen will be assigned to each of you, and you'll go in armed. The Kripo can't afford to lose anyone, especially since your training has cost the service a small fortune. If there's any rough stuff, let the Orpo lads handle it. They're the hired muscle, but we're the brains. So no heroics.' He paused and looked round to make sure his team knew he was serious. 'If there's shooting, don't hesitate to put the villains down. We can always get the information we need from some other toerag. We can't so easily replace any of you. Make sure you gather up any evidence that might be useful before the Orpo trample all over it. We've been hunting for the forgers for months. Let's do a good job and get them behind bars. Any questions?'

Persinger raised a hand. 'What are our orders if we encounter party officials in the company of the suspects?'

A sudden tension gripped the room. There was good reason to ask the question. It was not without precedent for party members to be involved in criminality. Indeed, they had thrived on it back in the days of the Republic. Some still did, and there was often an inclination for the police to look the other way rather than make enemies of people who had influence with the regime. Petty crimes could be overlooked, but not something as serious as forging ration coupons, Schenke decided. 'If you suspect they are involved with the crime ring, arrest them on my authority. I'll deal with the consequences.'

Expressions of relief appeared on the faces of some of his subordinates at his accepting the responsibility for such arrests.

'Anyone else? No? Then prepare your weapons and head down to the mess room. The uniformed men assigned to you will be waiting there. As soon as Hauser and I have divided up the names and handed out the lists, you can get going. That's all.'

The briefing broke up and Schenke headed back to his desk. Hauser went to fetch the list they had previously compiled and sat opposite his superior. He took out his notebook and pencil, then started reading out the names and assigning each of them to one of the Kripo officers. Schenke made a few adjustments, ensuring the toughest criminals were left to his more experienced men.

Outside the partition, the rest of the section put on their pistol holsters and then their jackets and coats before making for the door. Liebwitz was the last to go. He sat at his desk, focusing his attention on checking the action of his Luger before he loaded a magazine, thumbed the safety catch, and holstered the weapon in the custom holster he wore to the side of his chest, where it fitted snugly under his leather coat and was easy to draw in an emergency. He stood and tested it twice before he was satisfied, then left the office.

As the door closed behind him, the telephone on Schenke's desk rang. He picked up the receiver.

'Inspector Schenke.'

'You sound so formal, darling.'

'Ah, Karin, it's you.' He could not help smiling.

Hauser indicated the door and cocked an eyebrow, but Schenke shook his head.

'What can I do for you?'

'Right now, not much,' she responded seductively. 'Later, maybe. I'm calling about today's appointment. My friend has found a place that suits our needs. The upstairs lounge at Dorfman's. You know it?'

'Yes.'

'I'll meet you there at one thirty. Our guests will join us about the same time.'

Schenke was relieved at her discretion. Anyone listening in to the call would have found no reason to be suspicious about their brief exchange.

'Fine, I'll see you then.'

He replaced the receiver. Hauser was affecting not to pay attention, and Schenke said, 'We're meeting for lunch.'

'Good. She's a lovely girl, sir. You should make an honest woman of her.'

'Work for the future, my friend. Let's get these forgers first, eh?'

As he was reaching for his notebook, the phone rang again. Assuming that it was Karin calling back, he spoke in a casual tone. 'Yes?'

A male voice responded. 'I have a call for you from the Reich Security Main Office, sir. Connecting you now.'

There was a click and a short delay before a different voice came on the line. One that Schenke recognised instantly: Heydrich, the head of the Reich Security Main Office. He felt a cold tremor ripple down his spine.

'Am I speaking to Inspector Schenke?'

'Yes, sir.' He sat up straighter and indicated to Hauser that he should leave.

'I take it you know my voice?' There was a hint of amusement as Heydrich continued. 'Ah, but then we met just before Christmas, didn't we?'

'Yes, sir.' Schenke recalled the occasion at the conclusion of the murder case that had been solved at the end of the previous year.

'Let's skip the niceties, Schenke. Just a moment . . .' There was a rustle of paper and Heydrich issued a muffled order to someone in his office before he spoke into the telephone again. 'It's come to my attention that you have shown some interest in the death of SS Reich Doctor Schmesler. A suicide, I believe?'

'That is the officially recorded decision, sir.'

'I take it you disagree?'

'I found some inconsistencies in the evidence.'

'I imagine a man of your calibre would. That is to your credit as a professional criminal investigator, Schenke. However, a decision has been made and a verdict of suicide is the official outcome. The final outcome.' The last words were spoken with emphasis. 'Do I make myself clear?'

'Yes . . .'

'That's good. Then I don't expect to hear anything further about the Schmesler incident. If I do hear that you are asking further questions, I will be displeased, Inspector. Do you understand what that means?'

'Yes, sir.'

'Then there will be no need for any further warning about keeping your nose out of the matter. Good day. Heil Hitler.'

The line went dead, and Schenke replaced the receiver. He paused a moment in thought over the words Heydrich had used; *any further warning*. Up until that moment Schenke had been convinced that his abduction had been Heydrich's work to scare him off. Now he was not so sure. 'Further warning' implied that the threat made at the end of the telephone call was the first warning. But if Heydrich was not behind the abduction, then who had been? Schenke's brow creased in frustration, as he could not think of anyone else who might have been responsible. Whatever the true reason for Schmesler's death, the message from Heydrich was clear. If Schenke crossed the line that had been drawn, he would share the same fate as the doctor. As would Ruth.

'Shit . . .' he muttered.

Chapter Fourteen

Schenke had been shaken by his conversation with Heydrich. Fortunately he was able to calm himself in the empty office as the rest of the section went out to begin rounding up those wanted in connection with the forgery case. As noon came and went, he braced himself for the encounter with Ruth. He was not certain that she would agree to abandon the search for Schmesler's killers, even when she learned about what had happened to Schenke, and the warning from Heydrich.

He made his way down the street towards the toy shop, pausing fifty paces short and stopping to look in the window of a pawn shop filled with bric-a-brac surrendered by those desperate to make ends meet. But his eyes were focused on the reflection in the glass, searching for any sign that he was being observed from the other side of the street. Turning his head slightly, he checked left and right too, but no one appeared to be following or watching him.

He continued towards the toy shop and saw that the swastika in the neighbouring doorway had been erased. Ruth had got the message and should be there soon. He backed into the entrance of the closed shop and waited.

Over the next few minutes, several women walked past on either side of the street, but none of them was Ruth. The freezing air bit at his cheeks, and he rubbed his hands together vigorously to fight off the cold. To his right, he saw a stout figure in the black cap and quilted overalls of a coal deliveryman approaching, face smudged with coal dust. The man paused by the toy shop, and Schenke frowned, worried in case Ruth appeared and they had to wait to speak until the deliveryman had continued on his way.

'Good to see you, Horst.'

His head snapped round, and it took a moment before he recognised her features through the disguise.

'Don't stare at me!' she hissed. 'You want to attract everyone's attention?'

He moved to the toy shop window, keeping some distance between them so that they might look more like strangers. 'I didn't realise it was you.'

'Obviously, and that's a good thing.'

'Where did you get the idea for that disguise?'

'Disguise? These are my work clothes. I had a night shift at Siemens, working the boilers. Seems that only the dirtiest jobs are reserved for Jews these days. What's happened?'

Schenke related the previous evening's abduction and Heydrich's follow-up threat. 'We can't risk looking into Schmesler's death any more. I'm sorry, but you'll have to explain things to Brigitte.'

'No. I won't.'

His eyes widened. 'What are you thinking? They threatened my life. What do you imagine they'll do to you if they discover you're in on it too? If they're willing to murder a Kripo inspector, they won't think twice about killing a Jew.'

'I don't really care. Since the party's taken almost everything away from me, I haven't got as much at stake as you.'

'You've got your life.'

'For how much longer? How soon do you think it'll be before they clear us out of the capital for good and send us east? I don't have any illusions about what that might entail. Meanwhile, I'll do my best to find those responsible for the death of Brigitte's husband.' She looked at him directly. 'I've made a start. One of his friends from the hospital where he used to work paid a visit to Brigitte to offer his condolences. They talked about the job Manfred went to after leaving the hospital. Something to do with racial hygiene in one of the Reich Security Main Office's departments. Manfred didn't give any further details to his friend, other than that it was important work on a confidential project sanctioned from the very top. If we can find out what he was up to, it might point us in the right direction . . . Assuming you still have the stomach for it.'

Schenke glanced round to see if they were being watched before he responded. 'You're going to stick with this, aren't you? No matter what I told you about Heydrich's warning.'

'Yes.'

'There's nothing I can do to persuade you to leave it alone?'

She smiled sadly. 'No.'

Despite Heydrich's scarcely veiled threat, there was still the fact that a man had been murdered, and it was Schenke's duty to find out why and who was responsible. If he baulked at that now, he knew he would never forgive himself, despite the dangers facing him. He paused for a moment, surprised at the decision he had reached. There was pride and elation, too, at this proof that he was prepared to take such risks along with

Ruth. If that was true of them then surely it was true of others and he drew some comfort from the thought.

'Shit. All right then. See what else you can find out, but take no risks. I'll keep my head down for a few days to make Heydrich think his threat has worked. Besides, I have another matter that needs looking into. As long as I attend to that, his thugs will leave me alone. Once it feels safe, I'll see what I can discover about Schmesler's work. We can do this, Ruth. But we have to be damned careful how we go about it. Understand?'

She nodded.

'If you have the slightest suspicion that you are being watched, go into hiding and get a message to me. I'll see what I can do about providing for you until it is safe to come out again. Do you have anywhere you can go in an emergency?'

'There's always somewhere, for a price, or a service. I have some U-Boot contacts.'

He frowned. 'U-Boot?'

'That's what those Jews who abandon their identity and disappear below the surface of society are calling themselves. Provided you know the right people, you can get stolen or forged documents.'

'I'm not sure you should be telling me this,' Schenke replied. 'I'm on the hunt for some forgers at the moment. You'd better be careful in case the same people who are printing fake ration coupons are providing identity documents on the side.'

'Noted.' Ruth looked around. 'We've been talking too long. I'd better go. I'll keep an eye out for the mark.' She nodded towards the closed-up shop and then looked at Schenke speculatively. 'You're a good man. Riding to my rescue like a knight of old. The situation has a touch of *Ivanhoe* about it, don't you think?'

'I wouldn't know. I've never read it.'

'That's too bad. Goodbye, Horst.'

'Until the next time, you mean.'

She smiled sadly. 'Who can say?'

She turned away and strode off, looking just like any other manual worker as she made her way to the junction, crossed the street and disappeared from view.

Schenke began to walk steadily in the direction of the Dorfman hotel, where he was due to meet Karin and the couple Shirer had mentioned. Now that Ruth had gone, he was consumed by concern for her safety. If Schmesler had been working under the direction of someone at the very top of the party, these were dangerous waters indeed.

The hotel was on one of the less fashionable shopping streets in Pankow. In the second half of the previous century, heavy industry had moved to the area, and the smoke and grime in the air had driven away those who could afford to move to a more pleasant neighbourhood. The Dorfman's smart clientele was gradually replaced by travelling salesmen, budget-conscious tourists, philanderers and working-class newly-weds briefly sampling a taste of modest luxury before returning to their dingy rooms in crowded tenement blocks. There was a faded gentility to the place, with sumptuous curtains, carpets and gilded columns in the reception hall, but even a cursory inspection revealed threadbare material and worn patches on the carpets, while paint flaked on the columns and ceilings. There was also the musty scent of decay, familiar to so many outdated buildings in the twilight years of their splendour.

Schenke stepped through the revolving doors into the lobby. The counter was to his left, behind which stood a tall elderly man in a mauve double-breasted jacket. A boy, similarly dressed, waited at the far end of the counter, hands held behind his back, ready for instructions. Sofas and chairs were arranged around low tables across the lobby, and on the wall opposite the counter was a large fireplace of yellowed marble. A small pile of logs was burning in the centre of an iron grate; judging from the coats still being worn by the handful of guests seated nearby, it was giving out little heat. The war had stripped the hotel of most of its custom, and the parsimony of the fire indicated that it was suffering financially. Schenke scrutinised the people seated in the lobby, but none seemed suspicious, and no one had followed him in from the street.

Pulling off his gloves, he strode across the lobby to the carpeted staircase at the rear, and climbed to the lounge on the second floor, with its large windows overlooking the street. It was noticeably warmer here, thanks to two gas fires turned up to their top setting. A woman was arranging her sheet music at a piano in the corner ready to entertain a score of customers seated at small tables. Some were smoking, adding to the seedy odour of the place. There were a few couples, and a group of five loud men drinking beer as they swapped stories. Schenke put them down as salesmen.

In the far corner, away from the heaters, Karin sat on a sofa. She saw him at once and smiled as he made his way across to her. If this had been a social lunch, Schenke's heart would have lifted, but his senses were on edge in anticipation of the meeting. Noticing that she had chosen a spot with two sofas facing each other either side of a coffee table, he slipped into the space beside her and took off his hat before giving her a quick kiss.

'You look tired,' she said. 'How's the lip?'

'Sore. But nothing like as sore as my arm. Those bastards knew what they were about.'

'You should run yourself a hot bath when you get home tonight. That might go some way towards helping to ease the pain.'

The way she phrased the suggestion caught his attention. 'You won't be there?'

'I am having dinner with my uncle tonight. I think he's going to give me the talk about young women not sharing an apartment with their men before they are married. He's been very good to me. I don't want to cause any friction by making it seem as if I have all but moved in with you. Even if I have.' She touched his cheek. 'I hope you don't mind, darling.'

'As long as you come back tomorrow,' he replied as he glanced at the clock above the bar. It was the appointed time.

'She should be here any moment,' Karin reassured him.

'She?'

'Johanna Scholtz.'

'Is there a father?'

'Yes, but he refused to get involved. William said Johanna is determined to speak to you. She hasn't told her husband she's coming here.'

'To be honest, I really wish she wasn't. Given what else is going on.'

'I understand. But at least you have a chance of giving them some justice, even if you can't do the same for Brigitte Schmesler.'

'Assuming there's anything to investigate.'

'If you decide there isn't, maybe that alone will be some source of comfort to her. Either way, it may help the family.'

'Do you have any other details for me?'

'Sorry, I should have told you earlier. Johanna is a volunteer nurse, and Gottfried, her husband, is a school teacher. The girl who died was their only child. And . . . Ah, I think she has arrived.' Karin nodded subtly, and Schenke turned to see a short, thin woman wearing a black coat and a hat with a small red feather sticking out at an angle. She looked to be in her mid thirties.

Karin beckoned to her, and she made for the corner of the lounge. Schenke stood up, and there was a formal exchange of handshakes as Karin made the introductions.

'Please sit down.' She indicated the sofa opposite. When all three were seated, she continued, 'I'm going to order some hot chocolate for us all. Is that all right?'

Johanna gave a polite nod. 'Thank you.'

Karin called over a waiter to give the order. Once he had returned to the bar, she spoke again, in a voice low enough not to be overheard but not so low as to appear furtive.

'Horst is the police investigator Mr Shirer told you about. If anyone can help you, he can.'

Schenke cleared his throat. 'Before this goes any further, I need to make my position clear. I will listen to what you have to say, and I will have some questions, but if in my judgement there's nothing the Kripo can do about the matter, it ends there.'

'What if I was to pay you to investigate it in your own time?' the woman suggested.

He felt a flush of irritation. 'I am not a private detective, Frau Scholtz. I am a professional police officer employed by the state, and my time is taken up with investigating serious crimes.'

Johanna leaned forward. 'But serious crimes have been committed here, Inspector.'

'That remains to be seen,' Schenke replied. 'From what Shirer has told me, it might be a matter of coincidence. With this unusually cold winter, there will be more deaths amongst those most vulnerable to illness. That may be true of your child.'

'Our Greta was a healthy little girl!'

'Please stay calm.'

'Calm?' She glared at him. 'How can I be calm? They murdered Greta. She was a good girl. A German. Not subhuman.'

With mounting horror, he saw the tears glistening in her eyes as her voice rose in a shrill cry.

'Our daughter was murdered!'

Chapter Fifteen

At the sound of Johanna's raised voice, several of the other people in the lounge turned to stare. The laughter of the five men around the table died away as they looked across. Karin leaned forward, took Johanna's hand and spoke softly.

'My dear, you must control yourself. We can't bring Greta back. All we can hope for is that she gets justice. That's what the inspector is here to deal with.' She glanced at Schenke. 'Isn't that right?'

Schenke felt uncomfortable being put on the spot. Johanna's outburst had unsettled him, and he wished he had never agreed to Shirer's request. He forced himself to adopt an understanding tone as he replied. 'If the law has been broken, it's my job to see that those guilty are held accountable.'

'See?' Karin said. 'Now let's do right by Greta, eh?'

Johanna lowered her gaze as her shoulders slumped. 'I'm sorry, Inspector . . . It's still very painful for us to talk about. It's shattered our world.'

Schenke doubted they would ever come to terms with it. He knew from previous experience the raw emotion that the loss of a child engendered in parents. He had seen the helpless anguish of those who felt their hearts had been torn from their bodies, leaving behind an aching void that would never be filled. In the numbness that remained, the only comfort was the effort of maintaining a routine and trying not to think.

A moment later, the waiter came over with a tray and laid it on the table. As he leaned close to Schenke, he muttered quietly. 'Sir, the lounge manager asks if the lady is all right.'

'It's a family matter. A loss.'

'My condolences. Would you prefer to move to a private room?'

'No,' Karin intervened. 'We'll be fine here, thank you.'

The man hesitated briefly, and Schenke realised that he had made the offer in order not to discomfort the other customers, rather than out of consideration for a distraught woman.

'You can go,' he said coldly. 'Don't disturb us again.'

'Yes, sir.'

Schenke eased one of the cups of hot chocolate across the table. 'Drink some of that, Frau Scholtz. It'll do you good. Then you can tell me your story, when you are ready.'

She nodded her thanks and began to unbutton her coat now that the warmth of the room was making itself felt. As she pulled the folds apart to reveal a neat grey jacket, there was the glint of something round and metallic on her lapel before the edge of the coat covered it again. She picked up her cup and saucer and sipped the chocolate as she collected her thoughts. Eventually she began.

'Greta was born ten years ago. It was not an easy birth. The doctor who came to our home was young, and he decided it would be best to induce labour. We agreed to it, Gottfried and I. He could not bear to see me in such torment. Anyway, Greta was delivered. The doctor pronounced her healthy, saw to my needs and gave me something to help with the pain and let me sleep. In the days that followed, we were delighted with our baby daughter. We hoped, we planned, to have more children a few years later, when we could afford a bigger apartment.

'But then after the first year, we began to notice that Greta was not like others the same age. She did not seem to respond to those around her. It took her nearly three years before she could walk, and words came very slowly. We became worried and took her to see a specialist. He examined her and did some tests and told us it was likely that her impairment was a result of something that had gone wrong during her birth, or it might be a hereditary condition. He told us there was nothing we could do about it. She would be simple-minded for the rest of her life, he said. He also advised us to think carefully about having any more children, in case we were the cause. No more children . . .' Johanna swallowed.

'We were devastated. We decided we could not cope with the thought of having another child like Greta. Don't misunderstand me, Inspector. We loved her as much as any parent could love their child. But we feared for what might become of her, especially when we were no longer there to care for her. In the meantime, we schooled her as well as we could, but she struggled in lessons, she spoke with difficulty. Despite that, she was a cheerful soul for the most part, and other children liked her.

'Then, a year ago, she began to have episodes when she fell into sudden rages and screamed for hours on end. Much as we loved her, it wore our nerves down. Our doctor told us that she needed special care, and recommended an institution near Potsdam, the Schiller clinic. She would be looked after there, and there would be other children she could befriend and play

149

with. He told us there were pleasant gardens, and the children were taught basic skills so that they might find work when they were old enough to leave. It sounded ideal, so we took Greta to see it. It was an old villa with a walled garden, the rooms were light and airy, and she loved it. She would be happy there, we thought, and it would be good for her to be with people who could tend to her needs better than us.'

'A moment,' Schenke interrupted. 'The doctor who recommended the Schiller clinic, was he known to you previously?'

'He is our family doctor. The one who delivered Greta.'

'I see.' He took out his notebook and flipped it open. 'I need his name and address.'

'Dr Lenger, 13 Brennerstrasse, Pankow.'

Schenke nodded and noted the details. 'Please continue.'

'Where was I?' Johanna frowned. 'Ah, yes. We were sure that Greta would be looked after, so we made arrangements to commit her there.'

'When was that?'

'September the tenth of last year.' Johanna reached into her bag and took out a photograph, setting it down in front of Schenke and Karin. 'I remember the date because we had this taken the day before.'

It was a studio photograph, the parents standing stiffly either side of a broadly smiling child with blonde hair tied back with a ribbon. Johanna was wearing the same jacket she wore now. Her husband was in a formal suit. A tall, thin man with a severe expression, close-cut dark hair and a brush moustache.

'It was Sunday when we took her to the clinic,' Johanna continued. 'It was raining hard. We took her after we'd been to church . . . God forgive me. My father let us use his car for

150

the journey. We had her clothes packed, together with a box of her favourite toys, and we settled her into her room and stayed with her until it was time for supper. The director of the clinic told us that it would be best if we did not see her for the first few weeks, to help her get used to her surroundings and the new faces. He said we could call each weekend for a report if we wished.

'It all seemed to go well at first. We were told she was happy and that she had made friends. Then, at the end of September, we visited her and discovered that she had made progress with some basic reading skills. We left it another month before we drove out to see her again. That time it was different. Greta had been moved from her room to a dormitory on a wing we had not seen before. There were bars on the windows,' Johanna added with a look of disgust.

'The director was busy, and it was one of the orderlies who told us that Greta's behaviour had changed. She had become moody and had attacked a member of staff, so she had been moved to the secure dormitory for a while. When we saw her sitting on her bed, she looked nervous, as if she was afraid of the orderly. She didn't say a word until he left the room. Then she told us she wasn't happy and that she wanted to leave the clinic and come home. We asked her what had changed to make her so sad, and she said that the children in the dormitory disappeared.'

'Disappeared?' Karin's brow furrowed. 'What did she mean by that?'

'She said that every few days, some of the children were taken out for a treat, and that sometimes they never returned. She said the other inmates spoke about a brown bus that came and took children away. The orderly we'd seen earlier had told

Greta that if she misbehaved again, the brown bus would come for her too. We couldn't get anything else out of her. She was too upset to talk; she just cried and moaned and begged us not to leave her there. When the time came for us to go, she clung to us and a nurse had to hold her back as we left.'

Johanna shuddered and reached for her drink, but just stared at the froth in the cup. 'Gottfried demanded to speak to the director before we drove home. We told him what Greta had said, and he reassured us that children passed through the dormitory all the time, and that they were returned to their rooms once their behaviour had improved.'

'What about this brown bus?' asked Schenke.

'He explained that it was provided by the Strength Through Joy organisation to take kids out for the day. You know, for walks in the forest, or picnics at the local lakes. That sort of thing. There was nothing sinister about it, and the children had just made up a tale about it to frighten each other. When I told him about the orderly using it as a threat, he said the man would be disciplined and that we should be reassured that the clinic did not tolerate that kind of behaviour from its staff. We still weren't happy about the situation and told him we wanted to take Greta home. He said that was not possible. She had been committed to the clinic by Dr Lenger, and he would have to sign her release documents before she could be discharged.'

'That doesn't sound right to me,' Schenke commented.

'It didn't sound right to us either, but Lenger confirmed it. A new law had been introduced shortly before regarding children with mental and physical conditions who had been committed to the care of institutions. The same law also required doctors to report all births of such children to the office of the Reich Health Leader. We demanded that Lenger prepare the papers to release Greta. He said that he would have to examine her records and consult with a colleague before he could sign them, and he'd let us know the moment they were ready. We waited for a few days before I called his office to ask the reason for the delay. He said it was in hand and that we had to be patient. Another week went by, and I called again. This time he said he had sent the papers to the Reich Health Leader's office for authorisation, and they would be returned as soon as they had received the official stamp.'

Johanna paused and closed her eyes. She cleared her throat softly before she spoke again.

'A day later, November the twelfth . . . that was the day we received a letter from the clinic to say that . . . that Greta had died. She had contracted pneumonia two weeks earlier and had not responded to treatment. I . . . We . . .' She stopped and lowered her head, unable to speak.

'Do you have the letter with you?' Schenke asked.

She opened her bag and took out a plain envelope, holding it with an expression torn between grief and horror.

He spoke gently. 'May I read it?'

She let him take it.

Schenke examined the envelope. The Scholtzes' address was on the front, beneath a franked postage stamp. There was no sender's address on the reverse, and the top had been neatly slit open with the blade of a letter opener. He extracted the letter inside and unfolded it, holding it up so that Karin could read it at the same time.

To G. & J. Scholtz,

It is with great sadness that I write to inform you of

the death of your daughter, Greta. She succumbed to pneumonia on 9 November after a short illness. Her condition deteriorated rapidly, and by the time medication was prescribed, it was too late to treat her.

It is the policy of the clinic to cremate the bodies of patients who have died on site. Greta's ashes have been preserved for you in a sealed urn. Should you wish to have them delivered to you, there is a nominal charge of ten Reichsmarks for the service, payable on delivery. The deceased's personal effects, in line with the clinic's regulations, have been sold to raise funds for other children in need.

Please accept the sincere condolences of myself and the staff of the clinic.

SS Reich Doctor W. Pieper

Schenke read the letter through a second time before he folded it and replaced it in the envelope, laying it on the table beside his cup of chocolate.

'You see?' Johanna's voice quivered with barely suppressed rage. 'They didn't even return her things to us. They made us pay for her ashes. It's as if she never lived.'

'What did you do about it?'

'What do you think? We buried her ashes in the family plot, and grieved.'

Schenke winced at the thoughtlessness of his question. He should have been clearer about its intention. 'I meant to ask, did you take the matter up with anyone?'

'Of course,' Johanna said. 'We were angry. We wanted answers. My husband demanded to speak to the director of the clinic, but he refused to take our calls. He had some meetings with a lawyer, but the lawyer said there was nothing that could be done under the law as it stood. I asked Dr Lenger for his opinion, and he said he was surprised that someone as healthy as Greta could have succumbed to pneumonia, but that it was possible there were complicating factors. It was a month later that the parents of a child Greta had known at her nursery class came to our house. They had heard about her death and told us that their son had died at the clinic a week earlier. We compared circumstances, and they were almost the same in every detail.'

'Almost?'

'They were told that their boy had died from tuberculosis.'

'That's a significant difference,' Schenke pointed out.

'True, but he had been sent to the same barred dormitory for what the clinic claimed was violent behaviour. He told his parents about the brown bus. They were not notified of his death until two weeks later, and the director dismissed their concerns as well.'

'It's possible that two such deaths were an unfortunate coincidence,' said Schenke.

Johanna smiled wearily. 'That's what Lenger told us. So I spoke to the parents of the other children at the school that we had got to know when Greta was younger. There were two more children who had been committed to the same clinic and whose deaths were very similar. Yesterday, I was told that a fifth child had died.'

'Five children,' Karin murmured. 'From the same nursery class?'

Johanna nodded. 'Within the space of three months. Tell me that's just a coincidence.'

Schenke raised an eyebrow. 'I admit, it is hard to regard it as such.'

She leaned closer, her gaze uncomfortably intense. 'Think about this, Inspector. I looked into the death notices in the local papers of children who attended other schools for the handicapped over the last three months, and spoke to some of the families concerned.' She reached into her bag and brought out a small bundle of newspaper clippings bound together with a staple, setting them down before Schenke. 'There were another eight deaths at that clinic during the same months. Eight . . . That makes thirteen in all, starting with our Greta. Do you still think it is a coincidence?'

Schenke felt a sense of dread seeping into his mind. He shook his head. 'No.'

'No,' Johanna repeated with emphasis. She paused a moment. 'Someone at the clinic is murdering our children. And the director and the others in charge refuse to acknowledge it and don't seem to care. It looks to me like they may even be protecting the killer.'

She picked up the death notices and folded them so that Schenke could see the name on one particular clipping: *Greta Scholtz. Passed from this world aged ten . . .*

'Our little girl was murdered, Inspector. Killed in cold blood and disposed of. All they gave us was her ashes . . . And she was only the beginning.'

Chapter Sixteen

When he returned to his office at the precinct, Schenke read through the death notices and the letter from the clinic, then placed the documents in the top drawer of his desk as he considered how to begin dealing with the matter. His mind still reeled at the fact that so many children had died at one institution in such a short space of time. He had given his word to Johanna Scholtz that he would investigate their deaths in an official capacity, but first he needed more information to lay before Kleist to be sure of getting permission to involve the Kripo. The director of the clinic was a member of the SS, and that required an extra burden of proof before it was safe to proceed. Another SS doctor, he reflected, like Schmesler.

It was tempting to infer a connection between the two, but that was motivated more by his dislike of the organisation than by any shred of available evidence. The deaths of Schmesler and the children were both almost certainly the result of murder, but that was the only point of comparison between the two cases.

The Schmesler case had been closed and the children's case had not even been authorised. Yet Schenke felt invested in both. That would surely prove an unhelpful distraction from the ongoing forgery investigation. He was going to need some help, someone he could trust and rely on. Only one member of his section fitted the bill – Sergeant Hauser.

None of the arresting parties had returned to the precinct yet, so there was a brief opportunity to talk it through while the two of them were the only people in the office.

'Hauser!' he called, and beckoned when the sergeant looked up from reading the newspaper at his desk.

With Hauser seated opposite, he went through what he had been told in the lounge at the Dorfman hotel, and produced the letter and death notices. He watched as Hauser read over them and then sat back.

'It's hard to believe. So many kids . . . The director's either a complete incompetent or he's in on it.' The sergeant shook his head. 'What kind of sick bastard would do such a thing?'

'The question is, how is it being done?' Schenke responded. 'The disposal of the bodies suggests that someone is covering up evidence of the cause of death. There's no chance of an autopsy to justify an inquest if there's no corpus delicti. The director must have signed the cremation orders. I'd be interested to hear his explanation.'

'Then we should start with him.'

'No. Not him. That might be too direct. We need a clearer picture before we tackle SS Reich Doctor Pieper.' Schenke thought for a moment. 'Dr Lenger. That's where we start. I want to know why he recommended committing Greta, and why he pointed them in the direction of the Schiller clinic.'

Hauser glanced at his wristwatch. 'Whatever we do, we're

going to have our hands full with the forgery investigation. It's not going to be easy to work round that.'

'I've had a thought about that.' Schenke smiled. 'I can buy us a little time to look into these deaths while we wait for some of our suspects in the forgery case to develop a more cooperative spirit.'

Hauser raised an eyebrow. 'Oh, how's that?'

'You'll see. I think you'll approve. Whether our Orpo colleagues will is a different matter.'

It was eight o'clock in the evening before the last of the arrest parties returned to the precinct and led their handcuffed prisoners into the yard at the back of the building. There were nearly fifty of them in all. Those who had arrived earlier and had endured some hours of the cold were trembling in the faint beams of light cast by the blackout slits in the lamps shining down into the yard. Several uniformed policemen armed with rifles were standing guard over the assorted suspects, all of whom had a criminal record. It was several degrees below freezing, and skeins of cloud stretched across the star-sprinkled night sky. Tiny crystals of ice swirled on a brisk breeze and stung exposed flesh like the finest of needles. Most of those arrested had been allowed to put on coats before they were handcuffed and led away, but a handful wore only the clothes they had been found in when the police arrived at their door. The latter were shivering uncontrollably and shouting loudly as they demanded blankets and to speak with the officer in charge.

Inside the Kripo office, Schenke's subordinates were warming themselves by the stove, swapping accounts of their arrests. Schenke put on his coat and hat and spoke to Hauser.

'Distribute the names of those we haven't yet found. The team can work in pairs and track down the remaining suspects tomorrow. Then send everyone home.'

'Yes, sir. Need me to remain afterwards?'

'No. I've got one final matter to deal with tonight, then I'm done.'

Hauser looked relieved.

'Get a good night's rest, Sergeant. We've got some work to do if we're going to get the investigation into the Schiller clinic up and running.'

They exchanged a nod before Schenke left the office and made his way downstairs to pick up a mug of hot ersatz coffee from the mess room. Then he stepped out into the yard and strolled towards the huddle of men caught in the bright lights, their breath swirling around their heads. There was a small reviewing platform to one side of the yard, a throwback to the days when the precinct had been an army barracks. Climbing the short flight of steps, he raised his steaming cup and took a sip as he regarded the prisoners. Hostile faces watched him, some with envious expressions. When he was sure he had their attention, he casually tossed what was left in the mug to one side.

'Gentlemen!' he began. 'For those who have not crossed my path before, I am Inspector Schenke of the Kripo. It does my heart good to see so many of you here to help us with our enquiries concerning the forged ration coupons. Now that most of the names on our list are present, I can let you know a few details about what will be happening over the next few days . . . or weeks.' He paused to glance around the small crowd. 'It may come as a surprise to you that the crime ring behind the forged coupons has caused some distress to the

160

upstanding people of Berlin. They are getting increasingly angry. Therefore, in the interests of saving you from the consequences of their ire, the police have decided to take you into protective custody.'

There was a series of loud groans from the handcuffed men, and a few angry shouts of protest. Schenke raised his hands and called for silence. 'You're all criminals, and I will not insult you by asking for your cooperation in answering our questions, or expecting you to tell us the truth. I know you'll lie to protect your comrades, and some of you will lie just to annoy us. With that in mind, you are going to enjoy a few days of police hospitality before we even begin to ask questions.'

He indicated the barred storerooms lining the rear of the yard. 'I've arranged some accommodation for the duration of your custody. There's no heating, but you'll find some old straw in some of the stalls that may help to keep the cold out. You will be fed rations at dawn and at the end of the day. Not enough to grow fat on, but enough to keep you alive. We'll start asking you for information in a few days' time. Those of you who offer help in tracking down the forgers will get better rations, if your information is accurate, and the chance to be set free. Any hard cases who refuse to answer questions to my satisfaction will be sent straight back to their cells until they see reason. That's all, gentlemen. Enjoy your first night here.' He tapped the brim of his hat in farewell.

At once there was a barrage of outraged cries from the prisoners, who surged towards him until the uniformed police thrust them back with their rifles. One of the officers slammed his butt into a prisoner's guts, and the man folded up and collapsed to his knees with a groan. Schenke nodded to himself. A bit of harsh treatment on top of the discomfort of living in the makeshift cells might spur some of the less hardened criminals to speak up when the time came to question them.

He left the uniformed police to herd the men into the stalls, removing their handcuffs as they passed over the threshold. There was nothing left for him to do at the precinct, and he set off back through the streets to his apartment block. The loom of the ice on the path and the shielded lights of vehicles passing by provided enough illumination for him to make his way along the pavement, avoiding other pedestrians. Despite the temperature, the novelty of the blackout had not yet worn off for many Berliners. There were groups of youngsters out, chatting excitedly as they passed by. There were couples too, more than likely out in the dark because their families disapproved, or they were having illicit affairs. There were also prostitutes, pickpockets and muggers taking advantage of the darkness.

When he reached the quieter streets of his neighbourhood, Schenke's thoughts returned to what he had learned from the encounter at the Dorfman hotel. The more the information had sunk in, the more appalled he had become at the prospect that someone at the clinic was murdering helpless children and disposing of their remains in such a ruthless fashion. More troubling was the apparent insouciance of the director, which made it all the more likely that he was involved in whatever was going on. Schenke had already been warned off investigating the death of Schmesler, and he doubted he would be forgiven by Heydrich if there was further danger of embarrassing the party.

As he turned into his own street, he glanced over his shoulder and saw that the pavement was empty save for a single dark figure some thirty paces behind him. A cigarette flared briefly and revealed a man in the coat and cap of a worker. Given his experience the previous night, Schenke had a heightened awareness of his surroundings, and even though the man might be an innocent passer-by, he was taking no chances.

The instant he had turned the corner, he rushed forward several paces and ducked into an alley that passed beneath the first apartment block into the courtyard beyond. Pressing himself against the brick wall, he calmed his breathing and waited. A moment later, he heard the soft crunch of boots on frozen snow, and a voice muttered softly, 'What the devil?'

The workman hurried past the alley, sparing a quick glance into the inky blackness before he strode on. Schenke waited to make sure he had not doubled back, then emerged cautiously and looked round the corner. The dark figure was visible a short distance further along the street. He broke into a trot, then stopped abruptly and looked at the buildings on both sides of the street. Flicking his cigarette butt into the road, he turned and headed back towards Schenke, still muttering to himself.

Schenke unbuttoned his coat and drew his pistol, holding it ready, left hand over the slide, as he waited. He let the man pass him before stepping out into the street.

'Looking for someone, friend?'

The man stopped and turned on his heel, one hand reaching into his coat.

Schenke pulled the slide back to chamber the first round and brought the pistol up. 'Don't!'

The man froze.

The growl of an approaching truck forced Schenke to raise his voice as he gave the order. 'Put your hands up! Slowly, back into the alley.'

The man did as he was told, and Schenke took a few steps closer to him. 'Who are you?'

There was no reply, and Schenke reached for the small torch he carried in his pocket. It was an awkward manoeuvre while keeping the man covered, and he fumbled for the opening to the pocket.

A narrow beam of light bloomed across the junction. Schenke had the brief impression of a stocky man about the same height as himself before the lorry rounded the corner. The shielded headlamps swept across the wall of the building opposite, then crossed the road and shone directly at Schenke before the driver corrected the oversteer. Schenke was momentarily dazzled. There was a thud of boots on ice, and when the lorry had passed by, he saw that the man had bolted towards the corner of the junction.

'Police! Stop!' he shouted.

The man ducked his head and ran on, disappearing round the corner. Schenke hurried after him, going wide in case his prey was lying in wait. But he was still fleeing, running down the street. Schenke hesitated for an instant, then took aim, going for the legs, squinting into the gloom as he sighted his target as best he could. He squeezed the trigger and there was a deafening crash. The man half spun, staggered a few steps and then ran on.

'Stop!' Schenke shouted, taking aim again, more carefully this time.

On the far side of the street, a small group of people had stopped at the sound of the shot, and the man suddenly changed direction and dashed across the road to place them between Schenke and himself.

'Damn you! Stop!' Schenke called out, then, 'Police! Stop that man!'

He ran on as fast as his leg would allow, raising the barrel so that an accidental shot would not strike anyone.

'Hey! Watch it!' There was a cry from the group on the other side of the road and a commotion amongst the dark figures there. Schenke rushed towards them.

'Hold him!' he shouted.

As he reached the group, a man surged up and slammed into him, knocking him to the pavement. He managed to keep hold of his gun as he yelled, 'I'm police, you fool! Stop the other one!' He scrambled to his feet, felt a hand try to assist him and shook it off. 'Get out of my way! Where is he?'

There was no reply, and he pushed his way through them. On the far side of the group, he saw the man running on, just visible against a handful of other figures moving at a walk. There was no chance of taking another shot without risking the life of an innocent passer-by.

Thumbing the safety catch, he lowered his pistol. He breathed in sharply and then snarled through gritted teeth, 'Shit . . .'

Chapter Seventeen

3 February

'Who do you think it was?' asked Hauser the following morning as he turned the pool car out of the yard and onto the street. He proceeded cautiously, as he had signed out the new Audi 920 that had only been assigned to the precinct two weeks earlier. It was Oberst Kleist's vehicle of choice, and the sergeant dared not be responsible for any scratches or dents in the gleaming bodywork while the car was out of the precinct.

'I can't say,' said Schenke. 'I didn't get the chance for a good look at him before he ran. Could be anyone. A member of the crime gang running the forged coupon racket. Or one of Heydrich's lads keeping an eye on me to make sure I don't go causing any more trouble over the Schmesler affair. Might even have been some lowlife out to rob me when he got me alone in a dark street.'

'Do you think that's likely?'

'After what's happened these last few days? No chance.'

'What did your Karin have to say about it?'

'She doesn't know yet. I didn't want to worry her.'

Hauser let out a low whistle. 'Wouldn't want to be in your

shoes when she eventually does find out.'

'There's no reason why she should.'

'Then you don't know women. They *always* find out. One way or another.'

Schenke reached for the dashboard dial to turn the heat up. 'There's another good reason to concern ourselves with the deaths at the clinic. It'll be safer to be seen to be investigating something unconnected to Schmesler's death, so it looks like I'm paying heed to the warning I was given.'

'I suppose that's one way of looking at it,' Hauser commented tersely.

Schenke glanced at him and noted his clenched jaw as he stared through the windshield at the road ahead. 'Something bothering you, Sergeant?'

Hauser did not reply immediately. 'If there's anything to what Frau Scholtz told you, then there's some sick bastard out there killing kids. That doesn't sit well with me.'

'I would have hoped that no murder sits well with you,' said Schenke.

'It ain't a matter for sarcasm, sir. If some criminal takes out another, that's one thing. Someone harming a child, that's quite different. You're not a father, so maybe you don't get it.'

'I suppose.'

'Whenever I see kids coming to harm in the course of my work, I can't help but think of my own. It scares me to think of anything happening to them.' Hauser shot a quick glance at him. 'You'll feel the same way when you have children.'

'That's not on the cards for me right now.'

'That was what I thought, then Helga went and got in the family way.'

'As far as I understand the process, it takes two to get in the family way . . .'

Hauser chuckled. 'All right, boss, so I played my part. But I tell you. The moment you have your first child, it changes you. Changes the way you see the world.'

The Audi slid on the icy surface before the sergeant corrected it and slowed down. Out of the side window Schenke saw three men in imperial greatcoats sitting on boxes outside a shop as they shared a bottle. Another reminder of the first great war, which had devastated Germany and replaced the monarchy with a hopelessly compromised republic that was too ready to collapse before the onslaught of Hitler and his followers.

'It can't be easy for you now there's a war on,' he mused. 'Every parent will have to worry about enemy bombers and such threats, on top of the usual worries.'

Hauser shrugged. 'So far, that's amounted to nothing. As long as the Frenchies continue dropping leaflets on Berlin, I'm happy. If they start using bombs, Helga and I have already decided that she and the kids are going to live with her parents on their farm. Fresh air and hard work will do them a power of good in any case. And I'll get a bit of peace around the apartment. Always a silver lining, eh?'

He was trying to lighten the mood, but both men were preoccupied, and they fell into silence as they made for the address where Dr Lenger had his premises. They passed into a workers' neighbourhood: grimy tenement blocks on either side, with stained windows and peeling door frames. Ice and frost rimed the window panes and gleamed dully in the bleak light of the winter's day. Lenger's surgery was on the first floor, above a furniture shop, and his sign hung from an iron frame that projected out from the wall.

'There.' Schenke indicated. 'Pull over and park behind the truck.'

Hauser eased the car alongside the pavement. Ahead of them was a covered lorry with a load of wooden chairs stacked inside. The two men climbed out of the Audi and glanced round at their surroundings.

'Classy area,' Hauser commented drily. 'I don't imagine our doctor is living the high life on what he earns here.'

There was a varnished door beside the furniture shop with Lenger's name on it, and Schenke led the way inside. A bell rang as the door opened and closed behind them, and the two policemen climbed a newly carpeted staircase.

'Seems he's doing rather better than you thought,' Schenke observed.

At the top of the stairs there was a waiting room with two large sofas either side of a window overlooking the street. A low table was set between them with a small pile of faded picture magazines. Opposite the entrance, a short corridor led to a door with a brass plate on it. To one side of the corridor was a counter, behind which sat a neatly dressed lady in her fifties. Even though there was a small stove to heat the room, she wore fingerless woollen gloves and a scarf. She looked up and nodded a greeting.

'Can I help you?'

'We're here to see Dr Lenger,' said Schenke.

'Do you have an appointment?'

Hauser gestured to the empty waiting room. 'Do we need one?'

'We work on an appointments basis here, sir,' the receptionist said firmly.

'Well we don't.' Hauser smiled and nodded towards the door at the end of the corridor. 'Is he in?'

'I'll find out if the doctor can see you,' she replied, and stood up.

'Don't trouble yourself.' Schenke strode past her desk and rapped on the door. Without waiting for a reply, he turned the handle and entered.

Lenger's office was panelled in a light-coloured wood. One wall was taken up by shelving for books and journals, while glass-fronted cabinets contained bottles and equipment. On the opposite wall hung large anatomical diagrams. The doctor's desk, a plain oak affair, was positioned at an angle to the window, with three chairs in front of it for patients. Lenger sat on the far side in a shiny leather seat, examining some forms. He was wearing a white jacket over a jersey, and he stood up with a puzzled expression as the two policemen entered his office. He was a short, round man in his early forties, with a fringe of dark hair around his bald head. The thick lenses in his wire-framed glasses made his watery grey eyes look large and bulging.

The receptionist scurried between Schenke and Hauser. 'I'm sorry, Doctor, these men just barged in. I couldn't stop them.'

Lenger spared her a brief frown before glaring at his visitors. 'Who the hell are you?'

Schenke held up his identity disc. 'Criminal Inspector Schenke, and my associate is Sergeant Hauser. We're from the Kripo section at Pankow.'

'Police? Is this about the break-in?'

'Break-in?'

'Yes, I reported it several days ago. They turned the place

over and stole some drugs. The work of young hooligans, no doubt.'

Schenke shook his head. 'We've not come about the robbery.'

'Then what are you doing here? What is the meaning of this? Barging into my office without any warning . . .' Lenger's cheeks quivered with anger.

'We're making enquiries about another matter,' Schenke said calmly. 'From the lack of patients waiting back there, I'd say we're not interrupting anything important. Are we?'

Lenger opened his mouth to reply, then hesitated and sighed irritably. 'Very well. Fräulein Gerstein, I'll speak to these men. You can leave us.'

The receptionist scowled at the two policemen before retreating into the corridor and closing the door behind her.

Lenger sat down. 'What do you want?'

Schenke crossed to one of the patients' chairs and sat down, while Hauser made for a small filing cabinet to one side of the desk and leaned back, crossing his arms.

'I have a few questions to ask you about one of your patients,' Schenke began. 'Greta Scholtz.'

Lenger nodded warily. 'I remember her. A sickly girl, simple in the head.'

'Sickly? That's not what her parents seem to think. And I imagine you would remember her, given that she died recently and her parents came to ask for your assistance in finding out what had happened to her. I understand you weren't very helpful.'

Lenger folded his hands together. 'They're troublemakers, those two. Their girl died of pneumonia, according to the death certificate they showed me. There's nothing so unusual about that. Children with congenital abnormalities are prone to early mortality. The Scholtzes turned up here demanding to see me and refusing to leave until they did. I tried to reassure them that there was nothing sinister about their daughter's death, but they refused to accept my word for it and accused the people at the clinic of having murdered her. It's complete nonsense and their behaviour was unacceptable. Especially given that Scholtz is a party member. He should have more faith in those who practise medicine for the good of the Reich.'

'They'd only recently discovered Greta had died,' Hauser said quietly. 'How would you expect them to behave?'

'With a little more dignity, frankly. And respect for my professional opinion.'

'You say she was sickly,' said Schenke. 'Did she have a history of illness?'

'She'd been simple since the day she was born.'

'So I understand, but I'm talking about her physical health. Was she sickly?'

Lenger paused before he replied. 'Not as such, I suppose.'

'Had she suffered from pneumonia before? Bronchitis? Any other such illness?'

'No,' he conceded. 'Not as far as I am aware. But that's not to say she didn't. In any case, that's not the reason why she was brought to see me. I was consulted about her behaviour, or rather lack of it.'

'And what did you make of her behaviour?'

'Look here, I don't have the records any more. They went to the clinic shortly after she was sent there. I can't recall all the details.'

'I'm sure you can recall most of the details. After all, it

wasn't so long ago, and the subsequent visit by her parents must have refreshed your memory. So, what can you tell us about her behaviour, Doctor?'

Lenger cleared his throat. 'Very well. Greta exhibited some characteristics of mental instability, significant mood swings and a failure to grasp the barest educational requirements of someone her age. Her mother was not coping well. Her father was burdened by professional demands and could not spare the time to support his wife. It was clear to me that the family would be better off if the girl was sent to an institution where she could be properly cared for. That was my advice to them.'

'I'm not sure how good that advice was,' said Hauser.

'Are you questioning my professional judgement?'

'Given the outcome, what do you think?'

'I'm a doctor, not a damned fortune-teller. How could I be expected to know she would die of pneumonia?'

'If that is what she died of.'

'That's what it says on the death certificate, Sergeant. Are you in the habit of second-guessing the medical establishment?'

'Do you think it was pneumonia that killed her?' asked Schenke.

'As opposed to what? Bubonic plague? Leprosy? Malaria? Why would I doubt it was pneumonia when that's what it says on the certificate? And even if there was some other cause, we'd never know, given that her body was cremated.'

'Quite.' Schenke nodded. 'That rather begs the question why it was felt necessary to cremate her. Hardly the sort of thing that happens on a regular basis, I'd have thought.'

'You'd have to ask the clinic about that. If there was any

risk of infection, they'd have a good enough reason.'

'If it was bubonic plague, maybe. But pneumonia?' Schenke said.

'My God!' Lenger snorted. 'I am surrounded by medical experts today. Look here, why don't you just stick to arresting thieves, rapists and vandals and leave treating the sick to those who are trained to heal, eh?'

'We would, if only there didn't seem to be a rather large cloud of doubt hanging over the decisions of the experts, yourself included, Doctor.'

Lenger's eyes narrowed. 'What are you accusing me of, exactly?'

'We're not here to accuse you of anything – yet. We're here to ask questions, like I said,' Schenke responded. 'But let's move on. I'm interested in why you recommended sending Greta to the Schiller clinic specifically. What was your reason for that?'

Lenger unfolded his hands and eased himself back into his seat, some of the tension in his body seeming to ease. 'It has a good reputation. It was near enough for the Scholtzes to visit without too much difficulty. In any case, the preference these days is that children – and adults too, for that matter – with mental or physical handicaps are institutionalised so that they can be given the proper care, away from normal society.'

'Preference?' Hauser intervened. 'Whose preference?'

Lenger gave a smile. 'Not so expert now, are we? Perhaps you haven't been keeping up with the latest bulletins of the medical profession? There's a lot of new literature on racial hygiene and the need to breed out any weaknesses in our people. For many years now the party has been discouraging procreation involving those with mental or physical deficiencies, on the basis that we can eliminate such failings. There are even those who think we can do the same with habitual criminals, the work-shy, prostitutes and vagrants – all those sorts of people. I'm not so sure about that. Strikes me that a short, sharp spell in the camps would be enough to cure those with such un-German attitudes.'

'I imagine so,' Schenke said, before turning the discussion back to the Scholtzes. 'I have to admit that I find it difficult to believe that most parents would agree to being parted from their children.'

'They probably don't like it. But the way things are going, they won't have much choice in the matter. All birth deform-ities and any subsequent discovery of mental deficiencies have to be reported by doctors these days. It doesn't take much imagination to realise that the party will use those records to identify and institutionalise all those who fail to meet the standards required to purify our race. And being the good party members that they are, the Scholtz couple will no doubt be expected to go along with it.'

'And what's in it for you?' asked Hauser.

Lenger turned to the sergeant with a scathing expression. 'Apart from it being the law, and believing that it's in the best interests of the families and the Fatherland?'

Schenke could see that the sergeant's expression had darkened, and he knew that Hauser's devotion to his duty was nothing compared to his devotion to his children. Lenger was on dangerous ground, and he must have realised it. His gaze wavered and he looked down at the forms on his blotter pad as he continued.

'Since you ask, I'll admit that they sweeten the pill by

paying a fee for every child we arrange to be institutionalised. That's what this form is for, as it happens. It's another child I am recommending for the clinic. Born blind, in this case, so there's no place for them in the new order. As the saying goes, it's a life not worth living . . .'

Schenke saw Hauser's fists clench and unclench. 'I see. I think we have all the information we need from you for the moment, Doctor.' He stood up. 'If we need to speak to you again, we'll come back. Don't leave Berlin without notifying the Pankow precinct first.'

'I would ask that you make an appointment next time, Inspector. I'm not happy about people barging in on me like I'm some kind of suspect.'

'As long as you're not.' Schenke touched the brim of his hat in farewell. 'Come, Sergeant.'

Hauser eased himself away from the filing cabinet and paused by the desk, eyes narrowed. 'If ever someone like you tried to take my kids away,' he growled, 'I'd beat them to a pulp.' He reached out and picked up the form, crumpling it into a ball and tossing it into the doctor's lap.

Lenger flinched as if it was a hand grenade.

'There,' said Hauser. 'I've saved the state a few Reichsmarks for the war effort.' He turned to follow Schenke out of the office, leaving the door open.

They left the surgery and descended the stairs, emerging into the sharp cold air of the street. Schenke breathed it in deeply to dispel the cloying sense of corruption and crushing ideological conformity that had permeated Lenger's office. He paused by the passenger door of the car. 'Want me to drive?'

'No, I signed it out. I need to look after it. Can't be letting some former racing driver take the wheel.'

As Hauser pulled away, Schenke glanced at his sergeant. 'I know it felt good, but did you have to do that?'

'It was either the form or him. The cold-hearted piece of shit.'

Schenke nodded. He knew Hauser well enough to believe it. Lenger had had a lucky escape.

Chapter Eighteen

There was silence as they drove back to the precinct. Some ten minutes after they had left Lenger's surgery, Hauser spoke again.

'I'm sorry, sir. I shouldn't have let that bastard get under my skin. A kid is a kid, no matter how they are made when they come into this world. It ain't Christian to hide them away and pretend they don't exist.'

'Like he said, the party has decided that only the best breeding stock can be used to produce the master race. You can't make an omelette . . . as they say.'

Hauser glanced at Schenke with a bitter expression. 'Don't be like that, sir. I joined the party because I thought it would be for the best. The Führer swore to make Germany powerful again. But I don't hold with playing God. I don't know how Lenger can make those kinds of decisions with a clear conscience.'

'He manages. I don't think you saw the picture from where you were standing. Him, his wife and two boys. Seems that Lenger is a family man, despite the way he treated Greta's parents. At the same time, he's a party man, and he has bought into the doctrine enough to blind him to the cost others have to pay to ensure the rise of the new Germany. It's pointless to judge him harshly when there are so many like him.'

Hauser considered this as the Audi stopped at a junction and he checked the way was clear before turning in the direction of the precinct. Schenke continued.

'I need to know that I can depend on you. You're going to have to put your personal feelings aside while we're investigating the deaths of the kids at the clinic.'

'With respect, sir, I've been in the service thirty years. I ain't going soft.'

They drove on for another minute or so before Schenke said, 'I got the impression that the doctor's involvement only goes as far as steering his patients towards the Schiller clinic and collecting his reward for doing so. I doubt he's ever visited the place.'

'Maybe,' Hauser responded. 'So what's the next step?'

'We need to pay a visit to the clinic and speak to the director.'

'He's going to have difficulty explaining away so many deaths, I'm thinking.'

'Unless there is a valid reason for what's happened. It may even be that it's just misfortune and the parents won't accept the truth.'

'You really believe that?'

'I'm not prepared to discount it if that's where the evidence seems to be leading us. Anyway, wouldn't you rather that was the case than have to deal with the prospect that someone has murdered the children?'

'Fair point . . . So when are we going to Potsdam?'

'This afternoon.'

'So soon?'

'We've only got a few days before we have to turn our attention to questioning the suspects in the forgery case. By then we should have a clear idea of what's been going on at the clinic. We'll head over there once I've had a chance to get some information about the place. We'll take Liebwitz with us.'

'Oh, sweet Jesus, why him?'

'He may not be the easiest company, but he doesn't miss any details.'

'Sure, if you want to guess how many beans there are in a jar, but he's not good with people. He can't read them like you and I can, sir.'

'That may be true, but I want to make sure we miss nothing. Between the three of us, we should be able to manage that.'

Hauser sighed. 'It's going to be a long day.'

Potsdam was only twenty kilometres from the heart of Berlin. The ice on the road and the restricted width caused by the banks of snow on either side made the journey feel long and laborious. Around them the forests and lakes were covered in a wintry mantle. The Havel river had frozen over, and the snow that covered the ice created a smooth, wide plane from bank to bank. A thin, freezing mist hung in ghostly patches along the waterway, and the passing scenery reminded Schenke of the landscape paintings hanging in the Old National Gallery. There was something uncanny, almost Gothic, about the countryside in the grip of this bitter winter, and he looked forward to returning to the familiar surroundings of the capital.

While Hauser drove, Schenke read out from the notes he had made during a phone conversation with an old university friend who had qualified as a paediatrician.

'The clinic was originally a spa constructed above the Havel towards the end of the last century. It used to attract some of the wealthiest people in Berlin. Then came the Kaiser's war, and the spa was turned into a military hospital until 1920, when it became an institution for the care and treatment of children suffering from mental or physical handicaps. Some interesting experiments were carried out there under the first director, my friend says.'

Liebwitz, sitting next to Hauser, glanced over his shoulder. 'What does he mean by interesting, sir?'

'The experiments were controversial. Some kind of shock treatment was used on the mental patients. That came to an end when the director was dismissed back in '29. The new director followed a more conventional approach. The running costs are mostly covered by a philanthropic fund set up by Gustav Krupp, the industrialist, and one of the biggest funders of the Nazi Party, and the parents of the children pay only a small monthly fee. That makes the Schiller clinic one of the most oversubscribed institutions in the area.'

'Must cost the Krupp family a fair bit,' commented Hauser.

'They can afford it. In any case, I wouldn't be too impressed by their apparent generosity. It seems Gustav is keen to keep children with defects out of public sight. That's why the family is happy to subsidise the Schiller clinic, as well as other institutions. If you want to promote the idea of the superiority of the Aryan race, it's easier to do if there aren't too many people who look out of place.'

'Any subsidy offered to a charitable body like an institution for the care of children is almost certainly deductible from company tax,' noted Liebwitz. 'Therefore a shrewd business strategy by the Krupp family. Indeed, a model of efficiency, in so far as political ambitions occasion a tax advantage, and the desire to save money reaps a political advantage.'

Schenke looked up from his notepad to try to see if the Scharführer had meant his comment to be an amusing observation, but Liebwitz was sitting with his back straight as he stared ahead.

'Yes . . . I suppose so,' Schenke responded.

Hauser snorted. 'Thank God for philanthropists, eh?'

It was after noon when they reached Potsdam, a quaint town in the shadow of the regimented tiers of the ornamental park of Sanssouci, the summer palace constructed by Frederick the Great. It had always struck Schenke as the kind of place that demonstrated how much a ruthlessly pragmatic Prussian upbringing would strangle any spirit of romantic inspiration. They drove through the quiet streets and crossed the bridge to the south side of the Havel, then continued for another few kilometres before they came to the signpost with the clinic's name.

Hauser turned off the main road onto a narrow track that led through a dense pine forest looming high on either side. The trees created sufficient gloom beneath their boughs that he was obliged to switch on the headlights. Despite the winding nature of the track, it had been kept clear of the snow that had managed to find its way through the trees; where it had drifted, the snow had been dug out and heaped to the side. The clinic was by no means cut off from the outside world as a result of the extreme winter conditions.

They turned a corner and emerged from the forest to be confronted by a large gatehouse. The wrought-iron gates were closed, but there was smoke trailing into the grey sky from the small cottage to one side. Hauser drew up and sounded the horn three times.

While they waited for a response, Schenke noted the wall, at least two metres high, that stretched as far as he could see along the edge of the forest on either side.

'Looks more like a prison than a children's home.'

'I think not,' said Liebwitz. 'Most of those I've seen were not dissimilar. It helps to keep the inmates contained. For their safety as well as the institution's convenience.'

Before Schenke could comment, the front door of the cottage opened and a figure trudged out, bending towards the window as Hauser wound it down. He was a thin man in his mid forties, wearing an old soldier's greatcoat, fingerless gloves and a Russian fur cap; Schenke guessed he might have been a veteran of the eastern front in the previous war.

'Do you have business at the clinic, sir?'

Hauser held up his badge. 'Police business. Open the gates, friend, and let us in.'

The keeper squinted at the badge, then nodded and made his way to the gate. Lifting the heavy iron latch, which grated as it moved, he leaned his shoulder against the iron railings and heaved them to one side, then waved the car through.

On the far side, they caught their first sight of the clinic across an open expanse of snow-covered parkland. Schenke had been expecting something that resembled a hospital. Instead he found himself gazing at what looked like a castle. Huge towers rose at each end of a three-storey structure, with battlements interspersed with decorative turrets. The towers and turrets were covered by conical roofs, and where melting snow had slid off, the tiles looked like the grey scales of some enormous fish or dragon.

He smiled grimly. 'Anyone getting the feeling they've seen this place before, in a horror movie?'

As they approached along the drive, he noticed an inner wire fence that surrounded the grounds immediately outside the building. Beyond it, a handful of figures were moving across the snow, some unmistakably children. There was another gate to negotiate at the fence, this time manned by a thickset man in a booth who leaned out of a window to address them as the car drew up. Hauser raised his badge once again.

'I haven't heard anything about the police being called out,' the man responded as he looked closely at the three occupants of the car.

Schenke leaned forward. 'We haven't been called out. We've come from Berlin to speak to the director.'

The man held up a clipboard. 'You're not on the list, sir. I'll have to phone through to ask for permission to let you in.'

Hauser raised his badge again. 'This bit of tin trumps your clipboard every time. Unless you want to make trouble for yourself,' he added in a faintly menacing tone. The man nodded nervously before leaving the booth to unlock the chain and slide the metal-framed gate aside.

Hauser negotiated the final stretch of the drive and parked alongside some other cars, vans and a brown bus to one side of the main entrance. Schenke felt a tremor as he recalled Johanna Scholtz's words about the vehicle.

As they climbed out of the Audi, Liebwitz glanced round at the wire fence surrounding them.

'Given how uncooperative they are with us, one wonders how difficult they make it for the parents to visit their children.'

Looking up at the facade of the building, Schenke noted

grilles in the windows of the upper floors, and saw several pale faces peering through the glass behind the steel bars. This was the first time he had ever been to such a place, and he could not shake off the overwhelming atmosphere of bleak misery. Some of that, he knew, was down to the wintry weather and the heavy clouds that covered the sky. More snow was on the way, and he was keen to ensure that they returned to Berlin before any of the roads were blocked.

He led the way across the gritted parking area to the colonnade that covered the entrance. Two sets of glass-panelled doors. A mat lay across the threshold of the reception hall, with boot scrapers on either side. Schenke ignored them as he crossed the black and white tiled floor towards the counter. A pair of men in white jackets were sitting behind it. The younger of the two rose as he saw the visitors.

Schenke already had his badge ready. 'Criminal Inspector Schenke. I need to speak to the director of the clinic.'

The receptionist, who Schenke could now see was no more than twenty, glanced at his seated companion, who raised a newspaper and pretended to have missed the appeal for direction.

'The director? Yes, sir.' The receptionist nodded and reached for a telephone on the desk behind the counter. He dialled a number, and there was a pause before Schenke heard a faint voice from the earpiece.

'Reception,' the youth announced. 'There are police officers here. They wish to speak to Doctor Pieper . . .' He listened to the response, then looked up at Schenke. 'What is the nature of your business?'

Schenke smiled politely. 'To ask the director a few questions. At once, if he'd be so kind.' He took the receiver from the young man's hand and replaced it in its cradle. 'So let's not waste any more time. You can take us to his office now.'

The other man lowered his newspaper and stood up with a firm expression. He was half a head taller than Schenke and built like a boxer, though admittedly one who had seen better days. He must have been at least fifty, but there was no fat around his midriff.

'Now then, sir, you can't just come in here and make such demands. The director's an important man, and a busy one.'

'No doubt, but we'll see him at once, and anyone who gets in our way might want to think about the prospect of spending the night in a cell before he obstructs police officers in carrying out their duties.'

The older man hesitated and stared back at Schenke for a moment before his piercing gaze switched to his companion. 'All right, Wilke lad, take them up.'

The youth slipped out of the narrow gap at the end of the counter and bowed his head to Schenke. 'If you'd follow me, sir?'

A wide flight of carpeted steps either side of the hall climbed to a gallery that ran along the rear wall, where high arched windows faced north. As they reached the top of the stairs, Schenke saw that the windows looked down from the rear of the building onto a balustraded terrace with steps to a broad expanse of formal gardens that stretched to the edge of a broad waterway, a tributary of the Havel, he realised.

'Nice view,' Hauser commented as he paused to admire it. 'Must be pleasant in summer. Swimming and so on.'

'There's no swimming. It's forbidden. It would endanger the inmates.'

'Even for staff?'

'The director feels it would set a bad example to the inmates.'

'The inmates are children,' Liebwitz said quietly.

'Yes, sir.' Wilke looked at the Gestapo man's forbiddingly gaunt features. 'Children, as you say. This way, please.'

He indicated a wide corridor lined with doors. A similar corridor led off from the other end of the gallery; each of them was some fifty metres in length, Schenke estimated. As they passed the doors, he glanced at the signs: they seemed to be a combination of treatment rooms, offices and stores.

'I take it there are no patients on this level?'

'No, sir. The inmates' . . . the children's accommodation is on the top floor and the ground floor – that's where the physically disabled have their rooms and dormitories.'

'What's the basement used for?' asked Liebwitz. 'I saw stairs leading down from the entrance lobby.'

'That's where the food is kept, the boilers, kitchens and so on, under the east wing.'

'And what about the other wing?' asked Schenke.

'The secure cells are there, sir. For the, uh, children, who are a danger to themselves and the other patients and staff.'

'I understood there was a secure dormitory for those children.'

'Most of the rooms and dormitories are secure, sir. There's only a handful of rooms in the open part of the clinic.'

'Window dressing,' Hauser muttered, just loud enough for Schenke to hear.

'Tell me.' Schenke addressed the youth. 'Do you get any visitors, other than the parents? Journalists for example?'

There was the slightest break in Wilke's stride before he replied. 'Hardly anyone apart from the parents ever comes here, sir.'

They reached the end of the corridor, where an archway led into the vast round tower. An elaborate spiral staircase wound up through the tower, and down to the lower floor and basement. There were rugs on the floor, and tapestries, shields and other faux-medieval decor hung on the curved stone walls.

A tall, thin woman in a dark jacket was waiting for them beside the staircase. She had grey hair tied back in a tight bun, and half-moon glasses.

'You are the policemen wishing to see Doctor Pieper?' Her tone was frosty.

'That's right.'

'Doctor Pieper is on the telephone at the moment. An urgent professional matter. I will tell him you are waiting for him the moment the call is concluded.'

She made a curt gesture towards some chairs arranged around a low table, then looked at the youth.

'That's all, Wilke. In future you will follow protocol and have visitors wait at reception. Understand?'

'Yes, Frau Ritter.'

'Isn't Huber on duty with you?'

'Yes, Frau Ritter.'

'Then tell him from me that he should have insisted our police guests wait until they were called up. This is a secure medical institution, not a hotel.'

Wilke winced and nodded before turning to hurry away.

Schenke felt a little sympathy for him. 'Don't be hard on the boy. I made him bring us up here.'

'So? *I* would never have let you get beyond the reception hall. Young Wilke has a lot to learn if he is to remain in our employment and avoid military service.'

Before Schenke could respond, she turned and strode off,

disappearing through a doorway but leaving the door open. He turned to his companions, and Hauser shook his head in wonder.

'What is this place? She calls it a medical institution. Feels more like a prison to me.'

Liebwitz arched an eyebrow. 'Prison? I wouldn't be surprised if it was worse than that, Sergeant. Much worse . . .'

Chapter Nineteen

There was something in Liebwitz's manner that Schenke had not seen before. The Gestapo man seemed ill at ease, and there was the faintest of frowns on his prominent forehead. Hauser had not noticed, and was busy looking at the ornaments on the walls.

'I'm starting to wonder if I'm in the wrong profession,' he sighed. 'Or maybe I need a sharp whack on the head so that I can have a little time in a place like this to rest and recover. What do you say, sir? Think it can be arranged?'

'With the thickness of your skull? No chance.'

Liebwitz's sharp eyes shifted speculatively to the sergeant's head. 'How hard a blow would be required?'

Schenke could not help a smile.

'Gentlemen!'

The three of them turned to see that a tall man in a dark blue suit had emerged from the room next to Frau Ritter's office. The director had wavy white hair and hazel eyes, and looked to be no more than forty, even though Schenke knew from his notes that he was at least fifteen years older than that. He smiled warmly. The first sign of anyone being pleased to see them since they'd reached the outside gate, Schenke mused as the man strode briskly towards them, hand outstretched.

'I'm sorry to keep you waiting, but I had to deal with a colleague. I'm Dr Wilhelm Pieper, director of the Schiller clinic.'

He must have known that he needed no introduction, and it came across as self-effacing. Schenke warmed to him slightly, even as he understood that the ploy was quite deliberate. He offered his hand and felt the doctor's powerful grip.

'Inspector Schenke, Pankow Kripo section. This is my sergeant, Hauser, and Scharführer Liebwitz.'

Pieper shook their hands in turn and added a friendly pat to Liebwitz's shoulder. 'Always good to greet a comrade of the SS.'

Liebwitz bowed his head with stiff formality. 'Thank you, Reich Doctor.'

The director turned back to Schenke. 'I appreciate that you have already shown your credentials to my colleagues, but for the sake of procedure, you understand . . .'

'Of course.' Schenke held up his badge, and Pieper looked at it carefully before smiling again.

'Thank you. It never harms to double check. Now then, I have to admit that I am curious to know why three members of the criminal police have driven out from Berlin to visit our little institution.'

'At the moment, I'm treating the matter in confidence, so I'd appreciate it if we could talk in private.' Schenke nodded to the open door, where the director's secretary was watching proceedings from behind her desk.

Pieper's smile faded a little. 'But of course. Please.'

He waved them into his office and called out from the

doorway, 'Frau Ritter, some coffee for our guests.'

'Yes, Doctor,' she replied before he closed the door gently.

A large desk sat in front of an arched window in the heavy medieval style of the rest of the building. Through the leaded glass, Schenke could see that it had started to snow again, and he felt his heart sink at the prospect of the drive back to Berlin. The walls were painted a warm ochre, and displayed framed certificates and photographs, including one of Pieper being handed a scroll by Rudolf Hess, the deputy leader of the party. Pieper saw his visitor looking at the picture.

'That's the day I received a commendation signed by the Führer.' He pointed to one of the framed documents. 'There. Quite an honour, and one that helped me secure this position.'

'Congratulations,' Schenke responded. 'What was the nature of the commendation?'

'Oh, merely acknowledgement for an article I wrote for *Das Schwarze Korps*. Please, gentlemen, be seated.'

Pieper rounded the desk, but stood with his back to the window as he took a cigarette from a box, struck a match and lit up. He indicated the box. 'Help yourselves, if you wish.'

The director's hospitality was already starting to wear thin, and the worsening weather made Schenke keen to conclude their business as swiftly as possible, so he declined the offer with a shake of his head and glanced at his subordinates to indicate that he spoke for them all. Pieper leaned against the radiator under the windowsill and drew on the cigarette before exhaling to one side.

'So, what's this private matter you wish to discuss?'

Schenke took out his notebook and pencil. 'You had a child here by the name of Greta Scholtz . . .'

Pieper rolled his eyes and tutted. 'I take it your visit is at the behest of Greta's parents. They've managed to turn a family tragedy into something of a minor cause célèbre, it appears.'

'Why do you say that?'

'Word gets round, Inspector. After they challenged me about the circumstances of their daughter's death, they tried to kick up a fuss about it back in Berlin. I'm afraid you and your comrades are not the first people to be harassed by the Scholtzes.'

'They didn't harass the police. They reported a crime, and given the nature of their allegations, I am naturally obliged to investigate.'

'A crime? And what crime would that be?'

Schenke fixed his eyes on the director as he replied. 'Murder.'

Pieper betrayed little in his reaction. Neither surprise nor anxiety. Merely curiosity. 'What murder? The girl died from pneumonia. I treated her myself and saw the symptoms. There is no crime to be solved here, Inspector, I can assure you of that. There is only the understandable grieving of the parents of a child taken before her time. I sympathise with their plight; however, it is not acceptable to turn grief into unfounded allegations. My staff and I work diligently to care for the children entrusted to us.'

Hauser intervened. 'Then how do you explain the deaths of the other children you, ah, cared for?'

'Other children?'

He nodded. 'The others who died here after Greta.'

Pieper gave a weary shrug. 'I feared that Scholtz would try to link her death to those tragedies, and here we are. But there's no crime there either. All of them died of illnesses. Natural causes.'

'So many in such a short space of time?' Hauser pressed him.

'It happens, Sergeant. No doubt the constitutions of the weaker children in my care are adversely affected by this damned freezing winter as well. I'm sure you will find the same pattern in other institutions in Germany.'

There was a knock on the door, and it opened before the director could reply. His secretary entered with a tray holding a large coffee pot and four fine china mugs. She set it down on the desk, and Schenke caught the rich aroma of real coffee, not the ersatz variety, which tasted of burnt toast.

'Thank you,' said Pieper. 'Could you bring me the files of the children who have died here over the last three months, starting with the Scholtz girl.'

'Yes, Director.'

Once she had closed the door, Pieper reached over the desk to pour the coffee. 'I apologise for the mugs, but we tend towards informality in some of the more inconsequential areas of our life here.' He settled back against the radiator. 'When Frau Ritter comes back with the files, you will see for yourself that the children's illnesses were documented from the outset, right up until the moment they died.'

'We'll see,' Schenke countered. 'However, there is the matter of how many of these children were sent here on the recommendation of a Berlin physician, Dr Lenger.'

'No great mystery there, Inspector. I know Lenger well. He's a good doctor. He only refers the most serious cases to the clinic. That is to say, those children with conditions that make them more vulnerable to illnesses than their healthy peers.'

'Greta's parents claimed that while their daughter had a

mental handicap, there were no problems with her physical health.'

'They would say that, wouldn't they? Given their groundless allegations. But I can assure you, the record will prove that she became a sickly child who swiftly succumbed to pneumonia.'

The door opened again, and the secretary entered carrying a bundle of folders, which she placed on the director's desk before departing. Schenke glanced at them. It had taken very little time for her to produce them, and he suspected they must have been readied in advance. In which case, Pieper may well have been warned about their coming to see him.

'Tell me, Doctor, have you spoken to Lenger today?'

'Lenger?' Pieper frowned, as if trying to recall. 'Yes, I believe I did. This morning, in fact.'

'Would that have been him you were speaking to while we were waiting outside?' Schenke probed.

The director hesitated for a moment. 'Yes . . . yes, in fact it was. We were continuing our earlier discussion concerning the case of another child who might benefit from being treated at the clinic.'

'Let's hope she fares better than Greta,' said Hauser.

Pieper's expression hardened. 'I don't care for your tone or your insinuation, Sergeant . . . What was your name again?'

'Hauser, sir. And I don't care that you don't care for my tone.'

Pieper stiffened, and the tip of his cigarette quivered. 'I hold SS rank and am a long-standing member of the party. You will treat me with the respect I am due, or I will report you to your superiors.' He turned to Schenke. 'And you, if you fail to control your subordinates.'

'The sergeant is also a party member,' Schenke responded.

195

'Sometimes he expresses himself bluntly, but it comes with the job. Now, if we might look at these files?'

'Be my guest,' Pieper replied. 'You may use the interview room next door while I return to my duties.'

'We may need to take them away with us.'

'Out of the question. They stay here at the clinic. If you want to remove them, you will need a signed order from a judge.'

'As you wish,' Schenke conceded.

'If you have any questions, please address them to my secretary in the first instance.'

There was no mistaking the fact that they had been dismissed, and Schenke picked up the files and led his men out of the director's office.

The room next door contained an oval table with eight chairs set around it, and a couch and a single chair at the far end beneath the window. Snow was blowing against the glass in swirling flurries, and the sky had darkened, so Schenke had to turn on the light. A single bulb in a shaded fitting above the table cast its glow over the polished surface. He glanced at his watch. Just after two o'clock. There would be barely enough time to examine the files and return to Berlin before nightfall.

Ordering Liebwitz to close the door, he set the files down before taking off his coat and hanging it over the back of one of the chairs. He divided the files up and slid two piles across to the others, who had seated themselves opposite.

'What are we looking for?' asked Liebwitz.

'Anything that stands out.'

'In what sense, sir?'

'Just read the documents, Scharführer. You'll know it when you see it.'

Schenke opened Greta Scholtz's file and began to read. It started with the referral from Lenger, together with a brief overview of Greta's previous medical history. There was an initial assessment of her physical health and her mental capacity, which was found to be 'subnormal'. She was assigned to a ward, and there followed several pages of observations from nursing staff and others assigned to provide her care. A few weeks after her arrival, there was a report signed by Pieper for the attention of the racial hygiene certification office in Berlin. It was countersigned by an unreadable signature with a plus sign next to it.

There followed a letter from Scholtz asking how his daughter was faring, then a treatment report that described some symptoms of a chest infection. Pieper had authorised 'Special Diet Plan D' and assigned an orderly to be responsible for Greta's care, identified as 'WH'. There were only two more pages in the file. A statement saying that Greta had died of pneumonia and that Pieper had authorised the donation of her effects to other inmates and staff, along with an instruction for her body to be cremated and her parents informed once that had been done. The last sheet was a carbon copy of the letter sent to Greta's mother and father telling them of her death.

Schenke closed the file and skimmed the next one, covering much the same ground for a twelve-year-old boy with a spine deformity. He looked across the table. 'Tell me, have either of you come across reference to a racial hygiene certification office?'

Hauser nodded, and Liebwitz rifled through the papers of the file he was still reading with his customary thoroughness. 'Yes, sir. I can't say I have ever heard of it.'

'Nor me,' said Schenke. 'Any luck with the signature?'

'Has to be another doctor with a scrawl like that,' said Hauser.

Schenke frowned. The information in the files was scant and unhelpful. Which was no doubt why Pieper had been happy for them to examine the documents.

Hauser pulled out a sheet. 'There's no detail about this Special Diet Plan either.'

'Just a moment.' Schenke rose and made his way to the secretary's office. She looked up the moment she was aware of his presence in the doorway.

'Well?'

'I need your help with some aspects of the files that need clarification.'

She sighed impatiently and stood, pulling the hem of her jacket down to avoid creases, then followed Schenke back to the interview room. He waved her to a chair at the end of the table, and she sat down and folded her arms. 'What do you need from me?'

'Some spirit of cooperation would be nice for a start.'

She stared back frigidly, but made no reply.

'Very well, then,' Schenke began. 'Let's start with Special Diet Plan D, since it's mentioned in all the files we have looked at so far. What does that entail?'

'I am not a nutritionist, Inspector, so I don't understand the precise details. But I've heard of it often enough. It's the standard set of meals provided by the clinic to those who are poorly or recuperating. You'll find that all those we care for are assigned a specific diet plan. There's nothing sinister about it.'

'I didn't say there was.' He glanced at Greta's file lying open in front of him. 'What about the racial hygiene certification office? What is their interest in the treatment of the children in these files?'

'The clinic, like all such institutions, is obliged to report on the condition of new inmates. We submit the information to Berlin, and they send the forms back once they have recorded the details in their files. That's as much as I understand about the process.'

'Do you have an address for this office?'

She shook her head. 'The director has one of the orderlies deliver the documents by hand once a week. He cycles to Potsdam and takes a bus from there. He picks up the returns at the same time.'

'I see . . .' Schenke did not like the opacity of the arrangement. He held up the countersigned sheet. 'Do you recognise this signature?'

Frau Ritter leaned forward and squinted briefly. 'I recognise it.'

'Whose name is it?'

'I don't know. I only said I recognised it – I can't read it. A not untypical aspect of working with physicians. You'd have to ask the director.'

'I will be sure to. Let's hope you can be more helpful with my final query. Who is the "WH" who was assigned to look after Greta Scholtz?'

Her lips compressed with distaste. 'That would be Werner Huber. He is the one the director usually assigns to care for the more troublesome inmates. Huber was a soldier in the last war. He understands the need for discipline.'

'Huber?' Liebwitz cocked his head to one side. 'Was that the same Huber at the reception counter?'

'That's him.'

'Then we'll need to speak to him too,' said Schenke. 'Send for him, please.'

'Not possible.' She glanced at the clock on the wall. 'His shift ended half an hour ago. He'll have gone by now.'

'Damn . . . That's too bad. We'll want to speak to him next time we're here.'

'Next time?'

'We'll be back to examine the records in detail, and to speak to the staff and inmates.'

'I'm not sure the director will agree to that. It's not good for the patients to see strangers about the place. It unsettles them.'

Schenke glanced at his watch. It was nearly three o'clock. They would have to leave soon to avoid driving back to Berlin in the dark.

'I need to speak with Pieper and arrange another time to continue our investigation here.'

For the first time, Frau Ritter smiled. 'I'm sorry but he's left too.'

'What?' Schenke felt his anger rising. 'When did he go?'

'While you were reading the files.'

'Why wasn't I told?'

'I wasn't aware that you would need to speak to him again today.'

'Where has he gone?'

'He has a social engagement in Berlin this evening. Perhaps you can call him in the morning to discuss a further visit, Inspector.'

He glared at her for a moment, but she did not flinch. There was nothing further that could be achieved today, Schenke realised. Not that much had been achieved at all, and he did not like it. The situation smacked of some kind of cover-up, and he resolved to dig deeper.

He stood up. 'We'll be back. Make sure you let Pieper know. Hauser, Liebwitz, let's get out of this place before I'm tempted to arrest someone for obstructing a police investigation.'

'That's no concern of mine, Inspector. I've cooperated with you.' Frau Ritter smiled again. 'Willingly. Have a safe drive back to Berlin.'

Chapter Twenty

A blizzard was blowing by the time the Audi reached the main road and turned towards Potsdam. The road was already covered with fresh snow, and it was hard to see even with the wipers working hard to clear the windscreen. There was little traffic, though now and again a flare of headlights in the gloom indicated the approach of a vehicle. Hauser reduced his speed to what felt like a crawl as he strained his eyes to make out the way ahead.

'At this rate, we're not going to get back to Berlin until the middle of the night,' Schenke commented.

'If you want to take the wheel, be my guest, sir,' the sergeant growled. 'I'll try and pick up the pace.'

'How far do you think it is to Potsdam?'

'No idea. Haven't seen a sign since we got back on the road.'

'One and a half kilometres,' said Liebwitz.

'How do you know that?' asked Schenke.

'I recalled that shrine we passed a moment back. It was approximately a kilometre and a half from the edge of the town, sir.'

Hauser risked a quick glance away from the road and raised an eyebrow doubtfully at Schenke. 'Sure you did.'

Liebwitz did not respond, but continued staring ahead.

Schenke could see through the side window that the boughs of the fir trees lining the road were weighed down by snow. The wind was causing it to drift in places, and it was clear that if the storm continued for much longer, the road would be impassable.

'We can stop in Potsdam until the blizzard has eased,' he decided. 'Better than being stuck out in the open.' He reached into his coat for his cigarettes. He rarely smoked any more, but right now, he felt the need for the soothing warmth of tobacco smoke. He held the packet up. 'Anyone?'

'No, sir,' Liebwitz replied.

Hauser grunted his assent, and there was silence between the men as Schenke lit a cigarette and handed it to the sergeant before lighting one for himself.

As the car advanced in low gear, Schenke's thoughts turned to the clinic. He was still furious with the way Pieper and his secretary had played them. Giving them virtually nothing to help advance the investigation and forcing them to arrange a return visit. No doubt they would use the time to hide documents; perhaps they even hoped to discourage Schenke enough to abandon the investigation. As things stood, there was little to go on but the parents' conviction that their children had died under suspicious circumstances. The official records presented a different view, however, and unless Schenke's section could unearth evidence of foul play, the formal account would stand and there would be no legal path forward for the parents to take.

He recalled the incident that had piqued his curiosity.

There had been something off in Liebwitz's behaviour the moment they'd reached the clinic. A hint of an emotional reaction to his surroundings that was unlike him. He had said nothing overtly troubling, and certainly not enough to give Schenke grounds to pry into his reaction, but something had unsettled him and Schenke felt compelled to try and draw it out. He tapped some ash into the tray and cleared his throat.

'Liebwitz . . .'

'Sir?'

'What did you make of the clinic director? You were very quiet back there, and I wondered if you had observed something the sergeant and I might have missed.'

But before the scharführer could respond, the car suddenly lurched. Hauser made to wrench the wheel with his wounded arm, crying out in pain as his fingers spasmed and lost their grip. The steering wheel shifted round violently as the offside front wheel struck an obstacle in the snow, and the car spun, throwing its passengers to the right as the Audi rolled onto its side, slid off the road with a grating rattle and slammed against a boulder.

Schenke was hurled against the door, the impact of the handle driving the air from his lungs. He lay gasping, hearing only the moan of the wind outside, the creak of the seat in front of him and a muffled groan from Liebwitz. The engine had stalled, and there was a faint pinging sound from somewhere. The sudden silence shocked him for a moment, then he caught the tang of petrol and wrestled himself into an upright position.

'Get out of the car. Get out!'

He grasped the handle above him and wrenched it to the side before thrusting the door open. Looking round the front seats, he saw Liebwitz pushing Hauser's body off him. Hauling himself out, he opened the driver's door and reached in, grabbing the sergeant's arm and straining to raise his heavy body as Liebwitz heaved from below. The stench of petrol was getting stronger, and the odour caused an acute mental image to burst into Schenke's mind: the moment after the crash of his Mercedes-Benz W25 at the Nürburgring circuit, his leg trapped in the wreckage as he waited to be cut free from the racing car. The terror lent him extra strength as he dragged Hauser clear before turning back to help Liebwitz. Smoke curled up behind the Scharführer as he scrambled out and fell to the ground beside Hauser.

'Grab him!' Schenke ordered, and together they manhandled the unconscious sergeant away from the car, struggling through drifts of deep snow.

They were no more than ten metres away when the petrol tank went up with a dull boom. Schenke threw himself down over Hauser's body to protect his comrade. He waited a few heartbeats before looking over his shoulder, and saw that the Audi was engulfed in raging flames amid gusts of whirling white flakes. The snow around the car was bathed in the lurid glow of the blaze.

There was a movement beside him as Liebwitz pushed himself up from where he had fallen. His face was caked with snow, and he spat it from around his nose and mouth. Schenke eased himself up too, and knelt beside Hauser. There was a deep cut across the bridge of the sergeant's nose, and blood trickled down his cheeks. Schenke cupped a handful of snow and rubbed it in Hauser's face to clear some of the blood away, and the icy sensation caused the sergeant to blink and roll his head to the side with an angry groan.

'Get off, you bastard!'

Schenke helped prop the sergeant up, and Hauser grimaced. 'What the hell happened?'

Schenke nodded at the burning vehicle. 'That. The car skidded. You lost control and over we went.'

Hauser's jaw sagged at the sight of the flames. 'Holy Mother of Christ,' he muttered. 'I hope they don't dock that from my pay.' Then he clenched his eyes shut and his body trembled. 'My head . . . Fuck.'

'Concussion,' said Liebwitz. 'His head may have struck the steering wheel when we rolled. And he's in shock.'

'Then we need to get to shelter and call for help,' Schenke decided. He took one of the sergeant's arms. 'Help me get him on his feet.'

They raised Hauser and swung his arms over their shoulders so that they could share the burden. Which way? thought Schenke. With luck they might be able to wave down another vehicle, but it was getting dark, and with the weather worsening, they had not seen any cars or lorries for a while.

Liebwitz spoke up. 'We're closer to Potsdam, sir. There was an inn on the edge of the town. They might have a phone. If not, I can go on and find one after the sergeant is safely out of this blizzard.'

'Let's get moving, then.'

Schenke took a last look at the burning car, then they moved off, following the line of the road between the banks of snow. Hauser was doing his best to walk, but every few steps he stumbled and his full weight fell on the shoulders of his companions. The last of the daylight faded into dusk. Amid the muted howl of the wind, snowflakes drove into their faces and the biting cold stung their exposed flesh.

It took over an hour to cover the first kilometre, as far as Schenke could estimate the distance. The snow had covered the road ankle deep, and where it had drifted, they had to wade up to their knees through mounds of the stuff. They saw no vehicles, nor were there any buildings to be seen, as forest lined most of the route. The cold and the effort of carrying Hauser began to make Schenke's bad leg ache, and each step caused a jarring pain to shoot up his thigh. He was not sure how much further he could go; only tough mental discipline and the resilience to focus on each step kept him struggling on through the blizzard.

'Sir, there's a light,' said Liebwitz at last.

Schenke glimpsed a pale glow some distance ahead through the darting snowflakes. He felt his spirits rise and gave Hauser a shake. 'We're almost there.'

The sergeant looked sidelong at him, and then his eyes rolled and he closed them with a groan.

As they drew closer, Schenke could make out three windows, and he realised how lucky they were to be far enough outside a town for the people who dwelt there not to be concerned about blackout regulations. They trudged on, and soon he saw that it was the roadside inn Liebwitz had remembered. There were tables and benches outside, and a log pile beside the door, now covered in a thick layer of snow. A lorry was parked out front, along with a car. Neither model was identifiable under their white mantles. A lantern swayed gently above the entrance, and as they reached the door, he heard voices within.

Steadying Hauser, he reached for the door and swung it open, and they stumbled into a small lobby, where coats hung on pegs and there was a stand for canes and walking sticks. Closing the door, he shut out the wind and snow, and for the first time he could hear his and his companions' rasping breathing. Then an inner door opened and a rotund man in a thick sweater stared at them.

'Thought I heard the door. Oh!' He caught sight of Hauser's bloodied face. 'What's happened?'

'In a moment.' Schenke eased him aside and they entered a large room with a low beamed ceiling. Flames flickered in the wrought-iron grate in a fireplace large enough to stand in. There was a counter along the rear of the room, with bottles of beer and some spirits on the shelves behind. Several customers, all men, were seated at the tables closest to the fire; they had all turned towards Schenke and his comrades.

'Let's get him over by the fire,' Schenke ordered, and he and Liebwitz eased Hauser down into a high-backed chair to one side of the fireplace. Schenke slumped onto a bench and took a moment to catch his breath; Liebwitz, some ten years younger and seemingly unperturbed by his labours, remained on his feet and removed his gloves before holding his hands out towards the flames to warm them.

'Now then.' The man who had opened the door regarded them curiously as he stuck his thumbs in his waistband. 'What's the story, friend?'

Schenke introduced himself and briefly explained about the crash before gesturing at Hauser. 'My sergeant's had a knock on the head. I need to get him seen to by a doctor. Do you have a phone?'

'I do.' The man nodded. 'But it ain't working. The line went down in a storm before Christmas and it hasn't been fixed. Besides, the nearest doctor is in Potsdam, and I doubt he'll be making any house calls tonight.'

Liebwitz turned to Schenke. 'Do you want me to find the

doctor and persuade him to come out, sir?'

Schenke thought for a moment, then shook his head. It would take hours to find the doctor and bring him back, and anyway, he baulked at the idea of sending the Gestapo man out into the snowstorm. 'We'll get him cleaned up here while we wait for conditions to improve.' He turned to the man he assumed was the innkeeper. 'Can you fetch me hot water and rags to clean the sergeant's cuts. And some spirits to warm us all up. Brandy will do.'

The innkeeper nodded. 'I can get my boy to bring you water. As for brandy, we haven't had that in a while, thanks to the war. But there's always schnapps.'

'Schnapps will do nicely.' Schenke nodded. Now that he had rested briefly, his left leg had started to tremble, and he struggled to prevent himself from shivering as the innkeeper made his way to the bar, calling out to someone in the rear of the building. He looked around at the customers, who had returned to their conversations, and saw that four of them were wearing the faded overalls of manual workers. Two others wore jackets and ties. As his eyes moved to the last customer, he recognised the face at once. It was the youth who had taken them up to meet the director at the clinic. What was his name? He searched his tired memory. Ah, yes. Wilke.

He nodded a greeting to the young man. Wilke looked away and drained his beer glass before standing up and turning towards the door.

'Going somewhere, lad?'

'Have to get home,' he mumbled.

'Best to wait until the snow's stopped,' said Schenke. 'I'll stand you another drink in the meantime.'

'No thanks . . . I've already had enough.' His voice was

indeed slightly slurred, and he was swaying a little. 'I . . . I'd better get going.'

Schenke's tone hardened. 'Not until we've had a little chat. Sit down.'

Wilke glanced at the door, as if trying to work up the courage to make a run for it.

'Don't even think about it,' said Schenke. 'You wouldn't get past my friend there.'

Liebwitz turned from the fire and stared at the young man. Wilke's body seemed to sag a little in resignation.

'I was told not to speak to you again.'

'Really? I wonder why. Who told you?'

'Doctor Pieper. Before he left.'

'I see.' Schenke gestured to the bench opposite him. 'Sit down, lad. We need to have a little talk about what's going on at the Schiller clinic.'

Chapter Twenty-One

Wilke sat back down, and Liebwitz stood between the young man and the door. A woman carrying a steaming bowl and some strips of towelling over her arm emerged from the doorway behind the counter and made for Hauser. Behind her came the innkeeper with a bottle and three small glasses. As she set the bowl down on the floor beside the sergeant, the light from the flames in the grate reflected off a pendant hanging around her neck. Then she straightened up and returned to the kitchen.

Schenke hesitated for a moment before his gaze shifted to the innkeeper. He indicated Wilke. 'We'll need another glass for our young friend there.'

'The lad's had more than is good for him already.'

'All the same, I think he'll need another drink.'

The innkeeper glanced towards Wilke, who was rocking slightly on the bench. 'Fair enough. But you'll be the ones answering to his mother if he's reeling drunk when he goes home.'

'I'll take that risk.'

Schenke took off his coat and hung it over the back of

Hauser's chair. The sergeant's face was smeared with dried blood, but the cut over his nose was no longer bleeding. Schenke picked up one of the strips of towelling and dipped it in the hot water, then began to wipe away the blood from Hauser's face. The sergeant stirred and opened his eyes.

'What the hell?' He made to rise, and then winced. 'Oh, my bloody head . . .' He slumped back and waited for the pain to recede. 'Where are we, sir? What happened?'

'One thing at a time, Sergeant. Let me get on with cleaning you up while I explain.'

Hauser nodded.

'You came to grief against the steering wheel when the car went over. Remember?'

He frowned. 'Oh, yes . . . We skidded and hit something.'

'That's right.'

'And the car? There was a fire.'

'The car went up in flames.'

'The Audi? It's gone?'

There was a hint of tragedy in Hauser's voice, and Schenke could not help a slight smile as he responded. 'Yes, but at least the three of us are alive and safe, eh?' He finished cleaning the sergeant's face. 'There. Now let's get that schnapps inside us.'

Once the innkeeper had provided the extra glass, Schenke poured from the bottle and handed the glasses round, the last one being for Wilke.

'Drink up.'

He set the example by downing his drink in one go, feeling the tingling fire of the liquid spread through his stomach. Hauser and Wilke followed suit, while Liebwitz, still standing, took a tentative sip.

'Another,' Schenke instructed as he refilled Wilke's glass. The youth hesitated. 'Drink it.'

Wilke did as he was told, then held the empty glass in his lap out of the inspector's reach.

Schenke set the bottle down and focused on the young orderly. 'Let's talk. I want to know what happened when your director left. I take it he went out by the main entrance?'

'Yes, he did.' Wilke nodded, the slur in his speech more pronounced. 'Me and Huber were at the counter when he came down the stairs, in a hurry like.'

'What time was this?'

'Half past two. I remember because he told Huber he should take the rest of the afternoon off. That's when I looked at the clock and saw the time. Huber should have been on until eight in the evening. Dr Pieper told him to make himself scarce.'

'Those were his words?'

'That's right. Exactly what he said. Then he asked me if you had asked any questions when I brought you up to his office. I said you'd wanted to know about the layout of the clinic. He asked if there was anything else and I said no. He told me that if ever the police came back to the clinic, I was to say nothing to them and to keep out of their way if I knew what was good for me. Then he said the snow was getting heavier and that if I was to make it back to Potsdam I'd better leave at once. A few minutes later, he left and I saw his car drive off. I set off shortly afterwards.'

'You have a car?'

'I wish I did. No, there's a path through the forest that's clear of snow most of the way to Potsdam. I walked back.'

'But not home. You came here.'

'Yes.'

'Why?'

Wilke looked uneasy. 'Sometimes I need a drink. Some days at work, you hear things, see things.'

'What kind of things? The kind of things you tell American journalists, for example?'

Wilke froze for an instant before he looked down at his feet. 'I should never have spoken to that bastard.'

'Then why did you? Did he pay you for the information?'

Wilke looked up and nodded guiltily. 'Look here, sir, I don't want to get people into trouble.' Wilke glanced round to make sure he would not be overheard by the other locals, then lowered his voice. 'It's a cushy number and the director says I'm a good worker. Good enough not to send to war. I . . . I don't want to lose my job.'

Schenke felt no sympathy for the young man. Not when so many others his age were being conscripted and sent to fight for the Fatherland. He forced himself to nod sympathetically. 'We're not trying to get you into trouble, Wilke. We just want to understand a bit more about how the clinic operates. That's all. If you answer my questions truthfully, there'll be no harm done.'

'And you'll not tell the director that I told you anything?'

'As long as you've done nothing wrong, you have nothing to worry about as far as I am concerned.'

'All right . . . all right then. What do you want to know?'

Schenke thought carefully for a moment. 'To start with, what is it that you see and hear at the clinic that concerns you so much?'

Wilke frowned and took a deep breath. 'They're just kids, sir. We call them inmates, but they're just kids. No older than

my little sister. Sure, they've come into this world with something wrong in their minds or bodies. But they're still kids and
they should be treated with kindness. It's not their fault that
nature made them the way they are. They deserve some
happiness. Especially as they're no longer with their families.'

'I agree.' Schenke nodded. 'So, is someone not treating
them well?'

Wilke's bottom lip trembled. 'When they first come to see
the clinic, they're put into the nice rooms to make them and
their parents think it's going to be a bit like home. But once
the parents have gone, most of them are moved to the secure
wards. They don't like the bars on the windows and they don't
like the noise. Some don't sleep, and cry all night. Some scream
until they're seen to by the senior orderlies.'

'Men like Huber, you mean?' Schenke suggested.

'Yes. He was a soldier in the last war. After that he was in a
Free Corps unit and joined the Steel Helmets. He talks about
the old days from time to time.' Wilke shuddered. 'He says he
has killed people. Well, Reds at least. He scares me.'

'Does he harm the children?'

'Yes . . .' Wilke whispered. 'Yes, he does. When they're
making too much noise, or they don't behave the way he wants
them to. Then he beats them and drags them to their beds and
handcuffs them to the frame.'

Hauser leaned forward. 'You've seen him do this?'

'Often enough.'

'Have you told anybody at the clinic?' asked Schenke. 'The
director? Or one of the senior staff?'

'I was afraid to tell the director, so I told his secretary.'

'And what did she do about it?'

'She told me that Huber was doing his job and that I'd

better not make any more complaints about him if I wanted to keep mine.'

The tremor in his bottom lip was getting worse, and Schenke took his glass and half filled it this time before pressing it back into his hand. 'You need that.'

'Thanks.' Wilke knocked it back.

Schenke continued. 'What do you know about something called Diet Plan D?'

'I've heard of it. It's the one they prepare for the kids who get ill. To help them recover.'

'What kind of diet is it? What are those children fed?'

'I don't know. I'm not allowed into that part of the clinic. Only the senior orderlies go into the secure wards. It's their job to take in the food and medication. I just deal with the kids on the general ward and the private rooms. But you can hear the noises from the secure wards from outside the building. Not so much now there are fewer of them there.'

'Fewer? Do you mean because of the patients who have died?'

'Died?' Wilke looked confused. 'We've only had one die in the last six months.'

Schenke exchanged a brief look with Liebwitz and Hauser. 'So why are there fewer of them?'

'It's because of the transfers.'

'What transfers would those be?'

'The kids whose conditions are serious enough that they need to be moved to other institutions. That's what Huber told me. He should know. He's the one that drives the bus.'

'What bus?'

'It's more than a bus really. It's been adapted so that there's no chance of the children opening any of the windows or doors from the inside. It wouldn't do for them to fall out during trips out. Huber is in charge of transfers between the Schiller clinic and other places. He also drives when the kids are taken out for the day.'

'He brings them back, then?'

'Of course. They're only allowed out for a day, because that's as much as they can cope with.'

'I see.' That did not quite square with what Greta's mother had told him, thought Schenke. Maybe Greta's fears about the brown bus had taken on a measure of exaggeration in the telling. 'What about those he transfers? Does he bring some of them back too?'

'No. The transfers are permanent. I mean, the kids who need better care aren't the kind who are ever going to improve. At least that's what Huber says . . .' Wilke suddenly placed a hand over his mouth and his shoulders lurched. 'I'm going to be sick.'

Schenke stood and pointed to the entrance. 'Outside.'

Wilke stumbled towards the door, Schenke guiding him with a firm hand on his shoulder. Outside, the wind had eased off and the snow was falling with a serene regularity in the quiet night. The young man bent over, hands on his knees, as he threw up with an unpleasant animal grunt that became more strained as he emptied his guts and retched, a thin trail of mucus swaying from his lips. Schenke was tempted to put some distance between them, but he did not want Wilke to make a bolt for it. With the pain in his leg and still not recovered from his earlier exertions, he would never keep up with him.

After a few minutes, the young man stopped and wiped his lips with his hand. Schenke patted him on the back. 'Better?'

217

'Yes, much.'

Without warning, Wilke's arm shot out and he snatched a short log from the wood pile, swinging it in a vicious arc at Schenke's head. Instinctively Schenke threw his hands up to protect himself. Taking the blow on his arm, he stumbled back, catching his heel on a bench and tumbling sideways into the snow. Although he was slightly winded by the impact, he struggled up into a kneeling position and saw Wilke running into the road in the direction of Potsdam.

'Hey! Stop, you fool!' he shouted after him. 'I'm not going to harm you!'

The young man glanced over his shoulder, nearly fell, recovered his balance and ran on.

The door of the inn swung open, and Liebwitz charged out into the snow, pistol drawn. 'Are you harmed, sir?'

'I'm fine. The lad's running for it.'

Liebwitz raised his Luger, cupping the butt, and tilted his head slightly as he took aim.

'Stop!' Schenke ordered. 'What do you think you are doing?'

Liebwitz looked round. 'I can hit him in the leg from here, sir.'

'No. For Christ's sake, we're only questioning him. You're in the Kripo now, not the Gestapo. We don't go round gunning people down just because they don't want to talk to us.'

A disappointed expression flitted across the Scharführer's face, and he turned back towards Wilke, but the night had swallowed the young man up and he was no longer visible. Liebwitz lowered his pistol and removed the magazine, cleared the round from the breech, inserted the bullet in the magazine and slipped it back into the sidearm with a soft click. It was all done with a smooth efficiency that indicated a supreme familiarity with such weapons. Schenke struggled back to his feet, breathing deeply to recover from the winding blow.

'What happened, sir?'

'He hit me with a piece of wood once he had finished puking,' Schenke explained, trying to conceal his injured pride. 'He was too quick for me.'

'Evidently.'

'We got as much out of him as we could. Let's go back inside.'

Hauser was leaning forward as they returned to the warmth of the fire. 'The lad?'

'Gone,' Schenke said, not keen to elaborate. 'If we need to ask any more questions, we can find him at the clinic easily enough.'

'If the director lets us talk to him, or he's willing to speak to us when he's sober.'

Schenke was aware that the other customers were casting hostile glances at them, and then the innkeeper came over.

'Paul Wilke is a good boy. He's well liked around here, so we don't take kindly to strangers coming in and giving him a hard time. Even the police. If you're going to question anyone about what's going on at the clinic, you should talk to that thug Huber.'

Schenke rubbed his bicep where he had been struck. 'What about Huber?'

'He's chosen my place as his drinking hole. Comes down here from the clinic a couple of nights a week.'

'He lives there?'

'I doubt anyone else would have him. If it weren't for the

fact that he drinks plenty and likes to show off and buy rounds for the other customers, I'd rather he went somewhere else.'

Hauser smiled wryly. 'Sounds like the kind of patron an innkeeper would relish.'

'It's one thing to buy a person a drink, another to spend the evening bragging about the money he's making and the skulls of the Reds he cracked back in the day.' The innkeeper nodded to the men drinking at the other tables, four of whom were playing cards. 'Farmers and factory workers mostly. We keep to ourselves and we don't like politics. Especially a certain kind of politics.'

'What kind of politics would that be?' asked Liebwitz.

The innkeeper stared at him but made no reply, and Schenke cursed his subordinate's innate curiosity and lack of sensitivity. He cleared his throat and turned the conversation back to Huber.

'Would you say he was spending more than you'd expect a man like him could afford?'

'Who knows where his money comes from, but he surely has more of it to spread about than any other orderly working at the clinic. My brother-in-law is the gatekeeper there, and he earns barely enough to get by.'

'Has Huber ever told you how he comes by the money?'

'Bonuses, he says.' The innkeeper snorted. 'Bonuses? What kind of clinic pays its orderlies a bonus? There's something else. From time to time he has jewellery and other small trinkets that he tries to sell. Nothing elaborate, and he's happy to accept almost any price for them.' He nodded towards the door behind the bar. 'I even bought a piece for the wife. Huber says he has a cousin who picks the stuff up from the Jewish black market in Berlin.'

'It's possible, I suppose,' said Schenke.

The innkeeper bent to pick up a few split logs from the wood basket to one side of the fireplace and laid them over the glowing embers. When he straightened, he stuck his thumbs back in his waistband and regarded the three policemen.

'It's stopped snowing. You'll be wanting to be on your way soon, I imagine.'

'We're not going to get anywhere in a burned-out wreck,' Schenke pointed out. 'And if the phone lines are down, we can't call anyone to fetch us. We'll sleep here tonight. We can walk into town in the morning.'

The innkeeper frowned. 'Look here, Inspector. My regular customers will be leaving in an hour or so and then I'll be closing up for the night. You can't stay here.'

'Why not? It's not as if we're going to steal anything. We just need shelter and somewhere to rest. No need for you to worry.'

Schenke could see that the man still wasn't happy with the idea, so he tried a different approach. 'In return, I won't report your breach of blackout regulations to the local authorities. I may be wrong – I have no idea how things are done in the countryside – but they might not approve of the light in your windows being visible for some distance . . . What do you think?'

The innkeeper grunted with frustration before nodding reluctantly. 'You can stay. But I want you out of here at first light.'

'Thank you.'

'And I don't want to see any of your faces on my premises ever again.'

'Or what?' Hauser challenged him.

The innkeeper voiced no response, simply wagged a finger in warning, then turned and made his way back behind the counter.

Hauser eased himself back into his chair and stretched his feet towards the hearth. 'We'll do well here tonight. A decent fire, some comfortable chairs, a deck of cards, drink on hand, comradely company – and Liebwitz, of course.'

Liebwitz turned to him with a confused expression. 'Is that an . . . insult?'

'Not at all.' Hauser smiled. 'It's called banter. If you missed out on that in the Gestapo, I'm sure you'll pick it up when you've had the chance to spend a few more months with the Kripo.'

'Banter?'

'Look it up in the manual when we get back to Pankow.'

Liebwitz looked hurt.

'Quiet, Hauser,' Schenke interrupted. 'Save it until we're back at the precinct. We've got work to do.'

'Work?' Hauser raised an eyebrow.

'Look it up in the manual when we get back to Pankow,' said Liebwitz in a monotone.

Hauser looked at him open-mouthed, and then roared with laughter. 'Ah! The boy can be taught! You know something, Scharführer Liebwitz, I believe I may well like you one day.'

Schenke shot his sergeant a warning look before he realised the other customers were still paying them little attention. He motioned to Liebwitz to sit down, and then spoke quietly.

'You'll stay here tonight, Hauser. If we're not back by morning, I want you to call in the Potsdam police.'

'Why? What the hell are you thinking of doing, sir?'

'When the woman came out with the bowl, did you notice the pendant she was wearing?'

Hauser shook his head.

'It looked familiar, but it took me a moment to place it. I've seen it before. It looked like one I saw in a photograph of Greta Scholtz. Quite unusual, so I doubt it's a mere coincidence. If it is the same one, how did she get hold of it?'

Liebwitz answered. 'Huber.'

'I think so. He sold it to her. He must have stolen it from Greta's personal effects after her death. Or taken it from her while she was still alive . . .'

'Or after he killed her, maybe,' Liebwitz suggested.

Hauser shook his head. 'That sounds like a bit of a leap to me. It may not even be the same pendant as the one in the photograph.'

'It looked very similar to me,' Schenke insisted. 'I want to know how Huber came by it. That means we need to get back inside the clinic before Huber, the director or anyone else has the chance to hide anything more from us.' He turned to Liebwitz. 'I'm not sure we can trust the innkeeper or his regulars. We'll wait until the place is closed up before we set off. Then we'll see what's really going on inside that damned clinic.'

Chapter Twenty-Two

They stopped at the edge of the forest path and looked down the road towards the main gate of the clinic. The sky had cleared and the stars gleamed against a pitch-black backdrop. Schenke squinted at the hands of his wristwatch.

'Ten minutes until eleven. We should have plenty of time to search the place before dawn.'

'If we can get in,' Liebwitz responded. 'And we aren't discovered.'

There were no lights in the windows of the gatekeeper's cottage, not even the slightest glimmer around the edges of the shutters, and Schenke decided that those within must have gone to bed.

'Let's go,' he said softly, and the two of them broke cover and hurried through the snow towards the gate. Slipping a hand through the bars, Schenke reached for the iron pin that held the slide bolt in place and tried to pull it out. The pin resisted, refusing to shift.

'Shit,' he snarled. 'It's frozen in place.'

He tried again, but the pin seemed immovable.

'We'll have to find some other way.' He looked along the

wall and then up at the top of the gate. There was a soft click, and he turned to see Liebwitz holding the pin in his gloved hand.

'You must have loosened it, sir. It came out quite easily.'

'Fine. Let's get the gate open.'

Liebwitz put the pin down beside the pillar and drew the bolt back slowly. As soon as it was clear of the bracket, Schenke pushed the gate open far enough for them to pass through the gap, then eased it back so that if the gatekeeper stirred and happened to look out of his window, nothing would appear out of place. They made their way down the drive towards the empty booth by the inner gate. Ahead of them the main building loomed up, dark and forbidding, and Schenke was reminded of the ghost stories he had enjoyed scaring himself with as a child. An anxious tremor chilled his spine. Only one light showed, a masked lamp in a bracket above the entrance. Now that the snowstorm had passed, there was no wind, and a sombre silence seemed to hang over the scene.

They were moving through the inner gate when Liebwitz froze, his head cocked to one side.

'What is it?' Schenke whispered.

'Listen.'

He strained his ears as he stared towards the dark mass of the building. Then he heard it: a faint wail, rising in pitch until it sounded like a scream, before it was abruptly cut off. There was a shout, a man's voice, followed by a brief silence, then the wail began again, louder this time, joined by another voice singing pitifully. Schenke felt his scalp begin to tingle, and was tempted to turn and get away from this place. He glanced at Liebwitz.

'Come on, perhaps some of the kids are restless. That's all it is.'

He took a step towards the entrance, but Liebwitz stood quite still.

'What's the matter?' Schenke asked. There was no reply, so he tapped his companion on the arm. Liebwitz recoiled as if he had been prodded with a heated iron, and gasped. Even in the faint loom of the snow, Schenke could make out the anxious expression on the other man's face. It was the first time he had seen him show any emotion, and it was unnerving. Schenke grasped him by the shoulders and felt the Gestapo man trembling.

'Scharführer Liebwitz, pull yourself together, dammit!'

Liebwitz clenched his eyes shut and took a few quick deep breaths before tugging himself free. He cleared his throat.

'I apologise, sir.'

'What the hell's wrong with you?'

'Nothing. I'm fine now.'

Schenke glared at him. 'You'd better be. Ready?'

'Yes, sir.' Liebwitz's voice was restored to its flat tone.

Schenke nodded towards the entrance, and they set off, the snow crunching softly beneath their shoes. As they drew closer, he could make out a handful of other voices, unmistakably those of children, some crying, some shouting, some even laughing. There was a dull glow visible through the glass in the doors, and he could see a small electric lamp on the reception counter. Beyond sat a man in profile, absorbed by the book in his hands.

Schenke moved to the side of the entrance and stood by the wall. 'We're going to have to find another way in. There has to be a service entrance or something.'

They worked their way along the exterior towards the tower at the end of the building where Pieper had his office, eyes and ears alert to any sign of danger. Just before the base of the tower bulged out, they came across a flight of steps that led down to a large metal door below ground level. Schenke tested the handle, only to discover the door was locked. They continued around the tower to the rear of the building, where there was an orangery. One of the windows was loose and secured by a simple catch.

'I'll deal with it,' said Liebwitz.

There was a metallic click and a dull gleam of steel as the blade of his flick knife snapped into place. Easing the point between the window and the flaking frame, he worked the catch free. Once they were both inside, Schenke closed the window and secured the latch.

A few hardy plants sat in large pots, somehow having survived the long weeks of sub-zero temperatures. The furniture in the orangery had been covered to protect it during the winter, and even though there were a few wall radiators, they must have been turned off, as the air inside the structure was almost as cold as that outside. Schenke tried the nearest door, and the handle turned easily. He opened it slowly, and they found themselves in a lounge area, with sofas and chairs arranged around low tables. It was markedly warmer in this room, and he could just make out the framed portraits hanging along the walls. He paused to get his bearings, then led the way across the room and opened the door as quietly as possible. There was a corridor outside, stretching left and right along the length of the building. He turned towards the tower. 'This way.'

There were no lights in the corridor. Liebwitz took out a

small torch and flicked the switch, shielding the beam with his hand so that there was just enough light to see their way ahead. They passed a handful of doors on either side before reaching the arched entrance to the base of the tower. Beyond was the spiral staircase. Schenke was about to set foot on the bottom step when he caught a waft of air from below, and a sharp chemical odour filled his nostrils.

'Smell that?' he whispered.

Liebwitz was still for a moment before he replied. 'Yes . . . Not sure I recognise it, sir. Should we look into it?'

'Later, if we get the chance. The priority is Pieper's study, and any records we can find. Come.'

They climbed slowly, easing their weight carefully from one foot to the other on the iron steps to be as quiet as possible. The first floor opened out onto what looked like a storage area, filled with wooden chests, bed frames and stacks of mattresses. The entrance lobby had had a high ceiling, Schenke recalled, so the offices must be on the next floor up. They kept going, and this time they emerged into the area Wilke had escorted them to the previous afternoon. Schenke paused to listen, but there was no sound of movement. Silence, apart from the ongoing faint noises of those children whose sleep had been disturbed. He briefly wondered how anyone could endure living in such a place.

The door to Pieper's office was not locked. They entered and shut it behind them. Heavy wooden shutters had been closed over the arched window, and Schenke decided it was safe to turn on the desk lamp. The light was enough to see the entire room. He glanced around before making for the filing cabinets to one side.

'You start from the right,' he told Liebwitz. 'We're looking for any reference to the names of the children who died here.'

He went to open the top drawer, but it was locked. A search of the desk did not reveal any keys, and Schenke cursed under his breath. Picking up a poker from its stand beside an unused fireplace that now held a planter filled with ferns, he jammed the tip into the gap by the lock.

'We don't have a warrant to do that, sir,' said Liebwitz.

'You weren't so particular when you volunteered to force the window,' Schenke pointed out. 'We don't have a warrant to search the office in the first place. Look here, Scharführer, we're investigating a number of possible murders. There are times when all policemen are faced with the need to break a lesser law in the interests of a higher justice.'

'The law is not a convenient contingency, sir.'

Schenke did not have time to debate the issue. 'I am your superior in rank. That means you have to obey my orders, regardless of the circumstances, and I am ordering you to force open these filing cabinets to search for evidence. You can work out the trade-off between discipline and legality when you have the luxury of time to do so. Now carry out my orders.'

'Yes, sir. But I may require written confirmation that I am acting under your authority should there be any subsequent inquiry into this matter.'

If any other member of his team had spoken those words, Schenke would have put it down to cowardice. In Liebwitz's case, he knew it was pedantry.

Schenke leaned his weight against the poker, clenched his teeth, and controlled his strength as he heaved so as not to do any more damage than was needed to break the lock. There was a sharp snap and the drawer jolted open a fraction. He removed the poker and handed it to Liebwitz. The latter put his torch down and went to work.

The files were arranged in alphabetical order, starting from the top drawer of the cabinet Schenke had opened. He quickly found the first of the files they had already examined and pulled it out to glance through it. There was no difference. Nothing had been added or taken out. He picked another name at random to compare the files. This child, a boy of fourteen, was described as 'simple-minded', and had been referred by a doctor from Mitte. Once again there was a form from the racial hygiene certification office, but this one had a dash instead of a cross, and there was a brief remark in the comment box that the boy was capable of physical labour. From the accompanying photograph, he looked fit enough, even though his expression was a little dull and his mouth hung open. But then the same was true of some of the Brownshirts Schenke had come across.

As he continued to work through the files, he saw that a handful of forms were marked with the same plus notation as the dead children's. Some of those children had been put on Diet Plan D, but there was no other obvious connection. More forms had only a dash and an occasional remark about suitability for manual work. When he reached the last of the files in the bottom drawer, he closed it with a sigh of frustration.

'There's nothing helpful here. How about you?'

Liebwitz had taken a small stack of files over to the desk, and seemed to have read most of them. Schenke crossed the room and sat down opposite him.

'Personnel files,' Liebwitz explained. 'All the staff files are here, except for the director's; his records are probably with whoever he answers to higher up the chain of command.

I've found only one other qualified doctor and four nurses so far. The rest are orderlies, watchmen, cooks, groundsmen and so on. I'd have expected a higher proportion of staff trained to deal with the kind of inmates there are here. Therapists and so on.'

'No doubt that's another way the clinic keeps its costs down,' Schenke commented. 'It's not the quality of care the parents were led to expect. It's starting to feel more like a prison than a children's home.'

'There's not as much distinction as you'd imagine, sir.' Liebwitz tapped two files he had put to one side. 'Wilke and Huber. The Wilke file is brief, as you might expect from someone his age. This is his first job. He was taken on because his father worked here for a number of years before retiring. His school records are sound; they say he is honest and hard-working. He was in a Catholic choral club before it was taken over by the party. There's no mention of him ever being in trouble with the police and no disciplinary action since he started work here. He would seem to be a model employee.'

'What about Huber?'

Liebwitz indicated the fatter of the two files. 'As you'd expect, he is a more interesting character. He fought in a Prussian Guard regiment in the previous war. He won an Iron Cross, second class, but was punished for theft, insubordination, being drunk on duty and fighting. After he was demobilised at the end of the war, he joined a Free Corps unit that helped put down the communist revolutionaries. He was accused of murder, but a judge dismissed the charges. He then enlisted with the Steel Helmets, and became a member of the party the year before it came to power. He's had a number of jobs since leaving the army, none of which he held for very long. Until

Dr Pieper offered him a job at the clinic. He works directly for Pieper and there's no record of any disciplinary issues.'

'So he suddenly became a conscientious worker, eh?' Schenke gave a dry chuckle. 'I find that hard to believe.'

'He's also been put in charge of administering Diet Plan D, sir. And been given responsibility for the clinic's patient transport.'

Schenke recalled what Wilke had told him about the brown bus being driven by Huber. 'Interesting. Go on.'

'It's not the most interesting thing, sir. You should see this.' Liebwitz opened the file and turned a few sheets before he found the one he was looking for and slid it towards his superior.

Schenke saw from the letterhead that it had come from the Reich Committee for the Scientific Registering of Serious Hereditary and Congenital Illnesses. It was dated November the previous year, and required Huber to report to the office in Berlin for training for additional duties. The training would be conducted by Albert Widmann of the Kripo forensic laboratory.

He looked up. 'Widmann? What the hell does he have to do with training the staff of children's homes?'

'There's no mention of that in the file, sir. But look at the signature at the bottom of the letter.'

Schenke scanned down over the administrative details of the course. Even though it looked as if it had been signed in a hurry, the name could still be read easily enough.

'SS Reich Doctor Schmesler . . .' Schenke rubbed his jaw. 'What the hell?'

He felt uneasy, as if the ground beneath him had shifted slightly and he was seeing things from a different point of view.

A host of questions began to flood into his mind. How exactly was Schmesler connected to the clinic? What was the role of this committee? Was there a connection between the murder of Schmesler and the deaths of the children from the clinic? Suddenly the danger of the Schmesler investigation reared up again and he felt afraid.

There was a click from behind him, and he saw Liebwitz glance up and begin to reach inside his coat.

'Don't!' a voice snarled. 'Raise your hands and keep them where I can see them, or I will shoot you where you are!'

Liebwitz calmly did as he was told, and Schenke followed suit as he turned to face the door. Huber was standing on the threshold, his left hand on the doorknob while his right gripped a pistol that was aimed at the two policemen.

Chapter Twenty-Three

'How fortunate that I am in the habit of doing the rounds last thing before I turn in, eh?' Huber moved into the room, keeping his pistol aimed at the two policemen, and took up position with his back to the wall, facing the end of the desk, so that he could keep both men in clear sight. His eyes were alert, and even though he was a good ten years older than Schenke, he was powerfully built and light on his feet. Even unarmed, he could be a dangerous man.

'Before anything more is said, I could shoot you both now and claim that I thought you were thieves when I came across you in the darkness.' Huber smiled. 'So don't get any ideas about trying heroics. All that will get you is a bullet in the skull. I've killed men before and I will not hesitate to do so again if I need to. Are we clear, gentlemen?'

'I understand,' said Liebwitz.

'First things first,' Huber continued. 'Your guns. I want them placed on the middle of the table. One at a time. You first, Inspector. Do it slowly.'

'We're not armed,' Schenke replied.

'Bullshit.'

He eased his hands down to his lapels and drew his coat and jacket apart to show that he was not wearing a holster. 'We only came here to ask questions. There was no need to carry firearms.'

Huber waved him back into his seat and turned to Liebwitz. 'Let's see you, friend.'

Liebwitz repeated his superior's actions before resuming his seat.

'Can we lower our hands now?' asked Schenke.

'No. I like them where they are.' Huber moved his gun so that it was in line with the middle of Schenke's chest. 'The first question is, where is the other cop? The ugly one?' He glanced at Liebwitz. 'I mean the really ugly one. And don't try and lie to me. I'll know if you do. So speak true.'

'All right . . .' Schenke thought quickly about his reply. 'Sergeant Hauser is waiting for us in Potsdam. If we don't return, he has orders to bring in the local police.'

Huber snorted with derision. 'A likely story! He's here somewhere. You'd better tell me where.'

'Apparently you are unable to determine if someone is speaking the truth after all,' Liebwitz observed.

Schenke gave him a warning look. 'Keep quiet, Scharführer.'

'Scharführer?' Huber cocked an eyebrow. 'SS?'

Liebwitz nodded.

Huber was still for a moment, and then shrugged. 'Cop or party man, makes no difference if they try to make me look small.'

Walking behind Liebwitz, he dealt him a savage blow above his ear with the butt of the pistol. Liebwitz gasped and reached a hand to the side of his head as Huber backed to his previous position.

'Keep those hands where I can see 'em!'

'He's bleeding,' Schenke protested.

The weapon had gouged the skin above Liebwitz's ear, and blood was running onto his shirt collar. He looked dazed at first, but then Schenke saw a furious glint in his eyes as his fingers curled into claws. For the first time he realised how terrifying the gaunt Gestapo man could appear when he was finally provoked into a rage, and now he was worried that his anger might get them both killed.

'Liebwitz.' He addressed him sharply. 'Calm yourself, man!'

For a moment the Scharführer looked as if he might spring to his feet and hurl himself at Huber, but then his self-control returned and his face eased back into its usual deadpan expression.

'That's better,' said Huber. 'Let's not have any trouble, eh? Now, about your friend, Hauser. Where is he?'

'I told you the truth. He's not here. I thought we might be taking a risk returning and needed a backup plan in case anything happened.'

'Well, it's happened. Assuming you're telling me the truth, where is he staying in Potsdam?' When Schenke made no reply, he added, 'If you think I won't find out what I need, you're fooling yourself, Inspector.'

'I'm not going to tell you anything. Whatever you do to me.'

'I imagine that's true. You might be a tough bastard to crack. But I'm not going to waste time trying to find out.' He pointed the gun at Liebwitz. 'It's going to work like this. You'll tell me what I need to know, or I'll hurt your SS man again . . . and again. If need be, I will shoot him if you don't speak up.' He raised the pistol and took aim at Liebwitz's head. 'Bang! Just like that.'

Schenke flinched. Huber banged his fist down on the end of the desk. 'Tell me where your friend is!'

'He's at police headquarters. If we're not back by dawn, they'll be coming here mob-handed. And they'll see through any excuse about mistaking us for burglars and gunning us down.'

'You think?' Huber grinned. 'Even if that's so, I happen to know people in the party who I've done favours for in the past. Important people. They'll back up my version of events, and I'll be a free man and you two will be dead. I'm the one who has the upper hand here. We'll play things my way. I'll deal with your friend later. Right now, I want to know what you're doing snooping around the clinic in the dead of night. What are you looking for?'

Schenke stared at him. 'There have been too many children dying at the clinic over recent months for it to be a coincidence. We're trying to find out why. What is the purpose of Diet Plan D?'

'Oh, come on! You're the criminal investigator. You can't tell me you haven't worked it out yet?'

'I want to hear it from you.'

'What's that going to prove?'

'Your responsibility for their deaths.'

'My responsibility?' Huber laughed. 'Dear God, you've no idea what you have got yourself involved in, have you?'

'I know about Greta Scholtz. She owned a pendant. A very distinctive pendant. The same pendant that's being worn by someone else now. Because you sold it to them after Greta was murdered.'

Huber's expression was difficult to read – somewhere between pity and contempt. 'You're going to find murder difficult to pin on me or anyone else involved.'

'Who else is in on it, then?' Schenke demanded. 'Pieper? Lenger?'

'Sure, why not? Them and many more, I dare say. I've got a good thing going with selling the kids' personal effects, and I ain't in a hurry to give that up.'

'You're in it for the money?'

'Money, yes. And other reasons.'

'What are you and your friends up to with the victims? Are you abusing them before they're killed? Is that it?'

Huber's smile faded and the blood drained from his face as his lips lifted in a snarl. 'Are you calling me some kind of pervert?'

'Well, aren't you? You and those others.'

Schenke saw the anger in the man's expression as he raised the gun.

'Shut your mouth! You say one more word on the subject and I swear to God I'll shoot you both dead here and now.'

There was a terrifying stillness to the moment. Schenke's heart pounded and he could hardly bring himself to breathe, as if the slightest movement might provoke Huber into pulling the trigger. The orderly's features were fixed in an expression of disgust. Then his lips parted and he breathed out through clenched teeth as he stepped away and took up position to one side of the door.

'Enough talk. On your feet!'

Schenke hesitated. 'Where are you taking us?'

'Somewhere you can't cause any mischief while we wait for Doctor Pieper to return and decide what's to be done with you.' Huber waggled the pistol. 'Move. Keep your hands up where I can see them.'

The two policemen rose and edged towards the door while Huber covered them, his trigger finger curled through the guard, ready to tighten at the slightest hint of trouble. Schenke was aware of the knife his colleague still had in his pocket, and willed Liebwitz not to attempt anything rash. At the same time, he hoped Huber would not risk getting close enough to search his prisoners thoroughly. He hesitated on the threshold.

'You are making a mistake, Huber. You won't get away with treating us like this. Put the gun away and let us go.'

'Shut your mouth. Unless you want me to clip your head, like your friend there.' Huber raised the butt of the pistol.

Schenke stepped out of reach and left the room, followed by Liebwitz. Outside, Huber pointed towards the staircase, then flicked on the light in the stairwell.

'Down you go. All the way to the bottom.'

Schenke led the way, the metal plates of the stairs ringing beneath his feet as he descended. The ground floor of the tower was filled with furniture and boxes. He could feel the temperature dropping as they entered the subterranean level of the building. At the bottom of the steps, the floor was paved with stone slabs and the surrounding walls were unadorned brick. The air was almost freezing, and smelt damp. There were more boxes here, and wooden racks where vegetables and fruit were stored.

'Move away from the stairs!' Huber ordered. 'Towards the tunnel. Go.'

The mouth of the tunnel was dark, and the light from the staircase penetrated only a short distance before giving way to complete darkness. Huber flicked another switch, and a string of dim bulbs glowed into life along one side, reaching out into the distance. The tunnel must stretch the entire length of the building, Schenke estimated. There were doors spaced out evenly on both sides. He paced forward, keeping his hands raised, and the others followed, their footsteps echoing off the sides of the tunnel. Through open archways on either side he caught glimpses of more storage places. Then there was that smell they had noticed earlier. A faint acrid tang that reminded him of disinfectant. The doors had grilled slots at eye level and down near the floor, like the prison cells back at the Pankow precinct.

'Stop there,' Huber ordered. 'Next door to your left. Open it and go inside.'

Schenke glanced at the recessed door two paces ahead. Unlike the others they had passed, this one was made of steel, painted the same dull grey as a warship. It was secured by a sturdy sliding bar clamped into position by a spring-loaded bolt. In the middle of the door was a small glass window with a rubber seal around the edges with a metal plate that could be slid across the window. It took both hands to draw back the bolt and lift the bar before he could pull the heavy door open. As he did so, he noticed that a further rubber seal ran around the edge of the frame.

Stepping over the rim, he entered a space some five metres in length by three across, and barely high enough to stand in, and moved to the far end as he was instructed. He saw that the walls and tiled floor were covered in a thick layer of the same grey paint. The air was freezing and his breath came in swirling plumes as he turned and waited for Liebwitz to join him. The disinfectant smell was more distinct now. Huber remained outside in the tunnel.

'That's it, gents. You can lower your arms now.'

'You can't imprison us like this,' Schenke protested. 'There will be consequences.'

'Really?' Huber smirked. 'I have a gun. Seems to me I can do what I like, Inspector. You'll stay here until Pieper decides what is to be done with you. Sleep tight.' He began to close the door.

'Wait!' Schenke called out. 'We'll freeze to death if you leave us in here.'

'No you won't. If the kids can survive a night in the cells, so can you.'

The door closed and the metal plate slid across the window cutting off the light from the tunnel. From the other side came the metallic clank of the lever being locked into place before there was a sharp click as the bolt completed the seal. The faint echoes of footsteps quickly faded, and then there was only the pitch black and the sound of the two men breathing.

'Have you got your torch?' asked Schenke.

'No, sir. It's back in the director's office.'

'What about a lighter? Or matches?'

'I don't smoke, sir.'

Schenke felt in his pockets for his own lighter, and then recalled that he had lost it when the car rolled. 'Shit . . .'

He tried to recall the details of the cell he had glimpsed before the door had closed, but it had appeared to be completely empty. He felt his way along the walls in case something had been overlooked. There was nothing except for a duct in the wall nearest the outside of the building that angled upwards. He peered up it, but there was no sign of any illumination, or any air stirring.

'Can anyone hear me?' he called out. He waited for a response before trying again and then giving up.

'Liebwitz, where are you?'

'Here, sir, by the door.'

Schenke felt his way along the wall to the corner and nearly stumbled over the Scharführer's raised knees.

'Sorry.'

Easing himself down beside the other man, he tucked his coat under his buttocks before pulling up his scarf and wrapping his arms around his knees as they edged together.

'We're in trouble . . .'

'So it would seem, sir.'

'If the cold doesn't do for us, Huber and his friends will, I fear.'

'It's possible.'

There was a dull, resigned edge to Liebwitz's voice, and yet he was trembling. That made him seem more human.

'We'll be all right, Scharführer. Sergeant Hauser will raise the alarm when we fail to return. Then the tables will be turned on that thug.'

'Yes, sir. I still have my knife. If I get the chance to use it, do I have your permission to act?'

'Act?'

'Kill Huber and whoever else is there when they return for us.'

'Let's not be too hasty. If it looks as though our lives are in danger, I'll give the order to strike. But not before. Understand?'

'Yes, sir.'

They sat huddled against the door in the freezing cell. After perhaps half an hour, the cold seeped into Schenke's bones and he began to shake. He hunched his head down lower into the folds of his scarf and tried to distract himself from his misery by thinking over the exchange with Huber in the director's office. The implication that there were others, perhaps many others, involved in the murder of the children was worrying. What if there was a ring of child-abusers, as Schenke suspected? What if it included people of influence? The kind who could make two policemen disappear without any fear of the consequences? And yet Huber's anger at the suggestion that he was some kind of pervert appeared genuine. What other motivation could he have for involvement in the deaths of the children? Despite what Schenke had heard at the inn about Huber flashing his money around, that surely would not be reward enough for the risk of being uncovered as a child-killer?

So many vexing questions, he reflected. And it was bloody cold. He could feel his fingers and toes starting to turn numb, as well as his rump. He stood up stiffly and began to move his feet as he hugged himself.

'How are you doing?'

'I am cold, sir,' Liebwitz replied.

'No surprises there.' Schenke forced a chuckle. 'Get up and move around. It'll help.'

'Yes, sir.'

He heard a shuffling as the other man stood, and then a rhythmic stepping as he marched on the spot.

'This is not a good place, sir,' Liebwitz muttered, with such feeling that Schenke turned in the direction of his companion's voice.

'What is troubling you so much? Ever since we set eyes on the clinic you've been behaving out of character. There was a moment back there, in the office, when I thought you were going to leap up and throw yourself at Huber. I've never seen such fury in your expression. What the hell was that about?'

Liebwitz was silent before he cleared his throat. 'I recognise this place, sir. Not the Schiller clinic specifically. I mean these institutions for children who don't fit in with society's expectations. I was sent to one as a child . . . I spent three years of my life moving between such places.'

Schenke had already had a feeling that something like this might have been behind his companion's unusual behaviour, but now that Liebwitz had confirmed the suspicion, it made sense.

'But why? Why would you of all people be sent to such an institution? You're one of the most intelligent and able police officers I have ever met. Good God, man, you have a doctorate and can shoot the balls off a fly at twenty paces.'

'I've never tried that, sir.'

'It's just a saying. But in all seriousness . . . why?'

'I did not speak for a long time when I was a child, sir. My parents thought there was something wrong with my mind. I was taken to see a doctor and then a psychologist and I was pronounced a congenital simpleton. My parents refused to accept the diagnosis. They decided to commit me to a clinic in the hope that I could be cured.'

'Why didn't you speak up?'

'I did not want to, sir. I was content with just observing my surroundings.'

Schenke shook his head and laughed nervously. 'That's madness.'

'I did not know that at the time. I thought I was quite normal. I had nothing against which to measure my mental state or capacity at that age.'

'I can't understand this. What happened to you when you were a . . .' Schenke struggled briefly for what felt like the right word, 'a patient.'

'At first the doctors tried to talk to me. They gave me reading tests. Simple material. My mother had already shown me words and sounded them out, and I had picked it up easily. So when they put children's books in front of me, I leafed through them quickly without much interest and they took that as further proof of my idiocy. After that, I was sent to another institution, where the treatment was more extreme. They used galvanism – electrical shock therapy – for some months.'

Schenke had heard of such measures and had thought they sounded more like torture than a cure. 'How old were you at the time?'

'Six years old, sir.'

'Six . . .' Schenke felt his stomach twist with disgust. 'Dear God.'

'It was a terrible time for me,' Liebwitz continued in his monotone. 'After six months they decided the treatment was not working. I was then pronounced incurable and sent to another institution. A far more uncomfortable place. I was amongst the crippled, the deformed and children described as insane or mentally deficient. Those tasked with looking after us were men like Huber. They were largely unsupervised and treated us cruelly. We were beaten if we caused trouble, and many of the children were sexually abused.' He coughed. 'The more I was mistreated, the more I withdrew into myself and lived in my mind, where I could order my thoughts and focus on anything but the people and places around me.'

'How did you get out?'

'My mother died just before my ninth birthday. She had been stricken with tuberculosis and my father had been forced to nurse her. I suppose it must have broken him. He died shortly after her. My uncle came to the home to break the news to me. I don't know why, but that was the first time I spoke. I cried and called out for my mother. My uncle was an educated man of means, a professor of mathematics at Frankfurt. He was horrified by the conditions at the institution and insisted on taking me home with him. He and his wife were childless. They raised me as their own. Encouraging me to speak and begin my academic education. That I did not fit in with my peers nor understand their jokes meant that I was always an outsider. I never minded, as I never much cared for people apart from my uncle and aunt. And I did my best to put my early memories out of my head. As if I had a box where I placed the dark years, closed the lid and locked it away. And that is how I have lived until now. Until you brought me to this place, sir. So now I can recall it all. Every detail . . .'

Schenke felt guilty, despite having had no way of knowing that he was thrusting Liebwitz back into a nightmare when he brought him along to the clinic to assist in the investigation.

'Liebwitz, I'm so sorry.'

'For what, sir? It was not your doing. How could you have anticipated such a thing? It is a matter I must find a way to deal with, once again. That is all.'

Schenke impulsively raised a hand to comfort the other man, and then hesitated. What good would it do? What could anyone do in the face of such a revelation that would make things better in any way? He considered that there might be something in this world even more dark and immoral than the Nazi regime. Liebwitz's experience was institutionalised evil.

As an innocent child he had been subjected to bullying, torture and cruelty.

'We might not be able to change your past, Scharführer, but we can put an end to whatever is taking place in this clinic and bring those responsible to justice.'

'I hope so, sir.' Liebwitz sighed. 'In the meantime, we must stay limber and alert for when Huber comes back for us. We must keep moving.'

Schenke heard footsteps as his companion began to pace up and down the far side of the cell. After a moment, he followed his example, hands shoved deep in his pockets, head down, through the long, cold hours of darkness as they waited for their fate to be decided.

Chapter Twenty-Four

4 February

By the time they heard footsteps approaching, both men were shivering uncontrollably. Schenke's leg was aching terribly, and every so often he had been forced to lean against the wall so that he could rub the limb vigorously to try and ease the pain. His discomfort was made worse by a headache that had got steadily worse during the night; he suspected it was caused by the acrid chemical odour that lingered in the clammy air. Liebwitz was suffering from a similar headache, but seemed less affected by the cold as he paced up and down relentlessly.

The footsteps stopped outside the door. There was a metallic rattle as the viewing plate snapped aside and a thin beam of light penetrated through the glass into the gloom before being partially cut off as the silhouette of a head leaned close to inspect the occupants of the cell. Then the slot was closed and there was a muffled exchange of voices in the tunnel. Schenke moved towards the door and felt for it with his hand before taking off his hat and pressing his ear to the icy metal.

He could make out Huber's voice, and then Pieper's, lower and not audible enough to catch the sense of his words. He waited a moment, but there were no other voices, and he drew back from the door and replaced his hat.

'There's two of them. Huber and Pieper. Ready your knife but keep it out of sight.'

'Yes, sir.'

There was a soft click, and then an instant later the sound of the door bolt being drawn back and the grating squeal of the lever being raised. As the door opened, light flooded into the cell, causing Schenke to blink and squint.

'Outside, now!' Pieper ordered harshly. 'I don't take kindly to being woken in the middle of the night and having to drive back here to deal with you two.'

Schenke's eyes were adjusting to the light quickly. He looked down at his watch and saw that it was just after six in the morning. He glared at the director. 'I think this has gone on long enough. Tell your heavy to put his gun away and take us somewhere warm where you can explain this outrage.'

Pieper chuckled. 'Brave words, Inspector. According to Huber, you claim that we should be surrounded by your sergeant and his reinforcements at any moment.' He looked both ways along the tunnel and shrugged. 'Oh dear. Seems you were bluffing.'

'Give him time,' Schenke replied.

'Indeed. And since we have a little time, I'd like to put a few questions to you before I decide what happens.' Pieper nodded towards the cell. 'But not in this place.'

He frowned as he caught sight of the dried blood on Liebwitz's collar and the streaks on his jaw and the side of his head.

'What's this, Huber? You said they'd not been harmed.'

'It was only a light tap,' Huber growled.

'It doesn't look that way.' Pieper turned his attention to Schenke. 'Let's go somewhere warmer. Back to my office, if you please. I imagine you know the way.'

He pointed in the direction of the tower, and Schenke set off, with Liebwitz at his shoulder.

'Now, sir?' Liebwitz whispered.

'No talking!' Huber snapped. 'Not unless you want me to belt you round the ear again.'

The four marched in silence back to the stairs and up to Pieper's office, where the director instructed the policemen to sit on the far side of his desk. Huber was stationed by the door, pistol at the ready, as his superior stood in front of the desk, arms crossed. The folders the policemen had been looking at some hours before were scattered across the surface.

'Time for questions . . .'

Schenke shook his head. 'Time to clean Liebwitz's wound. And I need a piss.'

It was true that he needed to relieve himself, but the more pressing need was to buy time for Hauser to appear, assuming the sergeant had been able to persuade the officer in charge at Potsdam to send his men.

'You should have gone in the cell. You'll have to wait.'

Schenke indicated the rug underneath his chair. 'Looks expensive. Be a shame to ruin it.'

Pieper's lip curled in disgust. 'You wouldn't do that.'

'Try me.'

The director sighed with exasperation and nodded to a door in the corner of his office. 'In there. One at a time, and leave the door open. Your friend first.'

Liebwitz went to the toilet and Schenke heard the sound of running water. While they waited, he looked up at Pieper.

'How do you think this is going to end? Do you think you can just make two Kripo officers disappear?'

'Stranger things have happened, and with a war on, I would imagine the authorities have higher priorities. Besides, I passed a wrecked car on the way here. It looked very much like the car that was outside the clinic when I left yesterday. It would not stretch credulity too far to add your bodies to the wreck and burn them too.'

Schenke swallowed. His mouth felt dry, but he kept his expression defiant. 'Aren't you forgetting Sergeant Hauser?'

'The poor survivor of the accident?' Pieper affected a sympathetic expression. 'I will say he is in a state of shock. The poor fellow must be confused by his ordeal after losing two close comrades ... If he says anything different, I'll deny it and put it down to the trauma. His word against ours. And with the war on and all, people have better things to concern themselves with than the ramblings of a bereaved sergeant.'

'You can't really believe you'd get away with it,' Schenke challenged him.

Pieper made an amused expression. 'Try me.'

He turned towards the toilet. 'You've had enough time. Come out and get back to your chair.'

Liebwitz emerged, beads of water on his stubbly cheeks. He had cleaned the blood from his face, and as he approached the desk, he opened his hand just enough so that Schenke could see the tip of the flick-knife blade protruding from his cuff into his palm. He sat down and Schenke rose to take his turn.

The toilet was a cramped room, with a lavatory and sink. The window was too small to offer any chance of escape, even if he were able to barricade the door. He relieved himself and washed his hands. As he turned to leave, he caught a glimpse of a distant pair of headlights through the window, before they disappeared. It gave him a glimmer of hope.

'What are you waiting for?' Huber demanded. 'Back to your place.'

When Schenke was settled, Pieper fixed his gaze on him. 'Why did you come back here last night? What were you looking for?'

'Evidence concerning the fate of the children who have died at your clinic. I want to know who was responsible for their deaths. Every name associated with whatever sick little scheme you and Huber are running here. I know there's more than just you two involved. I know there's money in it for Huber, and payments for those who send children here. We know about the special diet you put the kids on to hasten their deaths. We know that Huber takes the children away in a brown bus and that they never return. I know that Dr Schmesler was involved, and that's why you tried to scare me off by having your thugs abduct me and threaten to kill me if I looked any further into the circumstances of his death.'

There was a brief look of surprise on Pieper's face before he gave a dry chuckle. 'You've got that wrong, Inspector. I don't know anything about any abduction. Aside from that, you seem to know rather too much. More than is healthy for you. You have been sticking your nose in plenty of places where it is not wanted. And not in a strictly legal manner either, as tonight's raid on my files proves. I assume you were behind the break-in at Lenger's premises just after New Year as well?

'Lenger?' Schenke was caught off guard and exchanged a brief look with Liebwitz.

'Don't play the innocent,' said Pieper. 'I know it was you. Why else would you come to the clinic to confront me?' A brief look of doubt flitted across his face. 'If not you then who, eh?' He turned to Huber. 'I think we'll go with our initial plan. I don't fancy the prospect of taking the bodies to the car. Let's have them shot here. Mistaken for common burglars. A tragic accident and all that. Do it—'

Schenke's head snapped towards Liebwitz. 'Now!'

Liebwitz lurched upwards at the same time as Huber's pistol rose to take aim across the room. The Gestapo man's right arm whipped back and then forwards and his knife glimmered as it spun the length of the room. Huber's eyes widened in surprise, and he snatched a shot just before the point of the knife struck him squarely on the cheek. The narrow point tore into his flesh, and the impact jerked his head to the side. Splinters burst from the polished surface of the desk before the window pane behind it shattered.

The explosive report of the pistol filled the room and made Schenke's ears ring as he threw himself at Pieper. The director was crouched over and had no time to react as Schenke spun him round to face Huber and pinned his arms behind his back. His henchman had recovered his wits with alarming speed, and plucked the knife from his cheek with a howl of rage and pain, firing wildly at Liebwitz at the same time. The latter threw himself behind the desk as bullets smashed into the wooden panels and blew out more of the window panes. Freezing air swept into the room, swirling the acrid smoke hanging around the muzzle of the pistol.

'Stop!' Pieper shouted. 'Before you hit me, you damned fool!'

Huber responded to the order by turning his weapon

towards the director and Schenke, clasping his other hand to his cheek to try and stem the flow of blood.

Pieper's eyes stretched wide with fear. 'What are you doing?'

'Shut your mouth!' Huber barked. 'Let him go, Inspector. Do it or I'll shoot.'

'You'll hit me!' Pieper cried.

Schenke kept a tight hold of the director's arms and hunched his head down behind the other man's shoulders as he called out. 'Liebwitz, how many shots fired?'

'Six, sir. Two rounds left.'

'Two is all I need . . .' Huber advanced across the room.

At that moment, they heard the sound of shouts approaching the office and the clatter of boots on the staircase. Huber froze, a hunted look on his bloodied face. A second later, the door swung open and Hauser entered, pistol in hand. Behind him Schenke could see several uniformed police in greatcoats, weapons drawn.

Huber swung round, his own weapon levelled at the sergeant.

'Drop it,' Hauser ordered calmly. 'On the floor now, or I'll drill you through the head.'

Huber was still for a beat before he lowered his weapon and bent to place it on the ground. Schenke released his grip and thrust the director away from him, then turned towards the desk.

'Liebwitz? Are you all right?'

The Scharführer's head rose from the far side of the desk, and he stood up brushing the splinters from the lapels of his leather coat. 'No injuries, sir.'

'Glad to hear it.'

Liebwitz retrieved his knife as Hauser led the police squad

into the room. Picking up the handle, he looked at the blood on the blade with distaste, then bent and wiped it on the shoulder of Huber's jacket.

Schenke took a deep breath to calm himself before he spoke. 'Sergeant Hauser, arrest these men. The charge is murder.'

Chapter Twenty-Five

As he stood outside the front of the Schiller clinic, Hauser shook his head. 'You are joking?'

'Just following protocol, Sergeant.' Hauptmann Böeliche of the Potsdam station raised his chin before he continued. 'And it is the custom for a subordinate to acknowledge my rank, even if the subordinate concerned is a high and mighty member of the Kripo.'

Böeliche was a short, corpulent man in his fifties who was made more corpulent by the padded coat he wore. The collar was lined with fur, which emphasised the roundness of his face. He turned to the men guarding Pieper and Huber. The latter had a dressing over the wound in his cheek, and was glowering at Liebwitz as he stood shivering in the snow. 'Get them into the truck and take them back to the station. Put them in one of the cells until further orders.'

The uniformed policemen led the prisoners to the covered lorry and heaved them up onto the bed of the vehicle. The pale light of dawn lent the snow outside the clinic a cold blue hue. The crisp air was filled with swirls of exhaust from the running engines and the steamy breath of the pinched-faced officers crowded around the car and two lorries from the Potsdam station. A couple of the clinic staff stood in the porch watching proceedings with confused expressions. There were other faces behind the windows as several curious inmates stared down from their rooms.

Schenke looked on with frustration and not a little disgust. Böeliche was a petty-minded glory-hunter, a not uncommon quality in those middle-ranking officers of the uniformed police who had long since been passed over for promotion. It would be best to humour him and coax him into changing his mind.

He stepped in front of Hauser. 'Those two are key suspects in a Kripo investigation. They should be coming back to Pankow with us for questioning. I appreciate that the arrest was made on your patch with the help of you and your men, and I can assure you that I will be expressing my gratitude for your quick action when I report to my superiors. Now, if you could transfer them into our custody . . .'

Böeliche's expression was smug. 'I'd be delighted to, the moment I receive the correct paperwork through official channels. Until then, I will be conducting my own investigation into any crimes they may have committed, and if they are convicted, I will be sure to mention the small part you and your colleagues played in their apprehension. In the meantime, feel free to apply to have the prisoners transferred to your precinct.'

Schenke bit back on his anger and tried again. 'Look here, sir. We have already been gathering evidence on these men, and we're well on the road to establishing their guilt in respect of the murder of several children.'

'Then perhaps you'd be so kind as to send me the relevant

files to assist my interrogation of the suspects.'

'I can't do that, sir. They belong to the Kripo. You'd have to ask my superiors for access to the evidence.'

Böeliche shrugged. 'We seem to be at an impasse, Inspector. If only this had happened within your own jurisdiction, you'd be home and dry. As it is, it happened in mine, and I don't take kindly to criminal investigators from Berlin sticking their noses into my patch without having the courtesy of announcing their intentions to me first.'

'We only intended to question the director, sir. I had no idea things would lead to this. But it is vital that we take the prisoners back to Pankow to interrogate them there before they have a chance to fix their stories and try to escape justice. There's also the danger that there are others involved, and if we don't get their names from Pieper and Huber as soon as possible, they might get wind of the arrests and destroy evidence and go into hiding.'

Böeliche prodded a finger against Schenke's chest. 'Then I suggest you go back to Berlin and get started on the transfer papers.'

Schenke felt a powerful urge to punch the man in the face. 'I hope your actions don't compromise our work, sir. I doubt my superiors in Berlin would look favourably on anyone who hampered a murder investigation.'

'Save your threats, Inspector. I have my own connections in the party. Men who would bat aside a Kripo inspector with as little concern as swatting a fly. There's no purpose in prolonging this exchange of views. Do you wish to have one of my men drive you and your colleagues back to Pankow, or will you make your own arrangements?'

The thought of being beholden to this petty-minded

provincial policeman grated on Schenke's nerves, but it would be quicker to accept his offer than to call Pankow and have a car sent to fetch them. Time was precious, and he wanted to secure the prisoners as swiftly as possible.

'Well?' Böeliche goaded him.

'We'll take one of your cars.'

The Hauptmann looked sternly at Schenke but did not say anything. He did not have to.

Schenke gritted his teeth. 'I would be grateful if you would provide a car for us to return to Berlin, sir.'

'That's better.' Böeliche shouted an order to a man standing beside a battered-looking Opel, then tapped a finger to the brim of his cap in farewell. 'Good day, Inspector.'

He made his way to the other car, where one of his men opened the rear door for him. The remaining uniformed policemen climbed aboard the lorry, and when the last had settled on his bench, there was a loud slap on the back of the cab and the vehicle lurched into motion, heading for the gate. Böeliche's car followed.

Schenke and Hauser stared after them for a moment before Schenke gestured to his comrades.

'Wait for me in the car.'

'Where are you going, sir?' asked Hauser.

'To put a call through to Kleist. Hopefully I can persuade him to get the ball rolling on the transfer documents while we're driving back.'

As the car pulled out onto the road towards Potsdam, Schenke related to Hauser what had happened after they'd parted the previous night. As he concluded, the car was passing the inn, and all three passengers glanced at the snow-covered building.

'What about Wilke?' asked Liebwitz.

'I'll issue orders for him to be arrested and brought in for questioning,' Schenke replied. 'But we'll send someone from the section to do the job and make sure he's taken straight to Pankow before Böeliche gets wind of it and causes us any more problems. That's assuming Wilke hasn't panicked and gone into hiding.'

'Bloody Böeliche,' Hauser growled. 'Took some persuading before that bastard even agreed to bring his men to the clinic. I had to tell him that he might do well out of it if he helped bring the killers to justice. Didn't take much to start him thinking about his name in the Berlin newspapers. Sorry that didn't work out so well for us back there, sir. Böeliche's out for himself.'

Schenke saw the driver nod his head in silent agreement with the sergeant's assessment of the Potsdam officer.

'I didn't get the sense that Wilke was involved with the killings,' Hauser continued.

'Maybe not, but he's likely to have information that may help us if we speak to him again.' Schenke leaned back into the rear seat and yawned widely, sucking in cold air that made him cough. 'We need more information. I fear there's more behind these killings than I thought. The link to Schmesler concerns me . . . And there's the matter of Lenger.' He turned to Liebwitz. 'You remember? Pieper spoke about a break-in at Lenger's surgery. Lenger mentioned it to me and Hauser when we went to see him.'

'Pieper seemed to think the police might have been involved.' Liebwitz shook his head. 'I don't see why. The Kripo investigates crimes. We don't commit them.'

Hauser turned and caught his superior's eye, then looked at

the scharführer. 'That's right, lad. We never do that sort of thing, do we?'

Schenke was more taken with Liebwitz's choice of pronoun, and was once again gratified that the former Gestapo man now saw himself as belonging to the Kripo. It would be good not to have to worry about his new colleague's loyalties.

'The question is, who broke into Lenger's place?'

Hauser sucked in a breath. 'I'm not sure I really want to know the answer to that.'

'Why not?' asked Liebwitz.

'Dear God, were you born yesterday? No, don't even think about answering that. Listen, who do you think was responsible for abducting the inspector the other night?'

'I couldn't say for certain.'

'Take a guess.'

'Well, given that they warned him off the Schmesler case, and given what Pieper said about the break-in at Dr Lenger's surgery, it is possible that it was the same men.'

'And?' Hauser prompted wearily.

'If they are the same men, it is possible they were working for Heydrich, since he issued a similar warning to the inspector. SS most likely. Or SD.'

'Either way, not people we want to tangle with.'

Schenke noticed that the driver had glanced back quickly at the mention of the head of the Reich Security Main Office. He leaned forward and spoke quietly in the man's ear. 'Just concentrate on driving. You'll forget everything you've heard since we left the clinic if you know what's good for you. Understand?'

'Yes, sir.' The policeman nodded.

'Good.' Schenke sat back and addressed his colleagues.

'Best we say nothing more for now. I'm tired. We all are. Let's try and get some rest before we reach Pankow.'

He worked himself into the corner by the door, pulled the brim of his hat down and closed his eyes, though he doubted he would sleep given the jolting of the old car's suspension and his memories of the crash the previous night. He tried to force himself to think about sitting by a fire with his head in Karin's lap, but after a while he realised he was thinking about Ruth again. Whatever the connection might be between Schmesler's death and those of the children, it made the situation more dangerous for anyone trying to uncover the truth. He was afraid for Ruth, and hoped that he might yet persuade her to abandon pursuit of whoever had murdered her family friend.

It was late in the morning when they climbed stiffly out of the car outside the main entrance to the Pankow precinct. The sleepless night and the drama of the encounter with Huber and Pieper had left Schenke feeling drained, despite the fitful snatches of sleep he had eventually managed on the journey from the clinic. However, he could not permit himself to rest until the transfer of custody had been arranged.

As he led the way into the office, Frieda Echs hurried across to him with an anxious expression. 'Thank God you're back, sir.'

'What's happened?'

'Plenty. We've had several lawyers demanding to have their clients released from custody. Seems that half those bastards from the crime rings we've locked up have got a bent lawyer in their pocket ready to take us to task. It's not just lawyers. I had a call from a Gauleiter demanding to know why one of his friends in the party had been arrested. I said he'd have to wait until you returned so you could call him to explain.'

'Oh, thanks . . .'

'Goes with the rank, sir.'

'Anything else I should know about?'

She nodded. 'Kleist has the transfer orders ready.'

'He hasn't put the call through?' Schenke felt a flush of irritation at the delay. He had hoped that Huber and Pieper were already on their way from Potsdam. 'Shit . . .'

'There's one other thing, sir. Karin Canaris has called three times this morning to ask why you didn't call her last night.'

'What did you tell her?'

'I said you had left the office on official business.'

Schenke frowned. He felt guilty over causing Karin such concern. That was on top of the guilt he felt for not telling her about the shoot-out in the street.

'Some coffee for you and the others, sir?'

'You read our minds.' Hauser smiled.

'That's not much of a challenge, Sergeant,' Frieda replied. She glanced to Liebwitz, who gave a curt nod.

Schenke went to his desk, picked up the phone and dialled the number of his flat. The second tone had barely sounded before Karin answered. 'Horst?'

'Yes.'

'Thank God! Are you all right?'

'I'm fine. We got caught in the blizzard on the way back from Potsdam yesterday. That's why I couldn't get home.'

'Potsdam?'

'It's a long story. I'll tell you all about it later.'

'What happened?'

'Listen, Karin. I can't speak now. There's something I must do. I just needed you to know that I'm safe.'

'Will you be back tonight?'

'I . . . I hope so.'

'Horst—'

'Look, I have to go.'

'You can't treat me like this.'

'Karin, I must go.' He hung up, fearful that the call had made more trouble between them than it had resolved. He sighed in frustration as he returned to the main office.

'What now? Hauser asked as he took off his hat, opened his coat and warmed himself at the stove.

'I'll see Kleist and get our suspects sent over from Potsdam. I want you and Liebwitz to put in some calls and see what you can find out about the Committee for the Scientific Registering of . . .' He paused as he tried to recall the rest of the lengthy title.

'Serious Hereditary and Congenital Illnesses, sir,' said Liebwitz.

'Just so. Find out what you can, and see if there is any link to Schmesler and Lenger as well as our friends at the clinic.'

'Friends?'

'Just do it, Scharführer.'

'Yes, sir.'

As Schenke turned to leave the office, Echs returned with three steaming mugs on a round tray.

'Going already, sir?'

'I'll be back in a few minutes. Keep it hot for me.'

He made his way through the building to Kleist's office, exchanging an informal salute with the precinct commander's aide. 'I have a prisoner transfer authorisation to collect.'

'Yes, sir. The Oberst left it with me before he went to his meeting.' The aide reached for a form and handed it over. Schenke blinked the tiredness from his aching eyes and read through it quickly to ensure it was in order, nodding with satisfaction when he saw Kleist's spidery signature at the bottom of the second page. 'Good. I need to use your telephone.'

The aide pushed it across the desk towards him and Schenke dialled the switchboard to be put through to the Potsdam police. There was a brief delay on the crackling connection before it clicked.

'Potsdam police station, front desk.'

'This is Criminal Inspector Schenke at Pankow. I have an order signed by Oberst Kleist for the transfer of two men being held in your cells. You can pick up the papers when you deliver the prisoners.'

'Yes, sir. The names of the men?'

'Huber and Pieper.'

There was a pause before the man at the other end repeated, 'Huber and Pieper?'

Schenke felt an ominous sense of anticipation. 'So?'

'Well, sir, they were released over an hour ago.'

Schenke's hand closed tightly round the receiver as he pressed it to his ear. 'What? Who the hell was responsible for that? Böeliche?'

'No, sir. The order came from the Reich Security Main Office.'

A chill gripped the back of Schenke's neck. 'Under whose name?'

'SS Gruppenführer Heydrich, sir . . .'

265

Chapter Twenty-Six

Hauser lowered his head into his hands. 'Heydrich . . . We're slipping into deep water, sir. If that bastard's involved with whatever is going on with the kids and Schmesler, we have to get our noses out of it or he'll have our balls for paperweights. What the fuck are we going to do?'

Schenke winced at the image and leaned back in his chair as he considered their predicament. 'Right now, I don't know. We'll have to play it very carefully. No one has warned us off the investigation into the murder of the kids.'

'Not yet. But my gut tells me they will, and soon.'

'Then we'll deal with that when the moment comes. Until then, we steer clear of anything to do with Schmesler's death and concentrate on what's been going on at the clinic. With Huber and Pieper off the scene, we'll have to continue our enquiries elsewhere. From what Pieper said, it's clear that Lenger is involved. We'll need to speak to him again.' Schenke raised a hand to stifle a yawn before he continued. 'There's someone else we must question too.'

'You mean Widmann?'

'Yes. I want to know why his name was in Pieper's files. If

he's involved in the murders, this whole thing is getting too close to home for comfort. If we turn the light on one of our own forensic people, we're going to cause bad feeling in the Kripo ranks. Doesn't matter whether he's guilty of anything or not. That's how it goes. So we need to proceed carefully with Widmann. Especially if there is so much as a hint that we're overlapping with anything Heydrich's lads are involved with.'

'Amen,' Hauser agreed. 'What's the first step?'

'I want you to get to work with Liebwitz on looking into that committee. Use your sources in other precincts and departments to see what you can find out, but be discreet . . . You'd better handle the calls, rather than Liebwitz. Let me know what you've got when I get back.'

'Back?'

'There's someone I need to speak to.' Schenke got up and made for the door. As he passed Echs's desk, she glanced up and gave him a reproachful look.

'No need to ask. I already called Karin.'

'Very wise, sir. She sounds like a nice girl.' There was a slight mothering tone to his subordinate's voice. 'You don't get to meet many nice young women in our line of work.'

'I've met you,' Schenke replied with a slight grin.

He refastened his coat before he nodded a farewell and strode out of the office. He signed out an unmarked car and left the precinct, glancing in the mirrors to make sure he was not being followed by any of the handful of vehicles on the road. To be certain, he made a handful of sharp turns before returning to his original route. As yet he had no clear idea of who it was that might be following him, but the possibility that he could be tailed frightened him. Particularly in view of his destination.

He had been warned off the Schmesler case, but he needed to know if Brigitte Schmesler had any idea why her husband's name had come up in the files at the Schiller clinic. It was clear now that there was a connection, but quite how far Schmesler was complicit in the murder of the children was impossible to determine at the moment. There was also the question of why Heydrich's men were determined to prevent a thorough investigation into Schmesler's death. And why had his office authorised the release of Huber and Pieper? Heydrich had a hand in both cases, and that strongly suggested that the two cases were in fact one. If so, Schenke and his colleagues were in danger if they persisted with the hunt for the murderers of Greta Scholtz and the other children.

There was another purpose to his visit to the Schmesler residence. Ruth needed to be warned to abandon her enquiries into the murder and go into hiding until the situation became less dangerous. As for Schmesler, it seemed to Schenke that the good doctor might not be so good after all. He had been involved with the men who had killed the children in some manner. It was possible that he had been killed by someone who thought he knew enough to make him a threat. Someone who might be working for Heydrich. If that was so, there was a chance that the regime was trying to cover something up. Was an influential party member involved in some kind of child-abuse? Schenke wondered. Was that the reason why he had been abducted and warned to leave any inquiry into the cause of Schmesler's death well alone? At the same time, Heydrich's order to release Pieper and Huber was obviously intended to prevent them being questioned by the Kripo. What was it he did not want those two to divulge?

* * *

Schenke parked two streets away from the Schmeslers' house and pulled up his collar as he strode to the corner. He paused and raised his wrist, making a show of winding his watch as he scanned both sides of the street close to the house. As he had anticipated, the property was under observation. A black car was parked twenty metres from the house, behind a van. Even though the rear window was fogged by condensation, he could make out the shapes of the two men sitting inside.

He lowered his arm, looked both ways as if searching for someone, then turned and retraced his steps as far as the entrance of the service alley that ran behind the houses. High walls punctuated by gates ran the length of the alley, and he hurried along until he found the rear access to the Schmesler house. He glanced about him quickly, but there was no one in sight, so he slipped the latch of the gate and entered the yard. Some sheds and a garage stood to his right, while opposite, across the cobbled ground, were two coal bunkers, nearly empty, and some bins and small churns. A short flight of steps led up to a back door, and a narrow set descended to what was presumably a cellar.

Schenke climbed the steps to the rear door and pulled the brass knob at the side. A bell jangled inside the house. He waited a few seconds before he pulled the knob again, twice this time. A moment later there was a rattle as a bolt was slid back, and the door eased open fractionally until a security chain brought it to a halt. A woman's face appeared in the gap, looking at him suspiciously, and it took Schenke a moment to realise it was Brigitte Schmesler. Her hair was loose and streaked with grey and her face looked worn and lined.

'I didn't expect to see you again, Inspector. Haven't you given up trying to find out who killed my husband?'

'Let me in, please. I need to speak to you.'

She did not move, but stared back with her lips pressed in a thin, sour expression.

'It's urgent,' Schenke insisted.

Maybe it was something in his tone, or perhaps she had simply taken a measure of satisfaction at keeping him standing outside, but she eased the door to and slid the chain off before opening it and nodding at him to enter. As he closed the door behind him and slid the bolt back into place, he saw that they were standing in a small pantry with an opening leading into the kitchen. Shelves meagrely stocked with tins, jars, bottles and wooden boxes of root vegetables lined one wall. The shortages caused by the war and the harsh winter were starting to affect the households of even the better-off.

'This way,' Brigitte muttered.

As she led him into the kitchen, the warmth from the heavy iron cooker wrapped around him.

'Why are you here?' she demanded. 'Have you discovered something?'

'Yes.' Schenke removed his hat as he considered what he should tell her. 'First, I need to apologise.'

'Yes, I think you do.'

'That day my colleagues and I came round, we found evidence to suggest that your husband did not commit suicide.'

'Suggest? I think it was rather more conclusive than that.'

He nodded. 'It looked like he was shot at close range by a third party. That's what I told my superior when I reported our findings in order to get a fresh investigation started. Instead I was told there would be no investigation and the case was closed. The suicide verdict would stand. When I called to let you know, I did not want to give you false hope that there would be any further investigation. I'm sorry if I seemed brusque.'

'And yet you continued to act on your suspicions. By proxy. You chose to involve a vulnerable young woman to do your work for you.'

Schenke's guilt was pricked. 'Ruth . . . What has she told you?'

'That she was determined to do what she could to discover who was responsible for murdering my husband, given that the police refused to.' Brigitte gave a slight smile as she continued in a fond tone. 'She's a good girl, that one. And brave.' She looked up sharply. 'Which is more than can be said for some.'

Schenke resisted the temptation to defend himself. There was no time to be wasted. 'I need to ask you some questions about a related matter.'

'Why should I help you with that?'

'Because it has something to do with your husband's death, I'm certain of it.' He briefly explained about the fate of the children and the files he and Liebwitz had discovered at the clinic. 'Do you know if your husband knew Dr Pieper?'

'Pieper? Yes, I recall him mentioning the name. I believe they got to know each other through the party. Manfred was of the opinion that Pieper's political fervour was rather more evident than his medical competence. As you can imagine, they never became friends.'

'I see . . . Did your husband ever mention the Schiller clinic?'

She thought for a moment, then shook her head.

'What about a man named Huber?'

'No.'

'Widmann?'

She stirred. 'A fat man with a rather grim face? I know him. I've seen him a couple of times. He was here yesterday.'

'Yesterday?' Schenke started. 'What for?'

'He came with two SS men. He said some papers had been missed when they first came to collect Manfred's files after his death. They were only in his study for a short time, but they left it in a mess and damaged some of the furniture. They didn't take anything, as far as I could see. Just left without a word. No apologies. No offer to repair the damage. Thugs . . .'

Schenke tried to recall the details of the study when he had been there. There had been no sign of any files or documents. Perhaps they had been hidden. He fixed his gaze on Brigitte again. 'You mentioned you had seen Widmann more than once.'

'That's right. He came to the house a month or so before . . . before that night. He told Manfred he needed to speak to him. They were in his study for some hours before Widmann left.'

'Did your husband give you any idea why Widmann had visited the house?'

'No. I told you before, he didn't tell me much about his work. But I recall that Widmann sounded worried as he stood in the hall with my husband. Something about the test not working and they'd have to use another facility. Manfred said he would deal with it.' She paused and shook her head. 'That was the gist of it. As much as I remember.'

'Are you certain there's nothing more?'

'I'm sorry, that's all.'

Schenke tried to think how that piece of information might

fit in with what he already knew. But his tired mind was struggling. 'Might I have a glass of water?'

'I suppose so. There are glasses in the cupboard behind you.'

'Thanks.' He opened the door to a large cupboard. The higher shelf was stacked with plates, with plain glasses to one side. The bottom shelf was bare except for a small dish with a handful of tiny grey pellets in it. He paused as he caught a faint whiff of something acrid, and recoiled slightly before he took a glass and went to the kitchen sink.

'It's because of the rats,' said Brigitte.

'What?'

'In the cupboard. I saw your reaction,' she explained. 'Not the nicest of smells, but it gets the job done. Can't let the vermin take over the place.'

'Ah, I see.' Schenke filled the glass and drank as he gathered his thoughts. He drained it and set it down. 'You still have no idea where your husband was working, or who he was working for?'

'Oh, I know something about that now, I think. Ruth told me.'

Schenke tensed. 'How did she find out?'

'She was outside when Widmann and his thugs left the house. She followed them back to their car at a distance and overheard Widmann give the order to search Manfred's office at the Chancellery.'

He felt his heart quicken. 'The Chancellery? She was certain about that?'

'Yes. Quite certain.'

'Dear God . . .' He fought to suppress his alarm over the full significance of the information. Manfred Schmesler's office was in the very heart of government. 'Where is Ruth now? I must speak to her.'

'I . . . I don't know.' Brigitte worked her hands together. 'I've told you all I know. I think it's time for you to go. Leave me in peace.'

'Hear me out first,' Schenke said firmly, taking a step towards her before he continued. 'Ruth is in danger. We all are. There are people out there who are prepared to kill to hide their secrets. They don't care that I am a police officer; they are not afraid to murder me, or my colleagues. At least we have a fighting chance to drop the matter and save ourselves. Ruth doesn't. She's a Jew. The party would kill her in a heartbeat if they thought she might embarrass them. I have to warn her. Tell her to go into hiding and stay there until I am certain it is safe for her to emerge. I know she comes to see you often. I know your family and hers were good friends before the party seized power. She is close to you and you care for her.' He leaned forward earnestly. 'For her sake, I beg you to pass on my warning.'

'It seems I am not the only one who cares for her.'

Schenke blushed. His exhaustion had got the better of him and he had spoken with more feeling than he had intended. He felt a realisation stirring within him. Yes, he did care about Ruth. More deeply than he had previously allowed himself to think. That was a dangerous thing to admit to himself. Dangerous to him and certainly dangerous to her. Then a rush of guilt swept over him as he remembered Karin. He loved her, he reminded himself. He had proposed marriage to her. And yet there was this well of emotion for Ruth, a desire to protect her from the dangers of the world. Perhaps there was nothing more to it than that, he tried to reassure himself. After all, it was the moral thing to do. A man should stand up and protect the vulnerable.

Brigitte was reading his expression closely and could not help smiling. 'Ruth was right about you, Inspector. You are a good man. I can see you care for her, and you are close to her too. Closer than you admit.' She stepped towards the door that led into the rest of the house. 'It's all right. You're safe and can come out.'

A figure moved out of the shadows in the hall and into the glow of the kitchen light. Her slight frame was wrapped in a thick cardigan and a long woollen skirt. Her dark hair had been cut into a short bob.

'Hello, Horst.' Ruth smiled nervously.

'I take it you overheard every word.'

'Yes, every word.' Her smile was warmer now.

He returned it, relieved to see her again and that she was safe for the moment. He felt an urge to reach out and embrace her, and was only able restrain himself with difficulty. It would be dangerous for both of them to go down that path . . . So very dangerous.

Chapter Twenty-Seven

For a moment everyone was still, and then Schenke approached Ruth and took her hand. 'Thank God you are safe.'

He released her quickly before taking a step back and sitting on the edge of the scarred wooden table in the centre of the room. He forced himself to concentrate on the wider situation the three of them were caught within.

'It isn't safe for you to be here,' he said. 'The house is being watched.'

'I know. The car down the street. It's been there the last few days. Arrives at dawn and leaves at six in the evening, when another takes its place. Two men. If Brigitte leaves, one of them shadows her. If anyone comes to visit, one of them follows when they leave to find out who they are.' Ruth smiled. 'I've watched them long enough to know the routine.'

'Who knows you are here?'

'Just me,' Brigitte answered.

'What about your mother?' Schenke recalled the busybody from the time he had come to examine the crime scene. She struck him as the kind to confide big secrets to her close circle of friends.

'She doesn't know,' Brigitte reassured him.

'Any servants?'

'Not since before Christmas. Our maid contracted tuberculosis and is in hospital. It'll be a while before she returns to her duties. Ruth is safe here, I assure you. Only the two of us know she is sheltering in my home.'

'Good.' He thought a moment. 'Is there a hiding place? Where were you when Widmann called?'

'In the cellar. There's a recess behind one of the cupboards. I've piled spare blankets there and placed some clothes chests at the front, and there's just enough space for me to slip into the gap and lie still in an emergency.'

Schenke shook his head. 'If it came to a thorough search, you'd be found without too much trouble. If you were caught here, you'd be sent to a camp the moment they discovered you were Jewish. And you, Brigitte, they'd punish you for sheltering a Jew.'

And more, if they ever discovered who your father was, thought Schenke.

'I know the risks I am taking,' Brigitte replied defiantly. 'Ruth is like a daughter to me. I could not imagine refusing to shelter her and share my food with her. Now we must trust that you will do your best to protect her.'

'Your secret is safe with me.'

'We know,' said Ruth.

Schenke did not want to expose himself to any further revelation of his feelings and swiftly changed the subject. 'Are you certain about what you overheard Widmann say about the Chancellery?'

'I am sure of it. I was no further from him than I am you as I passed by. I heard his words clearly.'

'Then Schmesler was working directly for the party,' he mused. He turned to Brigitte. 'Have you ever heard of the Reich Committee for the Scientific Registering of Serious Hereditary and Congenital Illnesses?'

'That's a mouthful,' she said.

'Did Manfred ever mention the committee, or anything with a similar title?'

'No . . . I think I'd remember. What's it got to do with him?'

'It might have been who he was working for. What about Widmann? Did your husband ever speak about him before or after the visit to your house?'

'I asked him about Widmann afterwards, but Manfred said it was a confidential matter and he could not discuss it. They did not seem to be on friendly terms. I get the impression you know Widmann already.'

Schenke nodded. 'He's one of us. I mean, he's part of the criminal investigation department.'

'A policeman?' Ruth queried.

'More of a scientist really. He's on the staff at the Kripo's criminal research institute. He specialises in forensic chemistry.'

'Then what was he doing here?' Brigitte intervened. 'That's nothing to do with Manfred's area of expertise. Nothing at all.'

'Well, it doesn't sound like it was a social call. They must have been working on something together . . . maybe something connected with what was going on at the Schiller clinic.'

As he considered the possibilities, a dark thought occurred to him. There was something in the lengthy title of the Reich committee that suggested a more sinister purpose than simply registering birth defects. The party's doctrine was based on the idea of the superiority of the German race, and Schenke had occasionally heard radio programmes and read newspaper articles about the desirability of breeding out any weaknesses in the German people in order to produce better stock. What if some party members with medical backgrounds had decided to take the lead in the party's ambitions? What if they had created a small, secret network of like-minded people who were sending children to the clinic for Pieper to dispose of them? Of course the dirty work would be carried out by Huber, no stranger to killing and happy to profit from the personal effects of those he got rid of . . . As it all fell into place Schenke admitted to himself that he had been avoiding his suspicions. The horrific nature of the scheme had prevented him from even considering it possible before now.

'What's the matter?' asked Ruth, breaking into his thoughts. 'Your expression's worrying me. What is it?'

How could he tell them what he was thinking? That Manfred Schmesler was involved in a ring of ideologically driven child-murderers? This was not the kindly doctor Ruth regarded as a family friend. More sickening still was the prospect that Brigitte had unknowingly been married to a monster. Perhaps, though, she had suspected something. Enough not to want to know more, and to save her conscience from recognising the truth of her husband's activities. She would not be the first spouse to try to build a protective wall of ignorance around her in order to make it possible to remain with the person she loved. At the moment, though, Schenke had no absolute proof of his suspicions, and it would do more harm than good to voice them.

'I was trying to work out why Manfred was killed,' he said. 'It's the question we haven't come close to answering. I am certain it was because he knew something. Those men who took me would have done for me too if they had thought I'd shared what he knew. Pieper wanted me dead for the same reason.'

'Do you think Manfred had uncovered what was going on?' Brigitte asked.

The question was one step away from the darker vision that had formed in Schenke's mind, and he offered a safe response. 'It's possible. Maybe he found out something that Heydrich wanted to keep secret, and that's why he had to be silenced. That's why my superiors were ordered to make sure his death was put down to suicide. That's why Heydrich threatened me, and then had me abducted, questioned and intimidated.'

Ruth frowned. 'If Heydrich was willing to kill Manfred, surely he wouldn't have baulked at silencing you the same way. Why take the risk of letting you live?'

'I don't know . . . I've a feeling that he has a measure of respect for me.'

'Do you really think so?'

'It felt that way when I was summoned to his office to make a report at the end of last year.' Schenke recalled the encounter with Heydrich, and all he knew about the man. Heydrich had seemed impressed with him when they had met, but at the same time his reputation for iron-hearted ruthlessness made it seem unlikely that he would spare someone if there was any chance of that compromising something he regarded as a higher priority.

'I don't know.' He ran a hand through his hair. His eyelids

felt heavy and his thoughts were clouded by tiredness. He needed rest desperately. 'There are too many fragments I haven't been able to piece together yet. I need time to think.' He paused and fixed his attention on Ruth. 'You can't stay here. It's not safe.'

'We've had no trouble so far,' Brigitte countered. 'Ruth keeps out of sight during the day when she is not working or trying to help you find Manfred's killer, and very few people call at the door.'

'Widmann was here. What happens if he comes back and sees her in the window, or she makes a noise while he and his men are in the house? The slightest mistake and she could be discovered, and then no one would be able to save either of you.'

'Where else can the girl go?' Brigitte demanded. 'Berlin is a cold and friendless place for her people. They are half starved, denied coal, and only get by thanks to what they can find on the black market. And if they are caught infringing any of the Nazis' regulations, they are arrested and sent east to God knows what fate. I've heard rumours of how they are being treated in Poland that would make your hair stand on end, Inspector. I'm sure you have heard similar tales. I was raised to show compassion for the weak and vulnerable, and I will not betray those values. I know that if Manfred was alive, he would say the same thing. He would welcome Ruth into our home and offer her shelter.'

'Even though he was a member of the SS?' said Schenke.

'He joined the SS because his career depended on it. Just like almost every other doctor in Germany. In his heart he knew right from wrong. He only wanted the best for his country and the people around him. Including Ruth and her family.' She clutched a hand to her breast. 'I know this as surely as I breathe.'

Schenke felt a sick sensation in the pit of his stomach at the way in which so many of his fellow Germans dared not admit to the evils that were being carried out in their name, for fear of punishment or unbearable remorse. They had become accustomed to living with parallel moral codes. He was no better in many respects, no matter how he tried to tell himself that he had greater self-awareness than most other people. In some ways that made him feel worse, and there were times when he wished he could surrender to the ideology of the party and believe in it unquestioningly in order to achieve some peace of mind and drive away the doubt and guilt that preyed on his heart and mind.

'My Manfred was a good man, and I am honouring his memory by taking care of Ruth.' Brigitte smiled at the younger woman. 'You can stay here as long as you like.'

Ruth hugged her. 'You are so kind to me.' Then she drew back. 'Even so, Horst is right about the danger we face. I can't put you at risk. You have already lost so much recently. I'll need to find another place if those men in the car continue to keep watch on the house.'

Brigitte drew a breath to challenge her, but Ruth raised her hand. 'My mind is made up. I will always be grateful to you, and I may need to come back here from time to time. But only if I think there is little chance of putting you at risk.'

'As you wish, my girl. But do whatever you must to survive.'

She nodded with determination. 'I will outlive the Führer and his party and see better days in Germany again. However long that may take. This can't last for ever. Nothing does.'

Schenke felt moved by her strength of will. At the same

time, he found it hard to believe that a regime that had its people in such a stranglehold might not last for longer than she hoped. The prospect added to his burden of his weariness as he reached for his hat.

'Very well. I've said my piece. I must go.'

Brigitte caught his hand. 'What about my husband's murderer? You'll tell me if you find out anything, won't you?' she pleaded. 'If there's any news.'

'I'll do what I can,' he replied. She might not like to know what he'd discovered if his suspicions about her husband were proven correct. Perhaps it was better that some truths were not exposed. He would not be thanked by either of these women if it turned out that the doctor was involved in the killing of children. It was difficult to reconcile Schmesler being a good husband to Brigitte and a loyal friend to Ruth and her family while at the same time believing it was justifiable to build the future of Germany on the graves of children whose only fault was to be born into bodies that did not conform to the absolute requirements of the party.

He nodded a farewell and turned to leave the kitchen. As he opened the back door, he heard footsteps and turned to see Ruth hurrying after him. She took his hand and squeezed it. 'Stay safe, Horst.'

'You too.'

There was a moment's stillness, and then he leaned to kiss her on the forehead before tearing himself away so that he would not give in to further temptation.

He closed the door behind him before hurrying down the steps and out of the yard into the service alley. The light was already fading, and he went cautiously, looking for any sign of the men watching the house. It was bitterly cold. Too cold for anyone to be standing outside for any length of time. He was grateful that the severe winter had forced the men to stay in their car; in less extreme weather, they might have watched both the front and rear of the house.

Returning to the unmarked car, he started it up and drove back in the direction of the precinct. As he negotiated the traffic on the dusky streets, he thought back over his earlier deliberations about Schmesler and pondered how he was going to share them with Hauser and Liebwitz. They might dismiss his ideas as too far-fetched. Too dangerous. But what if they didn't? Then all three of them would be placing themselves in ever greater danger the closer they got to the heart of the crimes they were investigating.

When he reached the precinct, Schenke passed a black Mercedes parked beside the garages, its engine running. He returned his car to its parking space, handed the keys to the mechanic in the kiosk and signed the return sheet. There were shouts from the makeshift cells as some of the men brought in for questioning over the forgery case caught sight of him and voiced their anger. As he set off towards the rear entrance of the main building, two men in dark leather coats and hats climbed out of the Mercedes and moved to intercept him.

'Inspector Schenke?'

He stopped and turned towards them. 'Yes?'

They drew up an arm's length away on either side of him. They were tall men, powerfully built, and he felt the blood chill in his veins.

'What do you want?'

One of the men took out his Gestapo identity badge. 'You're to come with us.'

There was no request, no formal politeness, just the bold

assertion of authority that brooked no resistance of any kind.

'Where to?'

'Someone wants to speak to you.' The man pointed to the car. 'Get in.'

Chapter Twenty-Eight

'Where are we going?' Schenke asked as he sat in the back of the Mercedes between the two men. A third man was at the wheel, wearing the same dark coat. They could not have looked more like Gestapo henchmen if they'd tried, Schenke thought bitterly. As the car pulled away, he caught sight of Hauser emerging from the rear of the precinct building and looking around, a piece of paper in his hand. Then he was lost from sight as the Mercedes drove out of the yard and into the street.

'I said where are you taking me?' Schenke sat forward and tried to turn to face the man to his left, but he was immediately pushed back into his place.

'Sit still, sir,' the man to his right insisted. 'There's a good gentleman.'

Schenke made no further attempt to move as he spoke again. 'At least tell me who gave the order to arrest me.'

'I didn't say you were under arrest.'

'Then stop the car and let me out.'

'Can't do that, sir. We have our orders.'

'Whose orders?'

'You'll find out soon enough. Now do be quiet. I don't

286

want to have to hurt you just yet. That's our job for when the time comes.'

His matter-of-fact tone reminded Schenke of Liebwitz. It seemed that it was something instilled into the men of the Gestapo. There was a frightening detachment to the way he spoke, as if hurting people was a routine part of his day. It was enough to persuade Schenke to keep silent as he looked out of the window at the streets they were driving through.

As far as he could tell, they were heading south towards the centre of Berlin. It was likely that they were taking him to the Gestapo's headquarters on Prinz-Albrecht-Strasse, and he could not help dreading what awaited him there. It was no comfort to be told that he was not under arrest. It was just as likely that he would be held under the protective custody rule if they wished to keep him for any length of time. As fatalism took over, he was able to ease his fear to one side and clear his mind. There was little doubt the Gestapo were taking him in because it had something to do with either the Schmesler case or the child murders.

It was more likely to be the former, he reasoned. The warnings from Kleist, Heydrich and the men who had abducted him not to meddle in the suicide verdict had not been heeded as categorically as required; he had overstepped the mark and would have to answer for it. But answer to who? Müller, the head of the Gestapo? Or his superior, Heydrich? God forbid it went any higher than that. He had met Himmler only once, at a police officers' gathering in a beer cellar. Although the Reichsführer-SS had been jovial enough at the time, his manner had changed in an instant when a serving boy spilled some beer on his jacket. Schenke had never forgotten the murderous look in the man's eyes.

They entered Mitte and crossed a bridge over the Spree, and he realised that they were on Friedrichstrasse. A moment later, they turned right onto Unter den Linden, and he saw the dark mass of the Brandenburg Gate against the dying light of the sunset. As they approached the gate, the car slowed and the driver swung it round to pull up in front of the canopied entrance of the Adlon hotel. The man to Schenke's right opened the rear door and climbed out, beckoning to him.

'Let's go, Inspector.'

This was an unexpected turn of events, thought Schenke. He was convinced he'd be taken to Gestapo headquarters, rather than to the finest hotel in Berlin.

Once he had emerged from the car, the other man in the back joined them and took up his position at Schenke's side. The greatcoated doorman opened the glass-plated door for them. The panelled entrance had large radiators on either side, and the warm air wrapped around the three men as they made for the blacked-out doors leading into the lobby, where another doorman stood waiting. Here they were surrounded by light from the chandeliers hanging from the high ceilings. There were sounds of laughter and a hubbub of conversation from the scores of people sitting in the armchairs opposite the oak reception counter. Most of the men were in some kind of uniform, military or party, and there were several women with them, finely dressed.

The burly Gestapo man who had done the talking took Schenke's elbow and steered him towards the rear of the lobby, in the direction of the suite of rooms used for private parties and social events. They passed a few closed doors on either side, behind which Schenke could hear muffled voices. They stopped outside a pair of doors leading into one of the larger function rooms, and the Gestapo man glanced at him. 'Wait here.' He opened the door wide enough to slip inside and closed it behind him.

Schenke's weary mind was struggling to work out what was happening to him. To be taken by the Gestapo seldom betokened anything other than a sinister purpose, and yet here he was at the Adlon hotel. Despite the luxury of his surroundings, anxiety took hold of him once more.

The door opened and the Gestapo man came out and nodded to the next door along. 'In there.'

Schenke found himself in a service area for whatever function was taking place in the adjacent room. Tables along the far wall were laden with wine and spirit bottles, cigar boxes, and platters of cold meat, cheese and delicate-looking bread rolls. A table at the end was neatly piled with plates, cutlery and glasses in preparation for a small feast. Two white-coated stewards polishing items of cutlery paused to look round at the three men who had entered the room.

'Make yourself scarce,' the Gestapo man ordered. 'You'll be sent for when you're needed.'

The stewards hurried out. Now the only sounds were the voices from the party in the next room. Schenke fixed his eyes on the food and was aware of a gnawing hunger. He realised that he had not eaten since the previous day. Wandering over, he nodded at the nearest platters.

'Do you mind?'

The Gestapo heavy shrugged. 'Not in the least. Your funeral.'

Schenke took off his gloves and grabbed a roll and some slices of cold ham. He ate ravenously, not knowing when he might get the chance to eat again, let alone so well. Whoever the small feast was for was obviously influential enough not to be bothered by the rationing restrictions placed on ordinary people. One rule for them and another for us, Schenke reflected. As was always the case when there was no one to hold a regime to account.

Once he had finished his makeshift sandwich, he took an apple, crunching on it as he turned to his minders. 'I think it's time to tell me why I'm here and who gave the order.'

They regarded him impassively, and he felt his anger rising.

'Oh, come on! You've got me here. What harm is there in explaining why?'

When there was still no answer, he tossed the apple core onto the table and paced towards the doors to the next room. The nearer of the two Gestapo men hurried across to block him and pulled out a rubber truncheon.

'I wouldn't . . .'

Before the confrontation could go any further, the door handle turned with a soft click and Heydrich slipped into the room with a companion. Looking past them, Schenke caught a glimpse of a long dining table at which twenty or so men were sitting, soup bowls and glasses in front of them. One glanced up and met his gaze, the light from a chandelier glinting off the wire-framed glasses beneath the close-cut dark hair on his oval face with its weak chin. Schenke felt his guts turn to ice as the door closed.

Heydrich stopped two paces away and regarded him with a look of disapproval, and Schenke realised that his cheeks were covered in stubble and his coat was smeared with grime from the night before. The other man from the dining party was dressed in a plain dark suit and tie. He had thick black hair and wore glasses. Schenke did not recognise him, but if he was close to Heydrich and Himmler, he was also a man to be reckoned with and feared.

'Inspector Schenke,' Heydrich began. 'Just what have you been up to since we last spoke?'

'Sir, I—'

Heydrich raised a finger to silence him. 'I thought I had made it quite clear that you were to leave the Schmesler case alone. In fact, I recall ordering you to keep your nose out of the matter and telling you that that was the final warning I would give you. Did I not say that?'

'Yes, sir.'

'Then kindly tell me what you are up to, Inspector.'

'Sir?'

'What were you doing at the Schiller clinic?'

Schenke swiftly put his thoughts together. 'Investigating the deaths of a number of children there. It has nothing to do with Dr Schmesler, sir. It's a different case entirely.'

'A different case entirely?' Heydrich repeated with a faint smile. He turned to exchange a quick look with the other man, who raised an eyebrow and shrugged. 'You expect me to believe that?'

'It's true, sir. I was approached by the mother of one of the children, who was concerned about the circumstances of her daughter's death while she was an inmate of the clinic.'

'I see. What is the name of this family?'

Schenke hesitated.

'Don't think you can deceive me, Inspector. One way or another I will have all the information I need. The only question is how painlessly that information comes to me. Do we understand each other?'

'Yes, sir.'

'Just to be sure that you do . . . Kuntz, if you please.'

Before Schenke could react, the Gestapo man swung his rubber truncheon in a vicious arc that connected with his left thigh. Agony burst through the limb, and Schenke gasped as he staggered to one side.

'That was the leg you injured in your motor-racing accident, wasn't it?' Heydrich mused. 'Doubly painful therefore, I would imagine. So, the name?'

'Scholtz,' Schenke muttered through gritted teeth.

Heydrich nodded. 'So on the word of this Scholtz woman, you decide to launch an investigation and drive out to the clinic in the depths of winter to interrogate SS Doctor Pieper? That's very conscientious of you. Is this how you always act when a family approaches you with a bureaucratic grievance concerning the nature of a relative's death?'

'Like I said, there was more than one death involved,' Schenke replied as he leaned against the wall and grimaced at the pain in his leg. 'I had good reason to suspect foul play. And we secured evidence to support my suspicions. Pieper and one of his employees are directly involved in the deaths.'

'Pieper told me that's what you accused him of.' Heydrich crossed to the food table and picked a single grape from the fruit bowl, biting the end off and chewing slowly. 'Before he disappeared.'

Schenke frowned. 'Disappeared?'

'Please don't play the innocent, Inspector.'

'I don't understand, sir.'

'Kuntz . . .'

'No, wait!' Schenke backed away from the Gestapo man. 'I have no idea what you are talking about. I swear to God. The last time I saw Pieper and Huber they were being taken into custody by the Potsdam police.'

Heydrich gestured to his henchman to hold back. 'I know Pieper was being held in Potsdam. He called my office from the station, and I gave the order for his release before sending a car to pick both men up. When the car arrived, they had gone. Apparently another car had turned up with some men claiming to be from the Gestapo and took them away. I am aware that there was a disagreement between you and a Potsdam officer over the custody of your suspects. So it occurs to me that you might have sent some of your colleagues to fetch them.'

'No . . .' Schenke was confused. What the hell was going on?

'Where have you taken them?' Heydrich demanded.

'I haven't got them,' Schenke replied desperately. 'Ask Oberst Kleist. I had the paperwork ready for the transfer. I was going through the proper channels, I swear.'

'Kleist?'

'The commanding officer at Pankow. He'll confirm what I say. Why would I snatch them if I had an official document in my hand to take them into my custody?'

Heydrich considered this briefly, then stepped closer, thrusting his head forward as his eyes narrowed. 'You are saying you had nothing to do with their disappearance?'

'Yes, sir.'

'Liar!' he screamed, slapping Schenke brutally across the face. 'Who are you working for, you pig? *Who?*'

The sudden violence stunned Schenke for a moment before his anger surged to the surface.

'No one!' Schenke spat back. 'I'm just doing my damned job!'

The Gestapo men stepped close, but Heydrich shook his head. 'Your job, Inspector, is to catch criminals and keep your damned nose out of matters that don't concern you.'

'The murder of children concerns me.' Schenke glared at his superior.

Heydrich tilted his head back and stared at the ceiling. 'Let's suppose for a moment you are telling the truth. Then who the hell has taken Pieper?'

'I don't know. I had no reason to doubt it was the Gestapo, until now.' It occurred to Schenke that perhaps Heydrich was lying to him, and that he had indeed taken Pieper and Huber and was trying to lay a false trail. But why on earth would he do that? Heydrich was the man who knew where the bodies were buried, quite literally. Who could he possibly be afraid of to the extent that he would wish to hide his actions?

'Humour me,' Heydrich continued. 'Who else would want those two men?'

Schenke was skating on the thinnest of ice as he tried to respond. He cleared his throat nervously. 'Before I answer that, may I ask a question?'

Heydrich looked surprised. 'I'm not sure you grasp the nature of our relationship, Inspector.'

'I do, sir. Believe me. I am trying to get to the truth of this.'

'All right. Ask your question.'

'Three nights ago, after leaving the Kripo labs close to your headquarters, I was seized by some men who blindfolded me and took me to a warehouse not far from the Tempelhof airfield. They told me to steer clear of the Schmesler case. They said that if I persisted in looking into the matter, or was seen near Schmesler's house, I would be killed.' Schenke paused to read Heydrich's expression, but the other man's thin face gave nothing away. 'I assumed that they were working for you. Just as I assume that the two men in a car watching the late doctor's house are working for you. Tell me that I am wrong.'

Heydrich stroked his chin. Once again he exchanged a look with the man still standing by the door to the function room. 'What do you think?'

The man scrutinised Schenke for a moment before he spoke. 'If he's telling the truth, then someone is playing a very deep game, Reinhard.'

'Quite.' Heydrich fell silent as he ate the remaining half of the grape and considered what he had heard. He swallowed. 'Inspector, in answer to your question, I had nothing to do with your abduction. The men outside the house are not mine and I have no idea who has taken Pieper and Huber, nor where they are being held.'

'Then who is responsible?'

He shrugged. 'Whoever it is, they don't work for me.'

'Then who might they work for?' asked Schenke.

Heydrich smiled. 'You are the policeman. You work it out, and then you come and tell me the answer and I will deal with the matter. I suggest you do it quickly, before anyone else goes missing. Including yourself. See to it.' He turned and strode back to the double doors, and he and his companion rejoined the gathering.

Once the door had closed behind them, Schenke allowed himself a deep breath of relief. Then he looked round at the Gestapo men.

'I'm free to go, I take it?'

'You are not under arrest, so do what you like.'

Schenke considered telling them he'd like a lift home, but the thought of being in their company any longer was more than he could stomach. He helped himself to another roll and a chicken wing, and gave the black-coated men a wide berth as he left the room and hurried through the hotel and out into the street. Bitterly cold as the air was, he gulped the snack down gratefully as he made for the entrance of the U-Bahn station opposite.

Chapter Twenty-Nine

It was eight in the evening before he returned to his apartment. As he opened the door to his apartment, he heard Karin stirring in the living room, and a moment later she rushed out into the hall and ran into his arms.

'Horst, my God, I've been so worried!'

She held him tightly for a moment, and then turned her head and rose up on her toes to kiss him on the lips before pulling back. 'You look terrible.'

'Thanks.' He forced a smile. 'I'm shattered.'

'You look it.' Her brow wrinkled. 'What's happened? Where have you been the last two days? I tried calling you at the precinct, but they didn't know where you were. Nor your sergeant and the other one.'

'Liebwitz.'

She nodded. 'They said you just took off yesterday and there'd been no sign of you since. I thought . . . I thought . . .' She smiled nervously and shook her head. 'It doesn't matter. You're back now, and you're safe. That's all I care about.'

Given his encounter with Heydrich, Schenke did not want

to give voice to his concerns about being safe, and just smiled back. 'I need a drink.'

He closed the door and took off his outdoor clothing, then followed her into the living room. A moment later they were sitting on the sofa in front of the fire, each nursing a glass of brandy.

'Is this to do with the Scholtz girl?' Karin probed.

'Her and the other children. I took Hauser and Liebwitz with me to the Schiller clinic to question the director and his staff.'

'Did you find out anything?'

'More than I am comfortable with.' He took a sip, and the liquid burned his throat. He waited for the sensation to clear before he continued. 'I believe the children were murdered, but I'm not yet certain as to why or how. But I know who is responsible.'

He described what had happened the previous night and the morning that followed, leaving out any mention of Ruth. He still felt guilty over the revelation of his feelings for her, and the confusion of his emotions with regard to Karin. Now that he was back with her, he felt on safer ground and determined not to compromise his relationship with the woman he had asked to marry him.

'The director of the clinic and his man . . . they're still missing?' Karin asked.

'As far as I know.'

'And you have no idea who took them?'

'None. There's another party at work and they've completely blindsided me. I was sure Heydrich was behind it . . . It's all too easy to think that the regime is always responsible for such things.'

'With good reason,' Karin responded. 'They generally are.'

'Maybe, but I shouldn't have drawn hasty conclusions. A good criminal investigator cannot afford to let personal prejudices get in the way of analysing the evidence. They beat that into you during training. I've failed to do my job properly, and because of that, I've missed something. I know I have.'

'What if Heydrich was lying?' she asked. 'What if he did have you abducted? He's the one who told you to leave the Schmesler case alone.'

'That was after those men took me. Why would he issue another warning? It seemed excessive at the time.' Schenke shook his head and took another sip. 'I think he was telling the truth when he said he had nothing to do with it. And I think he was also telling the truth about Pieper and Huber, and the men watching the Schmesler house.'

'Then who *is* behind it?'

'I've been thinking that through on the way back from the Adlon. The reason for keeping me clear of the Schmesler case must be something to do with a cover-up. Either Schmesler knew something that could embarrass the regime or one of its senior figures, or he was responsible for whatever it was. Either way, he had to be silenced to put an end to the matter. Heydrich is complicit in the cover-up, but there's someone else involved and he doesn't know who that is any more than I do. It feels like infighting amongst party factions.'

'Good. Anything that sets those bastards at each other's throats is fine by me.'

Schenke looked at her with concern. Even though they were alone in the privacy of his flat, he could not help feeling a twinge of fear when she spoke so freely. She might well be the niece of Admiral Canaris and well connected to the elite of

German society, but that did not confer upon her immunity from persecution by the regime. He needed to divert the conversation away from such issues, and recalled that Karin's induction into the voluntary nursing corps was supposed to have taken place that day.

'Did you start work at the hospital?'

'Yes. I did think about staying here to wait for you to return, but the worry was driving me mad. I had to do something to occupy my mind.'

'How was your first day, then?' asked Schenke as he loosened his tie and refilled his glass.

Karin stared into the glowing coals in the fireplace. 'Not quite what I had hoped for. When I signed up as a volunteer nurse, I assumed the training would be concerned with taking care of our injured soldiers.'

'Seems like a reasonable expectation,' Schenke mused with a hint of irony. 'I take it that is not what happened.'

'Once we were in uniform, we were marched . . .' she glanced at Schenke, 'and I mean marched, like we were a bunch of bloody army recruits or something . . . Anyway, they marched us into the hospital canteen and made us wait until this party official turned up. A young type, good-looking, with a ready smile. I thought we were going to get a brief welcome before the training started. Not a bit of it. He told us he was there to give us a talk on the role of the nurse in Nazi Germany.' She shook her head. 'Honestly, Horst, you should have been there.'

She got up, standing erect, shoulders back and chin tilted at an angle, as she spoke in a booming voice. 'Ladies! The Führer is proud of you. In volunteering to serve the Reich, you have shown the dedication and self-sacrifice that is the defining characteristic of the Aryan race. You have chosen to join the struggle against our enemies that is being fought with the blood and courage of our fine young men in uniform. You are heroes all, in your own way. From this day forward it is your patriotic duty to care for our wounded and nurse them back to good health so that they can return to the fight with fresh hearts and fit bodies to continue the struggle for the supremacy of the sacred values and beliefs of our Nazi ideology!'

Schenke could not help chuckling at her imitation of the rhetoric of the party's officials. He had attended enough compulsory political education events in recent years to recognise the hectoring righteous tone.

'Fellow Germans!' she continued, thrusting her finger at the imagined audience. 'We live in historic times. The destiny of Germany is to rule the world, under our Führer, Adolf Hitler. No one can stand before the might of the German soldier, sailor and airman. No leader can surpass the military genius of the Führer, and the astonishing speed of our defeat of Poland is proof to the world that Germany is the pre-eminent power. Hail Victory! Heil Hitler!'

Thrusting her arm out, she snapped her slippered feet together soundlessly. She held the pose for a moment, then relaxed and flopped down beside Schenke and nuzzled into his shoulder. 'It went something like that.'

'Oh, I'm sure it did.'

'I was inclined to raise my hand at the end and ask, in all innocence, how it was that we were now allies of Russia when only a year ago they were the great evil we must defeat.'

'I'm glad you didn't.'

'If I had, he would only have denied that the party had meant what it said in the past. Or that it was all part of the

Führer's Great Plan and we must trust in his genius.'

'It's a wonder that such things can be said and so many people accept them without a thought. It's like the party is some fanatical religious cult and Hitler is their prophet, preaching that faith is stronger than fact.'

'You are hardly the first person to say that.'

'Of course, I understand that. I dare say many, maybe most, say the same thing. Only we dare not say it aloud, and certainly not in public. Compliance makes cowards of us all.'

She propped herself up and stared at him. 'Not all of us.'

He felt the familiar chill of anxiety at her words. 'Karin, what is the purpose of opposing something you have no chance of defeating? What is the purpose of being crushed under the boot of the Nazi Party like an ant? I am not saying things will not change. But for now, the party's hold on power is absolute, and they will destroy those who challenge them. If their grasp weakens and there is a real chance to depose them, then and only then is it reasonable to speak up.'

She shifted away from him and switched her gaze to the fireplace. 'And who will be the first to speak up if we have all consigned ourselves to the cowardice of silence? People need to know that they are not alone in opposing the party if those who truly love Germany are ever to rise up on the day that the regime is vulnerable.'

'On that day I will speak up.'

'And until then?'

'I will devote myself to hunting down criminals. It is a good thing that I do, whatever else may happen in the world.'

'And will that satisfy your conscience?' she demanded. 'Are you not prepared to do anything to defy the Nazis?'

Instinctively he raged at the accusation. He *had* defied the regime. He had knowingly helped Ruth evade the legal restrictions placed upon Jews. In doing so, he had broken the law, at considerable personal risk. Yet he could hardly justify himself to Karin. He did not trust himself to conceal his feelings about Ruth. For all her haughtiness, Karin was intelligent and perceptive. She would see through his explanation, and then suspicion would poison her thoughts and suggest deeds that Schenke had not engaged in, and it would be difficult to draw the poison out of the wound to the trust that had been established between them.

'My conscience is not at issue. I can live with what I choose to do,' he said. 'And it will spare me from a futile death – there is no virtue in futility. Do you think I am a coward?'

'I didn't say that.'

'But do you think it?'

'Ah, so now you reckon we should not be afraid to say what we really think?'

He frowned. 'That's not fair, my love.'

'Why not?' she challenged him. Neither spoke for a moment before she sighed wearily. 'I do not think you are a coward. But I am disappointed. There, I admit it.'

Schenke felt a dull crushing sensation around his heart at her words. He breathed deeply for a moment before standing and crossing to the fireplace to move the screen in front of the dying flames. Without looking at her he said, 'I'm going to bed.'

He left her alone in the living room and trudged down the short corridor to the bedroom, unsure how far such disagreements might imperil their relationship. There was a leaden despair in his stomach as he reflected on the values that divided them. She had wounded him to the core, and that was hard to live with. As was the shame that he was indeed afraid of the consequences of attempting to defy the regime. The Nazis thrived on the dissemination of terror just as much as the dissemination of crass patriotism. To Schenke it felt like he was afflicted by a morbid moral sickness. But then so were the millions who looked on at what was happening to their country in silence.

Abject weariness of the body and soul weighed heavily on him as he removed his jacket and tie. He sat down on the edge of the bed and took off his shoes before lying down and closing his eyes, intending to rest for no more than a few minutes before completing his undressing and slipping under the covers. Instead, he was fast asleep within a matter of seconds. A deep, dreamless sleep that was his only means of escape in the country that Germany had become.

Chapter Thirty

5 February

The shrill ringing of the telephone dragged Schenke out of his sleep, and he sat up with a groan. His head was aching and his body felt as if every muscle was made of lead. He winced at the pain in his thigh where the Gestapo thug had struck him the previous evening. It took a moment for the weary murk in his brain to clear, and then he glanced to the other side of the bed, but there was no sign of Karin. Beyond, he could see daylight rimming the edges of the blackout curtain, and he glanced down at his watch and saw that it was past eight thirty in the morning.

'Shit! Shit . . . shit . . .' he growled as he rose stiffly from the bed and realised that he was still dressed from the night before. The telephone continued to ring, and he hurried into the hall and snatched up the receiver from the small table halfway along.

'Schenke.'

The line crackled as Hauser spoke. 'Sir, are you all right?'

'Yes. Fine.'

'I apologise for calling you at home. It's just that we were expecting you in the office well over an hour ago. Given what's been going on, I wanted to make sure nothing had happened to you.'

Schenke hesitated, still struggling to think clearly. 'I'll brief you when I get in. I'm on my way.' He was about to put the receiver down when he recalled one of the more important details from the previous day. 'Hauser, are you still there?'

'Yes, sir.'

'I take it Liebwitz is too?'

'He was the first one in, of course.'

'Good. Get a car and pick me up at the apartment. I'll explain when you get here. Be quick.' He hung up and stopped to listen, but there was no sound of movement anywhere in the apartment.

Hurrying to the bathroom, he grimaced at his reflection in the mirror. He lathered up quickly and shaved the stubble off as best he could, wincing as he nicked the flesh beneath his chin. As he worked his way round his jaw, he recalled the previous night's discussion with Karin and the hurt he'd felt at her implied accusation of moral cowardice. Her insistence on a courage defined by abstract notions of conscience was dangerous under the present regime, and he wished fervently that she was not the kind of person who embraced ideals without applying reason.

He washed the lather off and dabbed his face dry with a towel, sighing with frustration when he saw the telltale blossom of scarlet where he had cut himself. There was nothing to be done but hope that it dried before he buttoned his collar and put on a tie. His work coat was smeared with dirt, so he fetched his best coat from the wardrobe in the bedroom. That was when he saw the folded sheet of paper on the small table on

Karin's side of the bed. He picked it up and quickly read the contents.

> My dearest Horst,
>
> I am sorry you were upset by my remarks to you this evening. I did not mean to hurt you. You were tired, and it was unfair to subject you to an interrogation of your political and moral values. That said, one day you will have to choose whether you will stand up and be counted amongst those who oppose the tyranny of the party, or whether you will merely be an onlooker. Be aware that in the case of tyranny, inaction puts you on the side of the tyrant.
>
> I think you need time alone to think about your values. I have returned to my uncle's apartment and will stay there for a few days. I hope that will be long enough for the air to clear between us.
>
> All my love,
> Karin

He felt a heavy weight descend on his heart as he stared at the note. There was anger too. Not directed at Karin, but at the age in which they lived and the way the grim shadow of the regime hung over almost every aspect of life. Ten years earlier, before the Nazis had seized power, there would never have been this painful difference between them. For a moment he gave vent to the hatred and contempt he felt for Hitler and his cabal of gangsters. They had made almost everyone helpless before their arrogant and ruthless abuse of power. They were beyond the reach of the law and all the decencies of a civilised nation, and answered to no one. Schenke loathed the feeling that he could do nothing about it. All the more so given how he had been wholly within Heydrich's power at the Adlon. A word from the SS Gruppenführer would have sealed his fate just as surely as a bullet to the head. Perhaps when Karin had faced a similar experience, she might have more sympathy for his point of view.

He refolded the note and tucked it into his pocket so that it made him feel closer to her while they resolved their differences. Hurrying to the kitchen, he drank some water to slake his thirst before pocketing a bar of chocolate he had been saving to share with her. Then he put on his coat, hat and scarf and left the apartment.

He waited in the lobby for the car to arrive. The block warden, Kuhle, entered from the street carrying a paper bag of groceries, and the two men exchanged a nod. There had never been any neighbourly spirit between them, and Schenke made little effort to curry favour with the lowly party official, unlike some of the other residents of the apartment block. Kuhle stopped at the foot of the staircase and turned.

'Inspector Schenke, a word, if you please?'

'I'm waiting to be picked up.'

'A brief word.' Kuhle smiled thinly. 'I'm giving a talk on the latest revisions to the blackout regulations and air-raid drill in my apartment tomorrow night. It's an important meeting. The Air Ministry has issued a briefing about the effects of the Russian bombing of towns in Finland, and has passed on some useful tips to us block wardens to share with those we are responsible for. I expect you to join us. There will be cakes afterwards.'

Another petty exercise in authority. As petty as it was pointless. Despite the occasional sounding of the air-raid sirens in the capital, the only thing the enemy had dropped on the city so far was propaganda pamphlets calling on the German people to rise up against Hitler and his regime. The pamphlets were more effective as firelighters than they were at inciting insurrection, thought Schenke.

'I will be there if duty permits,' he replied.

'I hope so, Inspector. After all, you missed the last talk, on being aware of enemy spies. Good day to you.' Kuhle touched the brim of his hat and turned to climb the stairs.

Schenke made a mental note that if the time ever came to stand up and be counted, he would take the blackout regulation booklet and ram it down the warden's throat.

There was the rumble of an engine outside and he turned to see Hauser pulling up in one of the pool cars. Liebwitz was sitting in the passenger seat, arms crossed, upright, and turned to dip his head in greeting as Schenke opened the rear door and climbed in. No one spoke until Schenke cleared his throat.

'I know I said an early start in the office. Don't ask.'

Hauser could not help grinning as he gave his superior a knowing look. 'Certainly not, sir. That's between you and the fair Karin.'

'Don't push it, Sergeant. Let's get going.'

'Where to, sir?'

'Lenger's surgery. The doctor's got some questions to answer.'

'Assuming he has anything to add to what he told us when we last spoke to him.'

'Oh, I think he has,' Schenke responded. 'Pieper accused us of breaking into Lenger's premises. Which implies there was something there that was worth taking. Now, it might have been the work of petty thieves, but given the way things are going with this investigation, it feels like too much of a coincidence to me. Particularly after my trip to the Adlon last night to see Heydrich.'

Hauser glanced over his shoulder as he put the car into gear and pulled away from the kerb. 'Jesus . . . What was that about?'

'I was snatched by his Gestapo friends waiting for me outside the precinct.'

'That would be after you returned the car to the garage,' said Liebwitz. 'I saw the entry on the booking sheet this morning.'

'Yes, I went to see Brigitte Schmesler to ask her some questions about her husband's work,' said Schenke, anxious to conceal the full truth from his colleagues. 'I was careful to make sure I was not seen entering her house.'

'Why not just telephone her, sir?'

'I didn't have the number.'

'I see.' Liebwitz nodded, seemingly satisfied by the explanation.

'What did Heydrich want?' Hauser asked.

Schenke was grateful for the change of subject.

'He demanded to know where we had taken Pieper and Huber. He also wanted to know why were still investigating Schmesler's death, despite his warning.'

'But we aren't,' said Liebwitz.

'Quite. But he seems to think we are. So he has as good as drawn us a line between the murder of those kids and what happened to Schmesler.'

'And what bollocks is that about Pieper and Huber?' asked Hauser. 'It was bloody Heydrich who gave the order for their release. His Gestapo goons picked them up from Potsdam.'

'That's not what he said. He accused me of having them snatched so the Kripo could interrogate them without having to wait for a transfer order. It's a damned shame Kleist didn't act as soon as I called it in. We'd have had Pieper and his pet thug in Pankow long before anyone else could have picked them up, and avoided Heydrich thinking we were behind it.'

'Why would he believe we'd do such a thing? Why would we risk getting ourselves in the shit by trying something like that?'

'Maybe Heydrich assumed we wanted them for the same reason he did. They could lead us to their friends. What they know is dangerous to the other people involved in their crimes. My guess is that it's dangerous to someone high up in the party. Why else would Heydrich be so anxious to get them out of the hands of the police?'

'It's possible the Gruppenführer is lying and the prisoners are in his custody,' said Liebwitz. 'In order to put us on the wrong track.'

'That had crossed my mind,' Schenke replied. 'But there's no reason for him to put us on the wrong track. If he already has Pieper and Huber, he has nothing to gain from having us chase our tails trying to find them. Heydrich didn't order me to let the matters be. In fact, I think he'd rather we found out who took them and why, and then all he has to do is clean the matter up and dispose of any unwanted witnesses.'

'Just as long as we're not amongst them,' said Hauser.

'Amen to that.' Schenke sat back and scratched his jaw at the spot where he had cut it. 'So the most pressing question is who has taken Pieper and Huber. I'm not sure we're going to like the answer. I've been trying to think this through. We know the children were murdered and we know Pieper and Huber were directly involved. We also have links to Lenger and Schmesler. It turns out that Schmesler was working for some committee based in one of the offices of the Chancellery. The Reich Committee for the Scientific Registering of Serious Hereditary and Congenital Illnesses.'

'When did you find that out?' asked Hauser.

'From the files Liebwitz and I examined in Pieper's office at the clinic.'

Schenke paused a moment as his weary mind connected the information. 'So, we've got some obscure committee with a very suggestive name employing Dr Schmesler. Then there's the payments being made to Lenger for recommending that children with a variety of mental and physical handicaps be committed to the Schiller clinic. The same children are put on special treatment programmes and succumb to pneumonia or similar fatal conditions. The bodies are disposed of before a coroner can inspect them.'

'Shit,' Hauser growled. 'I really don't like where this is headed. So what's Heydrich's angle? I hope to God he's not behind this. If he thought we'd found out he was responsible for killing the kids, we'd be joining them soon enough.'

Liebwitz glanced at him with a strained expression. 'The Gruppenführer is the supreme law enforcement officer in the Reich. That's unthinkable.'

'He's clearly a lot more than that, Scharführer. His first loyalty is to the party.'

Schenke interjected. 'Let's assume Heydrich isn't behind it. At the same time, there's no hiding the party's ambition to rid Germany of those individuals it thinks are degrading the Aryan race. They were open about the purpose of the Nuremberg

Laws, after all. It's no leap of logic to see that they want to strip out anyone who isn't a healthy Aryan.'

'But killing kids?' Hauser interjected. 'If that ever came out in public . . .'

'Precisely. But what if someone at the top let it be known that they were in favour of euthanising disabled kids. Not a policy as such. No written orders or anything that could ever be traced to them. And what if some zealous office-holder further down decided to get the ball rolling? A small freelance operation at first. But if it worked out, and they could demonstrate that the children could be disposed of without a public outcry, then that official would be in prime position to be promoted to take charge of rolling the scheme out across Germany.'

'No.' Hauser shook his head. 'I don't believe it.'

'Why not?' asked Liebwitz.

'Who would do such a thing? Who could live with it on their conscience? The party are politicians, not psychopaths or child-killers. Inspector, you're on the wrong track. You know how it is in our line of work. The simplest answer is generally the right one. In this case, I think we're looking at a handful of perverts who are killing the kids, while Huber has a nice sideline in selling their effects.'

'Maybe,' Schenke responded. 'I've considered that possibility. When I suggested that to Huber he was enraged by the very idea. Either way, it makes sense that Heydrich is keen to discover the truth. If they are paedophiles, he'll want them disposed of before word gets out that party members and SS officers were involved in the murders. If it is a freelance operation, he'll need to determine whether to take control of the scheme or close it down and get rid of the evidence. What will be foremost in his mind is making certain the party's reputation is not stained and that the matter is kept secret. Whatever it costs.'

Liebwitz tilted his head to one side and frowned.

'What is it, Scharführer?'

'I did not say anything, sir.'

'I know. Your silence is thunderous. Spit it out.'

'Yes, sir. If what you say is accurate, it seems logical that the men who abducted you, those who broke into Lenger's surgery and those who took Pieper and Huber are the same people.'

'Yes, so?'

'Then why were you spared? If they wanted to keep their operation secret from outsiders, surely it would have made sense to kill you.'

'Thank you for that thought, Scharführer. But yes, I agree. So why didn't they?'

When there was no answer from either of his colleagues, Schenke sighed and looked out of the window. 'Let's hope we can get something from Dr Lenger. At the moment, he's our only lead.'

Chapter Thirty-One

There was a van parked in the street outside Dr Lenger's surgery when Hauser drew up. The doors at the rear were open and there were several wooden boxes within. A sallow-faced man in a fur cap was leaning against the side of the van rolling a cigarette. He looked round as the three police officers climbed out of the car and approached him. When he spotted Liebwitz's black coat, he half turned away.

'Looks like someone's moving house,' Hauser called out.

The man nodded.

Hauser stopped in front of him and held up his badge. 'And who might that be?'

The man gestured up at the first floor. 'The doctor.'

'Really?' Hauser glanced at Schenke. 'Where are you taking his stuff?'

'Storage. Dr Lenger is leaving Berlin.'

'Is he now? When did he arrange for you to move his things?'

'Yesterday.' The removal man placed the cigarette in his mouth and fumbled in his pocket. 'Rush job. Lucky for him I was available at such short notice.'

Hauser took out a box of matches and the man nodded gratefully.

'We need to have a word with the doctor,' said Schenke. 'You can take a break and get on with the job once we've finished with him. You can do something for us at the same time. Keep an eye out for anyone who might be watching the place while we're in there. All right?'

The man assented, and Hauser led the way through the door and up the stairs to the surgery on the first floor. The door to the waiting room was open, and the two sofas and low table had been pushed to the side to make room for the packing boxes occupying the centre. There was no sign of the receptionist. A hacking cough came from the direction of Lenger's office, and Schenke stepped past Hauser and strode down the short corridor to the open door at the end. As he crossed the threshold, he saw that the framed diagrams and other pictures on the walls had been removed, and files and papers were piled on the desk. Lenger was standing with his back to the door, examining a sheet of handwritten notes, before he crumpled it up and tossed it into a basket next to the desk.

'Going somewhere?' asked Schenke as he stepped forward, eyeing the array of boxes near the desk. Hauser and Liebwitz followed him into the room.

Lenger spun round with a panicked expression, his eyes darting from the policemen to the doorway. He turned suddenly and grabbed at the handle of a drawer in the desk, but Liebwitz was too fast for him, sprinting across the room and slamming the drawer on the doctor's fingers. Lenger howled in pain, then staggered against the window frame, clutching his injured hand. 'Bastard.'

Liebwitz slid the drawer open and lifted out a small pistol

between his gloved finger and thumb. He held it up for the others to see.

'Hang on to that, Scharführer. It may constitute evidence.'

He picked up a large envelope to drop the weapon into before folding it over and tucking it into his side pocket.

'That's no way to greet us, Doctor,' said Schenke. 'Can't say I have much faith in your bedside manner if that's how you treat visitors.'

'What are you doing here?' Lenger demanded as he nursed his hand against his chest.

'On my last visit I told you we might have some more questions. Do you remember what I said just before we left?'

Lenger shook his head.

'Then let me remind you. I said you weren't to leave Berlin without notifying the precinct.' Schenke turned to Hauser. 'Have we received any such notification, Sergeant?'

'No, sir.'

Schenke fixed his gaze on the doctor once more. 'You can imagine how disappointed we are to find you packing up your business like this. Would you mind telling us where you intend to go?'

'I, er, I'm moving to Dresden, to my sister's home. She is worried that Berlin may be bombed by the enemy.'

'That was decided very quickly, it seems. Well, I like decisiveness. It's the kind of quality the Reich approves of these days. However, I can't help thinking that your sudden move might have been motivated by some other reason.'

Lenger's shoulders slumped fractionally.

'I'm right, aren't I? So let's not waste time with me asking you questions and you giving dishonest answers. My sergeant is very good at telling truth from lies, and the Scharführer has been thoroughly trained by the Gestapo in effective interrogation techniques. Isn't that so, Liebwitz?'

'Yes, sir.'

'Then let's begin.' Schenke's tone hardened. 'Why are you really leaving Berlin?'

Lenger's watery eyes closed for a moment before he replied. 'I was told to leave for my own good, or I would disappear like Dr Pieper.'

'Who told you?'

'A man on the telephone. He called me yesterday.'

'And do you always react in such an extreme manner to threatening telephone calls?'

'I knew who it was. The same man who came to my surgery several days ago with some other masked men. They told me that if I referred any more children to the Schiller clinic, they would kill me. They made me lie on the floor while they went through my files, and took some documents away with them. I was warned not to say a word about it to the police or anyone else, if I wanted to live.'

'You must have been very frightened,' Schenke said with feeling.

'I was terrified. What the hell have I done to warrant being treated this way? I'm a good man. I take my duty seriously, and it's outrageous that I should have been treated like that.' Lenger thrust a finger at Schenke. 'You're supposed to protect people from such criminals! That's what I pay my taxes for.'

'We do what we can, Doctor. The documents the men took. Do you recall what they were?'

'Of course. They were the latest returns I was preparing for the committee.'

Schenke felt his pulse quicken. 'What kind of returns?'

'The forms I submit for the children I recommend for the Schiller clinic. I don't get paid until the forms are processed.'

'And who processes them?' Schenke asked.

'That's confidential.'

'Not any more, it would seem. You send the forms to the committee at the Chancellery, right?'

A brief look of surprise passed over Lenger's features before he nodded. 'How do you know about the committee? I was told it was a secret.'

'Not from us,' Schenke responded. He decided to take another chance with his next question. 'And who are the forms sent to? Is it Dr Schmesler or one of the others?'

'Schmesler,' Lenger confirmed.

Schenke forced himself not to react. His mind was rushing over what he and his colleagues had discovered so far. The connection between the child-murders and Schmesler had been confirmed, and Schenke reasoned that it was the information on the forms that had led the men to Schmesler's home, where he was murdered.

'Schmesler is dead,' he announced. 'He was almost certainly killed by the men who came here.'

The blood drained from Lenger's face.

'The same men were also responsible for the kidnapping of Dr Pieper. He may already have been killed, like Schmesler. It's possible that they may come back for you, especially if they get to hear that we've been to see you. I know they have been keeping watch on those involved with the committee's activities.'

Lenger glanced out of the window.

'Doctor, it may be safest if you are taken into protective custody, given the circumstances.'

'No. I have to get out of Berlin. Find somewhere to hide until this goes away.'

'Where do you think you'll go? Who would hide you? The men who are after you have become desperate. They may have let you live last time, but the stakes are higher now. If they find you again, they *will* kill you. I imagine you'll be left dead in a ditch, just as Pieper and Huber are likely to end up.'

'You don't know that they're dead.'

'We don't know that they're not. What do you think, Doctor? Do you think they are still alive? Or have they gone the same way as Schmesler?'

Lenger grimaced and wrung his hands. 'Oh God, I didn't mean to get into this. It was just a little extra money. Schmesler promised me there was no risk. He told me I was doing a service for the Fatherland.'

'And now he's dead, who is going to protect you? I'll say it again. You'd be safer in protective custody. Do you want that or not?'

'Yes . . . yes I do,' Lenger conceded.

'Very well. Before we take you to the precinct, I'll need you to provide us with the files for all the children you have referred to the clinic.'

'Of course. Whatever you . . .' Lenger paused. 'Why?'

'We're looking for any detail that might help us track down the men who killed Schmesler and are behind the disappearance of Pieper. The same men who might be looking for you to make sure that all the loose ends are tied up.'

'You can have them. They're in there.' He nodded to the filing cabinet next to where Liebwitz was standing. 'May I?'

The Scharführer moved away from the filing cabinet. Lenger pulled the top drawer open and began to work his way through the contents, pulling out files and placing them on the corner of the desk behind him. Schenke fanned through them, opening the covers and glancing at the contents. All had a photo of the patient concerned clipped to the corner, and he felt a little wrench in his heart when he came across Greta Scholtz's picture.

He had gone through the first five or so files when he came across a picture that made him pause. A young girl, perhaps ten years old. She stared out of the photo with a vacant expression, and there was something about it that struck him as familiar. He knew he had seen the face before. He lifted the corner of the photo and read the entry beneath. *Kleist, Maria Hilda.*

'Kleist . . .' he muttered to himself. Then again, aloud, 'Kleist.'

Hauser and Liebwitz looked towards him, and Lenger paused in his work to glance round. Schenke held up the file so that the doctor could see the photo. 'Maria Kleist. Do you recall her case?'

'Of course. She died at the start of November, I believe.'

'What about her parents? Do you remember them?'

'Yes. Well, the mother at least. The father was unable to attend the consultation. He had work commitments. He is a policeman, like yourself. At the Pankow precinct, as I recall his wife saying. You might know him.'

'Oberst Kleist. Yes, I know him.'

Schenke's mind was reeling. Kleist had been determined to close the investigation into Schmesler's death. He had failed to put through the custody transfer in time to prevent Pieper and Huber's disappearance. What if he had passed on the information that they had been arrested and were being held in a cell in Potsdam? Maybe it was Kleist, posing as an official from Heydrich's headquarters, who had called the police in Potsdam to authorise the release. Piece by piece, everything seemed to be falling into place, and the identity of the shadowy group of men who had been responsible for menaces, abduction and death was becoming clear. Moreover, Schenke realised that if Pieper and Huber were still alive, they would not remain so for long if his deductions were correct.

'What has Kleist got to do with this?' asked Hauser.

'Everything.' Schenke swept up the folders and turned to Lenger. 'How many more files are there?'

Lenger handed another one over. 'This is the last.'

Schenke added it to the others and bundled them together. 'It's likely that every one of these is linked to Schmesler's killers. We have to get the files back to the precinct immediately. You're coming with us, Lenger. Get your coat and hat.'

Hauser held Lenger's arm as they emerged into the street. The removal man opened the door of his van as soon as he saw them.

'It's a funny thing, you were right about someone watching this place,' he said as he paused to take a drag on his cigarette. 'A car drove past slowly and stopped opposite. The man at the wheel opened the door and got out. I thought he was going to cross the road, but he just took one step and looked up – at the window, I'd say – then got back in the car and drove off.' He pointed down the street, and then squinted. 'That's him. Coming back this way.'

The other four men turned and saw a dark car accelerating towards them, heedless of the patches of ice still on the road.

'Down!' Schenke cried out, thrusting Lenger against the

side of the van before crouching to cover the doctor with his body. Hauser and Liebwitz followed suit.

The car roared by on the other side of the van, then flashed into sight further down the street, heading towards a group of workers walking in the other direction. The passenger window was open, and Schenke saw a man in a cap aiming a pistol back towards the van. There was a flash and a sharp detonating crack that echoed off the buildings either side of the street. The centre of the window of the furniture shop burst into glittering fragments, and the glass fell softly into the compacted snow on the pavement. The workers scrambled in all directions.

Liebwitz's Walther appeared in his hand, and he rose to his feet, knees and elbows flexed as he took aim.

'No shooting!' Schenke ordered, concerned about the workers being caught in any crossfire.

The Scharführer relaxed his stance but kept his firearm trained on the retreating car. The face had disappeared from the passenger window, and a moment later it was closed and the car braked before disappearing around the corner.

For an instant no one moved, and the only sounds were the fading noise of the car's engine and the strained breathing of the men sheltering by the van. The removal driver reached for his ignition key, but Schenke caught his arm.

'You're not finished here. Go up to the surgery and pack any documents you can find, any scraps of paper, into boxes. I want them delivered to Pankow precinct.'

The driver shook his head anxiously. 'I'm a tradesman. I'm not getting caught up in any bloody shooting!' He glanced past Schenke to Lenger, who was trembling uncontrollably. 'Get someone else to finish off, sir. I'll return the boxes already in the back when it's safe.' He reached for the keys again.

This time Schenke wrenched his arm, dragging him out of the cab and thrusting him face first into the side of the van. He tapped the name painted there. 'I know who you are. Now you'll do as I say, or I'll have your bollocks for cufflinks. Understand?'

'Yes, sir,' the driver mumbled, and Schenke released him.

He glanced along the street, but there was no sign of any further threat. The few people who had been out in the open were still sheltering where they had taken cover at the sound of the shot. Schenke patted Hauser's shoulder.

'Put Lenger in the car. Let's get out of here.'

Chapter Thirty-Two

As Hauser drove towards the precinct, Schenke glanced frequently through the narrow rear window to make sure that they were not being followed. Lenger sat hunched beside him, his lips moving in quiet snatches of prayer. Schenke's dislike of the doctor increased. How could a man who was complicit in the murder of children expect the protection and mercy of any god?

Liebwitz still had his Luger in his hand, with the safety catch on, in case there was another attack. He turned to Schenke. 'Sir, what has Oberst Kleist to do with our investigation?'

Schenke explained the connection between the file and the family photo in Kleist's office, and the meaning behind his failure to transfer the prisoners from Potsdam. 'He's been playing us all along, I'm certain of it.'

'What are we going to do?' asked Hauser. 'You can't just walk into his office and arrest him. The evidence isn't strong enough. Right now, the worst thing you can accuse him of is incompetence.'

'Then I'll have to break the chain of command.'

'What you do you mean, sir?'

'I'll need authority from Kleist's superiors to act.'

Hauser got the point at once. Above the precinct, police authority was routed through the Reich Security Main Office. 'Shit . . . Heydrich.'

'I don't have any choice. We need to get our hands on Kleist before he hears what happened at Lenger's place. The men in the car know we have Lenger. And if I'm right, we've got their identities.' He patted the bundle of files on the seat beside him.

Hauser glanced at him. 'If you're right, the men we're after are the parents of the murdered children.'

'Yes . . .'

'I'm not sure how I feel about that, given what Schmesler, Pieper and Huber have done. They've murdered kids, dammit. They deserve to be strung up. Some might say Kleist and his men are just seeking justice.'

'I know,' Schenke conceded. 'I don't disagree, Hauser. But we can't have people taking the law into their own hands. There has to be a proper investigation and then due legal process. What if we left justice to the victims and their families? What if they went after the wrong people? We'd run the risk of lynch-mob justice.'

'But they went after the right people, sir. That's the difference.'

'That may be true now, but what about the next time? We can't let it happen, Sergeant. Whatever we may feel about it. We have the law and law enforcers, or we have bloody chaos. The three of us have no choice. I don't like it any more than you do, but Kleist and his friends must be stopped. Are you forgetting that they threatened to kill me if I got in their way?

They'll be sure to realise that we're on their trail now and the police will be coming for them. One of the first things they will do is warn Kleist. We have to get to him before he can run for cover. I'll put a call in to Heydrich as soon as we reach the precinct. Liebwitz, I want you to find out where Kleist is and keep him under observation. If he leaves the building, follow him and report on where he goes the moment you get a chance.'

'Yes, sir. Am I authorised to shoot if I am detected and threatened?'

'Only if there is danger to your life.'

'Yes, sir.'

'What about me?' asked Hauser.

'I want you to get Lenger into a cell. Book him in under a false name and put him down as a person of interest in the forgery investigation. I'll send one of our section down to stand guard on the cell. Then join me. I'll want backup when I go for Kleist.' Schenke shook his head sadly and felt the need to further explain his earlier comment to Hauser. 'I wish to God we were not in this position, Sergeant. I'd come down hard on any police officer who broke the law under other circumstances, but this is different. The real evil lies with the likes of Pieper and Huber. I don't deny they deserve a bad end, but if we don't get to Kleist and his men before they kill Pieper and Huber then we'll never have a chance of discovering how far the ring of child-murderers extends.'

Hauser sped through the streets as fast as the icy conditions allowed. They reached the precinct and turned into the garage. Once Hauser had signed the car back in, they crossed the yard to the main building, heedless of the angry shouts from the prisoners still being held in the storerooms. Lenger looked towards the noise anxiously, and Hauser gave him a nudge to keep him moving.

'Relax, you're going to have preferential treatment: a nice cell to yourself in the basement. Must be at least five degrees less freezing than those poor sods' accommodation.'

They split up in the entrance hall of the precinct, with Hauser heading for the basement with his charge, Liebwitz covering the main entrance and Schenke hurrying up the stairs to the Kripo section office. He strode through towards his cubicle, ignoring the glances of those at their desks, and paused on the threshold.

'Persinger!'

'Sir?'

'Get down to the cells in the basement. Hauser's waiting for you there. He'll explain what you're to do. Go.'

'Yes, sir.'

He closed the door behind him, placed the files on his desk and picked up the receiver of his telephone, dialling the number for the switchboard at the Reich Security Main Office. There was a dull purring noise before the call connected.

'Put me through to Gruppenführer Heydrich's office.'

'Yes, sir.'

There was a delay before a male voice responded. 'Yes?'

'This is Criminal Inspector Schenke. I need to speak to the Gruppenführer. It's urgent.'

'Yes, sir. I believe he's in a meeting, but let me check. Please hold.'

Schenke recognised the filtering tactic used by Heydrich's staff to field all but the most necessary calls. He heard the phone being picked up, and a different voice spoke.

'Inspector Schenke? I'm the Gruppenführer's aide. How can I help you?'

'I must speak to Heydrich himself.'

'I'm afraid Gruppenführer Heydrich is not available to take your call at the mo—'

'Tell him it's to do with the matter we discussed last night.'

'Sir, as I said, he's unavailable.'

'Just tell him!' Schenke snapped. 'Trust me, if he finds out later that you fobbed me off, you'll be on the first truck to some godforsaken posting in Poland.'

'A moment, please.'

He waited again, drumming the fingers of his hand on the desk.

'Schenke . . .' The familiar silky, high-pitched voice made him straighten up instinctively. 'This had better be important, and be careful what you say over an open line.'

Careful? Schenke was surprised. If anybody had a safe telephone line in Berlin, surely it would be the head of the Reich's security services. The fact that even Heydrich was worried about being spied on had not occurred to him.

He cleared his throat. 'Sir, I think I have found one of the members of the group we discussed yesterday.'

'Think?'

He cursed his equivocation. Heydrich was a man who demanded directness in his subordinates.

'I know he's one of them.'

'Very good. Then arrest him and get him to name the rest of his gang.'

'I would, but there is a problem, sir. I need your authority to act.'

'Why?' Heydrich's tone was cool.

'The suspect is Oberst Kleist, commander of the Pankow precinct.'

There was a pause. 'Are you sure about this, Schenke? I know him. Kleist is one of the old guard. He was wounded at Hitler's side in the Munich coup. A favourite of the Führer, you understand? Are you quite certain?'

Schenke took a calming breath. 'Yes, sir. I need your authorisation to arrest him.'

'I see. Very well, you have my verbal authorisation. If anyone questions you, tell them to call my office. Keep me informed.'

There was a click and the line went dead. As Schenke replaced the receiver, he smiled cynically. A verbal authorisation meant that Heydrich could deny ever having given it if things went wrong. Well, there was no time to get it in writing.

He drew his pistol from its holster and loaded the magazine before replacing it. Adjusting his coat, he set off for the top of the staircase, where he waited for Hauser to join him. He was aware of the potential danger in which he was placing himself, as well as his closest colleagues. He resolved to take full responsibility for the consequences if things went badly, and hoped that would be enough to spare Hauser and Liebwitz from any action taken by Heydrich.

He heard footsteps, and turned to see Hauser climbing the stairs towards him.

'Lenger's safe, sir.'

'Good.' Schenke regarded the sergeant with fondness and respect. 'I can do this alone. I wouldn't want you or Liebwitz or anyone else in the section to suffer if—'

'We're wasting time, sir.' Hauser nodded towards the corridor. 'After you.'

Schenke smiled his gratitude and set off in the direction of Kleist's office, his mind fixed on the confrontation. His sense of grim purpose communicated itself to some of the uniformed police he passed at their desks, and several of them looked up curiously for a moment, wondering what brought the two Kripo officers into their part of the precinct.

They reached the anteroom to Kleist's office and marched past his aide's desk to the door.

'Wait!' the aide called out. 'What do you think you're doing?'

Hauser gave him a steely look. 'Our duty. Sit down.'

Schenke opened the door and entered. As soon as Hauser had joined him, he closed it behind them. Kleist had his telephone receiver in his hand and was in the process of dialling a number. His jaw sagged in shock for a moment before he slammed the receiver down and shot to his feet. 'What the hell is the meaning of this? Explain yourself, Inspector!'

Schenke approached the desk. 'Oberst Kleist, you have become a person of interest with respect to the abduction of SS Reich Doctor Pieper and a member of his staff. You are also implicated in the death of SS Reich Doctor Schmesler.'

Kleist's expression froze for an instant, and then he laughed. 'Is this some kind of joke, Schenke? Have you gone mad?'

'Yesterday I called you from the Schiller clinic first thing in the morning to urgently request the transfer of two prisoners from Potsdam to Pankow. You delayed acting on my request in order to speak to your accomplices. You called Potsdam claiming to be an officer from the Reich Security Main Office and told them that Gruppenführer Heydrich had ordered the release of the prisoners. Your accomplices, posing as Gestapo agents, then abducted the two men. So my first question is, where have Pieper and Huber been taken?'

Kleist eased himself back a half-step from his desk, a frown furrowing his forehead. 'What nonsense is this? How dare you barge into my office and make such accusations? I will have you arrested, charged with insubordination and kicked out of the Kripo. By the time I am finished with you, you'll be lucky to be a ranker in the river police on the sewer patrol!'

'Sit down,' Schenke responded.

'You impudent—'

'Shut your mouth!' Schenke roared. 'Sit down!'

The two men glared at each other for a moment, seeing who would back down first. The tension was broken when the door opened and Kleist's aide appeared. He glanced at the two Kripo officers and then looked to his superior.

'Sir, do you, ah, need assistance?'

'Get out,' said Hauser. 'Now. Before I make you.'

'Arrest these men!' Kleist shouted.

Schenke rounded on the aide. 'I am acting on the personal orders of SS-Gruppenführer Heydrich. He has authorised me to arrest and interrogate Oberst Kleist. Anyone attempting to interfere will be charged with obstruction and disciplined severely. If you wish to have confirmation of my orders, you should call Heydrich's staff at the Reich Security Main Office. Now get out.'

The threat was enough, and the aide backed out and closed the door behind him. Schenke and Hauser turned back to see that Kleist had opened his desk drawer and taken out an automatic pistol. He cocked the weapon before pointing it at Schenke.

'Hands up!'

Schenke began to reach for his holster, but Kleist thrust the pistol forward.

'Hands up, or I'll shoot you down where you stand!'

Schenke froze and slowly raised his hands.

'You too, Sergeant, and step out to the side so I can see you both clearly . . . That's better.'

'What do you think you're going to do?' asked Schenke. 'You can't get away with this. If anything happens to us, Heydrich will hunt you down. We both know what that means. You still have a wife and son. Think of them. Better that you surrender to me than to Heydrich.'

'It'll come to the same thing in the end.' Kleist slumped back into his chair and rested his elbow on the desk, still keeping the Kripo officers covered. His tense expression gave way to a look of weary resignation. 'I've been expecting this. Who betrayed me?'

'I have the names of all those involved in your plot. It's over, sir. All that remains is to take your confession and hand the evidence over to the prosecutor's office. Please put the gun down. You can't escape justice.'

'Justice?' Kleist spat back. 'How can you call this justice? Those bastards murdered our children. Schmesler, Pieper, Huber and the others. Schmesler has been made to pay the price. Pieper and Huber are next. Some of our group are still at large. They'll do all they can to finish the job and kill the other murderers before they're done.'

'Pieper and Huber are still alive?'

'Until we get what we need from them.'

'Where are they?'

'You think I'd tell you? Then you really are mad, Inspector. No, they will be kept hidden until they have revealed all they know, especially the remaining names of their circle. Then my friends will put a bullet in each of their heads and dump their bodies in a ditch, where the rats can have them.'

'That's not how we work, sir. We're policemen. We do it by the book. We are not judge, jury and executioner. We have sworn to uphold the law, not twist it to our purpose. You have broken that oath.'

'You think I care about the distinction between the law and justice? Sometimes a crime is so heinous that you cannot take the risk that the guilty will go free if the courts fail in their purpose. The man we have killed and the men we are going to kill are guilty, plain and simple. We are cutting out the middleman and doing what must be done. We're not criminals like them, Schenke. That's why you were allowed to walk free after we'd warned you.'

'What about Lenger? A warning wasn't enough for him. One of your accomplices took a shot at him this morning. But he's safe for now.'

'A pity. At first our leader argued that Lenger should be spared, since he only took money. I wanted him dead from the outset. Looks like some of the others have come down on my side. And since you've put us all in the shadow of the guillotine, we've nothing to lose.'

Schenke saw the wild glint in the man's eye, and saw his trigger finger twitch slightly. A cold jab of fear lurched up his spine.

'Sir, if you share what you know with us, the men responsible for your daughter's murder, and those of the other children, will pay for their crimes. I give you my word that I will do everything in my power to guarantee that.'

Kleist smiled sadly. 'I am touched by your devotion to duty,

Inspector. In another life, I would speak as you do. But we are not in that life. It was my little girl, my Maria, who those devils murdered. Are you a father?'

'No, sir.'

'Then what do you know of my grief? How can you understand the depth of the wound I suffered when Maria was taken from my family?' He paused and chewed his lip. 'You can't. Any more than you can grasp the pain of the others who were persuaded to join our group once I'd got the details of the victims from Lenger's files.'

Schenke frowned as he pieced this information together with what he knew already, and Kleist saw the look pass over his face.

'I broke into Lenger's office and went through his files to find out who else had suffered the loss of a child. I left the files on the floor, ransacked the place and stole a few drugs to make it look like a burglary. Then I spoke to all the fathers I could locate and sounded them out. Some refused to be involved. Most wanted justice.'

'Sir, I can barely imagine what your loss feels like. But this? All this? It is wrong. You know that.'

'Of course I do. I have given most of my life to the police force. I was serving when you were still in nappies, so I don't need a lecture from you about my duty. I've served long enough to see every vice, to see the faces of murder victims and the families of the victims. I've seen guilty men go free on a technicality. I've seen it all,' he concluded wearily. 'And I stomached it because that is what a policeman does. I did not question whether that was a good or a bad thing. It was the job. Or it was until Maria was murdered. She was a strong girl. Never sick in her life. Until she went into the Schiller clinic.

She was dead within two weeks, and I knew from the outset that she had been murdered. This time the job was not enough. This time I resolved that justice was more important.'

'Justice? Or revenge?'

'There's not as much difference between the two as you think.' Kleist stared at him, defying Schenke to disagree. 'Now you know. You have caught me, and I will be made to pay for what I have done. I can't change that. But there's one last thing I can do.' He stood up. 'On your knees. Keep your hands behind your heads. Do it.'

'He's going to kill us,' Hauser muttered. 'Sir?'

For an instant Schenke feared that his comrade was right. But Kleist reached for the phone with his other hand, and the gesture indicated that he had another purpose in mind.

'Do as he says, Sergeant.'

Schenke squatted down, bending his good leg first before easing himself down, wincing at the pain. At his side, Hauser followed suit. Satisfied that they posed no immediate threat, Kleist used his trigger finger to dial a number before training the weapon back on them. Schenke could hear the dialling tone. Then a crackle before a voice spoke faintly.

'It's Kleist,' said the Oberst. 'I'm afraid my number is up. I have my gun pointed at two Kripo officers who came to arrest me. They claim to have the names of everyone in the group . . . Yes, I fear so. Very soon . . . No, you are safe there for the moment, but you must deal with Pieper and Huber before it's too late . . .' He listened to the voice on the phone and nodded slowly. 'You too. Good luck and goodbye.'

When he replaced the receiver, he stared at Schenke for a moment, and then turned his gaze to Hauser.

'How about you, Sergeant? Married?'

336

'Yes, sir.'

'Kids?'

'Yes, sir.'

Kleist smiled gently. 'Then you understand.'

He stiffened his shoulders and opened his mouth wide before turning the pistol and bracing the barrel on his bottom lip, aiming up into his skull.

'*No!*' Schenke shouted, launching himself towards the desk.

Kleist pulled the trigger. His head lurched back, and blood, brains, bone fragments and gristle exploded behind him and sprayed across the wall and the framed picture of his family.

Chapter Thirty-Three

'Shot himself, you say?' Heydrich's voice at the other end of the line was without emotion.

'Yes, sir.'

'Very well, that's one down. How many more of them are there?'

Schenke took a moment to focus his thoughts. The image of Kleist's body slumped over his desk with the back of his head blown away was difficult to suppress. At the same time, Heydrich's tone made him feel an aching disgust at the Gruppenführer's dispassion. He forced himself to think clearly.

'We have files on ten children referred by Lenger to the Schiller clinic. Two are still alive, so we can discount their families. Of the others, it's likely that some were approached by Kleist's group and may have refused to join them.'

'They will need to be dealt with at a later date.'

'Dealt with?'

'If they were approached, they should have reported it to the police. If there is no record of that, they were complicit by omission and will be punished. Continue.'

'Ah, yes, sir. So we are looking at no more than seven others, now that Kleist is dead.' Schenke held up a piece of paper with a list of names. 'Scholtz, Breker, Aubin, Kappler, Oehler, Gruber and Haushofer. All have respectable backgrounds, Gruber's a lawyer. Three of them are party members. I've detailed several police squads, under the command of members of my section, to find and arrest all seven.'

'Good. When you have them all, I want them delivered to Gestapo headquarters, where Müller will deal with them.'

'Sir, the suspects should be interrogated here and their confessions taken before they are held for trial.'

'Trial?' Schenke caught the hint of amusement in Heydrich's voice as he repeated the word. 'Inspector, given that you have uncovered a group of men who have murdered a member of the SS and kidnapped and may have murdered a second, I hardly think the Reich owes them a trial.'

'Yes, sir.'

'That is all, then. Let me know when you have rounded up the last of these scoundrels.' Heydrich ended the call.

Schenke lowered the receiver and looked out of his cubicle to where Hauser was briefing the arrest squads, moving to each in turn as he gave out the details of the suspects. Schenke had used Heydrich's authority to take command of the precinct's uniformed police while Kleist's accomplices were hunted down. None of the other officers, even those superior to him in rank, had dared so far to challenge him. If there was any trouble, perhaps a shoot-out in which the police suffered casualties, he had little doubt that Heydrich would deny his part in the drama and leave him to suffer the consequences.

There were other matters that troubled him deeply. Foremost was his final exchange with Kleist before the latter had turned his pistol on himself. He had empathised with the agony that Kleist had suffered as a result of his child's murder, and despite his dedication to his profession, he understood the motivation of the men who had been moved to take justice into their own hands, regardless of due legal process. He tried to imagine what he would have done in their place. Would he have been tempted to step outside the law? He hoped not. But there was never any way to know until such a thing happened. Even the most resolute of men could be broken by experience.

He closed his eyes in thought. As for the men who had murdered the children, he harboured no such feelings of sympathy. They were monsters and deserved their end, whether that was administered by the fathers of their victims or by the state. Schmesler, Pieper and the others in their circle were driven by their ideology. In their eyes, the murders were justified in the lofty pursuit of racial purification. Schenke found it difficult to decide if that was worse than if they had simply been a gang of perverted child-abusers and murderers. He was sure that it made no difference to Kleist and his accomplices. Where murder of their children was concerned, the justification of the killers was irrelevant. No ideology could excuse them. If ideology became a licence to murder then how could there be any moral justification of such an ideology? He felt himself moving onto uncomfortable ground and sensed Karin looking over his shoulder and pointing to the obvious conclusion and where that must take him.

There was a rap on the glass door of the cubicle, and he snapped out of his reflections. Hauser opened the door and leaned in.

'The men are ready, sir. Any final instructions?'

Schenke understood what his subordinate was asking, and nodded. It would help if he said something to the officers to establish his authority, however temporary. He eased himself out of his chair and followed Hauser outside. Some forty or fifty uniformed police were crowded into the Kripo section office along with Schenke's team. All were looking towards him expectantly.

'I am sure word has got round about the death of Oberst Kleist. I do not know what rumours are being spread, but I believe you deserve the truth before you set out to arrest his accomplices. Kleist killed himself. As some of you will know, he lost his daughter late last year. She was murdered, and Kleist and some accomplices took it upon themselves to track down and kill those responsible. Kleist gave his life to the police force. Many here will have respected and admired him. His was a distinguished career. Exemplary, some would say. Until he chose to abandon his duty to uphold the law and embarked on a private crusade for revenge. I do not question that he felt driven to act as he did. But he broke the law, and no policeman worthy of the title can tolerate that, regardless of what we might believe in private.

'The men we are after might feel they have nothing to live for now that they are outside the law and fugitives from the police. They are armed, and it is likely that some will choose to resist. If you can, bring them in alive. If they present a mortal danger to you, do not hesitate to shoot them down. If we can take them alive, I hope that the pain they have endured over the murders of their children might go some way to mitigate their punishment when they are judged by those in authority.' He could not find any more words to add, and so concluded simply, 'Good luck.'

Hauser cleared his throat. 'You heard the inspector. Move out!'

The men made their way from the office and Hauser turned to his superior. 'Ready?'

'As I'll ever be.'

Schenke had chosen to find and arrest Gottfried Scholtz. It was because of the Scholtzes that Schenke had become involved, and he felt he owed it to Greta's father to give him every chance to surrender peacefully if he was involved with the revenge plot. Hauser, Liebwitz and four uniformed men made up the arrest squad.

'Everyone armed?' The others nodded, and Schenke gestured for them to follow him. 'Let's go.'

The Scholtz apartment was in the Heinersdorf district, in a modest middle-class neighbourhood. Their block was built around a courtyard that was used for deliveries and was also where the younger kids played under the watchful eyes of their parents. Even though it was over a decade since the murders that had inspired Fritz Lang's movie, *M*, about a child-killer stalking the streets, parents were still inclined to be vigilant. A further irony of the present case, Schenke reflected. It was not a furtive toad-faced pervert who was responsible for the murder of these children, but doctors. The very profession one assumed to be most concerned with the preservation of life.

As the small police van pulled up in the street outside the entrance, Schenke glanced at his watch. It was just before two in the afternoon. Scholtz should be at work, so they would have to discover the name and location of his school from his wife, if she was at home. If he was one of Kleist's group, he might well be in a secret location with the others, along with Pieper and Huber.

The team climbed out of the van and closed around Schenke in a loose ring as he gave his orders.

'I'll be going up to the apartment with the sergeant and the scharführer. I want two uniformed men waiting inside the front entrance, the other two in the courtyard at the back. You know what Scholtz looks like. If he's inside and gives us the slip, it's up to you to stop him getting away. If he enters the building, I want him arrested on the spot. Then call out for the rest of us. Clear?'

The others nodded. Schenke drew his coat to one side and unclipped the strap over the butt of his pistol in case it needed to be drawn swiftly. Hauser and Liebwitz followed suit. Then he led the way up the three steps to the entrance to the block and pushed open the glass-plated door. The floor of the lobby was tessellated, with a neat geometric pattern running along the edges. The stairs were at the far end, and a door stood ajar to the left. It was not much warmer inside than out. As the second policeman closed the door to the street, a woman in her sixties with her grey hair tied back in a bun emerged from the open door and regarded them expectantly.

'Are you the concierge?' Schenke asked.

She nodded. 'Are you here about the radio?'

'Radio?'

'Him in number fourteen. I've heard that he listens to foreign broadcasts. I called the police about it and—'

'No. We're looking for the Scholtz apartment. Number fifteen. Which floor?'

'Third. To the left once you reach the landing.'

'Are they at home?'

343

'She is. He's at work, or some such. Regular as clockwork he is. I see him leave at seven in the morning and he's back home at five thirty.' She made a face. 'That said, I haven't seen him for a couple of days. But I might have missed him if he used the courtyard door for some reason.'

Schenke turned to the two uniformed officers. 'Stay here. Keep alert.'

The three Kripo men made for the stairs and began the climb to the third floor. The sound of their footsteps echoed off the walls and would carry some distance, Schenke realised. He glanced up the stairwell every so often, but there was no sign of anyone above them. At the landing, he saw the corridor stretching out on both sides, with two pairs of doors in each section, eight flats in all. They turned left and walked as softly as they could until they reached number 15. Hauser moved to one side of the door, and gestured to the scharführer to take up position on the other.

'Ready?' Schenke said quietly, his right hand close to his pistol as he raised his left and rapped loudly on the varnished wood. There was no sound from within, and he tried again.

'Sir . . .' Liebwitz pointed to the bottom of the door, where a glimmer of light flickered slightly as someone moved inside the apartment.

'Open the door!' Schenke called out loudly. 'Police!'

He hammered this time, continuing until he heard the rattle of a chain. Stepping back, he reached for his pistol as he waited. There was a soft creak, and the door eased back to reveal the face of the woman he had met a few days earlier at the Dorfman. He saw that there was a bruise on her cheek, and another on her brow.

344

Johanna Scholtz regarded him cautiously. 'Inspector Schenke . . . Have you any news for us?'

'Where is your husband?'

'Gottfried is at work. He won't be home until six at the earliest.'

'We need to come in. Stand aside, please.'

She hesitated, and then gave a shrug before obeying the instruction, closing the door when the three men were crowded in the small hall of the flat. A window overlooking the street at the far end provided natural illumination for what was little more than a dim passage between the rooms. A telephone was fixed to the wall halfway along, between two framed oil paintings of rural scenes.

Johanna Scholtz retreated to the living room while Schenke and his men quickly searched the other rooms. When they had finished, they stood round her as she sat on the corner of the sofa.

'Where does your husband work?' Schenke demanded.

'The Gymnasium on Schleicher-Strasse. He is head of the history department,' she said with a hint of pride as she pointed to a picture of a stern-faced man standing with a group of smiling boys.

Schenke turned to Liebwitz. 'Call the school. Use the phone in the hall.' The scharführer left the room.

'When was the last time you saw him?' he continued.

'This morning.'

'The concierge says he hasn't been in or out of the apartment block for two days.'

'She's old, and her memory is going.'

'Not that old, and she strikes me as the kind with enough of an eye for detail that she could tell me the comings and

345

goings of every person in the block. So I'll ask again. Where is your husband?'

'I told you. Gottfried is at work.'

'If you are lying, you will face charges for obstruction. In addition to any other charges relating to what your husband has been up to.' It was a calculated provocation, and he saw a glimpse of alarm in her expression, but she folded her arms and said nothing.

Liebwitz came back into the room. 'Scholtz is not at the school. He hasn't been seen for three days. The principal's secretary said they had telephoned his wife, who said his mother had fallen seriously ill and he had gone to Leipzig to see her.'

Schenke turned to Johanna. 'Where is he?'

'Leipzig. Like your man just said.'

Tiredness was fraying Schenke's patience. 'Don't lie to me!' he snapped. 'We know about the murder of Dr Schmesler. We know your husband is involved with the fathers of other murdered children in dealing with those they hold responsible. Tell me where he is!'

She flinched, and then recovered her poise, her lips curling with contempt. 'Gottfried told me everything yesterday. He said he and the others would not have to deal with this matter if you had done your job. If you had got justice for our little girl. You failed us, and my husband did the right thing. I was wrong to ask for your help. When I told him what I'd done, this is what I got.' She indicated her bruised face. 'Damn you . . . I should never have spoken to you.'

'He isn't doing the right thing. He's on the wrong side of the law, and claiming that he's seeking justice for Greta will be no defence when he is held accountable for his actions. If I can find him before he makes matters worse, I will do what I can to see that he is treated as leniently as possible. He's a party man. And if he has a good record, that will weigh in his favour.'

'I'm not so sure. The men they are after are also party members. And that will surely go against him, Inspector.'

'Maybe. But if he kills anyone else, or tries to shoot it out, you can be certain that there will be no mercy for him. Is that what you want? To have him gunned down?'

'Of course not!' she spat back. 'We want justice!'

'I know that the police and others failed you before you came to me. We had a chance to work together to hunt down Greta's killers. But your husband chose to act outside the law, and now the children will not be the only ones to suffer. Your husband and his accomplices will also be victims, and their families will be grieving for those fathers along with their children. What a waste. What foolishness. All you will have achieved is to make widows of grieving mothers.' He shook his head and softened his voice. 'What good is that, Johanna? You have just compounded a terrible tragedy. That is all that will have been achieved.'

Her brow creased, and her face twisted into an expression of agony. Then she let out a keening groan and began to weep, her thin shoulders racked with grief as the pain and tension of recent months overwhelmed her.

Hauser eased himself down and put his arm around her shoulder. 'It's all right,' he murmured. 'You cry. No parent should have to endure this . . .'

She leaned into his chest, sobbing, and Schenke caught his eye and nodded.

'We want to help you,' Hauser continued. 'Don't let this situation rob you of your husband. You've both lost so much already. Come now, tell us where we can find him. I swear to you we'll do everything we can to make sure he and the others aren't harmed. Let's put an end to all the suffering, eh?' He took her hand and gave it a squeeze. 'Where is he, Johanna?'

She made to say something and choked. She tried again. 'The airfield . . . I heard him say it on the telephone . . . a few nights ago.'

'The airfield?' Schenke repeated. 'Tempelhof?'

She nodded. 'That's where you'll find them.'

'Where exactly?' asked Liebwitz.

'I don't know,' she mumbled. 'That's all I heard.'

'I think I know where,' said Schenke. 'And I know who to ask to make certain.'

Chapter Thirty-Four

Klaus Zebrinski had started his shift at the hangar only half an hour earlier. He had made himself a jug of coffee in the workshop in the corner and was sitting in front of the stove going over the work schedule sheet on the clipboard. The two technicians working under him were already labouring over the port engine of the Ju 52 in the hangar. The work was behind schedule and the engineering company that had won the contract to convert and service the Lufthansa aircraft for military purpose was under pressure from Goering's aviation ministry. Accordingly, a senior executive had passed on a harshly worded message from the ministry to the manager of the Tempelhof division, who in turn had torn a strip off the man in charge of this particular hangar, who had had an angry word with the shift foremen. Zebrinski was not unduly concerned. With a war on, many of the younger technicians had been conscripted, and skilled aircraft maintenance workers were in short supply. They were hardly going to be sacked if they slipped a little behind schedule.

He was interrupted by a knock on the outside door of the workshop. Putting his coffee down, he made his way to the door as another knock sounded.

'Coming!' he shouted, and then muttered, 'Damned impatient bastard.'

Sliding the bolt back, he opened the door and peered outside. The sun was setting amid thin streaks of cloud to the west, washing the sky with lurid pink rays. Three covered trucks had pulled up a short distance away along the apron in front of the vast complex. Their engines were running, and small clouds of exhaust billowed from their tail pipes. Closer to the door, a car was parked, and two men sat inside while a third was directly outside the door of the hangar.

'Remember me?' he asked.

Zebrinski looked Schenke up and down and nodded. 'The policeman from the other day, right? Sure I remember. What can I do for you?'

'I need your help.' It was well below freezing outside, and Schenke nodded in the direction of the stove. 'Out of the cold, if you don't mind. And I could use some more of your coffee.'

Zebrinski let his visitor in before closing the door. Schenke crossed to the stove and held out his gloved hands. 'You remember the last time I was here.'

'How could I forget? You were in a bad way, Inspector.'

Schenke smiled at the recollection of his rank. He picked up one of the empty mugs on a shelf beside the coffee jug and poured himself a small amount.

'Better now, though,' said Zebrinski. 'What brings you here?'

'You mentioned that you'd seen some men over by the Lufthansa stores.'

'That's right. So?'

'I need you to show me where.' Schenke took a sip of coffee.

'You know where they are.'

'I do. But I need someone who knows the layout. Someone who can find their way about in the dark if need be. I need you, Zebrinski. I need your help. Lives depend on it.'

'These men are dangerous, then?'

'Yes. And they're armed. But you'll be safe. I have twenty men waiting in those lorries outside.'

'Sounds like more fun than being stuck in here all night.' The engineer reached for his coat and began to pull it on over his stained overalls. 'All right, but you'll be the one responsible for any breakages or any other damage, clear? I don't want trouble with management. Those bastards are like a constant boil on your backside.'

'I'll take your word for it. Let's go.' Schenke drained the cup and set it down.

'A moment.' Zebrinski paced over to the inner door, opened it and called out to the mechanics working on the engine of the Junkers. 'I've been called away for a bit. You two crack on. No slacking, eh?'

One of them flapped a hand dismissively. 'As if.'

He closed the door. 'If we're depending on the likes of them, Germany might as well throw in the towel now.'

He planted a woollen hat on his head and pulled on his gloves. 'Let's go and find these men you're looking for.'

Schenke left Zebrinski to climb into the back seat of the car and made his way over to the lorries. The sergeants in charge of the squads emerged from the cabs and gathered round.

'We'll be going in across the open ground.' He indicated the line of sheds nearly a kilometre away on the far side of Tempelhof's perimeter. 'We'll wait until the light is almost gone before we set off.' He pointed to two of the sergeants. 'You will take your vehicles around either edge of the airfield and stop far enough away so that they don't hear your engines when you approach. From there you go on foot and set up a screen a hundred metres short of the sheds. Your job is to stop anyone trying to escape. Only shoot if necessary. I don't want stray rounds hitting the rest of us. Make sure any trigger-happy types understand that. All clear?'

The sergeants nodded.

'Then get those lorries moving.' He turned to the remaining sergeant. 'Let's have your lads out now.'

'Yes, sir.'

As the other vehicles rolled away in either direction towards the ends of the vast building, the section selected to support the Kripo officers climbed down, stamping their feet to try and stave off the biting cold. Each man had been issued with a rifle, and these they now slung on their shoulders as they waited for the order to advance. Some took out cigarettes and lit them up, the tips glowing brightly as they inhaled the warm smoke. The sun had just set, and a blue hue hung over the landscape. Two hangars were open at the western end of the terminal complex, and their light spilled out over the snow-covered apron outside. The aircraft within gleamed under the lamps as tiny figures moved about them, unaware of the drama about to be played out.

Schenke rapped on the window of the car, and Hauser, Liebwitz and Zebrinski got out.

'I take it you've introduced yourselves.'

Hauser grinned. 'Turns out this one served in the same regiment as my dad in the old imperial army. Small world, eh? Be good to have a proper soldier with us, rather than some of the younger Orpo lads over there.'

'Youngsters . . .' Zebrinski said. 'Heads all filled with party ideology these days, instead of a decent education.'

Schenke gave a brief smile. 'There'll be more than enough of us to deal with any trouble.' He looked at the fading light in the sky. 'It'll be dark in a few more minutes. Then we'll get going and put an end to this.'

'I hope you are right, sir,' said Liebwitz.

'What do you mean?'

The scharführer stared towards the Lufthansa depot in the distance. 'I'm not quite sure yet, sir. I feel there's still more to this than we know.'

'Maybe, but let's keep our minds on the matter at hand. I want this to go smoothly. I'll have the Orpo boys hold back when we reach the sheds. It's likely the men we're after will have someone keeping a lookout, so it'll just be the four of us that go in to find out where they're holding the prisoners. More than likely the same place where they interrogated me.'

'Pieper and Huber may already be dead,' said Hauser.

'It's possible, but I doubt it. Why would they be here if that was the case?'

'Johanna Scholtz could have been lying about that,' Liebwitz suggested.

'I don't think so. It's likely that Kleist's warning was passed on to the others. If I were in their shoes, I'd want to meet to discuss options. And if the prisoners are still alive, they'll need to decide their fate.' Schenke paused. 'I'm sure they're here.'

He looked up again. The light was fading quickly, and there was a faint rattle as the hangar doors at the other end of the building began to close, narrowing the beams of light they cast over the snow before they disappeared abruptly.

'It's time.' He turned to the sergeant. 'Get your men in line. Ten-metre gaps. And load up.'

The orders were relayed, and the uniformed policemen took a last drag on the cigarettes and flicked the butts into the snow. Then they unshouldered their rifles and took clips from their pouches to load into the weapons, a task made more difficult by having to wear gloves.

'Safety on!' the sergeant cautioned, then spread the men out, a row of dark figures against the dull loom of the snow. When they were in position, Schenke and his party advanced ten paces ahead of them.

Schenke looked back. 'No one opens fire unless I give the order.' He took a long breath, then waved his arm in the direction of the sheds.

The line rippled forward, the Orpo men holding their rifles at the ready as their boots crunched softly into the calf-deep snow. Schenke kept the pace slow and steady in order to give the other squads time to take up their positions. The terminal complex began to fall behind them as dusk deepened.

As the dispersed line of men advanced over the open ground, Schenke became conscious of the first laboured breaths and the soft pounding of blood in his ears. His eyes strained to detect any movement from the buildings ahead, or any sound that might guide them towards the location they sought. At the same time, he was conscious that they would make an easy target for anyone hiding amid the shadows of the Lufthansa depot, particularly if armed with a rifle. It was almost as if he could feel the sights of a rifle being lined up on him. Any moment there could be a stab of flame, the savage impact of a bullet spinning him round before he even heard the crack of the shot. What went for him almost certainly went for the other policemen around him, and he fervently hoped that none of the younger men was jumpy enough to ignore his orders and fire at shadows.

'Zebrinski,' he said quietly. 'Which end did you see those men?'

'Away to the right.' The engineer raised an arm to point.

'Then we'll work our way in from the left and use the other sheds as cover.'

They continued to close in until Schenke noticed the glimmer of masked headlights to the left in the direction of the perimeter road that led to the depot. He caught the faint growl of an engine before it abruptly died away and the lights went out. A hundred paces further on, he saw lights to his right and heard the second police lorry. It kept coming, the noise of the engine intensifying as it crawled along.

'What's the fool doing?' Hauser hissed.

'Quiet!'

There was nothing they could do to stop the lorry, and Schenke feared it would give the game away. But as they watched, it drew to a halt, before reversing round and heading back the way it had come, the red tail lights twinkling in the gloom.

'Where's he think he's going?' asked Zebrinski. 'He's running from the fight.'

'No. He got too close and he's trying to make it look like he took a wrong turning. I dare say he unloaded the men before he turned round. He's got a cool head, that sergeant.'

A few minutes later, the depot buildings stretched out on each side, and Schenke raised his hand and ordered the others to halt.

'Sergeant!' he called out to the uniformed man immediately behind him. 'On me.'

The policeman came forward, surging through the snow, which was deeper on this side of the airfield. 'Sir?'

'I want your men to cover the ground in front of the sheds. Tell them to stay low, keep still and be quiet. Anyone who comes this way is to be challenged. If they try to fight it out, your men are to shoot to wound if they can. They're under your control from this point.'

'Yes, sir. Good luck.'

Schenke turned to the hangar foreman. 'You stick close to me whatever happens, understand? I don't want you wandering off and getting shot by accident.'

Zebrinski chuckled. 'I'll be right behind you.'

'Hauser.'

'Sir?'

'You follow our friend. Liebwitz at the back. Keep your eyes open and check both sides as we move. Ready? Let's go.'

Schenke went first, almost wading through the pristine mantle of snow, and the others followed in his deep footprints. They moved slowly, wits straining to detect any danger, until they reached the side of a small wooden shed and paused. To their left was one other building, with the rest stretching away to the right.

'What do we have that way?' asked Schenke.

Zebrinski took a moment to orientate himself. 'Some garages, then parts stores, workshops and a couple of small hangars, with old fuel tanks and open ground beyond.'

'Which would you choose if you had to hide up here for a few days?'

'Workshops would be your best bet. Easier to keep warm.'

'I agree.' Schenke eased his pistol out of its holster and pulled back the slide to chamber the first round. 'Ready your weapons.'

Hauser and Liebwitz followed suit.

'Check the safety catch.' He glanced at their dimly visible features. 'Same goes for you. No shooting unless I say. I'd rather we gave these men the chance to surrender and plead their case. They've endured enough already.'

'What if they don't surrender, sir?' asked Liebwitz. 'What if they choose to shoot it out?'

'Then we'll have no choice. Understand?'

Both men nodded their acknowledgement, and Schenke turned towards the end of the shed. At the corner, he paused and looked round cautiously. There were two fuel bowsers parked between them and the next cluster of buildings, but no sign of anyone else, and no sound apart from the soft sighs of their laboured breathing.

'All right, Zebrinski, I want you to lead us to the workshops. Keep us out of sight as far as you can. You're an old soldier, so you know where they're most likely to have posted a lookout.'

'I'll do my best, Inspector.'

Schenke gave way, and the engineer edged to the corner and peered round before scurrying across the snow to the nearest bowser, followed by the three policemen, hunched low, weapons ready as they glanced from side to side. Zebrinski pointed to a large building with a tower to their left that overlooked the open ground between their position and the next building.

'That's the old fire station,' he whispered. 'The hose drying tower would make a good lookout point, but it's been abandoned a long time. Be a cold spot to have to stand sentry duty. I doubt they'd use it.'

Schenke peered up at the looming structure. There was a

walkway at the top, but no sign of anyone outlined against the starry sky. 'We'll risk it. Keep moving.'

He patted the foreman on the back, and Zebrinski set off again at an easy trot, with the others close behind. Schenke felt his heart pounding, his ears straining for any noise above the shuffling creak of the snow underfoot.

They reached a low corrugated-steel warehouse, and Zebrinski edged along it a short distance before he found a door. Testing the handle, he found that it was unlocked. He eased it open, but it had moved barely wide enough to admit a man when there was a shrill grating squeal from the hinges.

Schenke felt his stomach leap before Zebrinski froze and the sound died away. All four looked about anxiously, listening for any response, but the quiet of the winter night was unbroken.

'Sweet Jesus . . .' Hauser muttered. 'That made me jump.'

Schenke nudged Zebrinski. 'Is there another way?'

'Sure, if you want to cross the open ground in front of the fire station, or move along the other side in full view of the end of the nearest workshop. If we go through the warehouse, we'll be out of sight, and the far end overlooks the aircraft apron in front of the main storehouse and workshop area.'

Schenke could see the sense of it. 'Let's go in.'

Zebrinski eased himself through the gap, and the others followed in turn, with Liebwitz at the rear. He made to close the door, but the slightest movement provoked another loud protest from the hinges.

'Leave it open,' Schenke ordered quietly.

'Sir, if the breeze catches it, the noise is bound to attract attention.'

'Then find something to wedge the damned thing.'

Liebwitz groped along the wall inside until he found a pile of empty sacks. He packed them under the bottom of the door until it was held firmly in place.

'Are there any windows in here?' Schenke asked as he took the torch out of his pocket and snapped the narrow beam on, pointing it at the floor.

There was a pause before Zebrinski answered.

'Yes. Follow me.'

He moved along the wall until he came to an interior door. It had been cheaply made from plywood, and gave way easily with only the slightest sound from the hinges. Inside, the torch picked out a long urinal and sinks on one wall, and cubicles on the other. There was a sour, musty smell in the freezing air.

Easing open one of the cubicles, Schenke saw the windows, a series of narrow openings with wire-reinforced glass secured by metal levers. He holstered his pistol, turned the torch off and put it back in his pocket.

'I'll go first. Then Zebrinski, followed by you two.'

He climbed onto the toilet seat to reach the lever, and pushed the window open. A waft of icy air bit into his exposed face, and he blinked as he pulled himself up and worked his way through the window, dropping into the deep snow that drifted against the wall outside the block. He rose quickly, brushing the snow from his face as he drew his gun, then looked round quickly before he spoke through the window.

'Zebrinski, out you come.'

The foreman dropped down beside Schenke, and the others followed quickly, Hauser grunting with effort as he struggled through the narrow gap. When the sergeant was back on his feet, the group edged along the rear of the latrine block, stopping just before the corner. Schenke waved them back, and then slowly looked round the end of the structure. There was a gap of ten metres to the closest workshops, and parked in front of the nearest one was a covered lorry and a van. A dull glow came from a small window high up on the workshop wall.

Schenke was about to draw back when there was a sudden bright glow at the end of the lorry as the man keeping watch there drew on his cigarette. It revealed his face, looking away from the workshop. Schenke scanned the area for any sign of a second man, but the lookout seemed to be on his own.

Edging back to the others, he described the layout ahead in a whisper before turning to Zebrinski. 'I assume there will be a large opening to the front of the workshop. Any other entrances?'

'No other doors. Just a window at the back. That's all.'

'Time for you to go. Make your way back to the end of the warehouse and then cut across the open ground to the police section. Tell them to close up on us here. Better make sure that you wave something when you reach them. Some of those lads look like they might shoot first before they offer a challenge.'

As Zebrinski set off, Schenke turned to the others, standing with their weapons drawn. 'One at a time. I'll go first. Wait until the lookout is turned away before you move.'

'And if he sees us, sir?' asked Liebwitz.

'We go in fast and hard and hope that the prisoners are still alive to be saved.'

'I won't lose any sleep if they shoot the bastards first,' Hauser growled.

Schenke rounded on him. 'I want them alive. All of them. We do everything we can to make that possible, Sergeant.'

He stared hard at Hauser to make sure that his point was driven home, then moved to the corner again and peered towards the lorry. The glowing cigarette had disappeared, and his straining eyes could not make out any sign of the man who had been there only a moment before. He was about to make a dash across the open ground to the workshop when he heard a drawn-out sigh close at hand, followed by the sound of a dull splash. Leaning forward and looking around the corner of the latrine block, he saw the lookout no more than three metres away, urinating against the wall, peering towards his feet, gloves in his mouth.

Schenke snatched the opportunity instinctively, bursting round the corner and sprinting towards the lookout. He looked round too late to defend himself, and the butt of Schenke's Walther struck him on the forehead. He reeled back, gloves dropping from his teeth as he made to shout a warning. A second blow landed before he could make a noise, and this time he fell backwards into the snow, arms thrown wide, still urinating over his trousers and midriff.

Schenke knelt down and felt for a weapon, finding a Luger in a holster under the man's arm. He pocketed it along with the spare clip in the pouch on the holster. As Hauser and Liebwitz came padding up, he reached for the man's hat lying in the snow close by and dropped it over his crotch.

'Out for the count.' Hauser prodded the body with his toe.

There was still no sign of any other lookout. Schenke pointed to the search lamp close to the driver's window of the lorry. 'Hauser, take up position by the truck. If there's any sign of trouble, turn the lamp on and get the beam on the workshop doors. Our targets will be dazzled and won't be able to tell that you're alone. Order anyone who comes out that way to throw aside their weapons and lie face down.'

'And you, sir?'

'We'll cover the windows at the back while we wait for the police to get here and close the trap.'

Schenke gestured to Liebwitz and made off towards the rear of the workshop. As they reached the corner, he could hear voices from inside the building. Raised voices, arguing, but indistinct as yet. As they worked their way along, he saw another glimmer of light, brighter this time. If this had been a more built-up area, there would surely have been blackout measures in place, but out here, screened by other buildings, there was no need to worry about drawing the attention of zealous blackout wardens. There was a dim pool of light on the snow around the window, and Schenke crouched low as he reached the peeling wooden frame.

'Liebwitz, stay this side and keep out of sight.'

He crept past the window and took up position on the far side before straightening up and peering in. Some of the panes were broken, and the rest were streaked with grime, but he could still see through into the interior of the workshop, and now he could clearly make out most of what was being said by the men within.

Pieper and Huber were sitting on chairs in the middle of the floor, their arms tied behind them. Gottfried Scholtz was standing guard over them, his pistol drawn and raised at waist level. Schenke recognised him from the photograph his wife had shown him and Karin. The three men were caught in the full glare of the electric lights hanging from the steel beam running the length of the workshop. A couple of metres in front of the chairs, suspended from the beam above an inspection pit, were two lengths of rope ending in hangman's nooses.

Chapter Thirty-Five

Schenke looked away from the nooses. Off to the side, within the pools of light cast from above, stood a small group of men. Schenke recognised the faces from family photos in the files taken from Lenger's office.

'Enough of this legal bullshit!' a voice called out. 'I say we hang the bastards now and get the hell out of Berlin while we can. The police know who we are. Kleist told you so. Every minute we sit here playing your legal games puts us in more danger. Let's get it done, and then it's every one of us for ourselves.'

Two of the others nodded their approval, but the man in the hat shook his head. 'We agreed when we began that this would be done properly. We agreed to follow the principles of justice. That's what makes us different from them.' He pointed towards the prisoners. 'Them and their friends in the party who have been protecting them. We do it by the book, and when the evidence has been presented, we decide whether they are guilty or not guilty. We took an oath.'

'Damn the oath!' the first man shouted. Schenke could place his face now. Dieter Oehler, father of one of the male victims. 'That was before those Kripo bastards hunted us down. We've no time to waste, Gruber.' He turned to the others. 'Let's put it to the vote, boys. Here and now. What do you say?'

All but one of the others nodded and grunted their support.

'Show of hands. Who says we've heard all we need to prove their guilt, and therefore we execute them now?' He thrust his own hand up and two of the others followed suit. Then he turned to Scholtz. 'What about you?'

Scholtz said, 'Hang them.'

'That's it,' Oehler said. 'Four to one.'

'What about Breker outside?' Gruber responded. 'He should have a say.'

'We don't need him. The vote is carried. We kill the bastards now.' Oehler stabbed a finger towards the men tied to the chairs.

Schenke could see the terrified expression on Pieper's face.

'You can't do this!' the director of the clinic said. 'It's murder!'

'Shut your mouth!' Oehler raged. 'You murdered our kids! This is justice. An eye for an eye.'

'It was not murder!' Pieper shouted back, his voice quavering but edged with indignation. 'We were ordered to carry out the killings. We were acting on behalf of the state. They were mercy killings. The Führer himself said they were lives not worth living. We were acting on his orders. I swear it.'

'Liar!' Oehler spat back. He strode across and delivered a vicious backhand to Pieper's cheek. 'How dare you accuse the Führer of such things?'

'It's true,' Pieper pleaded. 'You can confirm it easily enough. Call Obergruppenführer Bouhler at the Chancellery. He knows it all. Ask him about the programme. Ask him!'

Oehler looked at him with contempt. 'You'd say anything to save your skin, you vile piece of shit.' He struck the director again, and blood coursed from Pieper's nose. Oehler stepped back two paces. 'Any last words?'

'I swear I'm telling the truth!' Pieper cried out pitifully. 'We were carrying out orders. We're good men. Good Nazis. Doing our duty.'

Huber glanced at him. 'Stop your whining. We were dead from the moment these swine kidnapped us. So die with some dignity, damn you!' He spat on the floor at Oehler's feet, then sat stiffly, chin thrust out with his customary brutal arrogance. 'I admit I was one of those who killed your kids. And I killed many more. I did it for the Reich. It's you bastards who are the traitors here. You'll find out what happens to traitors once you are hunted down.'

Oehler shook his head. 'I've heard enough. Let's do it and get out of here. Scholtz, give me a hand. Pieper's first.'

'Wait!' Gruber opened his hands. 'I beg you. You heard him. This goes further than our children. There's more at stake. We have to expose the crimes of the party. That's why we've done all this.'

'I don't give a shit about that any more. Right now I just want revenge on the bastards who murdered my child.'

Schenke glanced in the direction of the policemen moving towards the workshop. They were too far away to intervene in time to save the prisoners.

Oehler grabbed Pieper's arm and dragged him to his feet. Shoving him towards one of the nooses, he slipped it roughly over his head.

'No!' Pieper shrieked. 'For pity's sake!'

'Where was your pity for our children?' Oehler demanded as he stepped behind his prisoner.

Schenke had seen enough. Smashing the nearest window pane with the butt of his gun, he aimed into the room as he shouted, 'Police! Raise your hands and drop your weapons!'

To his left, Liebwitz rose and also took aim as the men inside the workshop turned towards the window. For a heartbeat they stood frozen. Then Schenke repeated the order and there was a frenzied burst of action. Huber threw himself off his chair and crashed down onto his side on the floor. Oehler thrust Pieper forward, and the director stumbled over the edge of the inspection pit with a shriek that was abruptly cut off as the noose snapped tight around his neck. Gruber and the others snatched out their weapons; Schenke saw that one of the men had a sawn-off shotgun.

Oehler raised his weapon and looked up. There were two stabs of flame, and shattering crashes echoed round the workshop as he shot out the lights and plunged the interior into darkness.

'Open fire!' he roared, and there was a brilliant flash and percussive boom as the shotgun blew out several panes of glass between the two policemen.

Schenke was aware of a burning pain in his cheek, as if it had been pierced by a red-hot needle. There were more flashes as the other men blazed away at the windows and the thin corrugated metal of the walls close by. Their bullets burst through into the freezing night air, and Schenke felt one pluck at the folds of his coat as he tumbled away. More shards of glass fell on him, and he shielded his face with his hand. To his left, Liebwitz unleashed a full clip, aiming high so as to frighten the men inside into taking cover until the police squad could reach the scene. Then he scurried several paces away as a fusillade of bullets smashed through the wall where he had been standing. He calmly ejected the empty clip and fed in another magazine.

'Are you all right, sir?' he called across.

'I'm fine,' Schenke replied, looking out over the open ground beyond the buildings of the depot. He could see the first dark shapes of the backup squad of policemen hurrying towards the sound of the firing. On the other side of the workshop he heard an engine turning over, and for a moment he feared that some of the gang were making their escape, before he realised it must be Hauser. In the distance he could hear the sound of more vehicles starting up, and faint shouts as the other two squads responded to the shots and moved forward to close the trap.

There were a few more shots through the wall, then quiet, broken by the creak of the rope and the guttural choking sounds coming from Pieper. A voice sounded inside. 'Did we get 'em?'

Gruber called out to his companions by name to make sure they were all unharmed. Then Oehler shouted, 'There's only two of them out there. I'll keep their heads down. The rest of you get out of here. Go!'

'What about Huber?' Scholtz responded.

'Get him on his feet. We'll use him as a hostage.'

The engine on the other side of the workshop suddenly roared into life, and a moment later, the workshop doors burst apart as the lorry smashed through and the dazzling beam of the search lamp mounted on the driver's side swept across the interior, catching Gruber and the others in its glare. The vehicle hit a pillar and stalled. In the sudden quiet, Pieper writhed in the full glare of the beam of light, his shadow dancing grotesquely across the wall opposite.

'Police!' Hauser roared. 'Drop your weapons!'

Now that the first paralysing moment of surprise had passed, the men inside the workshop were keyed up to fight, and they rushed for cover amongst the machinery and piled storage boxes. One stood his ground and fired at the driver's cab of the lorry. Glass shattered, and Hauser returned fire. Two quick shots hit the gunman in the chest and cut him down.

Outside, Schenke and Liebwitz were back at the window, momentarily forgotten by the men facing the new threat. The shotgun boomed again, a jet of flame and sparks blasting in the direction of the lorry, and more glass shattered. Schenke felt a stab of dread for Hauser, but then the passenger door swung open and the sergeant rolled out and took cover to the rear of the vehicle as bullets smashed into the cab and the engine compartment.

Oehler rushed over to Scholtz as the latter struggled to get Huber upright. The prisoner was doing his best to stay on the ground. Oehler jammed the muzzle of the gun into his cheek and bellowed, 'Get up, or so help me I'll blow your brains out where you lie!' Huber needed no further warning, and struggled to his feet. With Scholtz steering him by the arm while Oehler covered their retreat, the three men made for the far side of the workshop.

The window panes near Schenke had been shot out, leaving a gap large enough for him to climb through. He swung a leg over the frame and hissed with pain as a shard of glass caught the material of his trousers and grazed his thigh. He threw his weight forward and tumbled inside, crawling swiftly to the shelter of some sturdy wooden crates filled with scrapped engine parts.

'One of the bastards came through the window! He went left.'

More shots crashed out, and the bright flashes lit up the ceiling of the workshop like fireworks against a cloudy night sky. Bullets smashed into the boxes and zipped overhead, and Schenke pressed himself into the ground. He was pinned down and felt foolish at his eagerness to prevent Oehler and Scholtz escaping with Huber. There might still be a chance to save Pieper, he decided, and risked a brief glimpse round the corner of the largest of the crates. The director was still moving feebly as his body swayed from side to side, and Schenke raised his pistol to take aim at the rope where it crossed the beam. There was a splintering crash just above his head as a bullet tore through the crate, and he ducked back into cover. *Shit . . .*

He called out to Liebwitz.

'Sir?'

'Save Pieper. Shoot the rope!'

'Yes, sir!'

There was a brief delay as Liebwitz took aim. His third shot nicked the rope, and frayed strands sprang apart. Then, with a dull twang, the rope parted and Pieper's swinging body dropped, his head striking the edge of the inspection pit before he disappeared from sight, the severed rope trailing behind him.

More shots were fired in Liebwitz's direction before all heard the sound of approaching vehicles and the shouts of the policemen closing in on the workshop.

'Get out!' Gruber shouted. 'Run!'

Two of the men broke cover and darted past the lorry as

they dashed for the opening between the shattered doors of the workshop.

'Halt!' Hauser shouted.

One of the men turned towards the sound and raised his pistol, but there was a flash from behind the lorry and the detonation of a shot, and the man spun and collapsed on the ground. As he writhed there, his comrade drew up and raised his hands.

'Throw down the gun!' Hauser's voice echoed, and the man tossed the pistol away. It clattered loudly on the ground.

Gruber and the man with the shotgun were holed up in the corner of the workshop, and the lawyer must have grasped that unless they made an attempt to escape at once, there was no chance to save themselves. They burst from cover, making for the window. The shotgun blasted again, and Schenke feared that Liebwitz would be caught by the deadly spray of lead shot. As soon as the second barrel was discharged, however, the Scharführer reappeared and fired twice, dropping the man with the shotgun. Gruber raised his pistol to take aim.

'Don't!' Schenke called out, but it was too late. Gruber fired, and an instant later Liebwitz's next shot struck him in the forehead, just below the rim of his hat. His head snapped back and he fell, arms outstretched, across the body of his comrade.

It took a moment for the ringing sound of the last shots to fade enough for Schenke to hear the receding footsteps of the last two gang members and their prisoner. He decided it was safe to emerge from cover, and scrambled to his feet. His priority was Pieper, and he raced over the open ground and down the short flight of steps into the inspection pit. Fumbling for his torch, he took it out of his pocket and turned it on. The beam fell on the director's contorted features: bulging blood-shot eyes, protruding tongue, and a deep bloody gash on the side of his skull where his head had struck the edge of the pit. There was no sign of breath in the cold air, and when Schenke took off his glove, loosened the noose and felt for a pulse, he found nothing.

'Dammit . . .' he muttered, putting his glove back on and snapping the torch off.

As he emerged from the pit, he saw that Liebwitz had climbed through the window and was loading a fresh clip in his pistol. Hauser had appeared from the rear of the lorry and kicked the weapon away from the injured man on the ground as he covered the one who had surrendered.

'We've got 'em, sir . . . Wait. Where's Huber?'

'There's two of them left,' Schenke replied. 'They've taken him with them. You stay here and watch these two until the Orpo lads arrive.'

He moved towards the darkness at the far end of the workshop, loading another clip as he moved towards Oehler, Scholtz and the surviving hostage. Taking out his torch again, he readied it in his left hand as he advanced warily, listening for his prey.

Chapter Thirty-Six

Ahead in the gloom at the far end of the workshop, Schenke could make out the shape of a biplane stripped of its engine. He moved to it and peered over the canvas-covered fuselage. At the opposite end of the workshop was a door; Scholtz was dragging Huber through it while Oehler covered their rear.

'Give up!' Schenke called out. 'The police have the depot surrounded. There's no escape!'

Oehler fired blindly towards the sound of his voice, and two rounds tore through the cockpit of the plane. Then he ducked out of the doorway and disappeared.

Schenke made his way around the rear of the aircraft and hurried over to the wall to one side of the door. He knew he would make an easy target if he rushed through it. There was a mop and bucket a short distance further along the wall, and he made for it, transferring the torch to his gun hand and slipping out of his coat. He arranged the coat over the head of the mop, then eased it across the opening. At once there was a burst of shots as both fugitives opened fire. The coat leaped under the impact and pulled the mop from his hand.

'We got him!' Scholtz called out.

'Shut up,' Oehler snapped. 'Keep moving. Get that pig up on his feet!'

Without his coat, Schenke was exposed to the cold breeze blowing in from outside and could not stop himself shivering as he snatched a glance out of the door. There were several large snow-covered mounds a short distance away, and beyond those what looked like an old control tower. Even in the darkness he could make out the trail of disturbed snow that indicated the direction taken by the fleeing men. He felt isolated and exposed. He was abandoning all he had learned from his training about the dangers of pursuing armed criminals alone. He knew he should wait for the uniformed police to arrive and close the trap, but he did not trust them to get there in time. Despite the loom of the snow and the dim starlight, there was plenty of cover and shadows that would help conceal the fugitives as they attempted to escape. He had to keep tracking them, keep close, until he could get help to bring the chase to an end.

Steeling his nerves, he darted out of the doorway and veered to one side, then changed direction abruptly and ran on to the shelter of the nearest mound and crouched down in cover as he looked about him, pistol raised. There was no sign of movement amid the soft sigh of the icy breeze blowing through the bare branches of some stunted trees growing along the edge of the depot. Hearing Huber curse in pain from the direction of the control tower, he moved on cautiously, following the tracks in the snow.

There was a sudden burst of noise as one of the Orpo lorries rounded the buildings behind the tower and sped past the mounds before Schenke could think to react and fire a shot to alert them to his presence. The same shot might equally alert the men he was tracking to the fact that he had not been hit in the doorway, he realised. He waited until the noise had faded, then continued threading his way past the snowy heaps on either side.

A sudden movement to his left caught his eye, and he saw a shape emerge between two piles of snow. There was a flash and a flat crack, but Schenke was already tumbling forward, and the bullet passed overhead. He could not roll into cover due to the depth of the snow and propped himself up on his elbow as he took aim in the direction of the shooter. But the man he assumed to be Oehler had gone. He rose into a crouch and surged through the snow in the opposite direction, hoping to work his way round towards the control tower without being ambushed again. Behind him he could faintly hear Hauser's voice warning the approaching Orpo men of the presence of police officers in the workshop.

As he reached the last of the mounds, Schenke saw a small strip of open ground before the entrance of the control tower – a pair of doors, one of which was ajar. The tracks led directly to the opening. It was too dangerous to risk the doorway, so he ran over to the treeline and scurried past the bare boughs to the other side of the building, where he found another, smaller door that was closed. Here was a chance to enter the building from an unexpected direction and take them by surprise. He tested the handle with his torch hand. It gave the slightest squeal of protest as it turned, and he pushed gently. The door gave easily, leaving a low parapet of snow on the threshold where it had drifted against the outside of the building. Holding his pistol in front of him and readying his torch, he stepped into the dark interior, eyes and ears straining.

He did not hear a sound as the pistol emerged from the shadow beside the door and the muzzle pressed hard into the side of his head.

'Lower your gun, slowly,' a voice said quietly. When Schenke hesitated, the muzzle was shoved against his head painfully. 'Do it.'

He lowered his Walther to the ground.

'Torch too.'

As soon as he had laid it down, the man struck him with the pistol butt, hard enough for Schenke to see dazzling white flashes. As his vision cleared, he saw the man scoop up his pistol and torch and then gesture towards the interior of the building. There was a soft click, and the torch illuminated a small lobby with a door at the end.

'In there.'

Still dazed, Schenke staggered to the door and pushed it open. There was a large square room on the other side, lined with tables, and ahead of him the open door he had seen a moment earlier. The torch beam picked out Huber on his knees in the corner, with Scholtz standing beside him, gun pressed into the angle between his neck and shoulder. A shove propelled Schenke to the opposite corner, and he reeled before recovering his balance and leaning against one of the tables.

'What are we going to do?' Scholtz demanded, his voice quavering with fear.

'Quiet, I'm trying to think.' Oehler went to the door and tried to close it, but the timbers had long since warped and no longer fitted the frame, so he had to leave a slight gap. He turned back into the room and shone the light at Schenke. 'Inspector Schenke. You just couldn't keep your nose out of it, could you? Kleist's orders and our warning weren't enough, it seems. Tell me how many men you have out there.'

There seemed no point in lying, Schenke reasoned. He had no need to exaggerate the number. 'Three sections. You can't escape.'

'We'll see about that. How are your men deployed?'

'The depot is surrounded. They're already searching the rest of the buildings. You've only got a few minutes before we're discovered. It's over. You either surrender to me now, or you'll have to shoot it out when my men find you.'

'Not while I have hostages. Including their leader,' said Oehler. 'Thanks for strengthening my hand, by the way.'

'Do you really think this changes anything?'

'If your friends want you to live, then yes. I'll demand one of your lorries and we'll be a long way from here before any reinforcements turn up.'

'And then where will you go? Your identities will be known to every police officer in Berlin. You can't hide for long. In any case, aren't you forgetting something?'

'What?'

'Two can play at your game. The first thing the Gestapo will do is arrest your families and hold them hostage. I dare say Heydrich will let it be known he'll give you twenty-four hours before he starts shooting your wives and any children you still have.'

'Holy Jesus, no . . .' Scholtz muttered.

There was a pause before Oehler spoke again. 'Why did you hunt us down, Schenke? You knew what this bastard and Pieper were up to. Since when does the police side with child-murderers?'

'We haven't sided with them. We needed Pieper and Huber

to help track down the rest of the men who murdered your children. You played into the hands of killers by taking the law into your own hands.'

'Yes, we took the law into our hands, because the police failed us,' Oehler countered. 'I already knew Gruber, and when I spoke to him about my suspicions over our kids' deaths and the authorities' refusal to do anything about it, he said we had to make sure justice was done ourselves. That was when we recruited the others.'

'And then you murdered Schmesler.'

'We executed Schmesler,' Oehler corrected him. 'Gruber and I went to his house and found him in his study. We informed him that our little court had found him guilty and he was to get on his knees while the sentence was carried out.'

'You shot him in the head. Cold-blooded murder is what I call that.'

'All execution is cold-blooded, Inspector. He deserved it. We were going to deal with the rest of them and put an end to the killing of children by that sick group of fanatics. Until you poked your nose in. Still, we got Schmesler. I dare say Pieper is dead, and this pig will be joining his boss the moment he has served his purpose as a hostage.'

'And me? Will you kill me too?'

'Maybe. But your best hope of coming out of this alive is not to give us any trouble.'

There was a dry chuckle, and the torch beam moved to Huber, whose expression had twisted into a contemptuous sneer.

'What's so damned funny?' Oehler demanded.

'You are. You and your pathetic little gang of avengers.

Do you think you will have solved anything by killing us? You think that will be the end of the killing? My God, you fools haven't got the slightest idea what is really going on, have you?'

'What are you saying?' Scholtz grabbed Huber's collar and shook it. 'Tell us!'

'You heard what Pieper said back in the workshop. Those murders weren't some freelance plot carried out by a handful of party insiders. You haven't put an end to anything. It's only just started. Our orders came straight from the top. From inside the Chancellery. Maybe even from the Führer himself. A chance to rid Germany of the useless mouths contaminating the Aryan race. That's what Pieper told me when I was recruited. It was our patriotic duty, he said.'

'You're lying,' Oehler interrupted.

'You think so? Let me tell you how we did it. You're going to kill me anyway, so I've nothing to gain from hiding the truth.'

'Shut your mouth!' Schenke snapped. He could tell that Scholtz and Oehler were close to gunning Huber down, and perhaps Schenke himself into the bargain.

Oehler swung his pistol towards him. 'Quiet, or you'll pay for it. Continue, pig.'

'Our technique was quite crude to begin with,' said Huber. 'The kids marked for death were put into a special ward and starved to the point where they either died of an illness or Pieper finished them off with an overdose of drugs. But it was too long a process to satisfy those running the programme. So some specialist from the police labs experimented with gas to find a more efficient way of getting rid of them.'

Schenke felt his guts twist as he made the connection. 'Widmann.'

Huber nodded. 'That's the one. Clever man, that. When we discovered that the gas lingered too long in the cellar, Widmann realised we needed a better solution. That was when he came up with the idea of the bus. We had it altered so that the kids could be securely locked inside while I drove to a quiet place. Then all I had to do was throw a lever and the exhaust from the engine was redirected inside the vehicle. It took half an hour and the job was done, then I drove the bodies on to the crematorium.'

Scholtz let out a groan. 'You bastard . . . you monster.' He moved in front of Huber and aimed his pistol into his face.

'Easy, Scholtz!' Oehler intervened. 'We need him alive for now.'

'Alive? After that? After what he said?'

Oehler stepped forward and gently pushed Scholtz's gun hand aside. 'When the time comes, I promise you'll get to put a bullet in his brain. But we'll need him to expose his accomplices and put an end to this.'

'Haven't you been listening?' Huber laughed again. 'The Schiller clinic is a drop in the bucket. The euthanasia programme is happening across Germany. Soon hundreds, then thousands of defective children will be put down. You've achieved nothing. You could never have stopped it. You don't have a clue about how deep this goes.'

'It's not true . . . Say it's not true!' Scholtz raged.

'If you don't believe me, ask Schenke what he thinks. He's smart enough to have figured it out, right, Inspector?'

Scholtz turned to Schenke, the gun wavering in his hand. Schenke's mouth felt dry, and he swallowed before he spoke. 'The smart thing to do is surrender. Let me take Huber in for questioning. Once we get his full story on the record, you can have your justice.'

'You fool.' Huber sniffed. 'You think the party will let this information go any further than those already in the know?'

'They killed my daughter,' Scholtz muttered. 'Murdered her like she was an animal sent to slaughter.'

'Not an animal,' said Huber. 'Just not an acceptable member of the Aryan race.'

'You bastard!' Oehler gasped. 'My son was a German! The same flesh as any other Aryan. He wasn't a gypsy, or a homo, or a dirty Jew, who all deserve to be exterminated like the rats they are! He was my son . . .'

For a moment, any sympathy that Schenke had harboured for Oehler was quashed by the unreasoning hatred of the man towards those he had spoken of. He felt nausea welling up inside him. There were so many like him, sick in the head. The high-ranking party members responsible for creating the euthanasia programme. Those who carried it out in blind furtherance of their ideology, like Schmesler, Pieper and Huber. And now those like Oehler, whose feeling for his fellow creatures was so stunted by his politics that it only extended to his closest family. Too blind to even grasp the irony that his fanatical support for the party had enabled the personal tragedy that had invaded his life. In the end, the only victims were the children themselves, and those parents, like Scholtz, who were motivated by grief and an understandable need for revenge.

'Lose the guns and get your hands up.' Hauser's voice broke the tension in the room. The door was open wide, and Schenke realised that the sergeant was using the darkness outside to conceal himself.

Oehler was the first to react, turning quickly and swinging the torch beam towards the door as he fired three shots in quick succession. There were two shots in response, tearing through his chest and hurling him backwards. The gun and the torch went flying, and the light beam flashed round the room before pointing over the floor towards Huber and Scholtz.

'Oehler!' Scholtz shouted. 'Oehler . . .'

'He's gone.' Schenke spoke calmly. 'You are the last of them. It's over. Put the gun down and surrender.'

Scholtz froze, his face twisted in incomprehension. He shook his head as he pointed his gun at Huber. 'He's lying . . . he has to be. The party would never do such a thing. The Führer would not allow it.'

'Do as the inspector says,' said Hauser. 'Do it now. Lower the gun.'

Scholtz turned to the open door, and his features resolved into a cold, uncompromising mask as he pressed the muzzle against Huber's forehead and pulled the trigger.

The two shots were almost instantaneous. Huber's head jerked back as the rear of his skull exploded across the table and wall. The bullet that killed Scholtz hit him below the ear, and his body collapsed across that of Huber, the two men united in death.

The freezing cold suddenly enfolded Schenke as he regarded the three bodies caught in the arc of the torch's light. He heard the crunch of Hauser's feet as the sergeant approached the entrance and stepped inside.

'It's all over then, sir. We've got two in cuffs back at the workshop. Here.' He tossed a coat to Schenke. 'Yours, I believe. Bullet holes and all.'

As Schenke gratefully put it on and fastened the buttons, he stared at Huber's face, his lips still seemingly locked in a cynical smile.

'How much of what he said did you hear?' he asked Hauser.

'Every word.'

'Then you must know it isn't over. It's only just started . . . God help us.'

Chapter Thirty-Seven

The lorry returned from the control tower with the last three bodies and laid them out beside the others in front of the smashed doors of the workshop. The cab spotlights of the other two vehicles illuminated the scene as the police picked up the weapons and searched the gang's hideout for any other evidence that might be relevant to the case and the likely prosecution of the two survivors, who had given their names as Breker and Kappler. Schenke was sitting in the cab of one of the lorries while Hauser cleaned the cuts on his face inflicted by broken glass during the shoot-out.

'Try and sit still, sir,' the sergeant said as he held up a piece of gauze soaked in disinfectant spirit from the medical box. 'You look like you've gone three rounds with Max Schmeling.'

'I feel more like Schmeling after Joe Louis had finished with him.'

'That's not very patriotic of you, sir.'

'But apposite.'

'I'm not sure Karin's going to approve of your appearance . . .'

Karin – she'd be worried sick by his fresh injuries, Schenke realised.

'We got off lightly. No dead or wounded on our side.'

'I suppose so,' Schenke said. He had failed to save the lives of Pieper and Huber and therefore the secret of the identities of the others involved in the murders of the children seemed to have died with the two men. That was the extent of his regret over their deaths. Any measure of sympathy he felt was reserved for the others, those who had chosen to take revenge on the murderers. Even Oehler, who was still a grieving father at the end of the day, despite his twisted views. Schenke's truest compassion was reserved for the children, the real victims in this whole sorry business. When the photos of their faces flickered into his consciousness from time to time, his heart filled with black despair over the circumstances of their deaths. They must have been terrified as they were taken from their families and cruelly treated by strangers until they were murdered. And now he was burdened with the chilling knowledge of Huber's claims about the euthanasia programme. If it was true . . . He forced himself to stop pursuing that line of thought. It would have to wait. There were other matters to attend to first.

'We'll need to arrange proper searches of those men's homes to see if there is any sign that others were involved.'

Hauser looked at the row of bodies lying in the glare of the lamps. He spoke quietly. 'Given what I overheard back there when Huber was spilling his guts, there are going to be bastards like him and Pieper operating right across the country. And they'll be doing it on the orders of someone at the top. I don't think that's good news for us, sir.'

'No . . . but at least we put a stop to this group.'

'Maybe we shouldn't have. Maybe we should go after the people they were after.'

Schenke had wondered how long it would take his sergeant to suggest something like this. There was a part of him that fervently desired that those in charge of the euthanasia programme be hunted down and prosecuted in full view of the public. Their deeds would horrify the nation so greatly that those in the party who had dreamed up the programme would never dare to contemplate its like again. But there were so many obstacles between such a desire and its fruition as to make it impossible, beyond any doubt. Even so, there must be some steps he could take to challenge it. The knowledge of such a monstrosity was as heavy a burden as any man could shoulder.

'Hauser, think it through,' he began. 'If Huber spoke the truth, who do you think we are up against? How long do you expect they would let us live if we treated them like the criminals they are and attempted to bring them to justice?'

The sergeant frowned. 'Are you suggesting we do nothing?'

'I'm suggesting that whatever we might do, we have to do it carefully. And whatever that is, it will be dangerous to us, and those closest to us.'

'But . . .' Hauser clenched his eyes shut. 'Shit . . . shit . . .' He seemed to sink into despair.

Watching his sergeant, Schenke was grateful that it was Hauser who had intervened at the control tower. If it had been Liebwitz, there would be no question about the scharführer's reaction. He would pursue the guilty within the party until his quest destroyed him. Or perhaps not. Maybe the very fact that the programme came from the top of the regime might make it unchallengeable in his eyes. Conversely, he might adopt the same reasoning as Schenke and resolve to fight the battles he could win rather than attempting the futile struggles that inevitably ended in annihilation. Now that he considered it, Schenke realised he did not understand Liebwitz well enough to know how he would react. All the more reason to be glad he was talking to Hauser.

'Listen to me, Sergeant. Three of the guilty men have been dealt with, but at least twice that many of their victims' parents are dead, or will be once Heydrich gets his hands on them. Maybe this incident will show the regime that they can't hide all their secrets. Maybe they'll close the programme down rather than run the risk of provoking more men like Gruber and his people. That is the best we can hope for at the moment. That is the measure of this fucked-up investigation.'

'You sound like you've been around Liebwitz too long. This is about right and wrong, sir. That's the only measure that counts at the end of the day.'

'But we're not at the end of the day. There will be a reckoning for the evil that is being done, but I fear that won't come for some time. Months . . . years . . . who can say? In which case, it is our duty to survive and bear witness. We can't do that if we're dead. It's a hard truth to live with. As hard as it comes. But we must continue to do our job and fight what evil we can within the system, because if we don't, who will?'

Even as he spoke, Schenke could not help asking himself the question – what if the system itself was the source of evil? What then?

Hauser was silent for a moment. 'I don't know if I can, sir. I have kids. When I think about Pieper's victims, I see my children's faces . . .'

A flicker of light at the periphery of his vision caught Schenke's attention, and he turned to see two vehicles approaching along the track that ran around the perimeter from the Tempelhof terminal. 'We've got company.'

'Who would that be? More of Gruber's lot?'

'No. We've accounted for those in Lenger's files.'

'Then maybe there are other cells . . .'

'It's possible,' Schenke conceded. But given the timing, it did not seem likely that the lawyer could have set up such a network. There was a more credible explanation of who was in the approaching vehicles. 'I think they're Heydrich's men.'

'How could they know about this so quickly?'

'How do you think? Someone at Pankow told them.'

'What are they doing here?'

Schenke thought quickly. 'Tidying up loose ends.' He turned to Hauser, his heartbeat quickening. They had only a few minutes before the distant vehicles reached them. 'You still in the mood to do some good? Listen . . .'

No more than a minute later, the two of them climbed out of the cab and Schenke called the uniformed sergeants over. 'We've done what we came to do. You and your lads have my thanks. It's a cold night and it's time to get back to Pankow before we freeze our bollocks off. Load the bodies and the prisoners into one of the lorries and leave that here for us. We'll bring them in. Your men can go in the other lorries; leave as soon as you are ready, and make sure you head off in that direction.' He pointed to the track opposite the one the vehicles were approaching on. 'Don't want you getting in the way of the reinforcements.'

The sergeants turned to look at the dim lights approaching.

'Reinforcements?' one queried.

'Gestapo,' Schenke responded. 'Always late on the scene whenever there's trouble, eh?'

He forced a laugh, and the other men smiled anxiously before turning away to carry out their orders, keen to get away before the approaching vehicles arrived.

'Wait. Anyone seen Zebrinski?'

One of the sergeants jerked his thumb in the direction of the terminal. 'He went off as soon as the firing started, sir.'

Schenke smiled. 'Very wise of him. All right, you have your orders. Get going.'

As soon as the Orpo lorries had disappeared between the buildings of the depot, Schenke hurried to the rear of the remaining vehicle and drew aside the canvas flap, shining his torch inside. The bodies were lying on the bed of the lorry, while the two prisoners were seated either side on the narrow wooden benches. They raised their hands to shield their eyes.

'Get out,' he ordered, stepping aside.

The two men hesitated.

'Get out now, if you want to live,' he snapped. 'My guess is the Gestapo will be here in a matter of minutes. Given what you have done, there's little doubt what's in store for you once you are in the cells at Prinz-Albrecht-Strasse.'

They did as they were told, the uninjured man supporting his wounded colleague. Schenke pointed to the shattered windows at the back of the workshop. 'Go out of the building that way and follow the tracks until you can find shelter in another building. After that, you're on your own. Get far away from Berlin. Don't contact any family or friends if you want to keep them out of danger. And if there's any immediate risk of you being captured, then for the sake of your families – and us – make sure you don't let yourselves be taken alive. Understand?'

One of the men looked at him suspiciously. 'Why are you letting us go?'

'Does it matter? Just go before it's too late. It's not us you have to worry about. Go!'

He gave the man a push, and the two of them crossed the floor of the workshop, climbed over the window frame and disappeared into the night. Schenke turned to Liebwitz, who had said nothing during the exchange and was regarding him with a curious expression.

'Scharführer, I need to know that I can trust you.'

'Sir?'

'Do you know why I let those men escape?'

'It would appear to have something to do with the moral imperative associated with the operation of justice, sir.'

Schenke could not help a grim smile. 'Indeed.'

'I understand their need for revenge, sir,' Liebwitz continued tonelessly. 'As you will appreciate.'

'Then I can rely on you not to tell anyone I allowed them to escape.'

'Yes, sir. But can you rely on those men not talking if they are caught alive?'

'After what they have been through, they deserve a chance to live. I cannot stomach handing them over to Heydrich's thugs. I trust they will not betray me.'

'Your grand gesture is a risk, sir.'

'I know. I will make sure the risk is mine alone if I am called to account.'

'Yes, sir.' Liebwitz was still for a moment. 'You are a good man, Inspector. That I have come to understand about you. I hope it will not be your undoing.'

He turned and walked to the cab and climbed in.

'That was unexpected.' Hauser whistled softly. 'I'd have thought our friend would have played this by the book.'

'He has his reasons. Personal reasons. Try not to goad him so much in future.'

Hauser nodded slowly. 'Fair enough.'

They could hear the growl of the approaching vehicles, and less than a minute later, the lights of a sleek car appeared between the buildings and caught the Kripo men and their vehicle in the narrow beams of the headlamps. A large covered lorry followed.

'Here we go,' Hauser muttered.

The vehicles slowed and drew up a short distance away. At once an order was barked, and men dropped from the rear of the lorry and spread out in a loose cordon in front of the workshop. A moment later, the rear door of the car opened and a bespectacled officer in a peaked cap climbed out. As he emerged into the pool of light cast by the search lamp on the Orpo vehicle, the silver insignia of the SS was visible on his collar, along with the small metal skull on the front of his cap. As he strode forward, Schenke recognised him at once. The man who had been with Heydrich at the Adlon hotel.

He drew up and glanced round briefly before fixing his gaze on Schenke.

'Someone at Pankow told us that you might need assistance. Where have the uniformed police gone?'

'I sent them back to the precinct.' Schenke indicated the distant lights of the Orpo lorries picking their way along the perimeter track. 'No sense in keeping them here after their job was over.'

'What happened here?'

'I'm afraid I don't know your name . . .'

The SS officer lifted his chin and indicated his insignia. 'You recognise the rank?'

'Yes . . . sir.'

'Better.' The man's lips twitched briefly. 'Obergruppenführer Bouhler . . .'

As he recognised the name Schenke felt his blood turn still colder.

'I imagine you are surprised to see an officer of my rank attending this incident. You should be. Take it as a measure of the seriousness with which the Reich Security Main Office regards this matter.'

'Yes, sir.'

'So, did you get them?'

'Yes, sir. The bodies are in the back. Unfortunately we were not able to save the prisoners. Dr Pieper and Huber were killed during the firefight with the gang members.'

'Show me.'

Schenke led the way and played his torch beam over the dead men. Bouhler glanced at them in silence for a moment.

'Good.'

'The leader seemed to be that man, sir.' Schenke aimed the torch at Gruber's head. 'A lawyer.'

'Lawyers, eh? They're a nuisance at the best of times. Worse when they get a bee in their bonnet about pursuing justice.' Bouhler shook his head, then turned away from the lorry and paced towards the shattered entrance to the workshop. Schenke followed, and they inspected the interior briefly by the light of the lorry's search lamp. The remaining noose still hung over the inspection pit.

'Inspector Schenke, now that you have tracked down and eliminated the gang responsible for Schmesler's death, the matter is closed.'

'Yes, sir.'

'There is a saying. Dead men tell no tales . . .'

'I've heard it said, sir.'

Bouhler turned to him. 'Did any of the gang have the opportunity to speak to you or the police officers involved in the incident at any stage?'

'No, sir. The shooting started as soon as we discovered their location and saw that they were about to execute their prisoners.'

'It's too bad that you were unable to save Pieper and Huber. Dr Pieper was a valued member of the SS and Huber was a good party comrade. They will be missed. I take it there is no way of knowing if they passed on any information to their captors, or anyone else, before they were killed?'

'No, sir.'

'I see. Then the matter of the children's deaths died with them all.'

'It would appear so.'

'In that case, all that remains is for you to submit your report directly to Heydrich's office tomorrow.'

'Yes, sir.'

'There will be no copy made of the report for the Kripo's files. You will submit the original, together with your notes. Every scrap of information to do with the case. Is that clear?'

'Yes, sir. But—'

'But nothing, Inspector. Dr Pieper and his associates were involved in criminal matters such that public knowledge of their acts would damage the reputation of the party and its functionaries. They were acting independently. The party knew nothing about their activities. Understand?'

'Yes, sir.'

'Germany is at war. Her people cannot afford to be distracted by a scandal involving the deaths of those unfortunate children. However, the guilty have been punished, and the parents who took the law into their own hands have paid for it with their lives. The matter is resolved. There is no need for it to be discussed any further once your report has been submitted. I expect you will be glad to put this unwholesome business behind you and get back to tackling other matters, Inspector.'

'I . . .'

'What is it, man?' An irritated expression formed on Bouhler's face. 'Do you have something else to say?'

Schenke forced himself to stay calm. 'No, sir.'

'Then I'll have my men take the bodies. We have a streamlined process for their disposal. It will save on any paperwork that would be required if they were dealt with by your section at Pankow. You can go.' Bouhler nodded over his shoulder. 'Get back to your desk and write your report.'

He turned away to shout his orders. One of his men backed the SS lorry up to the rear of the other vehicle, and his comrades hurriedly transferred the bodies across before climbing in and pulling up the tailgate. Bouhler tapped the brim of his peaked cap in farewell and got into his car before it drove off followed by the lorry.

'What now?' asked Hauser.

'Now we pray to God that they are so desperate to cover this up that they don't probe any further than the report I will write for them. If they question the police who were here tonight, or find those last two men, it won't go well for us, my friend.'

'You are something of a master in the use of understatement, sir.'

'Come, let's get away from this place.'

They climbed into the cab either side of Liebwitz. The Scharführer was hunched down to keep warm and staring ahead.

'Are you all right, Liebwitz?' Schenke asked as Hauser switched off the search lamp.

'Fine, sir.'

'I owe you more than an apology for letting those men go. I have put you in danger along with the sergeant and myself.'

'Yes, sir,' Liebwitz replied. He was silent before he continued. 'Sometimes danger is unavoidable, sir.'

'And you are willing to accept that?'

'Would it make any difference if I wasn't, sir?'

Hauser turned the ignition key and revved the engine as it caught. 'Good answer. You know something? For a Gestapo man, you're all right.'

Liebwitz looked at him and shrugged before turning and staring ahead once more.

'Back to the precinct, sir?' asked Hauser.

'Yes,' Schenke replied. Now that the crisis had passed, exhaustion had closed in on him, and his weary mind was struggling to think straight. 'Then home. We could all use some sleep.'

'Damn right.' Hauser slipped the gearstick into first, and the lorry edged forward over the snow.

Schenke stared blankly out of the window as the vehicle jolted along the icy track. He was not done for the night. There was one more task left for him before he could allow himself to rest.

Chapter Thirty-Eight

A clock chimed in a church tower somewhere as Schenke parked the pool car outside the Schmesler house. He turned the engine off and checked the time on his watch by the dim glow of the dashboard lights. Eleven o'clock. He flicked the switch and darkness filled the inside of the car.

He sat for a moment looking along the street, but there was no sign of the car that had been watching the house before. Tomorrow there would be fresh eyes on the house. Bouhler was sure to go after the families of those connected to Gruber's gang or their victims. Heydrich's men would turn up and search for any scraps of incriminating information. Fortunately the Gestapo's unswerving routine was to arrive at dawn, pounding on doors and brushing aside bleary-eyed occupants before turning their homes over. Schenke and those in the Schmesler house would be safe for a few hours.

He got out of the car, climbed the steps and pulled the doorbell knob. A dull jingle sounded from within, and he waited patiently for nearly a minute before a first-floor window opened a crack.

'Who is there?' asked Brigitte Schmesler.

'Schenke. Let me in.'

She hesitated. 'It's late . . .'

'There's no time to waste. Let me in.'

There was a muted exchange, and then the window was shut. A few moments later, the bolts slid back and he was admitted into the house. Once the door was closed and locked again, Brigitte turned on the hall light and he saw that she was wearing a fur coat over her dressing gown and nightdress. Further down the hall stood Ruth, similarly dressed. He felt a surge of affection as he saw her, and at the same time anxiety for her safety.

'Horst, what's the matter?' she asked. 'Why are you here at this hour?'

'You need to leave. Pack whatever belongings you have and be ready to go as soon as you can.'

'Why?' Brigitte demanded. 'What's going on?'

'Listen, I have to get Ruth out of here. It's almost certain that the Gestapo will be paying you a call in the morning. They'll want to search your house.'

'Another search?'

Schenke nodded. 'This time they will tear the place apart to make sure they miss nothing. If Ruth is here, they will take her away and she will be sent to the camps. It is likely that you'll suffer the same fate for sheltering a Jew, even if they don't discover the truth about your origins.'

Brigitte's eyes widened and she turned to Ruth. 'You told him?'

'Yes. I trust him. He won't tell anyone else.'

'Why?'

'He needed to understand why I was helping you.'

Brigitte lowered her head for a moment, then looked up at Schenke.

'Why are the Gestapo coming here?'

He sighed. He had anticipated her need to know, and now he would have to tell her the truth about her husband. 'I could use a hot drink.'

'Yes, of course.' She indicated the door at the rear of the hall. 'In the kitchen. The range keeps the room warm, and I have a little coffee left.'

'Sounds good.' Schenke smiled gratefully and followed her.

Ruth fell into step beside him. 'Do the Gestapo know I'm here?'

'No. At least I don't think so.' He took her hand and gave it a gentle squeeze. 'I'll take you somewhere you'll be safe for a few days until you find somewhere else to stay.'

He sat down at the kitchen table and took off his hat, then ran a hand through his hair. His eyes ached with tiredness. As Brigitte rummaged through a cupboard, Ruth sat opposite him with a worried expression.

'You look terrible.'

'Well thanks.'

'Have you been in an accident? Or a fight?'

'A fight.' He forced another smile. 'You should see the other man.'

'Horst, what's happened?'

On the drive from Tempelhof Schenke had had time to consider what to tell the two women. He had considered keeping the truth about Manfred from them. The fewer people who knew the truth the less likely it was to endanger them. But the enormity of what he had uncovered had to be known, he decided. At some point in the future there needed to be people who knew about the murders of the children to bear witness when the guilty were called to account. As terrible as the truth was for Brigitte and Ruth, they must share that burden.

Brigitte lifted the heavy lid over one of the heating plates and put the percolator down before sitting next to Ruth. Schenke was too tired to break the truth gently, and began simply.

'We got them. The men who killed your husband. We tracked them down to their hideout near the Tempelhof airfield. There was a shoot-out. The ringleader and most of his men are dead.'

Brigitte touched a hand to her mouth and gave a gasp before leaning closer. 'Who were they?'

'They were people whose children had been taken to clinics for the disabled and murdered there. They were seeking revenge against those they held responsible.'

Ruth frowned. 'What does that have to do with Manfred?'

Schenke met her gaze. 'The party have made it clear from the start that they believe the Aryan race has to be purified if it is to be strong. That is why they have forbidden marriage between Jews and Aryans. It is why they have sterilised those who were fathered by black troops when they occupied the Rhineland after the last war. They also want to remove those they refer to as "useless feeders" – the mentally and physically disabled – starting with children. All in the name of racial hygiene.'

He shifted his gaze to Brigitte. 'That's the area your husband specialised in. His most recent appointment was to an office set up by the Chancellery. A secret programme is being run from there. It's where Manfred had his office.' He paused. 'The purpose of the programme is to collate reports from doctors that give the names of children born with mental and physical defects. The reports were assessed by Manfred and some other doctors trusted by the regime, and those children deemed to be a burden on the state had a plus written on their papers. It meant they were marked for death at the clinic they were sent to . . .' He paused and shook his head sadly. 'I'm sorry, Frau Schmesler.'

'No.' She closed her eyes. 'No. It's not true. Not Manfred. He could never . . .'

'He could. And that's why he was killed by the fathers of his victims.'

'Wait,' Ruth intervened. 'How could you know all of this if it was a secret?'

'I had worked out most of it. I heard the rest from one of the men responsible for killing the children before he died tonight.'

'And how did these parents discover the truth?'

'There were too many deaths around the same time and under similar circumstances. Some parents became suspicious and banded together to find out the truth, then decided to take the law into their own hands and hunt down and kill those responsible. That's why they wanted to keep me from investigating Manfred's murder. To keep me from tracking them down in turn. If I'd known then what I know now, maybe I'd have backed off sooner and let them take care of your husband's accomplices . . . Maybe.'

Ruth shook her head. 'I've known Manfred since I was a child. He was a good man. He loved children. He would never have harmed them. Even after the party took power, he looked out for us. Me and my family . . . He was a good man,' she repeated lamely.

'Not always, it seems.'

The percolator started to bubble and steam, and Schenke took it off the hot plate and fetched some cups. He poured the coffee, then resumed his place, cupping his hands around the hot mug. Brigitte's head remained bowed as she tried to come to terms with what she had heard. Schenke took a careful sip. The coffee was bitter and unpleasant-tasting. The ersatz blend that failed to pass itself off as the real thing.

'What's going to happen now?' asked Ruth.

'Now?'

'You've found out what has been going on. You know about this euthanasia programme. Someone has to put a stop to it. The police must do something. It's murder.'

'It is murder,' Schenke agreed. 'And authorised at the top, maybe by Hitler himself. In which case it has to be kept a secret. That is how it works under the regime. Hitler decides what is within the law these days. No one can question him. If he has approved the programme, there is nothing that can be done to stop it. Nothing, you understand. I am powerless.'

'I want you to leave,' said Brigitte. She looked up with an angry expression. 'I want you out of my house.'

Schenke took another sip of the coffee and put the cup down. 'As you wish. Ruth, fetch your belongings.'

She had turned to Brigitte and taken her hand, torn between the need to comfort the other woman and the realisation that she must leave this house that she had been familiar with since she was a child.

'You need to go with him,' said Brigitte. 'I'll be fine, my girl. Go.'

Ruth leaned over to kiss her on the cheek, then rose and hurried towards the basement.

Schenke stood up. 'I'll wait for her by the front door.'

Brigitte waved him away with a flick of her hand. Schenke took a last look at her – at the sunken bow of her shoulders and the first heave of her chest as she fought back tears – then walked out of the kitchen and closed the door quietly behind him.

A few minutes later, Ruth joined him, dressed and carrying a battered-looking carpet bag. She paused and glanced back down the hall. 'I hope she can come to terms with what you told her. What if she tells anyone else?'

'She won't.'

'How can you be sure?'

'Would you? If Manfred was your husband . . . She will come to terms with it some day. Not for a long time, though. You can comfort her when it is safe for you to return.'

'Where are you taking me?'

He had already decided. Until he had patched up his disagreement with Karin his apartment would be safe enough.

'To my apartment. You can stay out of sight for a few days while we work out where you can go next.'

She looked at him. 'Your apartment?'

'Yes.' He felt awkward under her gaze. ' I just want to make sure you don't come to any harm.'

'And what about you? What would happen to a Kripo inspector who was discovered harbouring a Jew?'

'That's my problem. Let's go.'

They left the house and walked to the car. Schenke placed Ruth's bag on the back seat next to her. 'Stay low and keep out of sight. I don't want to have to answer awkward questions if one of my neighbours sees me driving up with a woman late at night.'

They completed the short journey in silence, and Schenke parked a short distance from the front entrance of his block. He turned to face her.

'We'll go in through the courtyard. Less chance of anyone seeing you that way. Last thing I want is our nosy concierge catching sight of you. Ready?'

She nodded.

They climbed out. Schenke locked the doors, then took her arm as they turned into the darkened alley that led under an arch into the courtyard. He used his torch to find his way to the rear entrance, then opened the door and glanced round the stairwell. All was quiet. He waved her forward and they climbed the stairs to his apartment. Once inside, he slipped the chain on the door and turned the lights on.

Ruth looked about her, taking in the details of the hall. 'Spare and tidy. Just what I would expect of a bachelor policeman.'

'How do you know I'm a bachelor?'

'No ring. No female touch to this place, and no chance of you bringing me here if you were married, obviously.'

'Fair enough.' He turned to indicate the doors. 'Kitchen, pantry, bathroom, living room, my study and the bedroom. You can take the bed. I'll be fine on the sofa.'

He faced her, and the two of them locked eyes in silence before Ruth rose on her tiptoes, put her hand around the back of his neck and kissed him on the lips. It lasted no more than a moment, but the warmth of her breath and the softness of her skin caused a thrill of excitement to course through

Schenke's veins. She began to draw back, but he caught her in his arms and held her there as he pressed his lips against hers, closing his eyes and surrendering to the bliss of momentarily putting aside all his troubles.

After a minute, they separated awkwardly.

'I'm sorry,' he said.

'What for?'

'I said I wouldn't expect any favours.'

'Is that what this is? That's not what it felt like.'

'It's not fair of me.'

'You did not force me to do anything I didn't want to do, Horst. Kiss me again.'

He hesitated.

'I want you to,' she said, stroking the back of his neck and making his flesh tingle.

'I can't.' He pulled himself away. 'There's someone else. At least, I hope there still is.'

He felt ashamed. He and Karin had argued. It was the kind of misunderstanding that couples patched up when their mutual resentment had subsided. And yet there was a part of him that was not sorry to have some time away from the occasional frictions that came with being with her.

'All right then.' Ruth smiled sadly. 'I won't force you.'

She walked down the hall to the bedroom and disappeared inside. Schenke went to the kitchen and poured himself a glass of water, downing it in a few easy gulps. He took off his outdoor clothes and hung them by the door before making for the cupboard in the hall where he kept spare bedding and towels. Taking out two blankets and a pillow, he made up a makeshift bed on the sofa. It was cold in the living room, but he was too tired to bother with lighting a fire. He took off his tie and his shoes, and loosened his shirt, then lay down and pulled the blankets over him.

He was angry with himself. He had only intended to have Ruth here for a few days until the danger of the Gestapo searching the Schmesler house had passed. He had not intended anything beyond offering her shelter. But he knew himself well enough to see through that self-deception. He was attracted to her. He wanted her, and the knowledge of that was frightening bearing in mind the danger it posed to both of them.

Despite his exhaustion, he was unable to sleep, partly due to the numbing cold that had seeped into his body. He rose to go to the hall cupboard and fetch another blanket. There was a soft click from the bedroom door, and Ruth was standing there in one of his thick hiking shirts, her bare legs crossed at the ankles.

'I hope you don't mind.' She touched the material over her chest. 'I found it in the wardrobe drawer. It's very cold.'

'It is.'

She looked at him. 'It'd be warmer for the two of us in your bed. You need sleep, Horst. You can't sleep if you are cold.'

'I—'

'Shh. I said you weren't forcing me to do anything. I want this. Now kiss me again.'

He put his arms around her and drew her close. This time they abandoned themselves to the kiss and the embrace that locked them together. As he held her Schenke was torn by feelings of guilt over his betrayal of Karin and anxiety over the madness of what they were doing.

'This is dangerous,' he whispered. 'So dangerous.'

'We live in dangerous times, Horst. It is better that we understand that and learn to live with danger if we are to survive.'

Then she moved away and led him towards the bed. She slid under the covers as Schenke undressed. He spread the spare blanket over the bed and stood naked.

'What are you waiting for?' Ruth said quietly. 'Come to me.'

Chapter Thirty-Nine

6 February

The telephone ringing in the hall drew Schenke out of a sleep in which he had been dreaming about walking in the Bavarian mountains on a hot summer day. He had stopped to rest by a tavern and have a beer and could hear children playing. He opened his eyes to find himself on his back looking up at the ceiling of his bedroom. The phone stopped and he wondered if it had been part of the dream. His mind felt dulled by a drowsy fog, and then he heard a sigh in his ear and a hand reached over his chest and stroked his shoulder.

At once he was wide awake, and turned to see Ruth lying beside him, strands of her dark hair across her eyes so that he could only see her nose and her lips, which moved gently as she murmured something under her breath. The events of the previous day, and more vividly, the previous evening, crashed back into his mind, and he quickly eased himself up.

'Mmm?' Ruth withdrew her arm and rolled away, then wriggled herself towards him so that her warm skin came into contact with his.

Schenke rubbed his forehead. He had a slight headache and was filled with unease about the previous night. Sleeping with

Ruth had been wrong in almost every way he could imagine, even if it had allowed him to forget the perils of the wider world and surrender to intimacy. He had betrayed Karin and he felt he had used Ruth, even though she had initiated their lovemaking.

The phone rang again. He slid out from under the covers into the cold air of the bedroom, snatching his dressing gown from the back of the door before padding out into the hall and picking up the receiver.

'Schenke,' he said quietly.

'Horst, it's me.'

He felt his blood run cold as he recognised her voice.

'Karin . . .'

'I've called your section office and I've called your flat. Are you all right?' The concern in her voice cut a fresh wound in his conscience. 'I've been so worried about you.'

'It's the investigation I've been dealing with . . . But it's over now.'

'Oh . . . the Scholtz child?'

'Yes.'

'Did you find anything out?'

'Yes.'

'And?'

How could he answer that given the tangle of horrors that had been unearthed? 'It was what they feared.'

'Did you find out who was responsible?'

'Yes.'

He heard a soft hiss like escaping steam at the other end of the line. 'What's wrong, Horst? When you talk in monosyllables, it worries me.'

'I'm sorry, I can't talk about this over an open line. I'm

tired. I'm not thinking straight. I'll be better when I've had a shower and something to eat.'

'Well don't let me stop you doing that,' she responded edgily.

'Karin, I'm sorry . . .'

'Sorry?'

He felt a sudden compulsion to confess. To get the truth out in the open and not be burdened by deceit. There was enough of that in the world without adding to the lies, pain and cruelty. At the same time, he did not want to have this conversation with Ruth in his apartment. She might be awake and listening, and he would then have to face her after the call was finished.

'I'm sorry I haven't time to go into all the details now. I can tell you everything when I next see you. We need to talk.'

'Yes, I think we do.' There was a tremor in her voice. 'Listen, Horst. I've decided to leave Berlin for a few weeks. I'm going to stay with some friends in Austria. I've been promising I'd go skiing with them for years, and now seems like a good time. It'll give both of us a chance to think about what we want from our relationship . . . Assuming that's what this is. I'm just not sure any more. You've been distant since before Christmas.'

'Have I?' Schenke recalled the murder investigation that had preoccupied him back then. It was when he had first met Ruth. 'Forgive me, Karin. It's not been an easy time. I've neglected you.'

'Yes, you damn well have.'

'I'll try and make it up to you when you get back to Berlin.'

She was silent for a few seconds before she continued. 'Is there someone else, Horst? Is that why you've been avoiding my calls the last few days?'

'No. I've been up to my neck in trouble. Haven't had a chance to speak to you before now.'

'I hope that's true. If not, I don't need you in my life. I'll find someone I can rely on.'

'Karin, listen—'

'I've listened enough,' she cut in over him. 'We'll speak when I get back.'

The line went dead, and he replaced the receiver before closing his eyes. 'Shit . . .'

'Was that her?'

He turned and saw Ruth standing on the threshold of the bedroom. She had pulled on his shirt again.

'Was that the woman you mentioned last night?'

'Yes. Her name's Karin.'

'From what I heard of your end of the conversation, you are in trouble.'

'Yes. I told her a few days ago that I wanted to marry her.'

Ruth regarded him with a pained expression. 'I shouldn't have let you bring me here last night.'

'Where else could you have gone at that hour?'

'I don't know. But it was a bad idea to come here. Even if I wanted to. Even if I wanted you.'

'I wanted you too.'

'What are we going to do now?'

Schenke's mind slipped gratefully into its usual practical way of thinking. 'You need to stay here for the time being. Help yourself to whatever you need, and get the fire lit and keep it going. Don't answer the door to anyone and don't make any noise. I don't want my neighbours getting curious.'

'What about Karin? What if she turns up when she gets back to Berlin and finds me here?'

410

He thought about how much Ruth could have gleaned from the telephone conversation she had overheard.

'She won't be back in Berlin for at least a month. That should be time enough for you to find a new place to live until it is safe to return to Brigitte. Meanwhile, you can stay here. Will you go back to your old job?'

'No chance of that. Too many questions to answer about my absence. I'll have to see what I can find at the Jewish labour exchange. One thing I can be certain of is that it'll be the same starvation wages and long hours and a foreman with wandering hands.'

'I'll do what I can to help.'

'Look after yourself, Horst. I'll survive.'

There was an edge to her voice, and he could understand her shift in mood. It was hard to live in a country where her people's citizenship, property and almost every civic right had been stolen from them. Last night they had been equals. Now, in the frozen light of dawn, they were divided by laws that the regime had driven between the so-called Aryans and those the Nazis defined as Jews.

'I have to get to the precinct,' Schenke said, making for the bedroom.

Ruth stepped aside, then sat on the bed and watched him as he dressed. Schenke did not shave or have anything to drink or eat in his hurry to quit the apartment. He paused at the door and looked back at her.

'We can talk when I return.'

'Talk? What about? I don't have any illusions about what the future holds for me. And there's very little you can do about it, Horst.'

He shook his head and left her, locking the apartment door

behind him and hurrying down the stairs and out into the street, where the icy air bit at his cheeks and shocked him into alertness.

There was a strange atmosphere of calm in the section office when Schenke arrived. The other Kripo personnel had been continuing their investigation into the forged ration coupons case while Schenke, Hauser and Liebwitz had been caught up in the turmoil of the last few days. Schenke sent Liebwitz to the cells to release Dr Lenger now that his life appeared to be no longer in danger.

The daily routine continued as before. Frieda Echs brought him a coffee and the day's digest of intelligence reports from the other Kripo offices in Berlin. There were the morning editions of the Berlin newspapers, the first of which carried a story about the eagerly anticipated launch of the *Bismarck*, the most powerful warship ever built – unsinkable, the headline boasted.

Schenke put the bundle aside and began to draft the report for Heydrich. It was a straightforward enough narrative of an investigation into the allegations made by parents of children who had died at the Schiller clinic. He made no mention of the euthanasia programme, and concluded that Gruber and the others had been eliminated after they had killed those they held responsible for the murder of their children. There were no further lines of enquiry, and therefore Schenke requested Heydrich's permission to close the case.

He had no doubt that Heydrich would agree. What happened after that would be out of his hands. He tried to quell the sick feeling in his soul. What was the point of solving one crime when an infinitely larger and monstrous injustice continued in secret? He recalled the words of one of his lecturers at the police academy. He had warned the young recruits that being a policeman entailed living with the knowledge that you could never defeat crime, but it was no excuse for giving up the fight. That advice rang hollow for those who worked in the shadow of the Nazi regime.

When he'd finished the report, he typed it out on his Olympia typewriter, without carbon copies. It was noon when he'd completed the job and signed his name to the report. He sealed it in an envelope and stamped the section's seal over the flap to ensure that any attempt to open it before it reached its destination would be detected.

Stepping outside his cubicle, he held the envelope up. 'Persinger!'

The detective looked up from the paperwork on his desk. 'Yes, sir?'

'Take this to Heydrich's secretary at the Reich Security Main Office.'

'Now, sir?' Persinger looked at the clock, no doubt noting that he was about to lose his lunch break.

'Immediately.'

Schenke returned to his desk and drew the forged ration coupon files in front of him. It was a relief to return to a more routine criminal investigation. Here was work he could carry out with a clear conscience and professional pride in his purpose. There was a distinct delineation between the criminals and their victims.

A knock at the door broke into his thoughts. Hauser stepped into the cubicle without waiting to be asked.

'I've had a call from a friend at the Mariendorf precinct, sir.'

'So?'

'I put the word out that we were interested in two names that had come up during the course of the forgery investigation. First thing this morning, before you arrived. Breker and Kappler.'

Schenke breathed in sharply. 'Why did you do that?'

'I figured that if they surfaced again, we'd get to hear about it before Heydrich's lot did, and that would buy us a little time to deal with the problem.' There was an edge to the sergeant's tone that implied how he intended to handle the matter if it ever arose.

'I see. That was a wise precaution. But you should have asked me first.'

'I was going to tell you as soon as you'd finished the report for Heydrich.'

'Well now I know. Thank you,' Schenke responded tersely. 'So what did your friend at Mariendorf have to say?'

'Two bodies were found beside the Teltow canal by the river police early this morning. They had both been shot through the head. A pistol was on the ground between them.'

'Breker and Kappler?'

Hauser nodded. 'They had their identity cards on them.'

Schenke was silent for a moment. 'The poor bastards didn't get very far. They must have known there was no chance of returning to their families, and with nowhere else to go . . . Wouldn't have been easy in any case, with one of them wounded.' He shook his head.

'That's how it looks to me. My friend says they'll have the bodies and records sent here for us to deal with.' Hauser regarded his superior. 'Two more victims of the crime ring we're looking for, is what I'm thinking.'

'Yes, that would be for the best.'

'Right. I'll handle the details, sir.'

'Thank you.' Schenke tapped the files in front of him. 'It's time we focused our attention on the forgery investigation in any case. Once you've called your friend back, we'll start the interrogation of the suspects we've been holding in the yard.'

'Yes, sir,' Hauser said. 'After a few nights in the cold, they'll be ready to sing like canaries.'

'I imagine so,' Schenke agreed. 'It'll be a welcome change from the last few days.'

Hauser stared at him for a beat before he replied. 'Like I said, you have a knack for understatement, sir.'

'It's something I've had to learn, Sergeant . . .'

Hauser turned away, and Schenke went back to preparing his notes for the first interrogation of the day.

Historical Note

When I research the period covering the rise and fall of Nazi Germany, it is sometimes hard to believe the bald statistics concerning the number of people murdered by the regime, nor is it easy to comprehend the cold-blooded manner in which those responsible went about it. Sometimes the sheer scale and breadth of the horrors inflicted by the Nazis is almost impossible to contemplate, and it is necessary to break the atrocity down in a way that allows people to connect with the victims in a more personal and empathetic way. That was the approach I took with this novel.

In order to understand what became known after the war as the 'Aktion T4' programme, we must be aware that this mass murder policy was the result of many years of conscious preparation, drawing on influences much wider than those located in Germany. A perversion of Darwin's theories of evolution gave rise to a growing number of works by scientists and pseudo-scientists advocating the removal of 'defective' humans, in order to take them out of the chain of heredity and thereby 'improve' humankind. Such notions were eagerly taken up across Europe and in the Americas, and provided febrile encouragement to the political programme of Adolf Hitler and his followers as early as the mid-1920s, when Hitler was already advocating the elimination of those he regarded as 'degenerates' ('*degeneriert*').

When the Nazi party seized power in 1933, they wasted no time in imposing their ideology on Germany. Besides the suppression of the media, the arrest, torture and murder of political rivals and the removal of Jewish civil rights, one of the first measures put in place was compulsory sterilization of certain groups. This was imposed on a wide range of those deemed degenerate: Roma people, prostitutes, the work-shy, habitual criminals, mixed-race people and those with incurable mental and physical disabilities. That same July, Hitler intended to pass laws to enable the killing of patients diagnosed with mental illness but was persuaded that such a move was too controversial. Even so, in 1935 he let it be known that, in the event of war, he would introduce such a measure, since the public's attention would be elsewhere and, in any case, in time of war, a few extra deaths would be easily missed amongst so many others. From 1937 a secret committee of the Nazi party was making plans for a euthanasia programme, seeding the notion through sympathetic articles in the Nazi-controlled press that portrayed the lives of people with disabilities as 'life not worthy of life' ('*Lebensunwertes Leben*').

The programme was activated in February 1939 when the father of Gerhard Kretschmar, a boy born with missing limbs, petitioned Hitler to have his son killed. The father had already approached a doctor in Leipzig asking him to end Gerhard's life but the doctor had refused on the basis that he might as a result be charged with murder. Having reviewed the case, Hitler sent his personal doctor, Karl Brandt, to arrange the murder of the child at the end of July. At the same time Hitler authorised Brandt to oversee the creation of a euthanasia programme. A month later, Hitler put an end to the sterilization program. Things had moved on from preventing reproduction by the 'degenerates' to eliminating them altogether. In October, Hitler signed an order empowering doctors to rid society of 'useless eaters' (*'unnütze Esser'*) by granting them a 'merciful death' (*'barmherziger Tod'*).

The programme was the responsibility of the Reich Committee for Scientific Registering of Serious Hereditary and Congenital Illnesses, whose structure and purpose were kept secret from the general public. The overall head of the programme was Philipp Bouhler, an SS officer, and one of the first members of the Nazi party. The section of the programme concerned with children was under the control of an SS doctor, Viktor Brack, and based at Tiergartenstrasse 4, from which the later name Aktion T4 derives. From the start the emphasis of the programme was on killing, not children already in institutions, but those who were still living at home with their families, before moving on to the elimination of those already institutionalised. Parents were coaxed by doctors to entrust their children to institutions where they would, supposedly, be better cared for. Once the children had been removed from their homes, they were subjected to various treatments ultimately intended to kill them. Some were injected with drugs that would progressively weaken them, while others were starved to death. Their deaths were passed off as the result of natural causes. Often, the bodies were cremated to destroy the evidence, and the parents were only then sent news of the death of their child. Considerable efforts were taken to conceal the scale of the killings; for example, Brack's officials kept a map in their office with pins placed in it for each child, to ensure there were not any suspicious clusters and that the victims were evenly spread out.

Very soon there was pressure to increase the numbers of those being eliminated. The German forces in Poland had already been engaged in mass murder of patients with mental illnesses of all ages, and had first started using poison gas on Polish inmates transported to Posen. Chemical expert Albert Widmann was brought in from the Kripo's forensic department to develop the most effective and efficient means of using gas (at this point carbon monoxide) to murder people, or, as they were described to him, 'beasts in human form'. Widmann oversaw the construction of a test unit at Brandenburg prison, where patients diagnosed with mental illness were gassed in batches of fifteen to twenty. The process took approximately twenty minutes to kill them.

The programme was rapidly expanded across Germany and for some time it was kept secret from those not directly involved. But suspicion began to be aroused when the number of deaths in institutions for those with particular illnesses and conditions swiftly climbed and a number of doctors, coroners, judges and Catholic priests began to protest. The American journalist William Shirer was aware of the programme very early on, but only gained concrete proof of its existence when he was contacted by a conscience-stricken official with the details in September 1940. Nonetheless, through a combination of denial, distraction, threats and ideological justification, the Nazi regime managed to prevent any effective opposition to the programme. By the end of the war, more than 80,000 people with disabilities had been murdered, over 5,000 of them children.

While the Holocaust is the most notorious crime committed by the Nazi party, it was through the euthanasia program that the Nazis first experimented with, then perfected, the means by which vast numbers of Jews, political opponents, Roma people, homosexuals and other victims were subsequently murdered. It was on the bodies of those helpless children that the most terrible atrocity of the twentieth century was built.

What was the fate of those responsible? Philipp Bouhler was captured by the Americans then committed suicide. Karl Brandt was tried and hanged in 1948, as was Viktor Brack. Albert Widmann escaped justice until 1959, when he was finally tried for his part in the programme and sentenced to six years in prison. He died in 1986. Even after the war, many of the doctors involved in the programme expressed their pride in what they portrayed as a process intended to improve the human race. In truth, all the above were the real 'beasts in human form'.

It is worth remembering that the Nazis were not alone in imposing compulsory sterilization. A mentioned earlier, the cause of improving racial purity had gained advocates in many countries. Between 1907 and 1939 the USA carried out over 60,000 compulsory sterilizations. In Europe, Switzerland, Denmark and Norway also embarked on similar programmes in the 1930s. In the case of Sweden, between 1935 and 1975, over 63,000 compulsory sterilizations took place. That is proportionately more, taking account of the relative populations, than Nazi Germany's 350,000. It is clear that some seeds of Nazi Germany's racial policies were sown in many other nations who were influenced by eugenics advocates from both ends of the political spectrum. We should not be so complacent as to assume that what happened in Nazi Germany could not be replicated somewhere else at another time.

I am sure that most who are reading this account of the Aktion T4 programme will share my despair that such things are possible. How could such inhumanity as that underlying the Aktion T4 programme and the Holocaust have existed on so vast a scale? I can think of no greater horror than the fate of the vulnerable children who were murdered in cold blood by the Nazis.

For those who are interested in finding out more, I would recommend the section on the Aktion T4 programme in Richard Evans' *The Third Reich at War* (Allen Lane, 2008), Michael Burleigh's *Death and Deliverance: 'Euthanasia' in Germany 1900–1945* (Cambridge University Press, 1994) and Henry Friedlander's *The Origins of Nazi Genocide* (University of North Carolina Press, 1994).

Simon Scarrow
August 2022